, al of

ject whos͟   ͟hybrid heart
this work is an͟   ͟assio͟   ͟Nietzschean enigma:
"how one becomes what one is". This debut signifies the taming of
an immense and soaring imagination in the figure of Pip Smith,
who—with cool command of form—is here both the falcon and
the falconer.'

LUKE CARMAN, author of *An Elegant Young Man*

'Pip Smith is a writer full to the brim with brio and vim. Her
fiction leaves nothing behind: every sentence wrings language for
its emotional and aesthetic possibilities. *Half Wild* is a remarkable
work of empathy: Smith has committed herself entirely to the
imaginative act, plonking us right down into the shoes, skin and
mind of a person who shed these same things time and again. We
live in an era where the reinvention of self is common, and even
encouraged; *Half Wild* reveals to us in dynamic prose that these
concerns are timeless and universal, that one of history's most excep-
tional chameleons could have been you, me or anyone we know.'

SAM COONEY, editor of *The Lifted Brow*

'Smith's writing is lucid and lovely; it's fearless—resonant with the
verve of another century and steadily surprising.'

STEVEN AMSTERDAM, author of *The Easy Way Out*

'A richly imagined and voiced novel that floats across time, and
through the shifting sands of identity. A buoyant, beautiful debut!'

DOMINIC SMITH, author of *The Last Painting of Sara de Vos*

HALF WILD

ABOUT THE AUTHOR

Pip is a writer of songs, poems and stories. Her first poetry collection, *Too Close for Comfort* (SUP), won the Helen Ann Bell Award in 2013. She ran the monthly writing event Penguin Plays Rough, for which she published and edited the multimedia anthology, *The Penguin Plays Rough Book of Short Stories*. She was a Faber Academy Writing a Novel scholarship recipient, has been a co-director of the National Young Writers' Festival, and holds a doctorate in creative arts from Western Sydney University. She is one quarter of garage band Imperial Broads and works in a bookshop.

HALF WILD

PIP SMITH

ALLEN&UNWIN
SYDNEY·MELBOURNE·AUCKLAND·LONDON

First published in 2017

Allen & Unwin
83 Alexander Street
Crows Nest NSW 2065
Australia
Phone: (61 2) 8425 0100
Email: info@allenandunwin.com
Web: www.allenandunwin.com

Cataloguing-in-Publication details are available
from the National Library of Australia
www.trove.nla.gov.au

ISBN 978 1 76029 464 9

Set in 12/18 pt Warnock Pro by Bookhouse, Sydney
Printed and bound in Australia by Griffin Press

10 9 8 7 6 5 4 3 2 1

She was just a half-wild creature who felt herself apart and different.

—Dr Herbert M. Moran, 1939

I was what other people made me.

—Eugenia Falleni, 1930

SYDNEY HOSPITAL, 9 JUNE 1938

—Who is she?

—Not sure. Female. Sixty, seventy maybe. Hit by a car up on Oxford Street.

—No purse?

—No. A wad of cash, though. A hundred pounds.

—Stolen?

—Probably.

—*What's your name, Mrs . . . ?* I don't think she can hear me.

—No, her eyelid twitched. Did you see that? Her eyelid twitched.

—*Mrs? Can you hear me? What is your name?*

JEAN FORD

My name, my name. What should we say my name is today, little Rita?

Today it's Jean I think, but tomorrow, when I find you, we'll christen me something new—something you can decide because my new life will be lived for you and no one else.

A name is a lie, Rita, remember that. If none of us had names, how would we remember who each other was? How would we call to each other from across the street? How would we attach a face to a name, a name to a bank account? I tell you, we couldn't. We couldn't even tell our own stories, because stories need heroes, and heroes would not hold together without a name, they would fall to jelly on the floor most likely, and wouldn't that be delicious?

Who I am, you cannot know,
for Jean Ford is my name.
Like Fords they make in factories,
my selves all look the same.

The doctors will think: a sensible name for a sensible woman, and let me out.

So call me Jean.

Can you hear me? I'm Jean—Jean Ford.

They can't hear me.

And there's a loud white pain flaring out from my hip and the back of my head that makes it hard to speak. Don't. No, stop. Morphine will only make me slip further away. I want to be inside this pain, because it's mine, because it proves this broken body's still got fight.

They are pressing into my wrist with their cold fingers. They are feeling for a pulse. They are saying numbers and writing on paper. Ha. Do monsters have pulses? I can hear someone fingering my banknotes. Don't you dare, don't you bloody dare, that's everything I've got.

What was it—almost twenty years ago now?—I was sent to die under a different name. I travelled to Long Bay Penitentiary like a celebrity, on a tram with tinted windows. Instead of a destination, the tram said *SPECIAL*. The woman next to me couldn't stop giggling. *Never thought I'd get called special, that's for sure.*

Inside the tram we didn't feel special. We got shoved ten at a time into compartments with seats for four and clung to the chicken-wire gates that fenced us in. A woman moaned the whole way there, like a cow torn away from her calf.

—*Ah shuddup Sandra, ya whiny bugger*—

Long Bay had never kept a woman about to hang and they weren't sure where to put me. They settled on a concrete cell, thirteen feet by seven. I got a mug and spoon, a shelf, and a single bulb hanging from the ceiling. I could've wrapped the light cord around my neck and jumped off the shelf I suppose, but what if the cord broke and left me lying on my back, more alive than dead, legs twitching like a poisoned cockroach?

I lay on my bed and stared at the ceiling. The cell was like a roomy coffin, and I was half convinced I was already dead when I heard a warder whisper outside my door: *Maybe they'll send her to Hall B in the men's.*

I could tell by the break in her voice what happened in Hall B.

They lowered their voices whenever they passed my cell, as if I was a ghost likely to haunt any poor sucker who pricked my ears. I probably would've, too, I was that hungry and sore about it.

They say you eat whatever you want when you're about to hang, but turns out this is a lie. They'd fed me Ration One for supper, the next best thing to dry bread and water. I suspect they didn't want to clean up my shit after I dropped. A constipated corpse is a tidy corpse, and doesn't leave a trace.

But everything leaves a trace. You mightn't be able to see those traces, but you can feel them, you can smell them. There are traces of me in you, and mark my words there are traces of me in the acid that burns the Crown Prosecutor's gullet at night, keeping him awake.

Wake up, Mrs; Mrs, wake up, a nurse is saying.

Ah, darling girl, I would if I could.

Now she is giving up, too. Her soft shoes pad across the floor.

The warders bit their nails when I looked them in the face. They barked occasionally, to remind me where I was, but it was hard for them to keep up the gruffness when I gave them no reason to complain. Mavis slipped a ball of tobacco into my pocket. May gave me an extra scoop of hominy on Sundays, and in early December a young warder slid back the hatch on my cell door.

Good news, love, she said. *There was a cabinet meeting. Your death sentence just got commuted to life.*

What? I didn't understand. What about the jury's decision? The lawyers' two-hour speeches? The months of preparation for the trial, and all along they could change their minds, just like that?

No premier wants a hanged woman on his hands, not now we can vote.

So it was life, then. Sentenced to life. It was worse in a way, but the women in the cells began to clap. The sound was water smacking stone; the drops accumulated and became rain. They clapped harder, they whooped and hollered—the cheers of women wild or poor enough to break the law are as close to rapture as a person can get now that churches don't mean much.

My cheeks were wet, my throat choked up; I hadn't cried like that in years.

Sister, the old woman is crying, I think.

The nurses are coming from all directions, needles out.

No, no more morphine.

Too bad. Jab.

And off I float. I've been trapped like this before, long ago now, but it's all coming back—

WHO SHE'D LIKE TO BE

WELLINGTON, NEW ZEALAND, 1885-1896

Mamma was always having babies. Sometimes I imagined they grew out her fingertips when she stood for too long in the sun, but they didn't. They crawled into her vagina when she sat on the toilet seat after Papà used it. That was why you always had to stand on the toilet seat and squat. Never sit.

And Mamma was a tailoress and a very hard worker. She worked every day of the week, and also cooked for us and cleaned the house and fixed our clothes except for when I did that, which was as often as she could make me. I tried not to be home too much in case she made me stitch flowers onto one of Ida's bonnets. Mamma said Ida couldn't stitch flowers onto her own bonnet because she was three and if you tried to make her she would put the needle in her eye or in your eye or try to eat it. I didn't know why bonnets needed flowers. If I had to stitch a horse costume, I would've done it. Or if I had to stitch something useful like trousers. But I didn't know why bonnets needed flowers, so I wouldn't do it.

When I came home after being outside for too long, Mamma would look at me as if she was experiencing great sorrow. When she stood up she held her back and sucked in through her teeth, as if the sorrow might leak out her back and pour all over the floor. Mamma always wore black, to accentuate the sorrow. She said she was in mourning for her lost babies, but she had more alive than she had dead, so you'd think that would make her want to wear more colour.

So far she had:

Me who was ten

Lisa who was nine but in Italy and didn't want to come and live with us

Federigo who would be five but was dead

Ida who was three

Rosie who was one

and Emily who was not anything yet.

Then there were others who died before they came out. There was no saying how many she'd have before she stopped.

I saw my last three sisters come out of Mamma and she was screaming and sweating and throwing her head around each time. Those three times were the only times I saw her hair out and all over the pillow, and she was yelling at me, *Ho troppo caldo! Tagliani i capelli, cazzo!* but Papà yelled, *Non brontolare!* from the other room. Each time Papà rushed in, asking, *È un maschio?* And each time Mamma said, *No, Luigi, hai una figlia.*

One of the times she gripped my arm so hard it bled where her nails went into the skin. I still have scars from it. They look like four empty cribs in a row.

Right, you. It's morning. Up.

It was still dark outside but Papà said it was morning, so it was morning.

Why aren't you fishing? I asked.

The sea is too high. Why aren't you helping your mother?

When there were high seas out on the harbour there were high seas inside Papà, too. He'd walk through the house with heavy feet, sometimes carrying buckets of water and a mop, which he'd drop in front of me without saying a word. Then his eyes would be a dark blue and you didn't say anything or else you got smacked. He never cared if I was out playing when he was fishing, but when there was no fishing he watched me closely, as if I was an insect he'd caught under a jar, and the jar made everything the insect did really big, but also kind of crooked.

If you're going to live under this roof you have to help around the house, said Papà, and he left the room but made sure the door was open so he could keep track of my getting-up progress with his ears.

Sometimes helping Mamma wasn't so bad. When we had to bottle passata at the end of summer my job was to put the teaspoon of salt into each bottle, but sometimes I got to fill the bottles with the red sauce. That was the best job, especially if you imagined you were a monster and the red was actually human blood that you planned to drink over the winter, when humans were harder to come by.

It was winter now and there was no passata to bottle, or bottles of blood to drink. There was only sewing in the dark, then school—long hours of chalk screech and out-of-bounds daylight.

When I was fully dressed I lay in bed with all my clothes on and tried to be invisible. *Maybe today I won't have to go to school*, I thought. *Maybe today I'll fix fishing nets with Papà instead.*

It was hard to tell how long it was before I could hear Papà's feet in the hallway. The steps were slow and even but loud, too, which meant he was trying to be terrifying.

Cosa. Ti. Ho. Detto?

The walls shook with his voice. Mice turned around in their nests, and in somewhere like Christchurch an earthquake shook the leaves off all the trees. I threw back the covers to show him I was fully dressed.

I did it all under the covers!

He wasn't impressed.

When I eventually came out to help the sun had already crawled into the sky and surprise surprise Mamma said she wanted me to stitch flowers onto one of Ida's bonnets. I opened my mouth to complain, but then Mamma rushed towards a chamber pot and filled it with vomit.

Fine, I said. *I'll do it.*

No, Nina, it's the new baby, Mamma said.

She looked pale and strained, and so, so tired.

I don't want to have babies when I grow up, I said.

Her face went still like the refrigerated pigs I once saw in the bond store at Queen's Wharf.

Well, what are you going to do? Mamma said. *Be a nun?*

No, I said. *I'm going to be a sailor, or a driver down the West Coast called Tally Ho, or a butcher boy like Harry Crawford.*

She ruffled my hair. She said I was a funny little joker. Then she said I'd better get my tally ho to school or she'd butcher me herself.

My teacher at the Sacred Heart school was a nun. Her name was Sister Katherine. She always had her head in a book about distant lands, so when she walked through the school she was really walking across the plains of Africa, or moving through a fish market in the Orient. You always had to say her name twice. First to bring her back to earth, and then to bring her over to you. It went like this:

Sister Katherine?

Hmmm?

Sister Katherine?

Oh! And she would jump and clutch her chest. *Yes, dear, what is it?*

Then she'd look at you with her eyes all misted over, as if someone was having a hot bath inside her head.

Sometimes she read to us from one of her books, but only when Father Kelly wasn't around. On this particular morning, she read out the first bit of *Frankenstein*, but just as it was getting good she stopped and made different people read different bits. I was scared she might ask me to read so I sat close behind a fat girl's back, but Sister Katherine saw and asked me to read next.

I was sweating and my eyes were doing that thing where they jump between lines. Sister Katherine was staring at me, saying, *Go on. Go. On,* between long pauses while everyone waited for me to start. Even the trees outside were waiting. The cicadas started chanting *read read read* faster and faster until someone threw a piece of chalk at my head and shouted, *You can't read!* Everyone laughed and the cicadas whirred and the trees bent down and brushed against the window, *ho ho ho.* Sister Katherine wasn't laughing, though. She had her finger pointing at me like a gun. *Out!* she shrieked. *Outside until I work out what to do with you!*

While I waited for Sister Katherine to calm down I did some experiments in the playground. I found a lizard and I also found a cicada that was the same thickness as the lizard. I pulled the head off the lizard and pulled the head off the cicada and then swapped them around, mainly so the lizard could see what it would be like to fly. I held the head in place with some pins I'd stolen from Mamma's sewing box and left the cicard and lizada behind a bush.

I knew Sister Katherine was behind me because all the insects in the playground were holding their breaths. Two cold fingers clamped my ear. I smelled talcum powder and old books and suddenly I was hauled onto my feet. Her flared nostrils were two trumpets sounding the start of a hunt. *I will make an example of you*, she said, and dragged me to see Father Kelly.

Show this child what happens to insolent children, she said, but Father Kelly told her to leave and shut the door. Then Father Kelly came up to where I was standing, squatted down and looked me in the eye.

You know, I've seen lots of insolent children in my time, he said. *And there is a difference between an insolent child and a child who was not meant for the schoolroom. I do not think you can be taught. You are one for riding horses and running about getting scabby knees, aren't you?*

And I said, *Yes*, because it seemed like that's what I was supposed to say.

But let me tell you this, he said. *You might find school difficult now, but it will only get harder for you if you cannot read and write. Particularly for a* . . . and then he talked a lot more. Out the window I could see the lizada hovering four feet off the ground. It wasn't even properly healed from its operation and already the lizada was learning how to fly.

Father Kelly held my chin and turned my face up so I had to look at him, and said, *Do you have a problem with your eyes, is that it?*

Up close I could see he had little red wriggly lines all over his cheeks and nose. That's why his face looked pink from a distance but up close it was lots of different colours—there was brown and some white splotches as well, and his moustache was yellow and white like the tail of a palomino horse.

You have to let me know, Nina. We might be able to help you, but you have to talk to me.

When I didn't say anything he breathed in very deeply and said, *Well then, if you won't let yourself be helped, good luck to you. You better go back to the classroom holding your backside, or Sister Katherine will think I have gone soft.*

At first I walked slowly in the direction of the classroom and then I looked over my shoulder and bolted towards the school gates. I cleared the fence in one leap and ran all the way up Adelaide Road and only stopped when I reached a high grassy hill. All I could do was grip my knees and pant, but it felt good to have that stale school air squeezed out of my lungs so nothing but life could flood back in.

When I looked up I saw that I'd made it all the way to the hill behind the public school in Newtown. I could hear groaning coming from behind a tree and my first thought was that it might be a wild pig, and my second thought was that it might be a man and a woman kissing, but then I saw it was a girl about my age, and smelled the vomit that was down her front. Her smock used to be white, but now she looked like a cake that had been dropped on the road in the rain.

Why did you vomit? I asked her, and she said, *Because I ate too many cakes.*

Why did you eat too many cakes? I asked, and she told me she got bored in arithmetic so she walked out and bought all the Wellington cakes the baker had in his shop and charged it to the head teacher. Then she sat up here and ate every single one because she couldn't think of anything better to do.

Oh, I said. *I hate cakes.*

She burped a bit of vomit into her mouth and tried to cover it with her hand, and then we both looked down into the playground of Newtown School.

Compared to Sacred Heart, Newtown School was a paradise. It sat in the middle of a dusty block as big as a desert, except for when it rained. Then it sat in the middle of a swamp full of diseases and everyone got to go on holidays. Because of all the rain in Wellington, they got to go on holidays a lot. They also had a holiday when the HMS *Nelson* was in port and when New Zealand played Australia in the cricket and whenever the head teacher Mr Lillington needed to go to the bank. Even from up on the hill we could hear two girls say, *Fuckit bumhole bugger shit*, to a teacher in the playground. He didn't say anything back, he stood in the mud as if he'd been struck by lightning, and the girls ran behind the building so they could throw scraps of rusted metal at him. Then he un-struck himself and kept walking around the playground with his hands behind his back as if he was thinking through a very hard bit of long division.

Is that your school? I asked the girl, and she said, *Yes.*

Do you like it? I asked, and she said, *Not really, no*, then pulled some grass out of the ground.

What's your favourite colour? I asked her.

Grey, probably, she said, which was a pretty good answer for a girl.

What's your name? I asked.

Amelia Grey, she said. *What's yours?*

Tally Ho, I said, and it felt like the beginning of something, when I said it out loud like that.

I didn't need to go to school anyway because I was going to be a butcher boy like Harry Crawford. All the butchers had boys who did deliveries for them and one of the best things was to watch them race through the streets. They'd hold the meat in one hand and whip their horse with the other, churning the street into a dust storm with their frenzied horses in the middle. It was like Arabia. And if the water cart had been through the street, patting the dirt down with the hose, that was even better. Everyone got splattered in mud, but no one cared. Shopkeepers would come out of their shops and stand on the side of the road to cheer them on. And if you got more than two butcher boys you'd get a real race, with bets going and everything. Old ladies flew off to either side of the road. Young ladies held their hats as if a Bible plague had come just to destroy all the hats. The butchers always pretended with the cops that they'd never asked their boys to ride like that through the streets, but if their boy won they couldn't wipe the smile off their face for the rest of the day and you'd get more change back for a ham hock than you expected.

Harry had won the race more than once but he never bragged about it, and he never said he won the race more than he had. Harry didn't need to brag or lie, because Harry knew that what he was and what he did was enough. He didn't need to be anything more.

On my first day of freedom I made as if I was going to school, but once I reached Adelaide Road I sunk back from the other Sacred Heart kids and went to Nonna and Nonno Buti's house instead. Nonno Buti was there playing chess with himself.

I said, *Nonno, why are you playing chess with no one?* And he said, *I AM NOT PLAYING CHESS WITH NO ONE, I AM PLAYING CHESS WITH MYSELF.*

Nonno Buti always yelled like that because he lost his hearing standing too close to explosions fighting in the Italian wars when he was younger.

Nonno Buti said that when he was in solitary confinement he played chess in his head. He played both sides. He said he did this to stay sane.

He said, *YOU MUST TRAIN YOURSELF TO IMAGINE CHESS MOVES INSTEAD OF TO THINK ABOUT THE FACT THAT YOUR CAPTORS DON'T UNDERSTAND YOU, OR THAT IT IS YOUR FAULT YOUR CAPTORS DON'T UNDERSTAND YOU, OR THAT YOU SHOULD BE MORE LIKE YOUR CAPTORS. QUESTO È MOLTO IMPORTANTE.*

He said he focused so hard on chess moves that bad thoughts couldn't get a leg in edgeways. And then, when he got out of prison and played grand masters at chess, he won, even though he hadn't played actual chess in ages.

I said, *But you aren't in prison, Nonno—you could play with Nonna.*

And he laughed and said, *HER BRAINS ARE TOO SOFT, ONLY GOOD FOR COOKING, HA HA HA.*

Brushing the horses in Nonno Buti's stable, I tried to remember how Harry Crawford rode his horse. I remembered how far he leaned forward over the saddle, how tightly he held the reins, how he moved with the horse as if he was flying inches above the horse's back. He was magnificent.

Nonno Buti let me practise jumping with his horse Geronimo. Only sitting in the saddle at first, then around the yard, then up and down the street. He was meant to call me Harry Crawford while I did it, but when he saw how I could jump the paling fence without that much of a run-up he blew on his hunting trumpet and shouted, *TALLY HO!*

But I could only ride like that if I was being Harry Crawford. Just like how Sister Katherine said that in Africa men ate other men, but they had to wear the skin of a cheetah to be able to do it.

Nonno said that if I didn't tell Nonna, I could take Geronimo out by myself.

I moved exactly like Harry Crawford on Geronimo as I slunk through the streets. No one could see us because there was nothing special to see—just a man and his horse, calling on a friend. The friend happened to be a ten-year-old girl playing hopscotch in the playground of Newtown School, but that was by the by. Amelia saw me tall and brave on Geronimo's slippery-dip back and ran straight over to join me.

We were out and blazing under the midday sun—me holding the reins, Amelia holding my waist—and it felt right to be part of the day like this. So much time had been wasted reciting the saints and pretending to learn how to read and all the while there were trees aching to be climbed and rivers thirsty for us to fling ourselves in, yodelling into the splash.

Now that our days weren't being marked by school bells and routines, time lurched forward, slowed down; everything happened at once, or nothing happened at all. Wise Geronimo knew that one thing had to come before the other, and he led us to the best climbing tree in Wellington. It was the best because there were hundreds of different ways you could climb it and the places where you put your feet were worn smooth like banister railings. Once you got to the top you could see into the back gardens of the biggest houses in Thorndon. They had statues and swings and podiums and mazes, not fishing nets spread out to dry that smelled like rotting sludge from the bottom of the ocean.

Me and Amelia could see into one garden that was full of ladies in white dresses. Their hats looked like lids. If you pulled them off there would be humbugs inside their heads. They moved across the grass like swans—but Amelia said it wasn't grass, it was a *lawn*—so they moved across the *lawn* like swans. And when they laughed they didn't snort or throw their heads back, they covered their mouths with their hands as if laughing was a sneeze that might give you typhoid.

Some of them were holding lace umbrellas even though it wasn't raining and some of them were holding tiny teacups on tiny plates or were nibbling the corner of tiny white triangles but peeling their lips back first so that they didn't get crumbs on their faces. Everything was tiny and breakable, because being a lady was about not breaking things, and the winner was the person who couldn't break the tiniest thing.

There was a great climbing tree in the middle of the garden with the slow swan ladies in it, but no one was climbing it; they were too busy standing around, holding their tiny things.

Someone was playing a violin. It was a friend of Nonno Buti's. He was in a black suit with a gold chain on his waistcoat. He had his hair oiled, and he'd twisted the ends of his moustache so that it went up at the sides. Amelia Grey said he was trying too hard to look rich, like most Italians.

I don't try to look rich, I said.

No, she said, *but you know what I mean.*

Geronimo galloped us to the cricket and he cantered us to the wharf. Every day held a new adventure and word spread around Newtown School that we had started our own School of Life. We took on new recruits, but only the bravest survived.

We got a pig's bladder from the butcher in Newtown and even though it was still covered in blood and smelled like wee, it was great. You blew it up and tied off the end and it was tough, not like a balloon. You could kick it and punch it and use it to play rugby or you could fill it with water and squirt it at people when they walked past and they would be covered in bits of pig wee mixed with blood and water.

That time it was me, Amelia, the girls who said fuckit to the teacher at Newtown School, and a boy called Horatio de Courcey Martelli, but everyone called him Horse. I called the fuckit girls Fuckit and Buckit. I called the tall one who looked like a foal Fuckit and the short one who looked like a donkey Buckit. They didn't seem to mind. I think they got worse names at home.

We decided it was Amelia's birthday. Every day we took turns at having a birthday and walking into a shop saying, *Hi, mister, did you know it's Amelia's birthday?* or *Did you know it's Buckit's birthday?* and one in every three birthdays you would get a treat, or maybe even a penny but sometimes they would say, *Why aren't you at school?* and kick you out.

Because it was Amelia's birthday she had to blow the bladder up and wear it under her dress as if she was going to have a baby.

That was funny for a bit, but then it got boring, so we sat on the gutter waiting for the butcher boys. Amelia still had the bladder up her dress and it was getting warm and slimy like a real baby. I thought for a second that I would like to have a real baby with Amelia, and then Fuckit said, *Watch this.*

Fuckit undid a safety pin from the back of her pinafore and smashed it into Amelia's baby. It was horrible. There was a wheezing sound and Amelia's stomach started to shrivel. She looked down at it, stunned. There was a warm sweet rotten smell coming out of it. I pushed Fuckit so that she slipped on the blood and slumped in the gutter. Amelia looked down at the blood all over her dress as if she was about to swoon. I thought maybe Amelia needed to breathe, maybe I should undo the top of her smock so she could breathe. I went to rip open the top of her smock and she pushed me off, saying, *What are you doing?*

Her brain had gone soft. She couldn't see that I was on her side, that I was saving her.

Leave me alone! I didn't want the gross thing up my dress in the first place, she said, and pushed me away from her so I slipped on the bladder and landed in the gutter as well.

The road was grumbling, and I wondered if an earthquake was about to split the city in two. Fuckit and Buckit ran across the street with Amelia, stepping on my hair and my hand as they did. Only Horse was still there, helping me up.

The butcher boys are here, Tally Ho, come on, get up!

In the distance we could see Raines with a pig's head under his arm and Harry Crawford with two hams tied up by the trotters hanging around his neck. Their horses were really going for it—dipping their heads down and rearing them back up like waves crashing on a beach and rising up and crashing again.

Harry Crawford was winning as usual, but then he stopped. Right in the middle of the race. I saw him catch the eye of a woman standing on the side of the road. She was laughing and waving and was wearing a hat covered in daisies. Her hair was a mess underneath. It looked like something birds made their nests out of. I suppose she looked pretty, in the way weeds buzzing with flies are sometimes pretty, but just because she was smiling and waving Harry Crawford pulled out of the race.

No! What are you doing? I shouted at him. *Keep going, you were winning!* He was drunk on this woman with the bird's-nest hair. He pulled the horse up so that it swerved as it moved towards her and she plucked a flower out of her hat, reached up and put it in the string netted around his ham. Then he clutched his heart like someone had stabbed it with a javelin. It was all wrong. Harry Crawford had never put a woman before a race.

Without Harry being Harry, I wasn't sure how to be me. I felt naked riding around on Geronimo's back, and preferred to take my gang into tunnels and caves: dark underground places, where cicadas buried themselves until their shells were hard as steel.

We found a pipe. It was huge. You could stand up in it and not even bang your head. You could shout into it and then hear yourself shout back, like there was another you standing at the other end of the pipe. It smelled a bit, but you got used to it. It had green slime growing around its mouth where it emptied into the harbour, which made the rocks beneath it slippery and dangerous and so much more exciting than school.

You had to see who could get across the rocks the fastest without falling into what came out of the pipe. It was usually me. If you fell in you had to sing 'Ave Maria' while gargling the water that dribbled out of the pipe.

In summer after lots of rain the pipe got so full that water bubbled out the manholes in Te Aro and all the people had to go from house to house in boats. I wished that happened in Newtown. Then Papà could fish in bed and the sheets could be sails and the pasta hanging up could be seaweed and we could all float around the house by lying on our backs blowing water up into the air, pretending to be whales.

Once I saw a dead cat come out the pipe. It had a worm growing in its eye. You would think the cat would be soft but I hugged it and it was stiff.

After that I got sick, and Fuckit got cholera and almost died, so no one was allowed down there anymore.

Buckit said it was my fault Fuckit almost died because I made her drink the pipe water after she fell off the rocks, but it was her own stupid fault for falling when she knew the rules, and none of us could see the disease in the water anyway. They never did come back to the pipe after that.

Fear seeped into our gang. Fuckit and Buckit went back to the boring safety of the schoolroom. Me and Amelia thought we could make our new headquarters the rocks under the Taranaki wharf, but Horse was scared of drowning. He could climb right up to the top of a mast whenever we played the ship game, but he couldn't swim. He was also scared of going to the toilet anywhere that wasn't at his house. He was happy to run through Newtown School with his willy out shouting, *I'VE GOT MY WILLY OUT!* but if he needed to go to the toilet he held it in until he got home. You could tell when he was holding it because he jiggled around and if you said, *Do you need to go to the toilet?* he'd say, *No,* and then you'd say, *Yes you do, you're squirming*, and he'd say, *No I'm not, I'm dancing*, and move his hands around to make it look more like he was dancing. Then when he was anywhere near home he'd run faster than a witch with her hair on fire and as soon as he was behind the front gate he would piss right into the flowerbed, letting out a massive sigh. That's why their camellia bush was dead on one side and their front gate always smelled like wee.

Just because you're behind the front gate doesn't mean no one can see you, I said to him. I was standing on the other side of the gate. I reached out and touched him on the shoulder to prove my point. He flinched, as if my arm had reached out from another world.

I know that, he said, but he always went round the back after that.

It was amazing how much people thought you couldn't see—like the ladies picking their noses in carriages trotting by because they thought they were in a sealed capsule that you couldn't see into. Or because it didn't count if poor people saw you pick your nose.

And later, so many people wouldn't see what was right in front of them.

Nonno Buti made a box for a rich Chinaman on the West Coast. It was a box with secret compartments so the Chinaman could hide his gold nuggets from the government.

We were standing in the back of Nonno Buti's workshop, admiring it. The box was lizard green, as big as an ice chest, and sitting in the middle of the workshop floor.

He said, *TALLY HO, TELL ME HOW MANY COMPARTMENTS THERE ARE IN THIS BOX!* but I was so amazed by the box I couldn't move. *DAI*, he said, pushing me forward, *APRILA!*

Nonno Buti stepped back and watched me approach the box with great care, then open and close all four of its compartments, breathe on the varnish, and tap each surface for spring-activated doors or secret hollow pockets. When I looked back up at him he was smiling so hard that tears were squeezing out the wrinkles at the sides of his eyes.

There are four compartments, I said, and Nonno Buti almost choked on his own laugh, he was that excited.

NO, TALLY HO, THERE ARE TEN!

It had taken Nonno Buti three months to make because he wanted it to be perfect, but now it was perfect and late, so he needed a coachman to send it down to Greymouth quick smart.

I asked Nonno Buti who the coachman was going to be. Was it going to be Papà? Or Harry Crawford? But he said, *NO, TALLY HO, YOU ARE THE ONLY COACHMAN UP TO THE JOB.*

It was going to be me!

He had that wild look he got when he was really excited. Like he wasn't really here, like he was riding around on shooting stars up in the solar system. That's when Nonno Buti was the most fun to be around and came up with his best ideas—the wooden whale with lots of little Jonah-shaped oyster forks inside its belly for instance, or the saltshaker which was actually a bald man's head with terrible dandruff.

He said I could have Geronimo to keep if I thought I could make the trip in a week.

A week? But I've never even been there before!

I KNOW, TALLY HO, BUT AFTER YOU'VE FOUND YOUR WAY THERE IN A WEEK YOU WILL MOST CERTAINLY KNOW HOW TO GET THERE IN LESS THAN A WEEK IN THE FUTURE, WON'T YOU!

He said it not like a question, but like a fact:

The altitude of Mount Cook is 12,341 feet.

The capital of Italy is Rome.

Tally Ho will ride a horse to the West Coast in less than a week.

All that night I lay awake thinking of a horse that could get me to the West Coast. I decided I'd need a horse that had an extra flap of skin which could be tied up on its back, or untied and buttoned onto its legs to make fins. That way, when the flap was tied up above its back, it could conceal its gills when on land, and then when the fins were buttoned down it would be able to breathe underwater when we crossed the Cook Strait. It would also have a head like a seal so that it could swim really fast, and would be blue so that it didn't look out of place with the other fish.

I'd seen a blue person before. Well, not really a person. A baby. It was my little brother who was born in Wanganui before we moved to Wellington. He slept the wrong way up in his cradle and in the morning he was blue. I asked Papà why the baby was blue and Papà whacked me across the back of my head with his shoe. Mamma was sobbing in the kitchen and boiling cloths to put on the baby to make him hot again, and I had to hold the baby and breathe on it. Papà was trying to get his feet in his shoes without undoing the laces so he could get to the doctor, but he didn't have a horse so he had to steal the neighbour's new bicycle. He'd never ridden a bicycle before but he learned straight away that morning. I always think about Papà on the stolen bicycle when I'm trying to do something I don't know how to do. I think: *If you don't get it right a baby will die*, and then I work it out straight away.

When we were in Wanganui Papà was a fisherman like he is now, but back then Mamma and me would go down and meet him in the afternoon when the water was white as milk and the sky was the colour of jam. The fish piled up on the wharf made one big monster with a hundred eyes and sometimes tentacles, too, and broken jaws on all of its faces.

Once they really did catch a monster. It was a giant blue fish that was as long as Papà and five times as fat. It took ten men to drag it up onto the beach and its whole right eye was as big as my head. The fish was very surprised to find that things could live out of the water. He was trying to work out where the coral and seaweed had gone, and why everything was pressed down onto the ground and not floating around his head like it usually was.

A man saw me staring into the eye of the fish and asked me if I knew why it was blue. I said no, and he said it was because it had turned into a man-fish after being a brown woman-fish.

Why are the women-fish brown? I asked, and he shrugged and said he didn't know, they were just more boring.

When the baby turned blue I asked Papà if it was turning into a man-fish. Papà didn't reply, he only had strength left to steal the neighbour's bicycle and work out how to ride it. And guess what colour the bicycle was? It was brown, not blue, and by the time Papà came back the baby was grey.

The morning after Nonno Buti gave me my West Coast assignment I went straight to his house. Nonno Buti was at work but Nonna was in the kitchen cutting up an octopus for cacciucco. I stood in the doorway of the kitchen for a second and waited for her to ask me what I was up to. She didn't.

I sighed loudly, and she reached up to untie the sage that was hanging in the window. Then I nuzzled my head between her bosom and the arm she was using to cut off the tentacles. Nonna had a lot of bosom, so this manoeuvre could cause suffocation if I didn't push her bosom in with my forehead to create an air pocket for my mouth.

Nonna still didn't ask me anything. She gave me a leaf of sage to eat and kept cutting. It was hard to speak with my face so close to an octopus massacre, so I had to pull my head out, swallow the sage and tell Nonna that I was going to become a cart driver on the West Coast.

She threw the octopus head in a tub and asked, *What, when you grow up?* and I said, *No, next week, to deliver a secret box to a Chinaman.*

Straight away Nonna said *Buti!* under her breath and wiped her black hands on her apron. The inky streaks make it look like she was ready for war.

When I visited Nonno Buti at his workshop the next day I could see that he was very sad, as if the stars he'd been riding around on in the solar system had finally crashed into the ocean and now he was deep under the water where the giant fish had been. He said, *Mi dispiace, Tally Ho, you cannot take Geronimo out anymore. You will have to wait until you are older before you can make deliveries for me.*

I wasn't worried, though. Nonno Buti once told me that anything was possible if you imagined it hard enough, it just mightn't happen the way you expected. He wanted to be the first man on the moon when he was a kid, for instance, but he ended up in New Zealand working next door to a man who sold telescopes, which was close enough.

When Papà came home that night he was thrown into the room by a fierce wind, but it wasn't a southerly or a northerly, it was coming from inside him and it was pushing him towards me.

I was sitting on the floor shelling peas into a bucket. I could have sat at the table, but I liked sitting on the floor because I could fold my legs up like a foal.

He stopped in front of me. The wind was still pushing, but he was standing still so the wind was running circles up against the inside of his face, making it red.

What are you doing? he said.

I thought it was obvious.

Shelling peas, I said.

He picked me up by the back of my collar. The front of the collar choked up under my chin. Then he walked me out the back door still holding me up like this, like I might actually be a foal who didn't know how to use its legs yet.

When we were out the back he looked around. He wasn't sure which way to go next, so we stopped there, near the back door. It slammed shut, and I jumped because I thought for a second that I'd been smacked, but it was only the door. Nothing hurt.

Do you know who I spoke to down at the jetty? he asked me.

It wasn't a question I was supposed to know the answer to, but I had to say something otherwise I'd get whacked, so I said, *No.*

Sister Katherine is who. And do you know what Sister Katherine said to me?

No.

She said, 'I hope your daughter is feeling better, everyone misses her so.' Have you been sick?

I coughed because my throat felt scratchy after the collar had crushed it. Also to check if I was sick. Maybe I was sick. There was still time. I opened my mouth and tried to catch some pollen on my tonsils.

Pitiful, Papà said. *Why aren't you going to school? We bring you to this country for a better life, and you are not going to school. Why? What are you going to do?*

This time I wasn't supposed to answer. I could have told him it was alright, that I was going to be a coachman on the West Coast, but he didn't want to know. His eyes weren't saying, *Tell me the answer,* his eyes were scared, like he was looking in a mirror and saw a monster—half lizard, half cicada—open its wings to fly away.

Papà said if I was going to run around like a boy instead of going to school then I would have to work like a boy and see how I liked it.

I nodded, and looked at my shoes, and tried to act punished.

We sailed to Rona Bay on the side of the harbour where the jungles were full of warriors and the sands were golden and flying fish leaped out of the water and into your boat, sacrificing themselves for your dinner. At first the other fishermen were quiet because there was a kid who kept jumping around and they wanted to talk about the women back in Italy and fights and horses, not be on their best behaviour.

Ah, don't worry, Nina is tough as old boots, Papà said, but he looked more worried than them because we both knew his old boots needed to be resoled every month and weren't very tough at all.

When we started sailing over to Rona Bay the moon was up and the sound of waves licking the boat made all the fishermen feel as small as prawns, so they talked to make themselves feel less edible. A man called Bert did most of the talking. He told me he came here by accident when he was fourteen after he was shipwrecked in a place where people wore gold in their noses and rode elephants through the streets. He got on a ship he thought was going to Australia but instead it came here.

Why didn't you stay there and have a pet elephant? I asked, and he said, *Because I wanted to see what life would be like at the end of the earth.*

It turned out life at the end of the earth was the same as it was in Italy but colder and with less military service.

If I'd been allowed to talk I would have told the other fisherman that I already knew how to row properly. You don't sit down like you see New Zealanders do, you stand up like they do in Venice. Then you can row for hours. But instead the other men talked and I sat next to Papà while he tied knots in his dragnet. I held the net up so it didn't get tangled, but Papà touched me on the arm and said, *No, don't hold it like that. Give it to me, it will be quicker.*

When we got to Rona Bay, the other men took the smaller boats around past the rocks, and Papà and I stayed in the big boat out in the harbour. He was quiet and I was trying to think of things to say. A penguin swam past with its head sticking up out of the water.

Look, Papà, a penguin! I said.

He nodded. After I said it, it seemed like a stupid thing to say. He could see that it was a penguin. He knew what a penguin looked like.

Good weather for fishing! I said. I hoped it was good weather for fishing. I wanted to show him that I knew.

I watched Papà move the rudder. He was squinting out into the horizon. The sun wasn't all the way up yet, but the clouds were bright in that way that made you feel like you had soap in your eyes. He wasn't even looking at his hand move the rudder. Papà could do lots of things without looking. He could tie a knot by flicking his wrist and twisting the rope around his fingers, and sometimes he would reach out for a rope and tug it out from the blunt metal teeth that were holding it down, and then give it a pull, or loosen it, and the sail would flick around to the other side of the boat.

That was tacking. Tacking is when you change direction. And reefing is when you pull in the sail so it has less of a belly and the boat doesn't capsize. And port means left and starboard means right. If the sail gets loud and thrashes around like a horse going crazy, that means you're pointing into the wind and you need to make a decision about which way you're going to turn. I was trying to think of a way of showing Papà that I knew these things, but he was looking at where the birds were circling above the water with a tight look on his face that meant, *Don't talk, I'm thinking very hard.*

The wind was strong. We only had one sail up and it was reefed, so it wasn't even all the way up. The wind was strong enough that the boat was tipped over to the side and we had to lean in the other direction to balance things out. Then Papà said, *Take the helm.* He said it without even looking at me. *Take the helm*, like I would know exactly what to do. I couldn't believe it. I stared at him, and he said, *Sbrigati, cambia il vento*, so I held the rudder with two hands, in case I accidentally let go with one of them.

I was steering the whole boat. I could have taken it out of the bay. I could have sailed to Australia or Italy or Ireland, but Papà said, *Pull the rudder to windward. To windward! Subito!*

I couldn't remember if windward was the way the wind was going, or where the wind was coming from. I moved the rudder to the direction that the wind was coming from. Which was the starboard side. The right side. East.

No, Nina! Windward! he said. He pushed me off the rudder and moved it all the way to the port side, so far over that it touched the side of the boat. The sail started flailing around and I hoped what I'd done didn't mean we were going to drown. I looked out for more penguins so Papà couldn't see my lip begin to quiver.

I saw one. Another one by itself, with its head straining up out of the water. He was looking really hard for something, anything, but he couldn't see us.

We caught warehou mostly, and seaweed, and an octopus and three dead tree branches. We caught the penguin, too. It was tangled in the net with a fish gripped in its beak. It was frightened, but it wouldn't let go of the fish. I had to grab the penguin on the body holding the wings down. It made a high, wheezy noise and tried to wriggle out of my hands, which meant *The net is wrapped twice around my left wing, please be careful.*

Here, let me do it, Papà said, reaching over.

No, I can do it, I said. I already had his head half untangled. But Papà brushed me aside with his arm so that I slipped off the seat and the penguin pecked him on the finger. He said, *Cazzo del uccello!* and ripped it out of the net so that it got a deep cut in its wing, and threw it back into the sea. The penguin swam away with its head straining forward, squawking an alarm signal to all the other birds in the harbour. *Don't go near that boat, they will try to rip your wings off.*

See? Papà said. *You would have hurt yourself.*

On our way back to Wellington, I didn't feel like doing anything but watch the mountains in the very far distance. Bert saw me looking and told me that on the other side of those mountains was the West Coast. He said you could find gold in the ground there, but it was very wild country and you had to be careful not to get eaten by pigs. You could have a Maori guide, which helped you not get eaten by pigs, but it raised your chances of getting eaten by Maoris.

Mamma always said that when we first came to Wanganui the Maoris used to come to her door. They would trade a whole wild pig for a cake of soap, then eat it like cheese. Mamma laughed every time she told that story, but she forgot that she couldn't speak English when she got off the boat and once bought cheese instead of soap from the grocer.

The other fishermen sang songs about Napoli and cried about leaving their mammas, even though they were grown men. *Then why did you leave?* I asked them, and they shook their heads as if to say I could never possibly understand.

When we took the fish to the Taranaki wharf the fishmongers saw how dark the other fishermen were and wouldn't buy the fish from us. The other men were Italians like us, but because they were from the south they looked more like Greeks. We were from the north and if we kept our mouths shut and stayed out of the sun we looked like regular New Zealanders. Even so, the fishmongers waited for the Scottish fishermen. Papà wrapped two big warehou in newspaper to take home and threw all the rest into the harbour right in front of the fishmongers' eyes. He said Italians once ruled the earth. Italians built the roads in Scotland, but it was too long ago for anyone to remember.

The sky was the colour of cloudy lemonade and getting clearer by the second as we walked along the waterfront with our two fish. There were so many ships. At least one of them had to be a pirate ship. There were clippers and steamers and barques and full-rigged ships. They squished their fenders against the dock, *creak creak*, as if their fenders were fat pigs with secrets and the ships were holding them up against the dock until they gave up and told everything. There were piles of boxes and crates and barrels too, and sometimes men in coats buttoned all the way up walking with legs stiff as guns, making sure nothing got stolen. Then there were the men huddled behind the gates, waiting for work. There were thousands of them, it seemed, and who should I see in the throng of hungry men but Harry Crawford.

Papà, look! I said, and Papà said, *What now?*

Isn't that the butcher boy from Newtown, Papà? Why would he need to line up down here?

Well, the man's got to eat, Papà said. *He can't survive on scraps from the butcher. You're lucky you have a papà to feed you fish at a time like this.*

But I'm a fisherman now, I said. *I can feed myself.*

He shook his head and said, *No, Nina. That's enough of these silly games. Tomorrow, you will help your Mamma instead.*

Between washing my sisters' pinafores and mending Papà's trousers, Amelia and I continued to rampage around the place— but secretly, so Papà would never notice. I snuck out and threw a rock at Amelia Grey's window and said, *Ngarl nymph thoro!* which meant *Hurry up, let's go to the quay!* in the language we made up. Amelia took forever to come outside. I knew she was there because her blind was all the way up which was code for *I am at home*, so I sat on the bit of the paling fence where there weren't any palings and waited.

A woman looked at me through the lace curtains of Amelia's living room window. It was probably her mother, but I couldn't be sure.

When Amelia finally came out she was wearing a white dress with a waistband like the swan ladies, not the smock she usually wore. She had her hair down and brushed. It was wavy and golden and some of it was pinned up underneath a flower. It was a real flower. A bee the size of my thumb was hovering near it, preparing to land. I went to swipe it away, but she said it didn't matter. She said she couldn't come out anyway because she was getting ready to go to a new college for ladies.

Do you want to go to the quay afterwards? I asked her, but Amelia had already gone inside and shut the door.

I went down to the quay with Horse instead.

To the West Coast! I cried, and we snuck on board a Norwegian barque to play the ship game. Horse was Captain Martello and I was First Mate Eugene, but Horse spent most of his time sitting inside the giant coils of rope on deck. He was weird like that. He would always find small spaces to sit in. He said it made him feel safe. I didn't need to sit in small spaces to feel safe. I knew I would never feel safe. My skin would always prickle as if one layer had been ripped off and my nerves were flailing around like tentacles. Amelia Grey didn't need to sit in small spaces to feel safe either. Amelia Grey had a safe feeling inside her wherever she went, as if she believed nothing bad would ever happen to her, which is probably why nothing bad ever did.

When I got home there were tomatoes spread out on trays in the grass, tomatoes lined up along the top of the front fence, tomatoes on the roof, seeds up, and the sun was reaching down saying, *Grow, grow!* and the tomatoes were saying, *No, fuck off, we don't want to!* and shrivelling up instead. There were trays with tomatoes on them balanced on top of the pumpkin vine in the vegetable garden, and tomatoes instead of fishing nets spread out across the grass, and inside someone was moaning. The house looked whiter than usual. It looked sick.

In the kitchen there was a puddle of something red on the floor—some of it bright tomato red and some of it dark wine red. Papà was pacing the corridor and I could hear that the moans were Mamma's and were coming from the bedroom.

What's wrong with Mamma? I asked.

And Papà said, *What do you think? It's time for the baby!*

When I opened the bedroom door Mamma reached out for me. Her hair was out again, and mussed up all over the pillow. You'd think it would be easy for her after having had so many babies, but she was wailing like she was going to be sick. *Tiralo fuori!* she said. *Get it out!* Nonna was standing at the end of the bed, looking between Mamma's legs, ready to catch in case it shot out like a cannonball.

And then it did.

It shot out. The baby couldn't wait any longer.

The other babies had held on to the inside of Mamma for as long as they possibly could, but this baby wasn't afraid of anything. The baby didn't even cry. The baby laughed and clutched at Nonna's hair. The baby was strong and wouldn't let go. The baby tried to eat the hair. The baby had a deep voice. The baby was a boy.

Un maschio! Un maschio! Nonna cried out.

Papà couldn't help himself, he flung the bedroom door open and clutched the boy, covering him with fat tears and kisses.

Un maschio! Finalmente! he said and took the boy to Mamma and covered her with tears and kisses too.

All that day people were coming over with fried eggplant and crayfish and mullets in tomato sauce. They drank their way through Papà's wine. They slapped him on the back. Every now and then Papà would come back down to earth, look at me and say, *Where are your sisters? Go and play with your sisters.*

When Father Kelly came, it was decided the baby was going to be called William. A solid name for a solid New Zealander boy, and from that moment on I knew I would hate him forever.

Mamma was scared Baby William would die because all her other boy babies had died, and so she tiptoed around him always, as if he was nothing but a phantasm that might vanish if she ever sneezed or gave him the wrong food for breakfast. *Oh, don't wake William. No, don't give him an apple, he doesn't like those. No, he doesn't like honey on bread, don't even think about putting honey on that bread,* she'd say, and William would look back at her with an idiot look on his face because he was a baby and that's what babies do. Mamma never ruffled my hair or called me a funny joker anymore, she was too busy trying to work out exactly what Baby William wanted at all times in case he died and she had to live the rest of her life thinking perhaps she hadn't paid enough attention to how much he did or didn't like apples or honey on bread. And if you were scraping the burned bits out of the bottom of a pan when you were doing the washing-up, it was all *No! No! Cosa fai? You'll wake Baby William!* in a whisper loud enough to wake Baby William and then whose fault was that but yours if he started screaming? I couldn't stand it anymore.

I could dislike honey on bread too if it would make her like me better and meant I could get out of cleaning the whole kitchen after every meal, but I knew it wouldn't. After a year of washing Baby William's nappies and mashing Baby William's food so it would come out orange-brown and putrid in another nappy moments later, I packed a few things. I took a can of sardines. I took some bread and a bottle of wine in case I might need to trade it for something. Then I walked. I walked until my feet bled and kept walking until my feet couldn't bleed anymore and the bones stuck out of my feet. I didn't stop until I arrived in Miramar, where a tall chimney injected the clouds in the sky full of smoke, and thought, *Yes, that's what I'll do. I'll get a job and earn more than Papà. That'll show them.*

I walked up the driveway of the place with the chimney, right past a dray being drawn by four horses. The dray they were tugging was heavy with bricks and the horses had stopped in the middle of the driveway saying, *Why should we bother when the sun is out and the grass is long and delicious?* but then the driver whipped them and they said, *Oh, that's right, we'd forgotten about the whip,* and kept pulling.

I walked past the horses, through the main gate and right to the edge of the brickworks. It was crawling with men snuffling through mud like pigs. There were no hats or babies for miles and I thought, *Yes, this is the place for me.*

I found the man who was pointing and ordering people around the most, thinking that would be the man who was in charge, and I said, *Will you give me a job please, Sir?*

And Sir said, *What—to a girl?* and started laughing and looking around him as if he was expecting a chorus of people to erupt into laughter with him, but there was no one there, they were all in the quarry working.

Well, I was going to show him too.

I walked out of the quarry, past the whipped horses who were still hemming and hawing over the deliciousness of the uneaten grass, and continued to walk when the dark spilled into the sky, and kept walking until I saw the dark dissolve around a lit-up house.

I went up to the front door of the house and—holding the bottle of wine out in front of me so they wouldn't think I was a beggar—knocked on the door.

A mother answered the door. She looked distracted. I could tell she was a mother because I could hear a baby crying in the background. She turned to it and said, *Oh William, hush now!* and I thought, *Not another fucking William, they are everywhere.*

I made to leave but then the mother smiled down at me. She wasn't wearing flowers in her hat, she was wearing no hat at all, and only had a few teeth. She clearly couldn't afford dentures or couldn't be bothered looking pretty anymore seeing as she already had a husband and a baby.

I said, *Please, ma'am, do you have any scissors?*

She laughed and said, *What do you want scissors for, girl?*

Behind her a young boy of about my age ran towards the sound of the screaming baby. I said to the mother I'd give her this very fine Italian wine in exchange for the use of her scissors. She stopped and considered this for a second, which seemed to take all the energy she had because she froze and looked up into the top right corner of her head where all her thoughts were already tucked into bed for the night. Finally her eyes came back downstairs into her face and she said, *Oh, alright, you seem to be a fairly harmless girl to me.* Then she screamed at the boy, *JOE, COME 'N' SHOW THIS GIRL WHERE THE SCISSORS ARE KEPT, WILL YA?*

Joe came up to the door. He had a tooth missing. He had hair sticking up in all the wrong places. He had pants that were too big and rolled up at the ankles and a shirt that looked like it had been worn by seven generations of potato farmers and braces that were holding up the too-big pants. His mamma went to stop the baby from screaming, so Joe and I were left to stand there and look at each other. I was sure he'd never seen a girl before just as I'd never seen a boy with lashes so dark and soft they belonged to the eyes of a mare.

I remembered what Amelia once said about boys being only after one thing and said, *Hey Joe, have you ever been with a woman before?*

He stared. Then blinked. *I'm twelve,* he said.

Well, these are uncertain times, Joe, you don't know what's going to happen next. They say we're all about to become communists so you better get a feel while you've still got the chance.

Um, the scissors are above the sink in the shed—you can get them yourself if you want, Joe said, then turned to go back inside.

Oh no, Joe, I don't think I could possibly reach them by myself, I said, grabbing him by the sleeve. *Why, I'm just a little girl.*

Joe frowned as if he was trying to work out how to spell *parallel* or *gnome* and finally said, *Oh, alright,* then led me around the side of the house to the shed.

The shed wasn't really a shed, it was more like three bits of metal propped up around a tap. Above the tap there was a plank of wood with nails sticking out, a tool dangling from each one. He reached up and lifted the scissors off their nail, and as he did I could see that the hair around the back of his neck curled like the feathers on the bum of a duck.

He turned around and there I was, standing in the doorway of the shed, not about to move away for anyone, especially not him.

Now, Joe, I said, *if you take off your trousers, I'll take off my dress.*

I thought you wanted the scissors, he said.

I did and I still do, but I thought I'd give you a present first.

Why would taking off my trousers be a pres—, he started to say, but I lifted my dress straight up and he stopped talking.

I couldn't see him because I had my skirts in front of my face but I knew he was standing there with his jaw dangling by its hinges and I said, *What, Joe, you never seen a naked woman before?*

But Joe wasn't staring, he was looking at the scissors, scraping off the rust. *Yep*, he said, *I see my mum naked all the time.*

But mums aren't really women, are they, especially not yours. She doesn't look like this, does she? and Joe squinted up at me.

So, I said, *if you cut off my hair, I'll let you stick your penis in here*, and I put my fingers in my vagina.

Why would I want to do that? he said. *Why didn't you just ask me to cut your hair?*

Will you cut it then? Will you cut it like yours? I asked.

My dad did it when he was drunk.

I think it looks perfect, exactly as it is.

Joe looked at me, all hopeful, saying, *Really?* and I did my sweetest smile yet and said, *Yes, Joe, really.*

He cut my hair off with only five snips of the scissors and when he snipped the last snip I held his hand that was holding the scissors and turned around so that the scissors were being held between us, a silver lily with dangerous sharp leaves, and pushed my hands all the way down until the scissors were pointing straight at his penis, which was when I said, *Take your pants off right now.*

He opened his mouth and started to shout *M—*

But before he could say *—ummy* I shoved the scissors closer— but not too close because I didn't want to rip a hole in what would soon be my new trousers.

He took off his trousers and took off his shirt and kicked them over to the corner, so I took off my dress and did the same.

We both stood there in our underclothes and maybe it was the wind bringing out the goosebumps on my arms, or maybe it was the blue shadows that dragged under his eyes, but I suddenly felt horrible.

I'm sorry, I said.

It's cold, he said, and started to cry.

His singlet was grey with stains in a way that made his skin bright white and the moon lit him so he glowed like a saint or a rabbit that was about to get skinned.

You can put my dress on now, if you like, I said.

He started laughing. He laughed so hard, snot bubbled out his nose.

No way, I'm not a girl! Yuck! he said, then popped the bubble of snot with his tongue, and licked up the remains.

Right, I said, and stopped feeling sorry for him. I put on the trousers and the shirt, and left him shivering by the tap. They fit perfectly, like Joe was the one who'd stolen them from me all along.

I slept behind a mulberry bush on the side of the road, and as soon as I woke I went back to the brickworks for another try at a job. I found the man who'd been doing all the pointing and ordering around.

I need some work, I said.

Oh, we're a boy now are we?

Yep, I said, *I've always been a boy, they dressed me wrong before.*

Well I can't pay you the full amount. Only a ha'penny a day, or the real boys will get jealous.

When he smiled, I saw that his teeth were brown pebbles. The spit in his mouth was mud.

Working in the brickworks was easy enough. I didn't understand why they thought only men could pat clay into wooden blocks and bake it in an oven. It was like baking bread, except instead of carefully measuring out ingredients you pulled fistfuls of clay out of the ground and whacked it into a mould. Actually, it was hard in that your muscles ached, the sun smacked you on the back of the neck and you worked in a permanently hunched position so that by the time the sun went down you were convinced you'd never stand up to see the horizon again, but in comparison to home it was like skipping through a field full of butterflies, all of them pouring honey in your mouth whenever you opened it to breathe.

The other workmen didn't talk much because if they did their clay faces would crumble back into the quarry and they'd lose the cigarettes from their mouths. We worked in silence until I got something wrong and one of the clay men ripped the wrong thing out of my hand to make it right, then went back to smoking and getting his arms half covered in red mud the way they ached to be.

Later the men sat around and made a cup of tea and lit a fresh ciggie. They still didn't say much, but when they did it was a joke at someone else's expense. Only the sissies didn't know how to take it.

One man with a smoke-grey beard and depressing operas droning on in his eyes looked up at me over his tea and said, *What, you can't be more than ten years old, boy.*

No, I'm thirteen years old; further away from the grave than you, I said, because you had to show them you could fight back.

His eyes lit up for a new comedy scene and he said, *Oh really?* then picked me up as easy as he would pick a mangy cat out of the bin and threw me down into the bottom of the quarry. I was sure something must have broken—how could you fall that far and not break anything?—but being young and made of rubber, everything sprang back into place.

Looks like that's pretty close to a grave to me, he said, and the other blokes laughed, even the man with the pebble teeth.

They want me dead, I thought. *I have to leave before this quarry really does become my grave.* But when I climbed out of the quarry the man who threw me down slapped me on the back so that I almost fell back in. Another man handed me a tin mug half filled with grey-white water he called tea.

Ah, ya little bugger, he said. *You're alright.*

When the clay dust hovering above the quarry turned dark red, red as the sky, and all the other men were packing up their things and getting ready to leave, I stayed back and cleaned my tools for a third time. *I bet they haven't even noticed I'm gone*, I thought. Papà would be fishing extra late trying to provide enough for a son, and Mamma would have her giant breast shoved in her new son's face. The son would be fat and stupid and laughing at something only an idiot would laugh at—its own poo, for instance, or a dribble of vomit—and meanwhile my sisters would be cooking and cleaning the house even though they were only six and four and three years old.

I felt a hand on my shoulder.

Eh, son, said the man with the pebble teeth. *I think it's time you went home now.*

He gave me a whole penny for my work, not the ha'penny he said he was going to pay me.

I don't have a home, I said.

The man sighed. *You can't go telling me that or I'll have to take you to one of them industrial schools.*

My face went slack. I could feel a twinge of tears and had to do everything I could to make them go away. I thought of horses. Harry Crawford's horse. Harry Crawford winning the race. How I'd be just like him one day. How could I go back to sitting hunched over spelling tests while slow nuns shuffled around dreaming up more things that could be counted as sins, and outside the trees grew slowly and the flowers budded slowly and the grass never grew at all because it kept getting cut before it could even start? The thought of it made me feel dead already.

I'd rather be buried alive in this quarry, I said to Mr Pebble Teeth.

He smiled but frowned at the same time, as if he was trying to push the smile right off his face.

Alright son, he said. *How about you bring your father by tomorrow, and if he says you can work then you can work.*

I decided to walk back from Miramar, sticking by the water as much as possible. You never knew if there'd be a pirate ship looking for a new deck boy a mile offshore. *Arr, you there, me matey,* they'd call out through a conch the size of a ham, *come over 'ere and help me feed the parrots—they be awfully restless this evenin' with the storm brewin'.* I'd run down the hill, climb over the rocks and swim out to the ship. They'd throw a rope down but before it even hit the water I'd swing right up and land on deck.

Unfortunately, while working out the names of my future parrots (Hello Sailor, Peaches, Echo, Long John), I'd managed to get back to Coromandel Street. I stood outside the front gate of my house and couldn't seem to move. Baby William was crying. Mamma was saying, *Shhh, shhhh.* Someone dropped a plate in the washing-up tub and Papà said, *ATTENTA, TI SVEGLIERAI IL,* which had the neighbour's dog barking its face off. I felt like a thief, standing there on the outside of my gate thinking, *Who are these people? I've never met them before in my life.*

I slept in the pumpkins. It was a clear night with no wind for a change, and I wanted to sleep outside. Bedrooms would be too small for the size of my dreams now that they'd be full of the stuff of the wide working world. There'd be men made of clay rising up from the earth to replace all the sissy men who couldn't handle life out here at the edge of the world, and there'd be parrots with wings made of my own hacked-off hair and women with no teeth smiling and saying, *Life's alright once you burn all the hats.* But before I dreamed these things I thought of Harry Crawford. His polished shoes were glinting slightly north of the Southern Cross and between all his fingers and toes were lit, hand-rolled cigarettes. His mouth was a wisp of cloud saying, *She'll be right, mate.*

Who's 'she'? I asked him.

He looked stunned for a second. *It's a phrase that you say,* he said.

But it must have started somewhere. What happened to her that made people worried she wouldn't be right?

That's funny, Harry Crawford said. *I never thought about that before.* He took a drag from one of his cigarettes before adding, *Maybe she had a hard time giving birth, or something like that, whoever she was.*

Harry, I said, *why don't you ride your horse anymore? Why don't you race the other butcher boys?*

Harry Crawford wriggled his toes in his shoes, making them glimmer, and said, *I'm all tangled up with a woman now, matey.*

Have to earn proper money if I even want to think about having a family.

Why would you want to think about that? Why don't you go to Australia? Become a drover or a jackaroo?

Harry Crawford shook his head. *I doubt there'd be any woman in the world as beautiful as mine,* he said, which annoyed me so much I couldn't talk to him anymore, let alone sleep. How did he know what there was and wasn't out in the world? There could be an island in the Pacific full of women with skin made out of real chocolate with raisins for nipples for all he knew; he'd never left this place to find out. This was like how Father Kelly would look out of his window and sigh and say, *How can people refuse to believe in God when—look at the harbour so still! And the hills rising up on either side of her like a brilliant green chorus praising God! How else could a world so miraculous come into existence if it weren't for Our Lord making it so?* I knew Father Kelly was too dull to dream up anything other than the hill behind Thorndon, Mount Victoria, and a bit of flat water in between. He'd never be able to imagine a place so miraculous it made your chest fizz like spit in sherbet every time you walked outside. It was as if there was a large stone on the top of Father Kelly's head stopping him from imagining what you can't see with your eyes. But now Harry Crawford, too. Maybe he could only see his life play out as far as the butcher's on Constable Street. Maybe he'll always get the same cheap mince and stop in on Mrs Wilson for a brandy snap sometimes, and only dream of the woman with the messy hair, even after she leaves him for Raines, and he finds that the stiff patterns of his life only flow with life again after downing seven beers. That was what happened to men here. They saw themselves as frontier men, but really they turned the wild and unknown into something safe that looked a bit like Glasgow.

I couldn't sleep knowing Harry Crawford was as feeble as that. I needed to start the whole vision over again, this time with Harry Crawford's shoes glinting not because they were polished, but because he was sitting in a paddock in front of a fire he'd made with his own hands out of a few cow pats and dried driftwood collected from the beach. Yes, this new Harry Crawford sat there with his legs spread, saying, *Ah, matey, did I tell you about the time I was on a trading vessel in the Pacific? The women there! Nipples sweet as raisins! Skin like chocolate! And what, save Mary, has happened to your hair?*

What? I said.

Mamma was standing with the sun rising behind her, Baby William on one hip and a tub of washing on the other, looking like she was about to drop them both before the image of her daughter asleep in the pumpkins, wearing some filthy boy's trousers and her hair all cut off.

Mamma didn't drop the washing and she certainly didn't drop Baby William. She looked at me with sadness, as if I was a poor replacement for her little girl, then bent down slowly, sucking the air through her teeth so I knew how much it pained her, carrying the weight of the baby and the weight of the wet washing in addition to the weight of the world. She placed the tub of washing in front of me and said, *Peg this up, will you, I have to feed William his second breakfast, he's such a hungry growing boy.*

Rosie and Ida were standing in the back doorway, staring like they'd had their brains eaten out by termites while I was gone. I walked past them, past Papà, took a loaf of bread off the kitchen table and a tin of sardines from the pantry, gripped a salami that was hanging above the stove and yanked it down. Papà winced as if I'd gelded him.

O, signore! he said.

I see, I said. *You only notice me when I'm a boy.*

With that I turned to leave, but Papà materialised in front of me.

Fine. You want to work? You can get a job.

Really?

Yes. He looked up to see if God was watching him lie.

No more housework?

No more house—well, only in the morning. And after dinner.

That's great news, Papà, because I already found a job, but I need you to come and give permission.

He nodded. Maybe it was a twitch. Papà no longer looked like a man who knew how to make craypots and fishing nets. He'd become the nervous director of a nativity play and our house was the set. It had to be perfect for the guest of honour, none other than Baby William himself.

I walked into the room I shared with Ida to get my things for work and found that our bed had vanished and in its place stood a crib with two small idiot hands clutching at the bars, the body they were attached to bouncing up and down as if being in prison was a delirious thrill.

Where's my bed? I asked the idiot creature, and it said, *Gaarrglrg.*

What have you done with my bed, you devil's spawn? I said, and behind me Mamma muttered, *Madonna mia! Forgive my daughter for the things she says, she has become possessed.*

My things had been moved into the other girls' room—four of us squished together in two small beds. It was a miracle of geometry. I pulled the pillowcase off my pillow, threw in the salami and the bread and said, *I'm going to work, and I'm going whether you'll come and give permission or not.*

Work? Rosie said, her eyes large and anxious. *No one works on a Sunday, it's a sin.*

Sunday? It's not Sunday!

Yes it is, and it's time for Mass, Ida said.

They were both wearing explosions of lace with blue sashes around their waists. They had bonnets on their heads, covered in so many flowers a bee would have overdosed with joy. Mamma was standing in the bedroom doorway pressing Baby William's face into her breast. *Drink me up, drink my life's blood dry. God knows the rest of them will if you don't.*

Rosie pulled what used to be my best Sunday dress out of my pile of things on the mattress, except it wasn't white anymore, it was pink.

Scusa, Mamma said without looking sorry. *Ida tried to scrub the beetroot in with the laundry, so now your sheets and things have gone pink.*

Ida giggled. *You hate pink.*

The window was locked and they were clustered in the doorway. There was no escaping the dress. I would've pushed past Mamma but William went *schlup schlup schlup blergh* and vomited onto her chest. She laughed as if she was being tickled. *Ohhhh! Quanto sei carino*, she said, *you funny little joker.* Then she ran her finger through the vomit and licked it off, *Num num num.*

With me in pink spliced between my white frilly sisters on the back of Nonno Buti's dray we looked like a chunk of coconut ice being dragged through the streets of Newtown. We may as well have held up a sign which said LOOK EVERYONE, HERE COME THE ITALIANS with Mamma sitting up the front clutching a baby boy to her chest, her head veiled and lashes low, hoping she looked the very image of the Virgin Mary now that she had a son. Beside me my sisters were saying:

I'm going to live in a cave and only say the rosary until I die.

Me too.

And my hands and knees will be hard like the skin of a camel from all the praying.

Mine too.

Mamma said, *That's right, girls, now let's remember the rosary in English so we can show Father Kelly.*

And then everyone said, *HailMaryfullofgracetheLordiswiththee-blessedartThouamongstwomenandblessedisthefruitofThywomb-JesusHolyMarymotherofGodprayforussinnersnowandatthehour-ofourdeathamen.*

They sounded like a swarm of hypnotised bees and I wondered if the cart was going too fast to make a run for it, but as soon as I worked out where I'd run Mamma dug her nails into my arm.

You're not going anywhere, Nina.

Mass was three hours of watching men in dress-ups swing brass balls around and getting wept on by all the depressed Virgin Marys stuck up in the windows. Were they bored or sad? It was hard to tell. There were babies everywhere, too, big paintings of babies and next to them crosses, as if to say, *Don't get too excited, babies, this is where you're headed next.*

Through the smoke and the mutterings of *Domini corpus dominum porpoise* I felt something akin to a cold wet leaf blown in the face. It was a glance from Horse on the other side of the aisle.

I like your pink dress and your new haircut, his eyes were saying.

Fuck you, mine said back.

There was no relief. Standing outside on the cold stone steps afterwards Rosie tugged on Sister Katherine's gown and begged, *Tell us again about all the saints who share our names and how they died.*

Well, Sister Katherine said, her eyes fogging up, *there was St Emilia, she died in a cave, and then there was St Rosalina, she died in her house after getting sick and the skin on her hands and knees was like the skin on a camel from all the praying, and then there was St Rose who also died in a cave—*

As Sister Katherine went on and on I could see a tiger-yellow waistcoat flash between the black and grey parishioners. It got wilder and brighter as it moved closer. Inside the waistcoat was a man. He had hair that flopped into his eyes and a sideways smile aimed right at me. When he was standing next to me he leaned in close and whispered, *Have these people always been insane?*

How did he know what I was thinking?

It's written all over your face, he said.

From that Sunday on, for a year at least, I always saw that man at Mass. I'd feel him watching as I tied up Nonno Buti's horses, as I untied the horses, as I slipped away to give the horses a piece of the body of Christ stolen from the biscuit tin on the altar. I don't know why he needed to direct all of his good looks at me, when any number of girls would have shaved off their ringlets if it meant he'd notice them for five whole seconds.

When everyone decided that Rosie was old enough to marry God, we squeezed into Nonna and Nonno Buti's house after Mass to celebrate. The women were in the kitchen trying to be helpful but there were three times as many women as men so there were mountains of cream-filled cakes, and biscuits balancing on top of the cakes and icing sugar dusted over the whole lot and only four men to eat them—Papà, Nonno Buti, Father Kelly and Little William. Even though it was Rosie's party the four men sat in the middle of the backyard while Ida and the women stood around them, watching them eat, offering a tray of biscuits, or rushing forward to brush the crumbs off their fat tummies. As a special case, Mamma was allowed to sit in the middle with the men, but only because she had Little William on her lap, sucking the filth off the hem of her skirt.

I wasn't standing anywhere near the men. I was sitting by the front window watching the smell of cakes draw more men up the front steps. Horse came with his uncle, and so did the musician I saw in the garden at Thorndon. Then there he was: the man in the yellow waistcoat. He arrived astride a palomino gelding—twelve hands high at least—swung his leg over, lashed the horse to the fence, then moved up the front steps in an easy glide. As he entered the house his eyes struck mine. Something lit up in them like a flash of lightning a million miles away and I turned my face before anything inside me could catch on fire.

Nonna saw, though.

She said, *He's got lovely eyes, don't you think, Eugenia?*

I didn't say anything. She knew I didn't respond when people called me Eugenia, but she kept calling me that anyway. Papà came into the front room, greeted the man in the yellow waistcoat as if he were a prince, and together they went out onto the street. Through the window I watched them speak. Papà was excited, the man was calm and collected. Then Papà shook the man's hand, and walked very quickly in the direction of our house.

Eugenia? Nonna said. *Not talking today?*

She put a hand on each of my shoulders and bent down to my level.

There's no shame in your name. It's the same name as mine. It's the same name as Santa Eugenia, and do you know what she did?

Died in a cave?

No. I don't know where she died, but when she was alive she was the daughter of the governor of Egypt and fled her father's house dressed as a boy—not so different to your little adventure, eh? Then she became a Christian. She even became an abbot!

Nonna said 'even' the way you would if you were saying, *God even loves hideous monsters like you!*

Nonna's face was so close I could see her moustache. It was made up of black hairs that got paler at the tips, as if they were frozen halfway through an invisibility trick. *Women loved Santa Eugenia. One woman tried to make love to her, and when Eugenia said no the woman accused her of adultery—*

I tried to ignore the howls in the pit of my stomach but the ghosts of millions of women who spent their lives sitting in a cave wishing they were dead so they could be with Jesus were hard to ignore.

Nonna was talking for too long and I felt faint. The dead saints grew louder, crying over their wasted lives. *I didn't realise life was all I had and now look, I'm dead I'm dead I'm deader than dead!*

—then Santa Eugenia had to appear in court before none other than her own father as judge, and all was forgiven. Being a woman saved her from death. You see, it isn't so bad all the time . . .

Nonna saw what she thought was deep understanding in my still face, and straightened up as slowly and confidently as if she'd been announced the winner of all the prizes at the church picnic. She'd got through to me. She knew she was the only one who could.

But when I stood up there was a deep red stain on my seat. I touched the back of my dress and saw that my fingers were brushed with blood. The howls hadn't been the howls of saints stabbing themselves in the stomachs over their wasted lives, they'd come from my own body saying, *Well, you're a woman now, even if you don't want to be, ha ha ha,* and blowing blood bubbles into my knickers out of spite. Nonna put a cushion on the chair where

I'd been sitting, smiled with a tear in her eye and shuffled me into her bedroom.

Through the window I could hear the men eating and the women saying how well the men were eating. Nonna folded a piece of cloth and showed me how to place it in the bottom of my knickers.

The good news is you won't be wearing smocks anymore, but the bad news is this means no more adventures in trousers for you! She winked, as if trousers had only been a clever place to hide in a game of hide-and-seek.

A nice full skirt will cover the new bulk in your knickers, I think, she said, and pulled a heavy mass of grey cloth out of the trunk at the end of her bed. It looked like something you put dead bodies in before throwing them into the sea.

We returned home to find that our backyard was no longer blanketed with fishing nets. Instead there were bits of wood and bales of hay. Broken bits of Papà's fishing boat were strewn about the place, and the boat's ribs were showing. It looked like Papà was trying to build himself into a rotting whale.

What are you doing, Papà?

As he hammered he shouted into the wood that he was sick of having no one to help him, that he was sick of the men at the Taranaki wharf treating him like offal, that he was going to start a carrier's business, and that would show them.

Tied up to the lemon tree were four palomino geldings. Papà had borrowed money from a hotelier—he wouldn't say his name— to buy the four geldings, but couldn't afford the wood for a stable so he'd had to take an axe to his own boat.

I walked towards the horses with my palm out for sniffing, and the horses nodded in approval. There are simple things you can do for a horse that don't involve talking or trying to be a certain way. You can put a stick in a tin of molasses and cover the stick with hay and give it to the horse as a treat. You can brush the horse, and pay attention to the way its coat shivers or doesn't. When I brushed Papà's horses it was as gentle and easy as breathing. That was all a person needed to do: brush a horse and say things to the horse that you knew it wouldn't understand and it would nod, not because it understood, but because it was adjusting its neck muscles, and that was fine also. I wished I'd been born a horse into a family of horses instead of whatever monstrous in-between thing I was.

While Papà hammered I saddled and harnessed the horses to show Papà that I was better with horses than anyone he knew, but when he saw me with them he ripped the reins from my fingers and said, *No, Nina! You will never get a husband like this.*

I refused to sleep in the glorified laundry heap with the other girls so I slept out in the pumpkins near the horses, my insides wringing themselves of blood as I did. In the morning old beer bottles were lined up in rows on the kitchen table, and over breakfast Mamma announced she was getting ready to bottle the passata again. She looked straight past me. *Would you like to help?* she asked Ida and Rosie and Emily.

I didn't have time for passata anyway. If my insides were going to turn on me like this, I'd have to find my own way back to the quarry before it was too late and I was married off or pregnant or dead.

Mamma must have heard me thinking, because she put on her sweetest voice yet and said, *While the girls get started on the sauce, I thought I might take you out to find a job.*

Really?! I was excited for a second, until I realised she was wearing her church-going clothes. No one would go to a brickworks in church-going clothes. *This does not bode well*, I thought. *This does not bode well at all.*

With Little William clinging to her skirt, Mamma took me to a white picket fence in Thorndon. It grinned like an underbite.

This isn't a brickworks, I said, my insides twisting and burning. *This is the opposite of a brickworks.*

A domestic, Mamma said, *is a better job for you.*

A domestic what?

Oh, she said. *It'll be just like what you're used to at home.*

Four babies always trying to win a screaming competition?

She looked nervous. *Maybe. And laundry to fold, and beds to make.*

She gave me two tentative kisses goodbye and as she did a thick coating of dust fell over the brickworks and the West Coast and all the hopes and dreams I'd ever had. They sneezed, then coughed, then died. A domestic. I'd never heard of a more boring job in my life.

Inside the mauve house the ceiling was so high you could've fit five horses stacked one on top of the other between it and the top of your head. I felt small and stupid in my heavy grey skirt with my hair up underneath something you could use to make cheese. The housekeeper was compulsively dusting in the corner, thinking, *This little madam is definitely a thief just look at her grubby fingers they've been in every coat pocket this side of town.*

And I was thinking, *I wonder when she'll stop dusting that one china horse over and over again.*

Finally the Lady of the House came in the front door. She peeled off her gloves as if she was trying to peel a peach without breaking the skin.

Can you fold a sheet? she asked me.

Yes.

Can you do hospital corners on a bed?

Yes.

Then the girl's hired, she said.

The housekeeper dropped the tiny horse she was dusting and it bounced across the rug, landing on her mistress's right foot.

The Lady of the House eyed it as if the housekeeper had just vomited the horse onto her shoe. *Are your hands getting the shakes again, Mrs Pryce?*

No, ma'am. I'm sorry.

If Mrs Pryce's hands weren't shaking before, they definitely were now. One was jittering all over the doorknob like a spider having a nervous breakdown; it just couldn't get a grip at all.

Mrs Pryce, you'll need to show the girl where the sheets are kept, the Lady said.

Mrs Pryce looked at me then. Her eyes were two currants someone had picked out of a scone, but one was slightly bigger so maybe that one was a raisin.

Right, she said. *Follow me, child.*

We walked down a wooden staircase, through a small blue door, around a corner, and down another wooden staircase that got narrower and darker as we went. Every third step or so creaked and Mrs Pryce reached her hand back and gripped my arm, saying, *For*

God's sake only step where I step or we'll lose our second laundry maid for the week.

At the bottom she thumped open a door with her hip. Steam coughed out of the room and Mrs Pryce bowed her head, praying to the God of Steam. Even I had to dip my head on the way in, the doorway was that small.

The ceiling was high but you couldn't see how high because the steam gathered above our heads into clouds. It smelled like clean sheets and soap and all you could see were walls made of stacked, folded sheets reaching high up into the clouds.

Where are we? I asked Mrs Pryce.

In the laundry, where do you think you silly girl. She moved down one of the corridors made by the sheets. *Come along or you'll lose me!*

I had to run to catch up, and as I did my footfalls made the sheet corridors shake.

Careful now, we don't want to have to refold all this, do we?

She said *we* as if she really meant *you*.

No, I said. *We don't.*

We finally stopped in front of a table. On the left of the table was a mountain of crumpled sheets, so clean they were the bluish-white of icebergs.

You will fold these, and when you've finished you will collect the dry sheets from the line and fold those.

Where's the—

You will find the line out there, she said, and pointed out the window to where a line was strung up between the weathercock on the stable roof and the laundry. There were ten white sheets there, kicking around in the wind, trying to jump free of their pegs. Every now and then they kicked right up to reveal the stable behind them, and a boy leaning against the stable door.

Mrs Pryce's eyes grew darker and more shrivelled in her doughy white face. *That's our coachman*, she said.

On the next glimpse I could see that he was smoking a cigarette.

You'll find he doesn't often work, as the Lady of the House prefers to walk around the city. But even so, he gets paid twice what you will.

How much will I get paid?

Something in the order of a ha'penny a day, I'd imagine.

She spoke quietly, almost tenderly, and I wondered if she was speaking to a distant memory of her younger self. She shook the memory out of her head and her lips became thin, her face tight.

Well, it's been lovely chatting, but we mustn't let the Lady of the House know we've been larking around like this, she said, and disappeared between the walls of sheets.

I watched the boy out the window for a moment. He was stubbing out his cigarette, stretching, yawning, then lighting another. He did it all so slowly, as if he was proving just how slowly he could go. Between a fluttering of sheets Mrs Pryce's lips mouthed, *Chop, chop, girl*, so I stopped looking at the boy and started folding.

There were so many sheets. Smooth, white, clean-smelling and so, so boring. *Corner-to-corner, shake, fold. Corner-to-corner, shake, fold.* This was the rhythm of the folding of the sheets. It lulled you like a boat lulled you and once you were lulled you were on a ship. I could see St Eugenia climbing the rigging, looking back over her shoulder. But then the folding was done and the daydreams coughed under their thick coating of dust and were still again.

I went out into the courtyard to collect the dry washing off the line, and who should strike up a conversation with me but the slowest coach driver in the world.

You're new, he said, to prove how slow he was.

Yes, I said.

You like horses?

Yes.

Can I take you for a ride?

Maybe he isn't so bad after all, I thought, and followed him into the stable.

The stable was rich with the smell of sweet hay and leather. A horse was blowing air through his rubbery lips and restlessly moving the metal bit around in his mouth. It felt like Nonno Buti's stable in there, except for the boy's hand pinching me on the bum.

What are you doing? I asked him.

Taking you for a ride, he said. So I kicked him in the shins.

What did you do that for, you crazy bitch?

Give me your shirt, I said.

What? No—

Do it, I said, and kicked him again.

I lifted Nonna's bodybag skirt up, and pulled my knickers down. The folded rag was now soaked and warm and deep dark red.

Here, I said, throwing the rag at him. His chest and arms were smeared with blood. *Go and wash it in the laundry. I have more important work to do.*

The boy stumbled backwards and opened his mouth, ready to shout.

And if you tell anyone about this, I added, folding his shirt and placing it in my knickers the way Nonna had showed me, *I'll tell them that's my blood on your skin, and you'll be locked up for the rest of your life.*

Once the boy was gone I stroked the horse down the nose and the horse looked deep into my eyes. *Yes, Tally Ho*, the horse said, *I'm bored of this place, too. Let's make it to the West Coast together.*

An escapee laundry maid astride a stolen horse was not going to make it to the West Coast unseen. I needed Joe's pants, needed food, too, and had to make my escape before anyone noticed the missing horse.

At the end of Coromandel Street I lashed the horse to a tree, and slunk through the shadows with my skirts bundled up in my arms so I could move without falling on my face. I'd hidden Joe's pants behind our lemon tree, under an old crayfish basket that had been left by the fence to rot, but just as I was slinking around the side of the house to fetch them I was stopped short by the sight of a man standing by our back door. Even in the dusk I could see he was wearing a bright yellow waistcoat with a gold chain connecting his lonely right pocket to his lonely left.

Mi scusi, he said.

Excuse me?

You're excused, he said, and winked as if no one had ever made that joke before.

I watched him closely, and he watched me back. It was a competition between who would look away first, but I found myself walking towards him. He picked up my hand and kissed the back of it. His lips were two leeches searching for warmth.

Nina, he said. *I've heard so much about you. Good things, of course . . .*

Inside, I could hear Mamma laugh too loud, then cough. I looked though the open back door to see dinner laid out on the table amongst freshly polished cutlery and roses in vases and finery I never knew we owned. Mamma sat at one end of the table, sipping from a glass of wine with her pinkie raised.

What's wrong with your pinkie? I asked her, but she didn't hear me.

Ciao, bella! she said warmly, as if I was not her estranged daughter who slept in a pumpkin patch.

Mamma, what's the special occasion? I was suspicious of the way her eyes were moving between me and the man in the doorway.

I'll leave you two ladies to catch up, shall I? the man said, before disappearing out into the garden.

I could smell a rat if ever I had smelled a rotting festering rat before.

What are you plotting, Mamma?

She looked younger than she'd ever looked as she wet her lips and said, *He's very handsome, don't you think, Eugenia?*

I supposed I agreed. He was tall and moved the way a thoroughbred moves, without ever having to think about it. His hair came up off his forehead as if it was falling back in a swoon. He was handsome, I'd give him that, and when he came back from the garden he seemed too handsome, the house suddenly collapsible, as if it might faint at the sight of him.

I trust you found the facilities alright? Mamma said.

Facilities? I asked her.

Il gabinetto, she whispered to me behind her hand, but he was already laughing at me for not knowing what facilities meant.

I went behind a lemon tree, he said. *Ho sentito dire che fa bene ai limoni.*

Mamma giggled and gave me a coy look that said, *Those men and their wee, they will do it anywhere if you don't keep an eye on them!* Maybe I would've laughed too, but all I could think about were Joe's trousers now steaming in piss.

Before he sat down the man picked his trouser legs up at the knee. He did other manly things, too, like spread his legs slightly and lean forward so that his crotch pressed against the seat of his chair.

This is Mr Innocente, Mamma said, not looking away from the man. I felt sad for a moment, having never made her look so happy.

Where's Papà and the others? I asked Mamma.

Out somewhere, she said.

I can't remember what we ate or what we talked about, all I can remember is watching the way the man cut food without looking at his hands. I remember Mamma saying at one point, *Are you alright, Nina? You're quieter than normal.* I kept watching the man, and he occasionally shot me a dark look with sparks in it, the way the ocean sometimes has sparks in it at night. I remember at some point he said he owned a hotel in Auckland and had every intention of becoming rich. When he said *rich* it was hard not to believe he would. He was a man who walked through the world as if everything deserved to go right for him, and so everything probably would.

After dinner he stood and walked with me to the door. I watched him the whole way, wondering if I should be saying something or doing something, but he kissed me on both cheeks and said, *I hope to catch you in a more talkative mood next time.*

Once the door clicked shut the rest of the family erupted out of the bedrooms shrieking and giggling. Ida clutched me by the arm and asked, *What's he like? Are you in love with him? Did he kiss you on the mouth?* but Mamma was answering all their questions before I could take in a breath to say one word.

When the other girls were fast asleep, Mamma brought her mending out to where I was sitting on the back step.

Why don't you marry him? she said softly. *He's a nice man for you. He will look after you.*

I shook my head. *No, Mamma. I can't.*

Mamma sighed. She couldn't understand why a girl would waste an opportunity to have that handsome man stick his penis in her and move it around.

She put down her mending and held my face in her hands. It was gentle at first, until she gripped my jaw hard so I couldn't look away. I held her gaze to show her I wouldn't budge and, no, I was not afraid. I'd had enough. She didn't want what was best for me, she wanted what was best for Papà's business, or for her idea of who I should be.

If you want him to marry, why don't you marry him yourself? I said.

She slapped me hard across the face. She'd wanted to make me cry, but she was the one crying, she was the one holding her cheek.

You selfish girl, she said through her tears. *Always wanting what feels good, never wanting to help your family. I should have brought Lisa to this wretched place instead, she would never have treated us like this. You won't help us? Fine. Don't be surprised when you die alone.*

In pants reeking with Mr Innocente's piss I rode my new horse down to the water. Mamma's curse was lodged under my ribs, making me ride faster than any butcher boy ever had. My face was raw where the wind whipped the tear streaks down my cheeks and

Wellington rushed by in a blur until Harry Crawford materialised, sitting on the end of the Taranaki wharf. He'd been drinking, I could tell by the wild swing of his legs and the half-empty whisky bottle leaning against his thigh. Things hadn't gone right since they banned racing in the streets and now all that drive of his was left to loop back and give him liver disease.

I eased the horse back and dismounted, but didn't tie her up. We had an understanding. She'd never leave without me.

Can I have some of that? I asked Harry Crawford.

He handed me the whisky bottle and stifled a belch in the back of his throat.

What brings you down here? he asked.

I told him everything. I could marry a man with sparks in his eyes. We could ride horses together through the streets, but we probably wouldn't. I'd have his children and never go outside except to church and my head would be filled with babies and churches and talk of other people's babies at church. Perhaps we'd have fierce arguments and I'd win him over to my way of seeing the world, but I couldn't imagine this happening either.

Is he handsome? Harry Crawford asked.

Yes.

Is he clever?

Yes.

Is he good?

What do you mean by good?

Then fuck him, Harry Crawford said. *Fuck those charming bastards.*

That's the problem, I said. *I can't think of anything worse.*

Well, Harry Crawford said, *I think you know what to do.*

I put my hand on his. *Will you come with me?* I asked him.

I can't, mate, Harry Crawford said, and we sat side by side in silence, swigging from the bottle and watching a party of drunk night bathers *eek* their way into chilly Oriental Bay. We sat like this for some time until a rumble in the earth had both of us turn our heads. I wondered if an earthquake had struck, when a dust cloud followed by a herd of horses rushed towards the water. The horses of Wellington had broken out of their stables, and all they could think to do was make for the harbour. I didn't know they could swim, and by the looks on their horrified faces neither did they. They paddled around with their heads straining high, their eyes bulging out of their faces, thinking, *Where is the ground? How come our hooves aren't touching the ground?*

There were so many horses the party of bathers had to scamper out of the water, knees up. They stood shivering on their beach towels, looking helplessly back at the bay. *Good on you, horses,* I thought, *you deserve to go places they can't.* I looked over at Harry Crawford to say something, but he was not interested in the horses anymore. He was walking towards where another man and his wife were saying horrible things to each other, things no other animal had a language for.

I recognised the woman. She was the woman with wild hair Harry Crawford had stopped racing for all those years ago. I wished she'd turn around and see him standing there, saying nothing, loving her fiercely still.

My horse took a step towards me and nudged the back of my head. *It's time, Tally Ho, it's time.*

We took the midnight ferry, me and the horse. The ferry was a steam ship, so big all the water in the harbour ran away from it screaming, revealing more water behind it, which also ran away screaming. The ship moved through the water like this for hours until the darkness and the terror had been drained from the sea and it was an exhausted reflection of the pale morning sky. I thought running away would be the brave thing to do, but didn't realise how frightened brave people must be all the time.

The other passengers were curled up asleep on the ferry seats in their work clothes, but my heart was going *ohmygodohmy-godohmygod* in my ears so loudly there was no chance of sleep, not for days. The horse and I stood frozen on the deck of the ferry looking out at the beaten up water and let the wind slap us in the faces to remind us how un-asleep we were. The ship was moving me away from a place that didn't feel right no matter how hard I tried, towards a world that *had to* feel right, because if it didn't, what then? The West Coast of the South Island was a place so full of anger at itself it didn't know what to do other than rip trees out of the ground and pound them into the beaches on the back of big waves, or suddenly decide to make a man rich for no reason other than *Why not?* I'd find gold there, or I'd get eaten by a cannibal, or I'd climb a mountain, or I'd kill a man defending myself. Nothing else could happen to an angry person like me in an angry place like that. It would hate me and spit me out, or it would love me and spit bits of itself out for me to keep as gifts—there'd be no in between.

We arrived in the Marlborough Sounds at an hour when no one was awake, not even night animals. The mist over the Sounds was clammy with the breath of dead saints that had escaped from the dank *drip drip* of mountain caves and the cold wooden floorboards of their convent dormitories to breathe the tides in and let them out again, and mutter curses high up in the canopies of kauri trees. With nothing else to do at that hour, they breathed the ferry towards Picton and, as they did, crawled into the passengers' ears to explore the rooms and hallways of their souls, because hadn't they been duped into being on their own for long enough?

CHILD COACHMAN ACHIEVES RECORD TIME DRIVING FOUR DANGEROUS HORSES DOWN WEST COAST

◊

Hokitika, West Coast

At least one hundred thousand deceased saints have sighted a child coachman, around 16 years of age, successfully transport passengers from Picton to Hokitika in less than a week.

Despite the high speeds achieved by the coach as it traversed some of the most precarious terrain of the South Island, the passengers later proclaimed they had never before experienced such comfort while travelling. The child coachman performed many marvellous feats, at one moment fording a river without first plumbing its depths. The water allegedly covered the backs of the compliant horses and seeped through the floorboards of the coach, however no speed was lost nor doubts raised by the passengers as to their safety.

The child coachman's appearance was described as luminous, with delicate features belying his considerable strength and ability. As a token of his appreciation upon arrival at his destination, one Maori half-caste presented the coachman with the last remaining greenstone talisman from his ancestor's now-dormant quarry near Kumara.

Despite the near super-human time achieved by the child coachman, the saints insist they did not interfere. Once the coachman had arrived at Hokitika at one hour past midnight on the 13th instant, weary and in need of drink, two police officers placed the child coachman under arrest, on a charge of horse theft and vagrancy.

Afterlife Observer, 14 September 1891

The first thing I wanted to do when I got back was tell Nonno Buti about my adventure, but instead I had to be the policemen's hunting trophy for a whole afternoon. It was a wonder they didn't chop my head off and mount it on a plaque, they were that proud of themselves for having caught me. First they walked me through the Central Wellington Police Station with my hands cuffed behind my back and patted their proud stomachs as if it had been their stomachs that had smelled me out and caught me.

When the Lady of the House arrived they thought she'd rip me to shreds but instead she pinched me on the cheek and whispered, *I like a girl with a bit of pluck.* She walked back to where the police officers were still patting their stomachs and said in her loudest acting voice, *Now, never steal my horse again, young lady, do you hear?*

Home would be different.

WHAT TIME DID YOU MAKE? Nonno Buti asked me on the way home from the police station. He was up in the driver's seat with the reins in one hand, holding something under a hat on his knee with the other.

Made it in under a week! I said.

Nonno Buti whistled though his dentures and his leg started jiggling. *I KNEW YOU COULD DO IT!* he said. *HERE, I MADE THIS FOR YOU.*

He took the hat off his knee and revealed a wooden horse with wheels for feet. It was still rough and had not been glazed or sanded. I was sixteen by then, though I didn't look it; too old for such a toy, but I didn't say so because I could see he was happy to have made it for me.

PULL ITS REINS IN, he said.

I pulled its reins and the wooden horse's mouth and belly opened. Inside there was something yellow and shiny, like pus-infected organs.

What is it? I asked him.

PULL IT OUT, GO ON, he said.

It was a jockey's silk racing cap!

WHAT DO YOU THINK? Nonno Buti said. His eyes were all questions and exclamation marks, but my stomach dropped. My

West Coast assignment had been a test. He wanted me to race for him. He wanted me to make him money.

But I'm a girl, Nonno, I said.

WE COULD BE RICH! he shouted down Adelaide Road, but the way he said *rich* was the way a child wearing a tea towel as a turban says *rich*. He was too excited. I didn't believe him.

No, Nonno. They won't let me race, I'm a girl. They have doctors to check.

BALLE! he said. I didn't know what he thought was *balle*—the fact that I couldn't race or the fact that I was a girl. *WE'LL SHOW THEM!* he said.

I was starting to wonder about Nonno Buti. Maybe all his belief in my ability to make it to the West Coast had been the deluded ravings of an old man. But then I *had* made it there, so maybe all brave things need a delusion to get started.

I put the silk racing cap on as we pulled up outside my front gate.

Mamma and Papà and I stood at three points of a triangle in the kitchen, with my brother and sisters standing at the points of a bigger more complicated shape around us. Their arms were by their sides and their mouths were open, ready to catch drops of spraying blood. They were at a bear fight and I was the bear, but nothing happened for a long time. When no one could handle the suspense much longer Mamma said very softly, *Dove cazzo sei stata?*

Mr Innocente entered the room, and took Mamma's elbow with a sympathetic look on his face. He had a great catalogue of looks for his face and knew which one would work on which person at any given moment. He knew you had to give people what they needed to help them love you—and right now what Mamma needed was a kiss on each cheek and to be told she was right to feel sorrow, so he rubbed her back and said, *Non ti preoccupare, I enjoy a challenge.*

Good, she is too much for me, Mamma said, and started to sob. Even from the other side of the room I could see that her cheeks were dry. She was beating Mr Innocente at his own game and he didn't even know she was playing.

Papà walked slowly towards me and gripped me by the top of the arm.

Nina, he said, *running away will not help. If you do not marry him, we'll send you to the girls' home. You cannot keep living here, you will give your mother a brain fever,* and Mamma looked at me and winced to show how horrible that would be.

The girls' home was hidden behind a medieval fortress on Cuba Street. No one knew what happened behind its high walls, but wild girls went in and came out dead-eyed, singing hymns about shepherds. It was the most terrifying place a girl could go, but I couldn't marry Mr Innocente, and I told Papà so.

Papà's grip tightened and my right side lifted off the floor. He was all muscle and gristle; I didn't know he was that strong. He shook me then. I could feel my brain rattle in my skull, his nails pierce my skin, but the shaking I could take. It was the look he gave me that I couldn't bear.

In that one look I saw how he hated all the different parts of me, especially the parts I couldn't help being. What he hated most in me was the stubbornness he hated in himself, and I couldn't help that, I couldn't change that even if I tried.

He shook me for a long while. Some of the older children were crying and saying, *No, Papà!* but Mamma ushered them down the hall to their bedroom.

When Papà let me go the tips of his fingers were white like the fingertips of a frog. He must have noticed this too because he looked at his hands and said, *I am an animal.*

I thought, *No, Papà, you're not as good as that.*

I sat on the kitchen table staring at the window. It reflected me back as a crinkly creature, the kind that lives in a rock pool and I thought, *That's where I should be, at the bottom of the sea.*

The hours began to drag and melt. I had no idea what time it was when footsteps padded down the hallway. I turned to look and there was Ida, standing in the doorway in a nightie that was once mine. It was so small it only came to her knees and the buttons down the front strained against their holes. I turned back to face the window because I didn't want her to see the tear stains on my cheeks, but I didn't have the heart to tell her to go.

She sat on the table next to me, put her arms around me and squeezed. She had her head resting right where Papà had gripped my arm but I didn't tell her to move because it's a wonderful feeling, having someone squeeze all the hateful bits out of you until all that's left is good.

The rain finally broke in relief and Ida squeezed until the rain stopped, and the whirr of tiny frogs offered their voices up in the absence of rain.

Where did you go when you ran away? Ida asked.

The West Coast, I said, *and I've got this to show for it.*

I reached into my pocket to pull out a greenstone a Maori had given me, but it wasn't there.

Ida pulled my hair out from under my silk racing cap, and combed out the knots with her fingers. It was a strange feeling, letting her be tender like this, because usually she was one of Mamma's spies, recording everything I said to use against me later.

She did my hair up the way she'd seen ladies have it done in the salons along Lambton Quay and walked me over to the kitchen window. There, looking back at me, was not a sea creature but a young woman I didn't recognise.

See, Nina? You are beautiful. You're more beautiful than any of us.

The thought made my stomach turn, but it was late, and in the morning it would seem like we hadn't been tender with each other at all.

Mr Innocente came to my pumpkin patch in the night, took off my nightgown and my bloomers then ran his hands over my skin, saying, *Don't pretend you don't want this. Don't pretend you're not dreaming about this right now.*

I tried to squirm away but I was half asleep and too slow. He pulled me back and thrust himself into me and grunted each time he thrust. It hurt like hell but it hurt less if I lay still and dumb, as if my body was an alien thing something strange was happening to a long, long way away.

When your body is broken into, your spirit lifts up out of scar tissue like mist, evacuates all cricks and aches, and condenses in a distant room until whatever pain your body feels has passed.

There's a mirror in this room. You're reflected—you appear smaller there—manageable, understandable. You can be shaped and adjusted, set back on course. You can come to terms with yourself here and, when you do, the room's no longer needed, the walls crumble and your spirit rushes back into your body where it lives pressed up against the outside world, with a clumsy animal grace.

Innocente shuddered and rolled off, and I pulled my knees up to my chest to try to cover up the hollow sick feeling he'd left between the bones of my pelvis.

I was stinging down there and I knew that my vagina was a black hole. There were sparks coming out of it, like the ocean when it's disturbed at night.

There were two sparks coming from the house, too. They were Papà's eyes, watching.

I dreamed that I had a penis—I could feel it, all the nerve endings and everything, and Innocente had nothing but a hole, a black hole.

All that week, voices were heard through walls. Papà in a rage at Mr Innocente, saying, *She is no good to us, she is ruined, you have to take her now!*

We were married at a registry. Mamma gave Mr Innocente a case of last year's passata as a dowry. Or a bribe. Or a curse.

And on the train to Auckland, words streamed out of Mr Innocente's mouth and the carriage filled with coal soot.

I dreamed and when I woke, it was to the sound of a woman calling out from the other side of a door. *Apri la porta, Brasseli, so che ci sei dentro!*

Who's that? I said.

Mr Innocente froze in the sheets.

Who is that? I said again.

This is what I was explaining to you on the train, he said.

The woman screamed, *APRI LA PORTA, STRONZO BIGAMO!*

When I opened the door a woman I recognised, with black hair turning grey in places, slapped me across the face so hard I dropped the sheet I was holding around my naked body. She saw everything: my breasts, the gap between my legs. The stickiness on my thighs.

When I came to, the woman was rubbing a tincture under my nose. I tried to sit up and move away, but she held me back down.

Shhh, she said. *I don't blame you.*

What's happened? I asked her, lying in her arms. I was comfortable there. *What's happened?* I asked again, closing my eyes.

I am his wife. I'm your husband's wife, she said. I opened my eyes with a start. Of course, that's where I'd seen her before. She was a vision I'd had of myself, married and worn out with nothing in my head but everything I had lost.

My feet carried me over hills and through the back streets of towns. They pulled my legs through a pair of trousers I found somewhere, I don't know where. They walked for years, until my hair grew so long it fell out, and a new crop of hair grew back, short as a boy's. They carried me to a house that looked like mine with a shrine to boats out the back rising up from a ground covered in broad leaves and heavy, swollen balls. *You'd think it was a garden growing the heads of demented babies if you didn't know better*, I thought, as I fell down amongst them.

The night sky was a mess of twinkles, there were too many, I didn't know how the sailors saw any sense in them. I tried though. I took a deep breath and held my fingers up to make a window. I squinted my eyes and moved the window around until the stars clicked into place and there she was: St Eugenia herself in a pair of trousers, looking right at me.

Are you going to give me some advice? I asked.

What can I say? she said. *You're a disgrace to our name.*

What? I said. *But you're in trousers too!*

And look where it got me. Dead.

I rolled away from her, towards the pumpkin at my side. St Eugenia faded into the morning light, thank God, but Mamma was there instead, standing in a nightshirt with two new babies on her hips and her hair falling over their faces. There was too much hair and too much Mamma, she was everywhere I wasn't and surveying the garden as if I wasn't there. She walked back into the kitchen and shouted, *Ida, there's a good-sized pumpkin out here, bring the knife.*

She didn't know me anymore. She didn't know the difference between her own daughter and a squash.

Why had I come back to this place? Perhaps I'd been hoping to see Ida again, perhaps I'd thought she might pull me close to her, and we'd sit together as friends, not as sisters, but looking at her standing at the back door with a knife in her hand and her eyes redder than a crow's, I thought, *It's time to leave now, Tally Ho, at least until they've calmed down.*

With nowhere else to go I went to the brickworks, only it wasn't a brickworks anymore, but a manufactory that made drains. I wondered if I was at the right place, but the same men were there, crawling around as if looking for their lost eyes.

There was a man standing with his hands on his hips, ciggie in mouth, smoke pouring out of his nose as if the insides of his head were on fire and he was standing patiently, letting them burn. He stared into the clay pit, stared at his watch, stared up at the sun as it adventured up into the sky and then turned to stare at me. He smiled in a way that said, *You again*, and I smiled in a way that said, *I don't know what you're talking about. Please give me a job.*

We worked hard and it felt good, putting our bodies to use like that. Some of the men took off their shirts and the sun turned their backs as brown as the clay, but I left mine on even when it was soaked through with sweat.

I could've made pipes forever. It was a simple process and everyone knew their role and how to play it. The rest of the world was a dark, unfathomable place in which people put on brave faces and pretended to know how to get by.

When the sun started the slow fall out of the sky the other men worked faster, hoping to draw home time closer. I worked more slowly, hoping to push it away, but the slower I worked the faster the end of the day arrived. It didn't make sense. As the other men streamed out the manufactory gates, the man with the opera eyes passed me a towel and bucket of soapy water to wash myself down.

You alright? he asked.

Yes, I'm fine, I lied. I didn't know where I'd sleep, but was trying hard not to let the worry show.

You coming with us to the pub or what? he asked, and it was a question I'd never forget. *You coming with us to the pub or what?* as if there was no doubt in his head as to whether I was a girl or a boy or a fish or a turnip. I was a man, and I was invited to the pub, where men went.

At the pub the drainpipe men taught me everything they knew. All their jokes, and what to say when, and whose chair to kick out from under who. To Darkie we said, *If you go outside at night don't close your eyes or we'll lose you!* and to the chows that stumbled in from Haining Street we pulled back the skin next to our eyes and said, *Ching chong Chinaman!* which wasn't as good but we laughed as if it was.

The beer was a song and we sang it loud and proud in the streets of Wellington. It made us brave enough to show the world how much we loved it. We wanted everyone to love the world as much as us. We wanted the spinster Mrs Cockrain in her bonnet and black cape to come out in the streets and dance. We wanted her to see how funny her name was, and laugh with us. We threw stones at her house trying to get the walls to fall flat on the ground, *bam bam bam*, and leave her standing there in her cape. But she never did come out, because she was a bitter old spinster and our song was racing towards the chorus, so we left. We went to find the dancing bear on Garrett Street and we danced with the bear. It was on a chain and it was tired but it still eyed our delicious hands and jugulars, so two of us held the bear's head back and one of us held its jaws open by the teeth and another poured three pints straight down its wide red throat. It danced again, a slow syrupy dance, and made the chain around its ankle sound like a tambourine played at the bottom of the sea. We walked down Haining Street breathing in the opium smoke that leaked from the boarded-up windows and let visions hover in front of us like an empty suit of clothes held up by fairies. We said, *Oh thank you, fairies, thank you very much*, and stepped into those visions. We couldn't tell the difference anymore between a punch in the face and a hug that went wrong. We became a pack of puppies jumping over each other in the middle of the street because they were *our* streets, we owned them and we were afraid of nothing. Eventually we found ourselves in beds at night or on floors that belonged to one or another of us and in the morning someone's wife or sister or mother gave us porridge or bread and kicked us out the door when we needed to be on the road to the drainpipe manufactory again. Apart from the fear of getting too drunk, of dropping my guard, of taking a piss somewhere someone might see, it was the best week of my life.

Friday arrived. It must have been a Friday because the lads were outside with their hands clutched tightly around envelopes full of money. They were clustered around one man reading from a newspaper.

. . . in a drunken row which occurred in a house off Cuba Street, about one o'clock this morning, a man named Harry Crawford, a stevedore, lost his life.

What? I pushed myself to the front of the crowd. *What?!*

He read on: *Some persons walking down Cuba Street, about that hour, state that they heard a woman crying, 'Murder.' They followed her to the house of William George Raines, a stevedore, where on a verandah at the back they found Crawford lying dead, with a large bruise on his forehead . . . Detective Campbell, after making investigations, arrested Raines shortly before ten o'clock on a charge of wilful murder which will in all probability be resolved into a charge of manslaughter. Raines, who did not appear to have completely recovered from his drinking bout, was brought up at the Police Court this morning, and formally remanded . . . Crawford had been in ill-health for some time past, and was brought up on a charge of lunacy a short time ago . . .*

The men stared at their shuffling feet. No one knew what to say. Sound and the air itself was suddenly extracted from the world, and with that all the possible conversations I hadn't yet had with Harry Crawford collapsed into one dead soundless nothing. It was the first time I realised we wouldn't last forever; that everything wouldn't work out in the end unless someone made sure that it did.

You know what I think? the man with the sad eyes said. *I think we should go to the opera house, what do you boys reckon?*

We shrugged, shifted our weight from foot to foot. Opera had to be the last thing we felt like watching.

Boys, he said, *Lena's tits will make you feel better, I promise.*

Going to the opera house meant standing in a queue for tickets then standing in a queue for whisky then standing in a queue for ice-cream. I tried not to think about Harry Crawford sprawled across Raines's floor, with a bruise blooming on his temple. He'd never have died like that; I refused to believe he was even dead at all. Raines must have been playing a prank. He must have given the cops a different name for the dead man in his house.

Once we were armed with our whiskies and ice-creams we took the stairs by threes up into the gods. The gods was a place near the ceiling filled with people like us, offering food and drink at the altars of their stomachs. We elbowed our way to the front, so close to the stage we could almost reach out and rip the blue velvet curtain off its castors. We tried this of course, but it didn't work.

When a man's voice announced that a Miss Lena Salette would sing us a song the men around me stood up and called out, *Kiss me, darlin'!* before she'd even walked out on stage; they were that sure she'd be beautiful. It turned out she was a woman like any other and sang a song that any other woman could have sung, but the crowd cheered. Ladies in feathers shuffled across the stage. One of them tripped, but no one seemed to mind. A fat man and a thin man poked each other and joked. Behind their stiff smiles their brains worked hard at remembering their lines.

Two whiskies in and I began to understand. The thrill of the opera house was not what was happening on stage; it was being in the house itself. It was us, here, watching. Three whiskies in and it was announced that none other than Harry Crawford of New York, Ethiopian song-and-dance artist and legmania champion of the world, would now perform.

I turned to the man next to me. *Did he say Harry Crawford?* I asked, but the man could not hear me over the roar of the crowd.

The man they called Harry Crawford walked out on stage with his shoulders back and his face turned out to the audience. His face was covered in black greasepaint and his legs did things I'd never seen legs do. They could wrap around each other as if they were made of rubber. They could fly up and kick the man they belonged to in the face. Harry Crawford hadn't died—he'd changed into this all-singing, all-dancing octopus masquerading as a white man masquerading as a black man. He'd left this dull place for the world of other people's dreams. I looked around me and saw men laugh. Their drinks spilled and their ice-cream dribbled down their fronts but they didn't care. All that mattered was that someone had let the God in them loose to laugh in another man's face.

Outside the opera house I was shaking with my new discovery. The seagulls were shaking with it, even the drunk men on the streets were shaking and it was with fear. They knew that God was not up there, far away. Broken pieces of Him were inside their hearts, and inside the hearts of everyone else, too. When those pieces came close together God was released as one resounding chant, usually at the cricket. It was a depressing thought, that cricket chants were the best the God in us could come up with, and so men drank, to forget that God was not as wonderful as they had hoped.

Outside the opera house bits of God called out to other bits of God. The bits had different names, but they were all the same underneath.

Jack. Hey, Jack.

Harry. Oi, Harry!

Nina! Nina!

I turned around.

A swan lady was standing in front of me with her white hat tilted slightly over her eyes. When she looked up the smell of Wellington cakes rushed towards me—coconut and chocolate and cream.

Nina? Nina! It's me, she said.

I tried to look across the street as if I hadn't seen her.

Don't you remember me?

The men around us stopped talking. I was growing breasts and hips and eyelashes right in front of their eyes.

Sorry, who? I asked.

Amelia—Amelia Grey! We played on your grandfather's hobby horse together when we were girls, remember? What was its name? Jerry-Moe?

Oh, yes, my mouth said. *Geronimo. How could I forget?*

I knew it was you under those boy's clothes. What a laugh! Were you performing tonight?

The drainpipe men didn't know what to say. Their eyes lingered around my chest trying to see through my shirt. One boy leaned in and asked what the others didn't have the guts to say.

Hey, Nina, can I have a feel of your tits?

What woke me up was a knock on the door. Then footsteps. The *cluck cluck* of concerned women talking in hushed voices. Gasping, then agreeing, then clucking. I was on a floor that could've been any of the drainpipe men's floors. My shirt was open and my right breast had slipped free of its binding for anyone to see. I tried to remember all the seconds that had passed between my third whisky and waking up here, but my memory of the night was one nauseous wave surging towards the acid-bright morning.

I was buttoning up my shirt quick as my fingers would go when a woman bent over me with the sun radiating out from behind her head. She looked straight into my eye as if I was a puppy with a brick around its neck, and she'd come to drop me in a horse trough.

Excuse me, mister, er . . . miss . . . She didn't know what to call a man who'd suddenly turned into a woman, and quite frankly neither did I. *There is someone here from the army to see you.*

The army? I could see this woman was as worried as I was, so I let her walk me to the door, watching me the whole way there in case I turned into something else. A rabbit, perhaps. Or a dog.

In the doorway stood a steamship of a woman in a uniform. It wasn't a police uniform and it wasn't a hospital uniform—it was something that was trying to be all these things and more. She was bigger than most men, and could probably king-hit one with her thumb.

What's your name, dear? the woman asked.

I don't know, I said. *Does it matter?*

The woman raised her eyebrows and shook her head at the sight of such a poor unknowing wretch.

You're a woman, though, are you not?

Sometimes, I said.

Behind her eyes thoughts were turning over, *clunk clunk clunk: Clearly her time on the streets has put her under great distress; she doesn't know her own name and she can't even tell me if she's a woman or a man.*

Come here, child, she said, pulling me into a hug that was all elbows and epaulets in the eye. *Come with me. You cannot be forced to live like this anymore.*

She was right. My men, the drainpipe men, would never drink with me again.

Captain Gunnion led me to a fortress on Cuba Street. She called it a house, or the Pauline Home, but it was a fortress.

Let's have a cup of tea, she said, unlocking the six locks on the front gate. *And you can get everything off your chest.*

Behind the gate was a garden, if you could call it that. It consisted of plants growing in the shape of cubes. Women in uniforms walked past the cube plants with young girls who looked like they'd had their brains extracted. A nervous sound came from their mouths, and even the house at the end of the path made a shrill noise, as if its walls were lined with cicadas. In a distant room someone was practising a tuba. The notes drew a square in the sky, *bom, bom, bom, bom*, over and over until a piece of sky nearly fell out and shattered at my feet.

Captain Gunnion did not smell like onions. She smelled like soap—and not the flowery kind; the kind that made a person clean without going in for any fancy business. She sat at one end of a large table, next to another woman with wide, jittery eyes. She was younger and her hands moved restlessly, never sure where God wanted them to be.

Please, tell us your story from the beginning, the restless woman said. She looked worried my story might make her sad, but a little excited by that, too. *What this woman needs is to have a good cry,* I thought, *really let everything out,* so I didn't skimp on the melancholy, I went straight for it.

Do you know the story of Cinderella? I asked.

Yes, of course, she said.

Well, that's not far from the truth.

ROMANCE IN REAL LIFE. A BIGAMOUS MARRIAGE. A WOMAN DISGUISES HERSELF AS A BOY.

A representative of the *New Zealand Times* unearthed on Saturday a most extraordinary case, involving a bigamous marriage, the desertion of the victim, her plucky determination to obtain her own livelihood in a brickyard as a labourer, and her rescue from her uncongenial occupation by the Salvation Army. It appears that the girl, who is 21 years of age, is a native of Wellington, and resided up till nine months since with her parents in Wellington. According to her statement to the Salvation people, she led an unhappy life with her father and mother, and was relegated to the position of the family Cinderella. About nine months ago she met a specious scoundrel in Wellington, who took advantage of her innocence, and with him she went through a form of marriage. The newly-wedded couple immediately after the ceremony took their departure for Auckland, where, shortly afterwards, the unhappy bride ascertained that the man whom she believed was her husband was already married to another woman, and had by her a family. The poor girl at once, on ascertaining her lamentable position, left the fellow, and as speedily as she could returned to Wellington, where she vainly endeavoured to obtain employment, but, as she states, without acquainting her parents of her forlorn condition. In despair, the poor girl says she obtained a suit of boy's clothes, and got her hair cropped, and after several attempts, obtained work in a drainpipe manufactory. The girl entered upon her duties and gave the greatest satisfaction. She was attentive, worked hard, and took her first week's wages, and on the same evening accompanied several of her yard mates to the opera house. There she was seen by a friend of her family, who, being aware of her identity and her antecedents, acquainted the Salvation Army of the facts in connection with her sad case.

The captain in charge of the Pauline Home called at the girl's lodgings, and had little trouble in inducing her to enter the Home, pending her obtaining a situation more suitable and congenial to her sex than the one she was recently rescued from.

The Salvation Army people give the young woman an excellent character. They state she is modest in her demeanour and is in every sense of the term a good woman. The Salvation officer who supplied the particulars of this extraordinary case says the girl's appearance when she entered the Pauline Home would lead anyone to believe she was a good-looking lad of about 17 or 18 years of age.

Wanganui Chronicle, 24 July 1895

Well, I'm glad we found you before it was too late, Captain Gunnion said.

What would happen when it was too late? I wondered, but did not ask.

Deirdre! Captain Gunnion said to the restless woman. *Show the girl her bed, and where she will be working.*

Working? I asked.

Yes, working. This is not a hotel, young lady.

Sergeant Deirdre led me up the stairs to a hall with walls that looked as if they'd been painted with splatters of leftover pea soup. Branching off the hallway were rooms the size of drill halls with high, barred windows at one end, and inside each room were rows of beds with sheets tucked so tightly into the bedframes you could see the stitching on the mattresses underneath. Deirdre pointed to a bed far out in the distance, a bed that looked like every other bed, and told me, proudly, that it would be mine.

I think you'll be very happy here, she said, and patted me on the hand. I was glad one of us thought so.

Sergeant Deirdre let me put my things on the end of my bed, so that I'd be able to find it again in the sea of identical beds, and walked me down the hall towards the whirring sound I'd heard from outside. As we moved towards the door at the end of the hall I realised it was not the noise of cicadas, but metal machines with teeth. Deirdre opened the door to thirty sewing machines and behind them women and children bent down, carefully feeding the ravenous metal monsters.

IT'S QUITE ENJOYABLE ONCE YOU GET THE HANG OF IT, Deirdre shouted over the noise. *ALMOST LIKE YOU'RE FEEDING A VERY HUNGRY PET,* she said.

The women looked like husks of women. As they fed their hungry pets I could not shake the idea that they were unspooling from the inside and feeding them their own unravelled souls.

WHAT ARE THEY MAKING? I asked.

WHATEVER NEEDS MAKING. OUR UNIFORMS, OR SHEETS FOR THE HOSPITAL, OR THINGS TO SELL.

SELL?

HOW ELSE DO YOU THINK WE CAN AFFORD TO LIVE IN THIS BEAUTIFUL HOUSE! she yelled over the violent vibrations of floor and walls trying to shake the room free of this infestation of machines. *SOMETIMES WE EVEN MAKE ENOUGH TO BUY A NEW SEWING MACHINE!*

A fine dusting of plaster fell from the ceiling, sprinkling Deirdre's hair, but she didn't notice.

IT'S GOOD TO KEEP THE GIRLS BUSY—YOU KNOW, GIVES THEM PURPOSE, KEEPS THEIR MIND OFF THINGS.

Keeps their mind off what? I wondered. *How much happier they were before they'd been rescued?*

That night I lay on my bed wondering what Mamma's life would've been like if she'd had a sewing machine. She would've had more time, but for what? To take in more sewing? To make more babies? Now that there were more machines in the world, the people in it galloped ahead with renewed purpose, but they were moving so fast they were likely to gallop off the edge of the earth. Where was our efficiency supposed to take us? To an early retirement sitting in an armchair, watching the seconds peel away from more seconds underneath?

As I lay there, the women from the sewing room filed in. Their pale heads at the top of their dark dresses looked like moons floating around in search of a planet. Some of them had shaved heads. Some had peroxide blonde hair that was growing out. Some of them were scratching their arms and the back of their necks. Once they were in the room, they sat, as one, on the edge of their beds.

I hate this place, one woman moaned.

Shut up, another said. *This is what God wants for us, remember?*

She laughed. She kept laughing. The laugh turned into a sob.

Learn how to play a tuba and you're saved from this, a third woman said. *But you don't have a musical bone in your body, Martha, so tough luck for you, eh.*

If you can play the tuba, you're saved from what? I asked and forty eyes turned on me.

Who are you? Martha asked.

I'm—

You're the one who goes round dressed as a bloke, aren't ya? Now Martha was standing beside her bed with her clothes off. It was brave of her, I supposed, but I couldn't look. I could never be that brave.

That night, in my dream, I was suddenly cold. Someone had made a cut on my head along the hairline, gripped the flap of skin and ripped down, peeling my face right off. Electrical cables were attached to my nipples, and someone was standing beside a giant machine, about to flick a switch. I woke to find my covers had been pulled off, and one of the girls, the one with the blonde hair, was climbing into my bed. I tried to speak, but she put her hand on my mouth.

Shhh. This is what you like, isn't it, love? she said, rubbing her thumb over my nipple.

Where'd you get that idea? I mumbled through her hand, but it felt good, like gold dust glimmering in ripples out across my chest.

No fucking in the dorm! one of the girls shouted out.

Ah shuddup Sandra, ya whiny bugger.

You woke me up, you bitch!

The girl in my bed started suckling then, as if she were a child. Her face looked as calm as a child's. She'd become a baby, and I was the Virgin Mary—and no more a virgin than Mary was, either.

I felt sick. *These women are disturbed,* I thought, and replaced my nipple with her own thumb, rolled her out of bed and carried her back to her own.

I'm not a mother, I whispered to her. *I can't be a mother. To you or anyone else.*

After a breakfast of watery porridge, Sergeant Deirdre walked me to the sewing room. I wondered if it was worth it, to spend my days bowed down to the ravenous sewing machines, feeding them cloth in exchange for a bed and watery porridge, but where else could I go? The drainpipe men would've told everyone what a joke I was by now.

Outside, the tuba was still cutting squares in the air, and a drum joined in, to keep its corners straight.

Who's playing that? I asked Sergeant Deirdre.

Our girls in the band. They practise tirelessly, they practise so hard they have no time to enjoy their sewing with the other girls, she said, shaking her head.

And what would I have to do to join the band?

Well, you'd need to be able to play a musical instrument for a start, she said. *Can you play?*

I stopped in the middle of the hallway. *Yes. Yes, I can.*

She seemed surprised. *What can you play, dear?*

Anything you put in front of me.

She looked doubtful, then guilty for doubting. *Well, I'll speak to Captain Gunnion and see what she has to say.*

I stood at ease in the music room. Standing at ease, however, did not put a person at ease. It meant standing with your feet hip width apart, staring at the wall, while Captain Gunnion paced backwards and forwards in front of you. She'd have been happier as the captain of a ship, or in the army leading a charge of horses to kill everyone in sight, but she was stuck as the captain of a spiritual army, which was more wafty than she was built for, but better than being a nun.

Are you prepared to be a soldier of God and recruit the stray sinners on the streets to our cause? Captain Gunnion asked. The way she asked, there was only one answer.

Yes, Captain. I am prepared.

Well, show me what you can do.

I made my way around the music room, trying my luck with the different instruments. The tuba looked easy enough. All you were meant to do was put your lips to it and blow, but when I tried all that came out was the sound of an elephant getting its trunk stuck in a washing wringer.

STOP! she called out. *What are you doing? I thought you could play. Are you wasting my time?*

No, Captain. I used to play in the Catholic church, but since they turned me out on the streets with nowhere to go . . .

My hand was shaking. I was afraid she'd march me over to a sewing machine so ravenous it would stitch me into a cocoon and I'd only break out once I'd become a fully formed soldier of God. A sob caught in my throat. How had it come to this? How could I crawl out of this place? A tear rolled down my cheek and crashed onto the tiny metal cymbal of the tambourine at my feet.

Stop crying and pick it up, the captain said. *I'll show you how to play.*

Out in the streets on Friday nights we sang, *Why Are You Doubting and Fearing?* Children bought ice-creams and came to watch, mostly to see who was at the girls' home now and who was prettier back when they were drunk and a whore.

We played on the street corners, we played outside the pubs. We sang, *There's a Sea for Weary Souls* to the sailors as they walked from the quay to Courtenay Place. Through a pub window I could see the drainpipe men laughing and pushing each other into bar stools. One squinted at me as if I was a ghost come to haunt him. I looked away, and tapped my tambourine harder.

We passed the bear on Garrett Street. It was drunk and stumbling. We played *There Is a Better World, They Say* to give him hope that he might make it back to a Russian pine forest. He roared at the noise we made and was poked with a stick by his master as punishment.

We played at the cricket pitches on the weekend and we played at the shops. We played to an old drunk in slippers who wore a Red Indian headdress and the hide of a sheep strapped to his back. We sang, *Sinner, See Yon Light!*

What light? he yelled back. *What bloody light? It's the middle of the night, you fools!*

We sang, *We Have Each a Cross to Bear.*

Bear? I'm no bear! I'm a fucking sheep! Baa! Baa!

So we sang, *The Lord's My Shepherd* and he passed out in a horse trough.

No one had the guts to shut God's soldiers up, so we played through nearly every suburb of Wellington, until there was only one left: Newtown.

On the day we were due to play in Newtown I tried to be ill, but Captain Gunnion did not believe me.

I held my breath and tried to faint, but it didn't work. They shook their heads and said, *O will you not yield to God tonight?*

No! I coughed. *I can't!*

O lamb of God, thou wonderful sin bearer, the trumpet player said.

What are you saying? What are you talking about?

They were circling now, their instruments pointed at me like guns.

Come to the Saviour, come to the Saviour!

Dark is the way, sinner!

For our salvation, Jesus paid a wonderful price!

Alright! I said. *I'll go! I'll go!*

The captain chose a spot on the corner of Coromandel Street for us to play on, possibly because of the twelve brats standing on the opposite side of the road in the shadows. I could feel them staring at me as one many-armed creature waiting to pounce. But it didn't pounce. We sang about shepherds and we sang about sinners and I played the tambourine on every two and every four. The monster sat there in the dark, and breathed, and licked its twelve ice-creams, and listened.

Though we are sinners every one,

Jesus died!

And though our crown of peace is gone,

Jesus died!
We may be cleansed from every stain,
We may be crowned with peace again,
And in that land of bliss may reign,
Jesus died! Amen.

After we finished killing Jesus I told the rest of the band I'd meet them back at the Home. Captain Gunnion looked at me down the length of her nose.

Are you sure? she asked.

Yes, Captain, God is with me. I'll be fine.

I walked along Coromandel Street until I found myself outside Amelia's house. Two lights flickered inside, turning the windows gold. I looked at my grey skirt and blouse and felt as drab as river stones with the gold blasted out. I couldn't go to her door like this.

I heard my house from four doors away—the shrieks and giggles of brats being chased around the living room, the call that it was time for bed, Ida's voice, a woman's voice now.

The garden was dark. The tomato vines in the front yard breathed out their spiciness into the night air, making my nose itch. There was no moon spying on me, no million eyes of stars, but I knew this garden well. I'd be as invisible as one of Captain Gunnion's angels. So invisible I wouldn't even exist. I tiptoed around the side of the house and, as I did, stopped for a moment to look through the kitchen window. A woman was bent over a tub, washing dishes. She paused for a moment, and I slunk back into a shadow, but she'd only paused to push the hair out of her eyes with her wrist. She was fair, with red cheeks. Children clambered up onto the kitchen table behind her, leaped off, and clambered up again to throw spoons at other children on the floor. They were blonde, some of them. One of them had red hair. They were what my family would've been if they were Scottish or Irish or dropped in a vat of bleach. I'd never seen them before in my life.

Behind the lemon tree, under a rotting crayfish net, Joe's trousers had become a slimy city for slaters and worms. When I pulled them on, a hundred cold feet tickled my legs. Dust to dust, ashes to ashes, my life as a boy would rise from the grave. If my family could leave Eugenia for dead, then I could, too. For good this time, and with no regrets.

THE SHIP GAME

The first rule is, you have to be tough.

The second, you have to get to the top of the mast without stopping. The top of the mast is called the button. Everyone has to touch the button, or else they die.

Don't look down. If you look down, you'll think about falling, and if you think it, you might accidentally make it happen. Then you'll die.

Climb to the top looking only at your hands. It helps if you sing under your breath to prove just how easy it is to climb. Don't notice that the top of the mast sways like a spindly pine tree in the wind.

As soon as you touch the button, go straight back down. Maintain three points of contact while descending the rat bars. Talk to yourself under your breath. That's it. Right foot there. Good. Hands down a rung. Well done! Could your foot go there? No. There? Yes! Good work!

Afterwards, down below, your eyes will try to hold on to the fixtures in the ship and pin them down; your eyes will try to tell your brain that the fixtures aren't swaying, you're the one who's swaying; that you must be drunk; that you've been drunk for days. Don't pay any attention to your eyes, or you will vomit.

You will probably vomit anyway. You will probably spend the first three rounds of this game sitting under the main mast, gripping onto the railing that runs around the deckhouse, vomiting into a bucket. The bosun will step around you, sighing because of the extra work he has to do now that you're sick. The second mate will ignore you. The cook will tell you it's all in your head.

Someone might bring you a glass of water and a biscuit. Maybe a lick of molasses. They will watch you eat the biscuit, then watch as you vomit it back into the bucket.

Look up. Smear the vomit off your face and into your hair. Say sorry. Watch them shrug and walk off.

Another deckhand might lift you up, walk you to the bridge and say: *Take the helm, it will make you feel better.* Discover that helming really does make you feel better. You are no longer a piece of flint being blown around a ship, being blown around the ocean, being pulled around the world, being thrown around the sun. These circles hula hoop around *you*. *You* are at the centre of all these circles, because *you* are behind the wheel. Watch the sea just beneath the horizon in the direction you are heading. Wait for it to tell you grand things about existence.

Keep waiting.

Give up.

The sea won't tell you anything. It will just move. Always. Sometimes the waves will mimic the shape of the mountains shrinking behind the stern. As the mountains get smaller the waves will get bigger, sucking all the power from the mountains. Waves are more powerful than mountains, because they can loom up on your right, then shrink underneath you and reappear on your left as three smaller mountains. Waves are nightmare mountains.

When a bell rings, let the nightmare dissolve. It's time for dinner.

Eat in the lower mess. Discover the meaning of the word 'mess' when your plate slides across the table and flings mashed potato across the walls.

After dinner you try to sleep. You lie in your bunk stiffly, your hands and feet pressed against the ship and the leeboard, trying not to roll out of bed. Every two seconds there's a thud against the hull. Both your eyes are all pupil. Cannon fire? Icebergs? A twelve-foot shark trying to smash open the fo'c'sle and suck out the tender humans inside? Quite possibly. After each thud the ship quivers like a dog in a thunderstorm. You think: we are all going to die. There is no doubt. How can you swim through swells as high as this? Be honest: you can't. You are definitely going to die. You begin coming to terms with death. You think: it will be like sleeping through a dreamless sleep—unmemorable. You think, maybe this has been a dream anyway, and you will wake up to find that the thuds were made by your little sister kicking the bed.

At a quarter to four in the morning, someone who is not your little sister, dressed in oilskins, touches you on the shoulder. *Get up*, he says, *it's your watch*. Grip his arm. He is slippery with ocean spray. *Is it terrifying?* you ask. *Is this the end?* He throws your oilskins onto the bunk. *Get up*, he says. *You'll be fine.*

On the bridge, the wind blows the spume from the waves horizontally, right into your face. You think it's horizontal, but you have no idea what horizontal is anymore. Horizontal could be any number of directions that don't point straight down to the bottom of the sea. But right now, horizontal could include that direction too. On the bridge you can't feel the ship quiver. It gets doused by a wave and then bobs back up like an empty bottle of rum. Think: *DO THEY KNOW EVERYONE IN THE FO'C'SLE THINKS THEY ARE GOING TO DIE?*

You are travelling at 10 knots. 10.2 knots. 10.6 knots. At one point you are travelling at 11.2 knots. Having never been on a ship before you have no idea what a 'knot' is, but now you know that 11.2 knots is bloody ridiculously fast.

We're going too fast, you think. *We're out of control.* This is like those stories when the driver gets shot by Indians and the horses keep running across the hills, any which way, and the cart and the horses end up smashed to bits at the bottom of an abandoned quarry. Except instead of a quarry you'll end up smashed to bits at the bottom of the sea, and the horse would be a giant squid, sucking the meat off your bones.

The ship dives nose first into a gully made by two waves and you think no thoughts anymore; you just sit on the bench with your back against the controls and look at the mast. The mast looks high. Too high. It doesn't seem in proportion to the rest of the ship. Or the barque, that's what it should be called. You wonder if they checked this when they built it in somewhere exotic like Denmark or Norway. The mast looks heavy, too. And with all those sails up, and the yardarms, it must be even heavier. The ship dips to the right side, rolling over a wave. The ship dips to *starboard*, you think. That means right. You are becoming a sailor after all.

The next day the captain is quiet. You wonder if he is nervous about not knowing what he is doing. When you asked where you were headed he pointed to the map and said, *Here. No wait, here. Oh, I've lost it. No—here it is*, and pointed to Australia. Now you notice that there is a network of glances all around you. The captain is watching you quite closely, and everyone else watches the captain watch you.

The captain does nice things for you. When dolphins swim alongside the ship, he tells you stories about them. That the males have corkscrew penises and rape the females in a gang. He knows all sorts of facts about the animals you can see, the animals you can't. Even the animal you are.

AS FAR AS HE
CAN REMEMBER

SYDNEY, 5 JULY 1920

HARRY CRAWFORD

My name is Harry Leo Crawford and I was born in Scotland in 1875 to my father Harry Crawford and my mother Lizzie Crawford—

Wait a tick, they'll say. *Isn't your wife Lizzie Crawford?*

And I'll say, Yes, as it happens that's the same name as my wife now. She's Scottish too. Lizzie's a very common name there.

Or perhaps I'll start with how it was when I was a boy and we left Edinburgh for the one other corner of the world that looks the most like Edinburgh. Green and rough and windy and cold—but wilder, with Maori wars and glaciers and gold getting coughed up out of the ground. New Zealand's full of Scotsmen and women. When it's day in New Zealand it's night in Scotland and, yes, I've wondered before if New Zealand only exists when all of Scotland sleeps.

A boy who can't sit still can't be expected to live his life trapped in someone else's sleep. I ran races for the butchers, which was great fun of course, but when a boy like that grows into a man he gets to a point where he feels his muscles strain under his skin, as if he's actually a lion that somehow got born into the wrong body.

Wellington's too small for restless boys. What usually happens is they learn to dull their twitchiness right down by throwing back a few beers at the pub so the twitchiness can release itself as a loud story, a slap on another bloke's back, or a punch in someone else's face, until the pub closes or they black out—whatever comes first.

If New Zealand is the spirit of adventure squeezed into two small islands, then Australia is that same spirit stretched out as far as it can go.

When I was a child I thought the ground under Australia must've been nothing but snake tunnels and the surface was a dry wasteland where you'd see the occasional rusted-up water tank, skinny dog licking its balls, or hard man shooting a rabbit. If you wanted to be a hard man, Australia was the place to be one. New Zealand had mountains to climb and cattle to muster but Australia was tough, and it wasn't going to say sorry for anything. It was just there, and you could take it or leave it.

I wanted to take it alive. I couldn't keep living in a house that was trying to be a house in Scotland, with a mother who lived with her head drifting around in dreams of Scotland and a father who couldn't understand why the market hadn't made him rich yet. Besides, I'd got into a nasty altercation with a pissed bloke I'd once thought of as a friend, so I felt it was time to pack my things and tell the oldies I was leaving.

They didn't cry or beg their only son and child to stay. We weren't that sort of family I suppose. My father was a trader who always dressed the best he could manage, even in the hardest times, and my mother was a stiff upper lip sort of woman. Even so, the morning after I told them I was leaving she made haggis and blood sausage especially for me, and my father sipped his tea quietly until he could find it in himself to wish me luck. I could tell by the unusual hardness in his voice that he was trying not to show how much he needed me around, in case it caused too much of a fuss.

I was too young to realise I'd never see them again. Excited and nervous as I was, I don't really remember my passage over here. I barely remember the name of the ship. Maybe it was the SS *Australia*, maybe it wasn't.

I know I came direct to Sydney, and because I didn't have two pennies to rub together I had to work my passage. I spent most of my time in the boiler room working the pump. It was hot down there and time burned up like a fever. When you spend your days only sweating, never pissing, the booze hits you harder and comes back up more easily. It was always a mad fight for the dunny after a night on the piss. And it was a good idea to keep a crowbar under your pillow. Down in the pump room we were so far under the surface of the sea that we'd hear loud thuds against the hull and wonder about the sharks and giant squid with teeth trying to break in and go for us. But sometimes the thuds came from the inside. You didn't ask too many questions about that.

I remember spots slowly appearing on the faces of the men I worked with. By the time we saw the high yellow cliffs of Sydney some of the crew had let those spots take them over. And I remember thinking that the good thing about being a nobody is you're not important enough to sneeze on.

Anchored in the middle of the harbour, we were quarantined for two weeks, watching boats with yellow and white flags come from North Head for the bodies. Sydney sprawled all around us like a tart with her legs spread. *Come and get me boys*, she said, but we couldn't and the bitch knew it.

Once, a stiff dead sheep washed up against the hull, and sometimes the water frothed red, sometimes a brownish yellow, the colour of beer. And I thought: Well then, Sydney's also a city of restless men throwing their carcasses into the drink.

But no, of course I won't say it like that.

Where'd you work when you first got here? they'll ask. Temora, I'll say. *Why'd you only last two weeks?* And I'll say, Now you know as well as I do that men have the pub they go to and like dogs they like to know the smell of all the other men at that pub. They say Temora is Australia's friendliest country town, but there's friendly, and then there's climb-inside-your-head friendly. I had grand notions of going to the outback to become a drover, or better yet a jackaroo, but of course I wound up cleaning glasses in the Temora pub.

I like to keep myself to myself, but in Temora there were blokes who were all: *Where you from?* and *Crawford? I know a bloke by the name of Crawford from Edinburgh, wonder if you know him,* and *Wellington? My cousin grew up in Wellington,* as if there were only two people living in these places: you, and the bloke they're related to. Their questions crept in from all sides and then there you were, stuck in the middle with no way of getting out short of throwing a beer in their faces and running away.

In Temora, bugs crawled over the tiles in the loo. Flies and other flying things flung themselves at the gas lanterns. And outside there were flecks of dried grass blowing against the fence. They reminded me of something. A body being thrown against a toilet door. The queasiness of endless blue above and all around and no way out.

I preferred working in the city. The King's Head was the sort of place where suits and bar flies and working girls felt comfy sniffing each other up—the pub being on Park and Elizabeth streets, right in the middle of town.

When you're the new useful some men let their eyes follow you across the room, slow as the eyes of lizards. They watch you until they've grown accustomed to your smell and your ways. Some bar fly will lift their sorry head and say, *Tell us about this new one doing the glasses,* and the barmaid will say, *Don't know a thing about him,* loud enough for you to hear. That's when you carry on picking up glasses as if you're deaf.

Doing the tasks of your job is about a quarter of what your job actually is. All the rest of it is making everyone believe they couldn't live without you, and if I've learned anything in my life it's that everyone would be fine living without me, so I have to put on quite a show of polishing glasses with an extra twist of the wrist, and grunting when I change the heavy kegs.

In the city people cark it all the time and no one bats an eye. When I was working at the King's Head a bookmaker called George who lived upstairs shot himself in the head. No one knew why. Do you have to have a reason? Sometimes you're just full and it's time for lights out. Then a woman burned alive there in her bed. The only things that burned were the woman and the bed, and the version of the story that stuck was that she was reading a book called *The Resurrection* and fell asleep, then the bedclothes caught alight when the candle fell over and *whoosh*, up she went in flames. The licensee was shitty because now he was down one bed and one set of bedclothes and had nothing but a black bedframe and a pile of ash in exchange. He got her week's rent out of the room before the cops combed through her things, though, and he was proud he'd had the presence of mind to think of that.

You see, the great thing about cities is, the more people they have in them, the more you're left alone. Or the more you find yourself alone in them at least.

With all the ghosts lurking about the place I tried to get another job but it was tough, considering I can't read that well.

I listen, though. I listened to the snatches of things people thought were worth talking about, which was usually about how some woman burned alive and some bloke shot himself with a revolver and how the new useful swings his arms kind of funny don't you think, like he's trying too hard to look tough.

I did get another job where, thankfully, I didn't have to talk to as many people, but there were downsides, too, that almost put me off my food.

Back then Sydney's meat was killed on Glebe Island, connected to land by a bridge. There was something about the slaughterhouse being surrounded by water that helped the ladies of Sydney forget that their good fresh sausages came about thanks to some faceless men killing on their behalf.

The sheep, bullocks, pigs and cows were all killed differently and in different sheds leased by different butchers. I worked for most of them over the three years I was there, but never doing the actual killing. You had to be built like a bull yourself and be highly trained for that. My job was to hose down the floors or take the offal to the punt, but I watched enough times to know how to kill in fourteen minutes flat.

The bit I liked best was watching the men cut around the legs and tail and strip off the skin in one piece. The worst was watching the pigs get killed. When they got frightened, they got frightened in a real human way. They looked at you and screamed like they knew what was coming. Sometimes the butchers had to chase them round the room wielding the hammer over their heads for maximum force when they finally brought it down between the eyes. But this was bad news, because the more the pigs run around the more excited they get and you don't want your pig to get too excited because fear makes for bad meat.

When the pigs were cornered they leaned back on their hind haunches with their front trotters out in front of them, like an Arab praying or like a dog about to get whacked. Then the butchers hit them on the head with the hammer. Even though most of the men had been killing for ages it was hard not to let the pig's fear catch on, so they hit too hard sometimes, and sometimes more than once, and smashed their skulls in.

Now there are new tastes for American-style slaughtering, which is where you're meant to stun the pigs without smashing in their skulls, but God only knows how you're supposed to do that with nothing but a hammer. They'd never let you waste bullets on a pig.

They used to dump the innards and diseased livestock into the harbour right next to the abattoir, but women got hysterical if they saw their children bathing next to a sheep's lung, or when the beaches of their harbourside properties began to froth with red foam. Then there was the smell of fat that came out the chimney of the boiling-down room and mingled with the smoke from the ferries to make meat clouds that mustered over the harbour. But if Sydney wanted their meat killed the same day they ate it, and if they didn't want to pay extra for it to get frozen in the new expensive refrigeration rooms, this was the price they had to pay.

It was alright once you got over the shock of how human the pigs looked, hanging upside down in a row like women hanging from trapezes at the Tivoli. I tried to get over it by remembering I probably step on hundreds or thousands of ants every day and don't think twice about it. Still, it seems unfair to only get shocked when you're killing something that could, in a certain light, be mistaken for yourself.

Why'd you leave the meatworks? they'll ask, and I'll say: Look, after three years of blood and guts a man can either grow a thick skin or start turning off his meat, and I'm not one to be fussy about my food so it was time to work somewhere else.

At Perdriau's in Drummoyne the congealed blood of a tree goes in one end of the factory and comes out as so many bits and pieces of civilised life that I reckon if you took away everything in the world except for the things made of rubber you'd still have a pretty good shadow of what the world used to be like.

Inside the factory there were rows of men working machines and even girls working alongside men, but in different jobs. They would've taken on more girls if they could've, because they got paid half of what the men did, but they weren't up to the same kind of manual labour as the men, and quite frankly the quality of the products would have suffered.

There was one department where the men and the girls got to work together, and that was where they worked on inner tubes. A girl roughened the end of her tube. The man then took it from the girl, uncovered a bottle of mixture, brushed over the ends, closed her end tightly over his, and pressed them hard together under a hand roller.

Repeating the same task every day made it easy for your mind to wander. Watching the girls and the men work together, I was reminded of all the things that aren't made of rubber but could be: nipples when they're cold, a man's member when he's excited. Going from meat to rubber as quickly as I did, you realise how similar the two are.

I would've liked to work on the inner tubes, but I was too shy to ask, and then it was too late. No matter how useful rubber is, if there's a strike in five other industries, it becomes much harder to get buckets of resin from the Amazon to Drummoyne, and then you're laid off without a second thought.

Losing my job was a shock, and I was feeling mighty sorry for myself. There were a few bad weeks on the piss which I'd rather not go into, and then I had no choice but to go back to work, any work, and of course I wound up right where I started: at a pub. But by then I'd accumulated a few more knocks, and to tell you the truth I was grateful for the company of the women working there.

To be single all your life, all the way up to the age of forty-four, is no easy feat, especially as a man in this town. The war must've killed off half the men, or they're too busy playing with each other in the Hyde Park dunnies, or just playing with themselves in their own rooms, because there are lots more single women in Sydney than men.

Up until recently I didn't have time for a woman. I always thought they picked at your quiet moments, as if you were a dead sheep in a paddock. Even when they keep their mouths shut you can see them planning to bring the brilliance out in you, or add brilliance, by imagining you in a blue shirt that might bring out the blue in your eyes. And then as soon as they turn thirty they cut to the chase and throw themselves at any pair of balls. Their once-high standards are now sagging down around their ankles. If they used to want their future spouse to have an office job, now all they want is for him to be able to write his own name.

Not being able to write my name, I thought I was off the hook. But at that time my nights were long and sleepless. Dark minutes dragged and became gaping hours. I'd keep busy during the day in the hope that I'd fall fast asleep as soon as I was horizontal, but instead I'd lie with my eyes wide open, dog tired, bones aching, feet hot and swollen with blood, wondering if the touch of a woman's breasts against my back would make the endless night a warm pleasure instead of a terror. On my days off, I'd catch myself sitting in the park, watching young lovers giggle uncontrollably, and tried to remember the last time I made a woman laugh like that.

So I suppose I turned myself in—to the women, that is. If you let her, there's always one woman who'll do so many nice things for you, really go out of her way to ask you how you are or bring you a homemade lunch or mend a hole in your jacket, that you start getting trained to expect these kindnesses, like how wolves get turned into dogs.

I met my Lizzie when I was working at the Coogee Bay Hotel by the sea. There were worse places to work. During the dizzy summer months people played dress-ups out on the beach every night of the week and the St John's Ambulance men made a fake gold rush, burying gold nuggets in the sand and watching people go crazy digging up the beach trying to get them out again. Even from the beer garden I could watch the ocean's strange effect on women. They laughed at the waves as if they were cheeky fingers tickling them in their most sensitive areas. They let their hair out and leaned back into their deckchairs with their eyes shut, giving in to the sun's long slow full-body kiss. It made you want a woman, so you could kiss her like that.

After an early shift in summer it was a tradition for the other boys who worked at the Coogee Bay to take a running leap into the ocean.

Are ya coming, Crawford? they'd ask.

No. Don't swim, I'd say.

Don't swim or can't swim?

What's the difference to you?

Fair enough.

The conversation would go the same way every time, as if having a repeated routine with someone was halfway to knowing them.

That's Crawford, they said to the new Scottish office lady, *he don't swim.* They were confident they knew that about me, at least.

I was wiping down the bar, and she'd come out of the office to ask the barmaid whose timesheet had a tangled scrawl instead of a name at the bottom.

As the other men bolted out the door for the sea the barmaid whispered to her, *That'd be Harry Crawford. Can't read or write, the poor bastard.*

You could see the heart of that Scotswoman glow like a lamp. To her, I was a stray dog covered in blood and grass and shit, and she was going to clean me up and teach me how to read and write and maybe how to love her back. You could see her coming up with the whole plan in the second it took me to put the rag down on the bar and look up.

She was wearing a plain dress in a fresh yellow. Her hair was the colour of wood ash, and broken capillaries dusted her cheeks. She was forty-nine then, and thick around the middle; she didn't look like she was going to crimp and pinch me into shape. I stayed behind to give the tables another polish, and another, and another, hoping that when she was done for the day the two of us could take a stroll down the pier perhaps, until her tram was due to leave. She was a hard worker, because I polished every table in the front bar seven times before she locked up the office and stepped out in her summer hat.

It was January then, and even though it was evening it was bright on the concourse. Mermaids and pirates sat on the low walls and ate fish and chips, as if that's what mermaids and pirates did every day. Women slipped in and out of the water in less than they'd wear to bed. Kids who're usually seen and not heard shrieked across the beach wielding kewpie dolls over their heads as if they were about to kill a pig with them. Lizzie looked like a young girl, her eyes full of wonder and free of worry. The on-shore breeze whipped her hair about her face, giving me an excuse to touch it. We stopped under a pine tree and she startled when I tucked the hair back behind her ear, as if no one had ever touched her before. Then she smiled, showing her terrible teeth, and I smiled too.

When she stepped onto her tram, I caught a glimpse of how others saw her. No girls eyed her jealously. No blokes helped her step on board. She was politely stepped around, never to be thought of again, and I was glad for it because it meant I could have her all to myself.

We were married at the Canterbury Registry Office in September last year, and almost a year later we're still going strong. Being the twitchy sort, if someone asked me what I've done with my life I wouldn't know how to answer them. But there's a stillness in my wife that's as large as a cathedral. My twitchiness calms right down when I think of it.

Lizzie and I can spend hours sitting next to each other, not saying anything. Sometimes I wish I could sit next to her and do nothing but sneak looks at her calm face. Sometimes I wish

I never had to go to work, but then I'm glad to go to work, so I can have coming home to look forward to.

And the best part is, this woman loves me back. I can't believe it. She loves me so much she's convinced she's up the duff. I reckon she's going through her change of life, but when she gave me a kiss before I left for work this morning and said, *We're going to have a baby*, I wanted it to be true so much I almost believed it myself.

Now the cops have brought me to their dungeon office and it's time to talk. The interview room is small and the typist is not making eye contact with me. My palms are sweating and I can't breathe right. I should've seen this coming. Men in dark coats and hats pulled down to cover the face have been sitting in the corners of most places I've been drinking or working in this past week. I heard these men ask, *Have you seen a person goes by the name of Harry Crawford?* and what could I do but hide? I know as well as the next bloke how the cops work these days—they ask questions until a man doesn't know what he's answering, and next thing he knows they've put an entirely false story into his perfectly innocent mouth. Just like how it was during the great strike of 1917, when the police went into the homes of union leaders and picked up bags which were suddenly full of knives and guns that the union men had never seen before. *Oops, what's this then?* the cops said. *Oh ho ho, this will be going straight to the magistrate—what do you think, boys?* and all the rest of it. They should be magicians, not police officers, the way they pluck things out of the air is all I'm saying—

But so far, so good. I'm not crying, or shaking. I'm telling the big detective everything: how I came to be here, where I've worked.

I tell him my wife is the only personal friend I've had, male or female, since arriving in Australia.

The big man cracks a smirk. *Great story,* he says. *I might tell you that I've interviewed a young man named Harry Birkett, also his uncle and aunt, and I feel certain that you married Birkett's mother a few years back—*

TO ALL OUTSIDE APPEARANCES, AT LEAST

SYDNEY, AUSTRALIA

DRAMATIS PERSONAE

WAHROONGA/BALMAIN

Annie Birkett: Housekeeper at Dr Clarke's residence, also known as Daisy

Harry Birkett: Son of Annie Birkett

Harry Crawford: Scotsman, formerly of Wellington, New Zealand; Dr Clarke's general useful

Lily Nugent: Sister of Annie Birkett, resident of Kogarah

DRUMMOYNE

Clara Bone: Grocer on the corner of The Avenue; married to Ernest Bone

Lydia Parnell: Wife of Harry Crawford's colleague at Perdriau & Co. Rubber Works; friend and counsellor to Crawford

Emma Belbin: Resident of Rozelle; friend of Lydia Parnell

Jane Wigg: Resident at 7 The Avenue; neighbour to the Crawfords

WOOLLOOMOOLOO

Jack: Boarder at 103 Cathedral Street

Henrietta Schieblich: Landlady at 103 Cathedral Street

Eduard Schieblich: Violin teacher and husband of Henrietta Schieblich

Marcelina Bombelli: Resident at 156 Cathedral St; mother of Frank Bombelli and short-term carer for Harry Birkett

LANE COVE

Emily Hewitt: Office worker at the Cumberland Paper Board Mills

Ernest Clifford Howard: Apprentice at the Cumberland Paper Board Mills.

Constable Walsh: Constable at Lane Cove Police Station

Eliel Irene Carroll: Resident of Tambourine Bay and witness

DOUBLE BAY

Mrs (Granny) DeAngelis: Owner of the Italian laundry

Mr DeAngelis: Husband of Mrs DeAngelis

Josephine DeAngelis: Adopted granddaughter of Mrs DeAngelis

Nina: Mother of Josephine, employee at the Italian laundry

SYDNEY CITY

Sergeant Lillian Armfield: 'Matron' at Central Police Station, Sydney

Detective Sergeant Stewart Robson: Detective in charge of 'the man-woman case' at Central Police Station

Detective Bill Watkins: Detective working on 'the man-woman case' at Central Police Station

Maddocks Cohen: Solicitor for the defence at the hearing and the trial

Mr Gale: Magistrate presiding over the hearing

Roderick Kidston: Crown Prosecutor at the hearing

William Coyle, KC: Barrister for the Crown at the trial

William Cullen, KC: Judge presiding over the trial

Archibald McDonell: Barrister for the defence at the trial

LONG BAY

Dr Moran: Surgeon, Italophile, friend of William Coyle, KC, and author of the memoir *Viewless Winds*

STEWART ROBSON.
October, 1920.

I am Detective Sergeant stationed at Sydney.

I have had considerable experience of identifications
in police work generally.

Most decidedly it is the fact
that the police have to be particularly careful in securing identification.

They must be very careful.

If they arenot verycareful there is liable to be
trouble on both sides.

CRAWFORD, THE FAMILY MAN

WAHROONGA, 1910–1913

HARRY BIRKETT

Wahroonga Public School was full of the sons of doctors and lawyers who grew up in dark houses under the enormous trees of Sydney's Upper North Shore. Harry Bell Birkett was only the son of a doctor's widowed housekeeper, did not own a boat or a chemistry set, and so was only interesting to the boys with allergies who liked to take him on as a charitable project. But Harry knew that when he got home he'd have the whole doctor's house to play in as if it were his very own house, and the doctor would show him how to bowl a fast ball straight into the wicket as if he were his very own son.

Somewhere out in the world real men were fighting real pirates or driving wild horses across mountains honeycombed with gold mines. In Wahroonga you were lucky if you ever heard the dog from next door bark. There were lots of trees to climb, and strange insects to watch battle their way through a wilderness of lawn, and yellow and black spiders the size of your hand to dismember in a torture ceremony for an audience of stink beetles, but Harry sometimes wished that the spiders were pirates and the gum trees were the masts of ships and the grass was an ocean filled with sea monsters. The world could have burned down to the ground and you would never know it in Wahroonga. You mightn't even smell it. You would only notice that the sky at sunset was a bit more red and matched the curtains in a nice way.

Harry slept in the same room as his mother on a trundle bed at the foot of her own, but sometimes he would crawl up into her bed because she was very long and thin and he was only small then, and warm—just like a hot water bottle, she said—and those were his favourite nights.

Then they would lie awake talking. She would stroke back his hair and pull the thumb out of his mouth every time it found its way there, but she wouldn't reprimand him for it. She would tell him about all the possible futures they could have together once she'd saved enough money and they could leave.

'And what do you say about us owning a lolly shop?!' she would ask him and he would say, 'Oh wow, Mum, really?'

'Well, why not?' she would say, and then go on to describe all the different lollies they would have: chocolates with caramel centres and caramels with chocolate centres and liquorice in the shape of fish. Harry wanted to tell her they never needed to have this shop, that he would be happy to spend the rest of his life lying in his mother's bed imagining it, but he didn't, in case actually believing the lolly shop was going to happen was the only thing that made the dreaming of it possible.

One day in spring, when Harry and his mother were sitting on the kitchen steps sharing a packet of humbugs, Harry saw that a man on horseback was watching them from further up the path near the stables. He tugged his mother's skirt and pointed at the man but his mother didn't seem to care.

'Yes, Harry, that's the new useful. Shall we go and say hello?'

Harry didn't feel like sharing his mother with anyone that morning but did not have a good enough reason to say no, so he said yes.

The man was small with dark hair and a smooth face and the horse he was on top of let him sit on its back as if he were an important extension of the horse.

'What's your name?' Harry asked the man.

'Harry,' the man said.

Harry thought the man was playing a joke but no one laughed.

'But that's my name,' Harry said.

'Can I share it with you, squirt?' the man said with a wink.

Over the weeks that followed Harry couldn't work out what exactly made Harry the New Useful *useful*, but sometimes they called him a gardener and sometimes they called him a coachman, and sometimes he would take Harry the Squirt and his mother out for a ride on the doctor's dray, maybe to see the circus or to have a picnic down by the Lane Cove River on their day off.

Having two Harrys at the doctor's house was confusing, so sometimes Harry the younger was called 'squirt' or 'kid' or 'boy', and sometimes Harry's mother was called Daisy even though her name was Annie, and Harry the New Useful was called Harry Leo Crawford, but mostly just Crawford, because it was hard to imagine him being called anything else. Except 'father', which Harry the Squirt called him once by accident, and then blushed.

He blushed because Crawford was short and skinny, almost like a boy himself. He was not father material—he didn't even have a beard—and what if his mother heard him say 'father' and got the wrong idea? Crawford had probably crawled inside his head and made him say it. He was fishy like that. He had a New Zealand accent with a bit of something else thrown in. He was from Scotland, but he could only remember that place when he had haggis for breakfast because he'd left when he was very small. Just like how Harry Birkett couldn't remember his real father except for when he held his fork in his fist the way his strong, bearded father used to, but then that was only because his mother pointed it out.

Once Crawford arrived at the doctor's house, he seemed to always be where the things people missed or wanted should have been. Harry's old father was never around because he was dead, but Crawford was always around. He was there to help Harry and his trunk onto the cart when they finally left the doctor's house for good. He helped Harry's mother put her boxes next to Harry's trunk and he waved as they moved off down the driveway. And after the long ride down the highway to Balmain, there was Crawford again: holding the keys to the lolly shop Harry's mother had always wanted.

From the fingers of Crawford's other hand hung something limp and dirty. A single key, dangling on a ratty piece of string.

It could have been a key for a diary or a box, or a single shoebox room in a boarding house.

'Hello, neighbour,' Crawford said. 'I quit the doctor's too, and took a room just down the road.'

LILY NUGENT

The gravel driveway of Dr Clarke's house was as long as a country road. Daffodils sprang up out of the lawns on either side in a semblance of carefree clusters. Grey trunks of blue gums disappeared into cloud above the house like the columns of an ancient Greek acropolis. Why did one man and his wife need to live in a house the size of a small ancient city? Didn't the huge halls (not rooms) make them feel tiny in comparison? Didn't God feel further away? Everything about the place made Lily feel crass. The salmon pink of her dress felt tinned, not fresh.

As she walked down the driveway, she could smell horses, then hear voices, then see the roof of a wooden shack peeping over the top of a hedge. This must be the coachman's quarters, Lily thought, and turned around to find another path. But she could hear the shrill laugh of a small boy, then her sister's laugh, followed by a gruff leathery voice calling out: 'Daisy, come back!' She heard Annie's voice again, shouting: 'No, Crawford, I can't, Lily will be here any second!'

Lily stopped in the driveway, saw a bare patch in the hedge and bent down to look. Through the tangle of twigs she saw her sister running with her skirts hiked up above her knees, and her nephew with a fistful of leaves in his hand sneaking up behind a short man with unusual spade-like hands. The man was pretending not to see the boy, then turned around and walked towards the boy with the exaggerated strides of a monster. The boy was delightedly terrified, threw the leaves in the man's face with a scream and ran back towards the house, chasing his mother. The small man swiped at the leaves in his face with his spade hands and moaned after them: 'Daisy! Daisy!' He followed them, and Lily couldn't tell if he was exaggerating his steps or if he actually walked like that: like a man twice the size of himself.

'Who is Daisy?' Lily asked her sister, standing on the service door steps.

'Well hello to you too, dear sister!' Annie said, cheeks still flushed with rushing, a voice full of bubbles. She had grass on her shoulder, grass sticking out of her hair at all angles. She looked like an escapee from a pagan festival that had got a little too silly.

The short man came striding up the hill towards them with steps too big for his legs.

'Daisy,' he said to Annie in that leathery voice, 'you forgot your hat!'

He handed her a hat with five fresh daisies woven around the band. Annie saw them, and tried not to smile.

'I said, *Who is this Daisy?*' Lily asked again.

She did not like secrets, did not like thinking this man knew her sister better than she did herself, and she certainly did not like that such a place made her worry about the colour of her dress while Annie was rolling around in the hay.

'It's me, silly,' Annie said. 'I am Daisy. It's just a friendly name Mr Crawford has for me.' She looked sideways at the small man and flushed again, until she looked dangerously sunburned.

Standing there, watching Mr Crawford ruffle the hair on her nephew's head, Lily realised that he must have been the Don Juan of her sister's letters. This was the man taking Annie and her son out in the doctor's dray on their days off; this was the poor man who couldn't read; the man who was a miracle with horses.

Lily felt suddenly ill. She wanted the doctor to walk in now and sweep her sister off her feet. It had been known to happen. One in every hundred or so posh North Shore doctors had actually left their wives for their housekeepers or secretaries. She wished she had written that in her letters now. *Hold on, dear sister, the doctor might marry you one day!*

What a father young Harry would have had then! What a school he would have gone to! What a waste.

BALMAIN, 1913–1915

HARRY BIRKETT

The lolly shop looked exactly the way a lolly shop should look, except it was coated in a thick film of dust, as if it were buried in the memory of a dying old man. When the door blew shut the dust jumped off the jars as if the old man had coughed, and the jubes sang their colours out into the light before the dust settled over them once more.

The shop had been sold after two boys robbed its previous owner on the stickiest day of summer. A police officer (with a real revolver) had chased the boys for half a mile only to be stopped in the street by heart palpitations and the sight of the fugitives inching across the harbour in a dinghy.

Harry and his mother were determined to revitalise the mood of the place. They ordered new blue balls of chewing gum, butterscotch, toffees in the shape of cushions, bullseyes, American fudge, peanut brittle, real ice-cream cones, soft drinks with bubbles, rocky road chunks, and Cadbury's Dairy Milk chocolate all the way from England. Their lolly shop was going to be the lolly shop the whole of Balmain had as their favourite.

But one morning the joy Harry had in their project suddenly evaporated. As Harry's mother was pulling the boiled lollies apart with her fingers so they looked a bit fresher, she paused for a moment and said, 'Harry, how would you like it if Crawford came to live with us?'

She said it as if she were saying, 'How'd you like an ice-cream cone for breakfast?' But Harry wasn't fooled. There was something about Crawford that reminded Harry of the seaweed shadows that flickered beneath the waves at the beach; the ones you had to look at twice to make sure they weren't the shadows of sharks.

'He basically already does live with us.'

'Yes, but if we got married—'

'Married?!'

'—he could live here on a more permanent basis. What if he stayed the night, every night?'

'He already stays the night!'

Harry had seen Crawford step under the streetlight across the street with a bunch of flowers, or a brooch wrapped in tissue paper, or part of a pig carcass from his new job at the meatworks wrapped in a bloody white cloth. He had seen his mother look over each shoulder, checking for neighbours, then let Crawford in the shop, even after business hours.

'No, Harry, he stays until you've gone to bed and then comes back very early in the morning so it looks as if he stays the night, but he doesn't stay the night properly—only married people can stay the night properly.'

There was no spit in Harry's mouth anymore. His body had gone into a state of shock and had to conserve its energy in case he needed to run away very fast or punch his mother in the arm. His mother was lying to him about Crawford staying over. Maybe his mother lied about everything. Maybe she wasn't his mother at all.

For a whole week Harry couldn't talk to her. He would grab his breakfast from her, then eat it while hiding in the storage cupboard. In the dark, the jars of rainbow balls looked like eyeballs. Maybe his mother collected men's eyeballs. Maybe his real father's eyeballs were staring at him, warning him to leave. Maybe that's why she liked it when men looked at her, because she was imagining what their eyes would look like in a glass jar hidden in the cupboard.

When they walked to school together Harry walked on the opposite side of the road. When she came to pick him up he would walk straight past her as if she wasn't there. She was dead to Harry now. She looked like a ghost anyway, with her fair, almost see-through skin and blonde hair turning grey in places and long white skirts and white lace blouses that went right up to her chin. The worst thing was that Harry wouldn't be allowed to crawl into her bed anymore because the other Harry would be there, smelling of blood and meat from the meatworks and turning his mother into a slut.

After a few days of Harry's silent treatment there was a sadness that ran through his mother's voice so that it sounded like velvet rubbed the wrong way. And after a week of being ignored and not speaking herself, all the words she could have said spilled out of her at such a rate her face became red from lack of oxygen.

'Now listen, Harry, it's very hard running a shop on your own, especially as a woman, and Mr Crawford has promised to help around the place, he might not be the same as your father but he can always get a good leg of mutton and sometimes even lamb and I am going to marry him whether you like it or not.' Then she jabbed her new greenstone pin into the high lace collar of her blouse so hard that she gave a little gasp and looked at Harry as if it was his fault, as if everything was his fault, and cried.

Harry's mother did not often cry. The only other time he saw her cry was when she got the letter that said his father who no longer lived with them was dead, and even then Harry couldn't be sure that the tear running down her cheek wasn't sweat because it had been a hot day and she was wearing an awful lot of skirts.

Harry begrudgingly let his mother and Crawford marry on a hot February day in the Methodist church. He wore a sailor suit for the occasion, and felt as slimy inside it as a piece of corned beef left in the pot overnight. Aunt Lily was there with his two cousins who were not old enough to be fun or interesting, and so they spent the day hiding their faces in Aunt Lily's skirts whenever he got too close, or staring at Crawford in his borrowed suit and high starched collar as if he were a monster that had walked right out of a picture show to gobble them up.

After the wedding there was no big party with tiers of cakes and sandwiches. The adults went back to the shop to drink too much alcohol and then walked Aunt Lily and her kids back to the railway because the trams were too full and the fresh air was supposed to do everyone good.

That night, Harry heard creaks and pants and giggles and, 'Oh fuck, Harry,' through the thin walls. Hearing his mother call out his own name like that felt strange, even though he knew it wasn't meant for him. He wondered for a moment if he did wish she would scream like that for him, then shook the thought from his head and frowned himself to sleep.

LILY NUGENT

Balmain in February was so humid the flies moved through the air like paddle steamers slowly sinking—rising and sinking—in a stagnant river. Outside, the gardens were limp and inside the Methodist church the minister's red face looked as if it were freshly basted in fat. Flies buzzed in and out of his mouth as he opened and shut it: dying, before being born again.

'DO NOT FORGET,' the minister said, releasing three flies as he did, 'IN THE WORDS OF JESUS CHRIST: VERY TRULY I TELL YOU, NO ONE CAN SEE THE KINGDOM OF GOD WITHOUT BEING *BORN AGAIN*.'

The words resounded in the eaves of the empty church, shifting damp clumps of dust and lifting dozy pigeons out of their nests. The newly released flies flew up into the kingdom of God, which was now all around them, repeated, and repeated, and repeated.

Lily's little sister stood at the pulpit in a smart cream dress, but all Lily could see was how she flinched every now and then after being spat on by the minister's explosions of words.

'Why didn't you get married at the Anglican church?' Lily asked her sister after the service.

'There was too long a wait,' Annie said. 'And besides, Harry is a Scot, and you know how the Scots feel about anything from England.'

Another set of eyes might have seen how Annie had grown taller under the minister's shower of spit. Those same eyes might have seen Annie and Harry as two strains of apple trees, flourishing together under the Holy irrigation spraying from the presiding minister's mouth; the greenstone pinned to Annie's left breast a new green shoot; the heart-shaped pendant hanging on a chain around Annie's neck a precious metal replica of her own full heart.

On a chain around her neck, Lily thought. How appropriate for a woman's heart to be chained around her neck on her wedding day.

Lily suspected the wedding meant more to her new brother-in-law than it did to her sister. He had never been married before. Lily knew her sister was no great beauty, but standing at the pulpit, her new husband looked like a donkey that had woken to find himself in the arms of a fairy queen. He was blinking uncontrollably. His voice was gruffer than usual. He kept wiping his hands on his trousers and staring into her face as if it were a rare rainforest flower in the process of opening, yielding its midnight scent just for him.

Harry's voice broke the same morning the lolly shop coughed its last cough, rolled over, and died. When Aunt Lily turned up with the removalist and dray, his mother leaned against the doorway of the dead shop like something wilted, and watched Crawford carry out the things worth keeping.

'Don't worry, Mum—' Harry started to say, but when he said 'Mum' his voice jumped as if he were about to hiccup or cry. He wasn't about to cry, though. The adult in him was simply forcing itself through his boy body like Houdini bursting out of chains in a cage under the sea.

Aunt Lily was supervising the move and doing her best impersonation of a sugar bowl, with two hands on her hips, saying, 'Good boy, Harry,' every time he picked up a box. He wanted to say, 'I'm not a boy anymore, Lily, I'm a man now,' but he didn't in case she laughed at his voice seesawing between boyhood and manhood and pinched him on the cheek.

Tomorrow he would wake up in Aunt Lily's house and he would be a man with a man's voice. He would open his mouth to speak and deep tones would rumble through the house, shaking its foundations, demanding respect, and Crawford would not be there to stop him from finally being the man of the house he was supposed to be.

'I have no problem with you coming to stay until you find somewhere else, Annie, but I do have a problem with that gruff husband of yours and his girl, always lurking in corners like funnel-web spiders,' Aunt Lily's voice had said to Harry's mother down the post office telephone, loud enough for Harry to hear it through the telephone booth wall.

'His girl' was a dark fifteen-year-old who called herself Crawford's daughter. Her mother had died of consumption, she said, but this was the first any of them had heard about another woman. Crawford's girl was never really talked to or explained, and ever since she surprised them on the doorstep one night with the knowledge of her existence and a large, pregnant belly, Harry's mother looked permanently wan; her corsets were always too tight. The girl came to live with them whenever it suited her, then moved on once she'd eaten all their food and left a pile of dirty washing on the laundry floor. When it was time to sell up and move, Crawford's girl was, of course, nowhere to be seen.

Even though Crawford was short for a man, he turned out to be strong. Harry carted as many of the boxes to the dray as he could, but Crawford always carried more. Aunt Lily was the shortest and the smallest of them all but she was also the scariest, like a terrier in a family of labradors. She had a way of raising her eyebrows that could make a person say sorry without knowing why, and she especially liked to do this to Crawford, because she knew that if he and his trail of illegitimate children hadn't been lurking around, the shop would have been fine, just fine.

'How can it be,' Aunt Lily asked Crawford as she scrubbed the walls of the shop so hard the paint came off on the sponge, 'how can it be that there are hundreds of children in Balmain and yet this fine lolly shop—a children's paradise—is a deserted wasteland? How can that be? Someone must have scared them off, Crawford; someone must have scared them off.'

'Sorry, Lily,' Crawford said, because she had raised her eyebrows.

After all the furniture had been tied down to the dray, Harry sat with his mother on the kerb, holding her around the shoulders, and she looked up at the sky, waiting for it to fall. Crawford leaned on the dray with a cigarette hanging out one side of his mouth, while Aunt Lily walked through the shop to do a final check. There, on the empty counter, she found a kidney-shaped greenstone glinting like a sugared mint leaf. She picked it up between two gloved fingers, walked it outside and dropped it in Harry's mother's open palm.

'What's this?'

'Oh, Crawford gave me that,' Harry's mother said, as if he wasn't there to hear it. 'He was given it by a Maori when he rode horses up and down the West Coast of New Zealand.'

Who would have thought that the man skulking under the brim of his hat had driven horses up and down the wild West Coast of New Zealand?! He was a real man, then. The kind of man Harry always wished his own father had been.

In that moment, Crawford grew an inch, right before Harry's eyes.

DRUMMOYNE, 1915–1917

CLARA ANNIE BONE

Clara Bone the grocer's wife sat by the upstairs window studying Lyons Road below. Her cat, Prudence, prowled around her ankles. Ordinarily she would kick Prudence aside for being such a nuisance, but this Sunday she welcomed the feeling of an animal between her legs. It kept the wildness of her grief company, so she could sit back from it for once, and watch.

During the week customers had flicked their eyes between the prices on the blocks of butter and her composed face, as if she had personally been responsible for the war and the inflated cost of shipping. Of course, none of it was her fault, and she had to get by like everybody else. She had already made the supreme sacrifice by allowing her son to fight, and every day she regretted it, so she wasn't about to feel guilty about her profit margins or her new holiday cottage by the sea. The sea was a mindless thing, but it was a grand thing, too: deeper and more agile than the mind and the war and the thought of her son's body getting blown apart. Mr Bone had his garden. Well, she would have her trips to the sea.

The street, stark under its electric lights, was quieter on Sunday nights, and ran out in the direction of a sea she could only visit sometimes. She was tied to Drummoyne, but she supposed there were worse things to be tied to. Parachutes, for instance, falling out of planes.

From her window she could see a couple, new to the area, walk down the brightly lit road and turn into The Avenue. They walked arm in arm, a perfect specimen of young lovers—but closer inspection revealed irregularities. The woman was a great deal taller than the man, and thin to the point of being skinny. She looked as if she had fallen out of the world of ladies and lace and somehow found herself here, in this suburb of dressed-up workers' cottages. The man walked with a swing in his arm, a stride that over-shot the distance of a step and seemed to be holding something back behind the lips. Following the couple was a boy, slightly younger than her son would be now. And—was that a shadow, or a dark girl? A maid, perhaps? Mrs Bone pressed her nose up against the glass, but the scene flickered to black.

Another fuse blown in the streetlamps. Mrs Bone shook her head. Electric lights. She knew they would never last.

HARRY BIRKETT

When they stepped into their new brick house in Drummoyne, Crawford turned to Harry's mother and said, 'Look, Daisy, a separate dining room,' and she smiled as if he had said, 'Look, Daisy, a Persian elephant just for you.'

It seemed to Harry that the more well off you were, the more rooms you had for the different things you did. You could eat breakfast in the kitchen, but if you were well off you ate dinner in a dining room. Now that Crawford had a job at Perdriau's rubber factory and they were no longer living on a woman's wage they could afford to eat their dinner in a dining room.

At first it was fun pretending to be middle class. After school, Harry would walk down to Five Dock Bay at the end of their street. He passed through the empty sports field, where bicycles had been thrown against the brown grass as if bicycles were not things a person had to save money to buy. He passed a neat couple in new hats pushing a pram, the woman saying, 'There's no point farting about. You need to know what you want,' and the husband staring at the mangrove roots that reached up out of the water like the fingers of a drowning man. Under the surface of the water the oysters looked like exploded wedding dresses, singed and pickled in brine.

Drummoyne was a suburb of couples walking arm in arm along the edge of the bay as if they only ever spent their days walking— never screaming or dancing or fighting. On a single salary from the rubber factory, Harry's family could not afford to walk. They could hardly afford to live in their brick house with its separate dining room, and although Crawford and Harry's mother didn't exactly fight, they did have long conversations in raspy voices late into the night when they thought Harry was sleeping. They may have had more rooms to fill but they also had less room in their heads for any thoughts other than how they would next afford their groceries or rent.

Harry decided he did not want to be middle class if those were the things middle-class people thought about. *We can just eat brown bread, instead of white*, he could hear Crawford say on the other side of the bedroom wall. *And if my daughter comes back again, she'll pay her way, you watch. We'll eat corned beef instead of beef. I don't mind. Come here, let me kiss you. Please.*

At Perdriau's bits of machinery sporadically exploded, separating ears from heads and flinging the young women who worked there against the walls. Crawford only mended tyres there but still he'd come back stinking of rubber as if his limbs were slowly being replaced with the stuff. He would come back swearing, too, at the enamel mug he took to work when he dropped it in the sink, at his jacket if he got his elbow caught in the sleeve when he was trying to shake it off, at Harry if he ever tried to open the bathroom door when Crawford was soaking in the bath.

After a year of pretending, they had no choice but to downgrade to the weatherboard house at number five next door. If Crawford's girl ever showed up, she had to hand things over to pay for her time there: a brooch, or a scarf—who knew where she got them from. Harry had to get a job running messages for the grocer at the top of their street, and on Wednesdays Harry's mother would go out in her gabardine overcoat to do a bit of washing, or something like that.

Or something like that.

The phrase haunted the rooms of the house. Harry supposed the 'something like that' was mending, but he could never be sure. He just knew that when it was Wednesday, his mother returned home flushed in the cheeks and distracted, her head cluttered with things seen in the outside world collected on her day's adventure. He knew that on Wednesday, the evening meal was pork fritz and bread if anything at all, and when they ate Crawford would watch her face intently from the other side of the dining room table, trying to see if she was still what she said she was: his wife.

CLARA ANNIE BONE

The Crawfords' boy was intelligent, Clara could see that much. He knew exactly how to tessellate his mother's groceries so that they fitted perfectly in the wooden crate. She was so impressed with the boy's natural gift for packing, she could not help putting her hand on his shoulder and calling him 'Rabbit', as she used to call her own son.

'You better be careful, Rabbit, or I might give you a job and not let you leave,' she said, then gave him a gumball on the house.

The idea of a job made the boy stand up straight as a soldier.

'Hear that? A job, Harry!' his mother said, patting him on the head.

He pulled away, and ruffled his hair so that he stood apart from her: a grown-up, motherless man.

'That would be excellent,' his mother said to Clara, even though Clara was not talking to *her*, she was not doing this for *her*.

Clara could not help but have ham sandwiches ready when the boy came to help the following afternoon. And a little raspberry cordial. And a freckle, for after the sandwiches. She gave the boy so many treats he found it difficult to leave, and so when she opened the front door of the shop the next morning to find Mrs Crawford twisting the wicker handle of her basket in her hands, Clara was sure she was about to be reprimanded for keeping the boy for such long hours.

'I thought I could come and do a bit of work, or something like that, while your maid is away, as a favour,' she said. When the tall woman spoke, her teeth moved around in her mouth. Clara tried not to laugh.

She had kept doctors' houses before, Mrs Crawford said, ten times the size of her own, and missed the work, how it kept her mind off things. *What things?* Clara wanted to ask her. *Your son did not die in Ypres, what could your mind possibly need to be kept away from?*

But Clara didn't mind having Mrs Crawford around. It gave her a chance to observe the woman: how every day she'd almost drink them dry of tea, and how she rubbed the Brasso on the door handles so hard she nearly rubbed them clean off the doors. She always worked harder when she thought Clara was watching. But Clara was not watching her work; she was looking at the woman's skinny hips and small bust, and wondering how an intelligent boy like Harry was ever born from such a scrawny old hen.

'You aren't happy, are you, Mrs Crawford?' Clara said out loud to her one day while watching the woman scrub the steps so hard that her dentures fell out of her mouth.

Mrs Crawford grabbed her teeth and gobbled them up with her bare gums before Clara could see. But Clara did see.

'Moff wewwy, mo,' she said, and moved her tongue around in her mouth like a giraffe, then said again, 'Not very, no.'

Clara tried not to smile. 'Why is that, dear?'

'It is my husband. He—'

'Oh yes,' Clara said. 'That must be hard for you.'

It is funny, Clara thought, as she stepped over Mrs Crawford on her way up the stairs, how normal and happy people look at night, under the electric lights, from a distance.

HARRY BIRKETT

Harry's almost constant presence at the Bones' was misunderstood by his mother as an enthusiasm for work—which was not entirely wrong. Lifting sacks of flour was never more exhilarating than when Mrs Bone pointed to where they should go with her long white fingers. But in truth, Harry didn't want to stay at home only to find Crawford's girl in the kitchen, still drunk from the night before and using up the butter on the last of the bread. He didn't want to wake up in the morning to his mother kneeling beside his bed again, begging him in a whisper to try to keep Crawford at home when she next pays Aunt Lily a visit. Whatever schemes she was plotting, he wanted no part in them.

He preferred the harmless chaos at the Bones' shop. They kept seven different kinds of flour, and each sack had little moths that leaped out like soldiers jumping from planes shouting *Geronimooo!* Big cockroaches flew in the Bones' open window on hot nights and small cockroaches scurried across their counter when the store was locked up and no one was looking.

By mid-summer, they declared war. Mr Bone stalked through the shop like a German soldier spraying surfaces, gassing the small creatures to death, and Harry stayed upstairs in the Bones' apartment, setting mousetraps in Mrs Bone's wardrobe and looking out the windows Mrs Bone had polished after breathing on them with her ripe red mouth.

From the upstairs window Harry could see into his neighbours' yards. He could see Mrs Wigg at number seven leaving for her Eisteddfod committee meeting. He could see his own house through the red and green bristles of a bottlebrush tree—it seemed a prickly, empty place. It had no cockroaches, mice or moths, but it also didn't have their tiny, fluttering heartbeats, or give him the feeling of togetherness he had now with the Bones, armed to the teeth against their scuttling enemy forces. He watched as his mother rushed out the door with Crawford close behind her. He was supposed to be there, keeping Crawford distracted while she paid Aunt Lily a visit in Kogarah—Harry had forgotten—but it was too late to go home now. It would look far too suspicious.

Lily sat opposite her sister and uninvited brother-in-law as if she were interrogating them for war secrets. She did not intend to make them feel this way, but they sat so stiffly that Lily felt she'd been cast in the role of inquisitor without even knowing she had auditioned. They sweated as they sat, and the room burned with a mustard-yellow light that made the shadows of the objects in it larger and darker than the objects themselves.

Lily could see new etches radiating out from Annie's lips. She looked strained and tired—it was crippling her, all this withheld information.

'Annie, dear, you wrote saying you had something to tell me,' Lily suggested, holding her smile in place so that she did not look threatening.

Annie widened her eyes at her sister, sending messages Lily could not decipher, then looked at Crawford to see if he had noticed.

He had. Annie nibbled at her slab of teacake. Lily was sure Annie was chewing in code: *It's Crawford. Stop. Look at Crawford. Stop. Tell me what you see.*

Crawford was not much to look at. His eyebrows drooped down either side of his face, giving him the appearance of a worried cat: drenched and miserable. He did not touch his cake. He did not sip his tea. He sat and worried; looked from one sister to the other and worried some more.

Lily, who had spent a pleasant morning filling the house with teacake smells and guessing at the 'news' her sister's letter had promised (she was hoping for news of a baby, but was not about to hold her breath), now found that this unspoken 'news' had swollen to fill every corner of her house, giving the place the caustic air of a German trench. She wondered why Crawford had followed her sister here. She would have to get her alone if she were ever to find out.

'Annie, will you come and help me prepare the root vegetables? You always knew what to do with them.'

'Certainly,' Annie replied, and stood up so quickly her chair was thrown into the sideboard behind it, shattering a porcelain horse.

'Oh! I'm so sorry!' Annie said, looking as if she were about to cry.

Lily was not irritated, not really. She chose to see the accident more as an opportunity. 'Crawford, you'll find a dustpan out in the shed at the very back of the garden.'

Crawford looked at his wife. Annie seemed to be genuinely frazzled by the broken horse, and was now turning the pieces over in her hand as if they were the bloodied ears and legs of a real horse she had accidentally killed.

'Don't, Daisy, you'll cut yourself,' he said.

She snapped a look at him that suggested she would have happily smashed him to pieces, too, if Lily's nice things had not been at risk of getting damaged in the process.

'In the shed, you said?' Crawford asked Lily, and left without waiting for a response.

Once he was in the garden, Annie could not hold anything back any longer, and let out a low, rasping moan.

'Is it his daughter?' Lily asked, with a hand on her sister's back. 'Is she making a nuisance of herself again?'

Annie nodded, shook her head, nodded. She looked thin and frail and light, like the cockatoo carcass Lily had once seen washed up on the mudflats at Kogarah Bay and never forgotten. What had he done? What had that man done to her? Lily stood helpless before the awkward throes of her sister's body, saying simply: 'Shhhh. Shhhhh. It can't possibly be that bad.'

As she would soon find out, it *was* that bad.

Lily thanked God Mr Nugent had never given her cause to fall apart quite like this.

HARRY BIRKETT

After Harry's mother and Crawford came back from Aunt Lily's place, things seemed to settle down for a while. His mother was quieter, and doing her best to make a show of kindness. On a hot January afternoon, when Harry was let off work early to listen to what was left of the cricket on the wireless, he'd found his mother sitting on Crawford's lap on the front porch, sharing a bottle of ale. They already had the cricket on, and Australia had just hit a six, so Crawford poured six fingers of ale in a glass Harry's mother held in front of him, and he took six gulps straight from the bottle. Crawford was loving their new game, but Harry's mother's laugh had a shiver to it.

Crawford patted the milk crate next to them.

'Come join us, sport. We're killing it out on the green.'

Crawford looked part crushed underneath Harry's mother, but they seemed to take a liking to stretching out the summer afternoons with a bottle of ale on the front porch, nodding to whoever walked past. Harry took this as proof: women were complicated. One day they'd be jangling with you, the next they'd be sitting on your knee, sharing your beer, like nothing had ever been wrong.

When the dark came on before Harry had finished work, they seemed to use the cold as an excuse not to sit out the front like that, for everyone to see. And by the time spring came around, making everyone sneeze and go outdoors wearing too much or not enough and always the wrong thing, people started grumbling when they came into the shop. There was trouble with the unions, or there was trouble with the industrialists—it depended on who was doing the grumbling. One by one the unions went on strike. First it was the railways and tramways, then it was the miners, the wharfies. People started buying the older, cheaper flour in the store if they bought any flour at all.

Sure enough, Crawford lost his job at Perdriau's. It was because of the strike, he said to Harry's mother. There was no one left to send the rubber up the line. He stood before her in the kitchen like a scolded child, his hat clutched behind his back, like it was the hat's fault things had taken a turn for the worse.

Harry's mother did not snap him up like she might have done a few months before. Strangely enough, she almost seemed relieved. She turned to Harry and said, 'Well, my boy, now you're really the man of the house.'

Harry could have killed his mother for the shame that brought Crawford. He tried to catch his stepfather's eye, to show him he was sorry, but Crawford would not let his eye be caught.

If they fought, Harry was not there to hear it. The Bones were letting him stay for dinner now, to take the pressure off the pantry at home, and on the Eight-Hour Day weekend Mrs Bone was going to take him up to Collaroy, where the ocean was loud enough to drown everything out.

*

On the Friday morning before Eight-Hour Day, 1917, everyone in the Crawford house was distracted. Harry's mother was getting ready to go on a picnic with Crawford—picnics were supposed to keep the mood between couples pleasant—and Harry only had one more shift until he left for Collaroy. He was restless and didn't have a newspaper to read because Crawford was staring at it, pretending to look for a job. Harry shovelled his breakfast into his mouth and read the name blown into the glass bottle in front of him over and over.

Robert Robert Robert Robert Robert.

'Mum, who's Robert?' Harry asked when she took away the bottle to pack in the picnic basket, and he had nothing left to read.

'Oh, an old flame,' she said, smiling a warm milk smile.

Crawford shook the paper straight, but said nothing. Since he had lost his job they were living off Harry's wage, and Harry's mother seemed lighter, more distant, maybe even happier in her distant place than the real world made her. She hummed to herself as she put the dish scourer in the picnic basket, the sandwiches under the sink.

The ticking of the roof as it warmed in the morning sun made Crawford flinch. Maybe he was on edge because the mention of his name no longer made Harry's mother smile a warm milk smile. It made the little muscles on the side of her eyes contract, as if she was struggling to read a sign on the far side of a room.

HARRY BIRKETT

When Harry arrived home from Collaroy all he wanted to do was go to sleep and dream the long orange beach stretching out on either side of him again—its stealthy rips, the tough plants clinging to the dunes, Mrs Bone's wet swimming dress shaped around her clutchable thighs.

But when Harry walked up the front path he forgot all about the beach and Mrs Bone's hams. He forgot because the front door of his house was as open as a throat and a lantern in the kitchen was moving yellow light around in the hallway.

When Harry stepped into the room Crawford did not look up. He sat, staring into the wood grain eyes of the kitchen table as if trying to hypnotise it into life. One of his hands rested next to a bottle of whisky, the other beside an empty glass. About a quarter of the whisky was gone. Something was wrong; Crawford never drank whisky.

Harry stood and Crawford sat in the still house like this for some time. There were no night-birds calling to each other from the neighbours' trees and it was too cold for crickets. There was maybe the rustle and thump of a possum crashing through a tree onto the neighbour's roof but it could have been the sound of Harry's heart falling through his chest and thudding like a fish onto the floor.

'What's happened?' Harry asked.

Crawford said nothing.

'Where's my mother?' Harry asked.

'I don't know,' Crawford said, but the bottom had fallen out of his voice and Harry did not believe him.

'Where is she?' Harry asked again.

Crawford turned to Harry and for a moment Harry saw himself as Crawford might: standing there, pathetic in the twitching light, red and cringing in his adolescent limbs.

'She's gone to North Sydney with a Mrs Murray and her daughter,' Crawford said.

The boy and the man looked at each other for a long time. One of them was a jungle cat, the other its prey, and for the first time in his life Harry felt something fierce rise up in him. If the world champion boxer was standing before him at that moment, he would have automatically known how to pummel his jaw into a paste of teeth and tongue. He was the cat. He would not be the one to look away.

'Would you have a drop of whisky?' Crawford finally asked the boy.

'No,' Harry said, shook the visions from his head, and went to bed.

In the morning barely anything had changed. Crawford was still sitting at the kitchen table, his back towards the doorway, his right hand resting next to an empty glass, but the shadows had crawled back under the furniture and the whisky had practically disappeared from the bottle. It was sweating out of Crawford's skin instead.

This time, when Harry entered the room Crawford stood and swayed as if he were on a ship and clutched the chair to balance.

He looked at the catastrophe of fences, sunlight and clotheslines out the window and went to the stove to make tea.

Harry saw that Crawford's hand was shaking as he struck a match against the side of the matchbox. And when the flame took on the gas burner Crawford flinched and turned his face as if half expecting the flames to leap up towards the ceiling.

'Let me do that,' Harry said, 'you're too drunk.'

'Oh no. No, no.' Crawford shook his head hard.

'Did you fight with her?' Harry asked, hoping Crawford was so drunk he would forget to lie.

Crawford nodded.

'Did she say when she'd come home?' Harry asked.

'I don't know,' Crawford said, dropping the tea canister on the floor. 'No.'

'No, or you don't know?'

Crawford nodded, shrugged, wavered. He slowly lifted the kettle off the stove with a tea towel wrapped around both hands, as if the kettle held Harry's mother inside it, shrunk to the size of a pea. He lifted off the lid and looked inside.

'Here, let me do that,' Harry said again.

'*No!* Please. It's the least I can do for her now.'

At the shop, Harry wasn't noticing the rise and fall of Mrs Bone's full breasts when she breathed as much as usual. He was too busy talking himself out of the idea that his mother had left because of him. Maybe she had gone to see Robert. There was nothing holding her here anymore. Not her unemployed husband who had become a drunk, and definitely not her son, who'd drifted away into filthy, late-night dreams of Mrs Bone.

'I'm sorry, Mum,' Harry said to the new bottles of kerosene he was stacking on the storeroom shelves. 'I didn't think you'd notice.'

'What didn't you think I'd notice, Harry?'

It was a woman's voice, but it was not Harry's mother. It was Mrs Bone. He had replaced his mother with this white-necked, red-faced woman who looked—Harry now realised—more like a raw leg of mutton than the pin-up girl he'd thought she was.

'Your father came to say he wants you home at once,' her red mouth said. Harry had spent so much time imagining that mouth down where it could make him feel alive, and all the while his mother had retreated further and further away.

At home the scene was the same. Crawford was sitting in the same position with his back to the door, but now there was a green tablecloth on the kitchen table tingeing Crawford's smooth skin green, and there was a little pork fritz and bread and butter where the whisky bottle had been.

'Why did you want me to come home?' Harry asked. 'Is she back?'

But Crawford would not answer him. Instead, they ate, letting their knives and forks scrape against their plates and teeth to fill the empty room with sound.

After eating they cleared the table together, and washed up at the sink side by side. Crawford was sober now, but Harry could see the booze had opened up new rooms inside him. Rooms, or dark, musty dungeons at the bottom of spiral staircases. He wanted to hug the man, but knew he wouldn't. He would go to bed early and lie staring at the ceiling with his arms held stiffly by his sides. He was angry, because Crawford would not answer any of his questions, or even hold him, and he didn't know where to put his arms, they were so long and thin.

SYDNEY, WEDNESDAY, 3 OCTOBER 1917

HARRY BIRKETT

When the light in the sky was pallid and groggy, Harry was dragged up from the depths of sleep by Crawford shaking his shoulders saying, 'Get up as quick as you can.' Harry rolled over, but when he looked up to ask what was happening Crawford was gone. He could hear footsteps in the hall. Two sets. Then there was the sound of cans being slid off shelves in the kitchen and clattering into a bag. There was Crawford's voice and the voice of a boy. Once Harry had one side of his shirt tucked into his pants he walked down the hall, toes first. The house felt as fragile as blown glass. To walk suddenly or violently or even normally would have caused the house to crumble to bits.

From the dining room doorway he could see Crawford and the Parnell boy from a few blocks away clearing out the kitchen cupboards at a manic rate. Had the Germans come? There were no sounds of planes. Was there a flood? No, it was not raining, though the air felt hot and heavy, the clouds about to drip sweat.

'What are you doing?' Harry asked, but Crawford turned to the Parnell boy and said, 'The ice chest; don't forget to empty the ice chest.'

'What are you doing?' Harry asked again, stepping into the kitchen.

Now Crawford looked caught out. First he'd wanted Harry awake, now he wanted Harry gone—or did he even know what he wanted? He was acting like a panicked animal, urged forward by fear, not led by anything so thoughtful as a plan.

'Go back into the dining room,' Crawford snapped. 'I'll explain soon.'

From the dining room window, Harry watched the Parnell boy leave the house weighed down by a sack full of the groceries Harry had ordered and brought back from work only that week.

'Where's he taking our food?' Harry asked. He was fourteen now and as strong as Crawford, but in a nervous way, unused to his own strength.

'I've sold the furniture and there's a man coming for it and I want you to come to town with me,' Crawford said.

'What for?' Harry asked.

'Never mind, put your shoes on,' was the only answer he got.

Harry and Crawford followed the boy with the sack full of their food through the streets of Drummoyne. The light was more robust now and the men who worked some distance away were already moving towards the tram with their heads bent to the ground, watching their feet walk them there.

When they were in the Parnells' kitchen, Harry was told to sit at a table and wait for breakfast while Crawford and Mr Parnell went to another room to talk in hushed and hurried voices.

Breakfast, when it came, was bread and butter and beans stolen from their house. Mrs Parnell watched Harry eat, standing by with a pot of beans in her hand and spoon at the ready in case Harry needed more. The woman was looking at Harry as if she was about to cry on his behalf.

'Are you alright?' Harry asked her.

'That's sad news about your mother,' she said. 'I'm sure she loves you, she's just not thinking straight.'

'What news about my mother?' Harry asked. All he knew was that when Crawford lost his job his mother sulked and had probably yelled and now she'd taken off without a trace, without even a note. But then Crawford was in the doorway with a newspaper in one hand and the woman was looking at Crawford with her hand covering her mouth, saying, 'I'm sorry, I shouldn't have said anything.'

'I'll be back in an hour,' Crawford said, throwing the paper on the table in front of Harry so that the knife and fork jumped on his empty plate.

'What was that about my mother?' Harry asked the woman, but again she said, 'I'm sorry, I shouldn't have said anything,' then turned her back on him and wiped down the bench once more.

For a full hour Mrs Parnell fussed around Harry, clearing his plate, wiping down the table in front of him, sweeping the floor under his chair, leaning against the kitchen bench, watching him turn the pages of the paper. And for an hour Harry tried to read. He read every advertisement for false teeth and blood pills. He read about the revolution brewing in Russia, he read about how many Australian prisoners were held captive in Germany, he read about the price of eggs, but none of it was sinking in, because none of it had anything to do with his mother.

When Crawford returned, Harry was tugged out of the Parnells' house into a day fully alive and crawling with men on their way to the tram or the shipyards or the factories to work.

'Where are we going?' Harry asked, but he was not told. He was told instead to hurry up.

When they saw a tram pulling out of a stop on Bridge Street both Crawford and Harry ran for it, grabbed a side rail and swung themselves onto the carriage.

We're going to find mother and Robert, Harry thought, but he did not dare ask Crawford if this was right.

They got off at the railway and Crawford did not stop to get his bearings, look at street signs or the signs on the trams. He opened the palm of his hand and counted the coins there and then they walked, Harry noticed, in the direction of seagulls and salt.

The streets were full, but oddly quiet. Horses trotted past and men propped up doorways, smoking cigarettes, but none of them seemed to be making any noise. They walked through dark gullies of streets sunk between sandstone buildings until they reached the water sucking at the pylons of Circular Quay.

'Two tickets for Watson's Bay,' Crawford said to the man behind the ferry ticket counter. 'One way,' he added, and even though Harry had not spoken in some time, Crawford turned to him and said, 'We're going to take the tram back, in case you were wondering.'

As they waited for the ferry, Crawford sat on the edge of the bench, leg jiggling, eyes up. He seemed wary of the seagulls looking down at them from the tops of pylons and the roofs of buildings along the quay.

It was hard to make out the buildings on the other side of the harbour—where they ended and began—because the sky above the harbour was misted over with spume and fog and Harry couldn't think clearly. He could just see windows in the clouds—it looked like people lived in the clouds. Why had his mother left? Was it something he had said?

He asked Crawford: 'Was it something I said to her?'

Crawford said nothing. Perhaps he thought it was.

The ferry was small and though the harbour was flat and dark under the heavy clouds, the boat moved in a sickening way. Crawford leaned against the railing, looking out, as if worried the ferry might not know the way, and Harry slumped back, not only in the ferry seat, but inside himself, so that he watched Crawford from eyes inside his own.

The ferry curved around Garden Island, past boats pulling against their moorings like horses tied to fences, itching to run. They passed leisure yachts named after violent, hungry pursuits: *Buffalo Hunter*; *Moby-Dick*; *Pirate Queen*. They passed the green roughage of shrubbery and pipes cut out of the sandstone walls like sawn-off arteries, dribbling black water into the harbour. They passed houses tiered like syrup cakes. They passed fragments of regular lives lived in those grand houses: a maid collecting under-garments from a clothesline; a woman on an upstairs balcony, pacing backwards and forwards.

'What are we doing?' Harry asked, but the wind was loud and Crawford didn't register the sound of Harry's voice.

Up on a hill, a convent school and church with a dark spire spiked two clouds in the guts, but still the rain would not spill out.

They arrived at Watson's Bay at a time when only housewives and old men were out in their gardens or walking through the streets. It was a slow, weather-beaten outpost of Sydney and the wind stung through the weave of their jackets and the pores of their skin, making their bones thrill with cold. Crawford gripped Harry by the wrist and tugged him up the hill, through a park, until they were standing at the raw edge of the coast.

Down below, the Tasman was a deep wild blue, the blue of fish eyes, not the dirty green of the harbour, and the cliff face reaching up out of it was jagged, as if the country beyond this point had been dissolved, in one instant, by a freak acid wave. Along the top of the cliff, a fence kept people netted in, though the fence was rusted through with salt and was easily peeled back in places. Leading up to the fence, knife-sharp grasses strained against the wind. Trees bent back, flipping the silver undersides of their leaves at the sky. The only tall tree to be seen was a scraggy pine. Crawford climbed the path towards it and Harry followed.

'Where are we going?' Harry asked.

Crawford still said nothing. The wind carried a child's voice up from Watson's Bay below, then changed direction and brought with it only the slap of waves against rock.

Harry stopped in the middle of the path. 'Crawford! Stop walking. Please!'

But Crawford did not stop; he kept climbing the path and Harry had to run to catch up.

At the summit, part of the cliff hooked out and around into nothing, but in its crook a stubborn green succulent grew, its leaves swollen with the strain of clinging. 'Why are these fences here, wrecking the view?' Crawford said. 'Come over to the other side and throw rocks with me.'

Harry didn't move. From here he could see the hard rock platform below and how the waves shattered against it. The sandstone of the cliff they stood on looked as soft and collapsible as a skull, the grass on top as rough as salty, blood-matted hair.

'No, Crawford. I want to go back.'

Harry's eyes stung. The rain seemed to be falling upwards, right into them.

'I want to go back!' he yelled. 'Can you hear me? There are signs, can't you read the signs?'

But of course Crawford couldn't read the signs, because Crawford couldn't read, and now Harry was sobbing with frustration. Despite his height and his new strength he could not make Crawford leave or read the signs or tell him where his mother was. He could only retreat back into being a boy and he wouldn't let anyone touch him when he was like this, especially not Crawford, who was climbing between the rocks and the wind-whipped grass, trying to turn the cliff and the bitter wind into a game.

'Come up here, ya bugger! Come *on*!' Crawford called as if to a dog, but the thin veneer of fun crumbled easily in the wind and underneath his desperation was an ugly pulsing thing.

Harry stayed right where he was. Sobbing. Not even bothering to cover his face. He felt raw and pathetic and his snot and tears mixed with the spume, making his face sting where the wind struck it.

Crawford was not looking him in the face anyway, he was still walking here and there, finding stones to throw, then crawling through a gap in the fence and throwing them. The two went on like this: Harry sobbing, Crawford crawling in and out of the hole in the fence, collecting stones, throwing stones, trying to entice Harry into playing his game, until Harry went and sat on a rock—a numb, crumpled shell of a boy, embarrassed by his own tears. He watched an ant crawl up and fall off a twig again and again until eventually he noticed Crawford sitting beside him.

'You hungry, kid?'

Harry felt himself nod.

'You want to go get a pie?'

Harry nodded again.

'Alright, let's go and get a pie.'

On their way down the hill, Harry noticed the sapling of a pawpaw tree growing amidst a thicket of grass and prickles: a glimmer of the tropics in this bitter, wind-pummelled place.

'I thought we were going back by tram?' Harry said as they boarded the ferry back to Circular Quay.

'Changed my mind,' Crawford said.

But Harry suspected he hadn't changed his mind. His mind had been worn down.

It would be a full three-quarters of an hour before they could eat. The ferry would stop at Rose Bay and Double Bay and pass all the boats straining against their moorings and the grand houses with their elegant women trapped inside and Harry would have to sit there, so hungry his bones themselves felt hollow, his eyes heavy from crying, clutching his knees to his chest on the ferry bench. Crawford sat next to him and Harry thought he heard him say, 'I'm sorry, son. We'll find her.'

When they finally arrived at Sargents pie shop, Harry could have stuffed his face with every pie in the store and Crawford would have bought them all for him, too. Would you like a mince pie? Yes. With mushy peas? Yes. And a shepherd's pie? Yes. How about a pink cake? Or a lamington? Yes. Yes to both? Yes.

They walked up the hill towards the botanic gardens, their arms overflowing with pies and cakes as if they were heading straight for a bunker to live out the rest of the war.

They ate by the large fountain, where businessmen languished on the grass, reading the *Herald* and nibbling at their cut lunches between paragraphs. And they ate furiously—almost in silence but for the sucking of stray meat back into their mouths and the growling of their stomachs. Ibises and pigeons stalked the grass between Harry and Crawford, pecking at the pastry crumbs that escaped their hands and mouths. Even as he ate, Crawford appeared deep in thought.

'What are you thinking about?' Harry asked.

'I don't know. Eat your pie.'

'You must know what you're thinking about.'

'Come on,' Crawford said, but what he meant was, *She has left me as well. Leave me be.*

When the pies were finished, Crawford was silent. He stared, fixated, at the fountain.

Harry asked again, 'What are you thinking, Crawford? Tell me.'

'No, never mind—come on,' Crawford said, and made them move before their stomachs were ready, so that their steps were slow and their insides heavy as stone.

Harry suspected Crawford did not know where they were going. They walked in no direction in particular—or every direction at once—and it seemed like each corner turned was a new and different decision Crawford had made about what the day would bring. It was early afternoon now, but the sun was obscured by cloud so the whole sky glowed white. It could have been any time at all. And they seemed to be walking forever—the further they walked the more the minutes stretched out like pastry beneath their feet.

They eventually arrived at Sargents again but a different Sargents, on Castlereagh Street near the Southern Cross Hotel.

'But we already ate, Crawford,' Harry said.

'Did we?' Crawford seemed genuinely confused.

'Yes. Just then. And I'm so full now I can barely walk.'

Crawford reached into his pocket and pulled out a silver shilling. It glinted the same cold light as the distant, buried sun.

'Here,' Crawford said, flicking it to Harry, 'buy yourself a cup of tea. I'll be back for you in an hour,' and he crossed the street towards Hyde Park without once looking back over his shoulder.

He waited for Crawford under the awning of the shop and watched as the clouds finally filled the sky with a fine rain. The rain was so delicate it spun in the air like snow, dusting the wings of the pigeons lined along the lampposts. They shook themselves and as they did turned the rain into spray, and by the time Crawford was back the spray had become rain again, pooling in puddles on the street.

The man and the teenager stood close together—almost touching—under a ledge at the side of the building. Crawford leaned his head back against the stone, shut his eyes and breathed out. It seemed to Harry like the first time Crawford had breathed all day.

'Let's wait for this to pass,' Crawford said, and Harry couldn't tell if he meant the rain or the breathing or what.

When the roar of the rain had given in to the sound of birds shrieking in the fig trees in the park, both Crawford and Harry moved out from under the ledge and followed the tramlines out of the city. They walked with more purpose now—the tram lines giving them direction—and eventually they arrived at a house with four windows flashing purple and white.

Crawford put a hand on Harry's shoulder.

'I'm going to leave you at this boarding house for the night,' he said, and walked back towards the tramline, the way they had come.

A screech of bats tore the sky open above their heads and Harry glanced up. He looked over Crawford's way to see if he had noticed the sound, but he had gone. All that was left of the scene were two tram tracks, white with water and afternoon light, never touching, chasing each other to the quay.

JACK, THE BOARDER

WOOLLOOMOOLOO, OCTOBER–NOVEMBER 1917

HENRIETTA

She is ready to leave the house with her hat pulled low over her eyes and her laundry bag balanced on her hip when a sharp rap at the door has her spill tea towels and soiled undergarments all over the floor. *'Ach du scheiße!'* she swears at a sweat-stained singlet. She is already overdue at the police station by an hour. What if that's them now, come to check up on her?

Peeking out at the man on her front step she can't see much. He has his back to her and the silhouette of his face, turned towards the Domain, is blurred by a cloud of cigarette smoke. But she can see that this gaunt man in grey trousers, a mismatched coat and worn hat is clearly not—to her great relief—an officer of the police.

'Yes?' she asks the man.

His face is drawn, the bags under his eyes are purple with sleeplessness. 'I need a place to stay for a few nights.'

'I see.' She needs more tenants, but these days one has to be so careful. 'And who might you be?' she asks, but in the same instant he asks, 'You do run a boarding house, don't you?' and in the confusion they both look at each other, waiting to see who'll answer first.

'I am Mrs Shipley,' she says, doing her best to soften her consonants. 'Und you?'

'I'm sorry?'

'Your name?'

'Oh,' he says. 'Jack.'

She unlatches the door and steps back into the hallway, apologising for the mess as she does. He'd given her a fright, she says. That was all. The police is usually very clean. The place, rather.

The man, who can't move for the tumble of boxes and bags he's standing amongst, looks like he hasn't eaten in days. No, he's nothing to be frightened of. An opium eater, maybe, but he doesn't appear to be the patriotic type. And was that a slight accent she could hear? Maybe he's a Boer?

Now he is rattling off requirements, instructions. He needs a single room, with two beds. One for his stepson. He needs help with these boxes. And full board, too, once he gets himself a job. The transaction is swift and straightforward, because he's left the boy at another boarding house up in Paddington and has to get back to him, quick—and she has the laundry to wash, she says, gesturing to the mess on the floor to make sure he has no doubt laundry's the reason she is leaving the house. She shows Jack his room—the front room, bright, with nothing in it but two bare cot beds thrust against opposite walls—bundles up the laundry, and leaves.

At the corner of Crown Street, she hides the heavy laundry bag behind a bin, and looks back at the house to check no one has seen. Jack's on the front step with a fresh cigarette hanging off his lip. He's looking up towards the cathedral as a violin trill lifts from her husband's music room at the top of their terrace and tangles in the smoke from his cigarette. Thank God her husband has not yet been taken away. She cannot deal with people like this on her own, she simply does not have the nerve for it.

JACK

At first the woman is just an eye, wide open and scared.

She calls herself Mrs Shipley, but gets her words mixed up in that way foreigners do. And there's something fishy about how she opens the door. She opens it just a crack, and asks what I want before opening the door an inch further.

The hallway's covered in dirty laundry. She's nervous about it, tries to block my view. I look at her and the look says, *Smile at me. Go on, we're the same, you and me.* But she doesn't smile back.

The house smells of vinegar, and of something sweet also—I can't put my finger on it. Lamps are burning at their lowest gas mark; some corners of the hall throb with light, others fade into blackness. It's a tomb, this place, and it's restless with ghosts.

The foreign woman drops my suitcases and opens the door onto a bright room with nothing in it but two bare beds. There's a window.

No curtain. It looks out over Cathedral Street below. The foreign lady has given us a front room, then. Good. I think that's good.

I haven't been sleeping. At night, I'm wide awake. During the day, I drift around in a fog. I'm not sure how things get done, but they do get done. Somehow I made it here. Decisions are being made through me, as if I'm being dreamed by someone else, and in this dream I'm a man who knows to pack up the house in Drummoyne, leave the keys for the landlord at the grocer, take the boy Harry, deflect all questions of his mother, and leave for a place where everyone lives as if they've been packed at a cannery.

But the boxes. Where are they? Out on the front steps where anyone might find them. When I open the front door there's my green box, full of her lace, her things, curtains she left half mended. My green box, bending the light towards it. A violin scale floats down from the open upstairs window above, and it strikes me what the sweet, vinegary smell is that lingers in the house. It's the smell of cabbage farts and pig's blood. It's a German house, full of German smells. I almost laugh. No one will trust the word of a German woman, especially not the police.

HENRIETTA

Standing in her kitchen with a letter held high between herself and the sun, Henrietta hears footsteps, then a cough, and turns to see a boy in the doorway.

'Hello there,' she says, hiding the letter in her apron pocket.

'Hello,' says the boy. He's looking up at her with the frightened eyes of a dog about to be hit. The poor thing can't be more than fourteen.

She stretches her hand out towards him. 'It's alright,' she says, 'I don't bite.'

The boy has his eyes trained on the biscuit tin on the kitchen bench. He must be starving. How strange that she should be reading a letter from her son and then turn to find a boy—about as tall as her son had been ten years ago, and as fair—standing before her. She must have dreamed him up. She fetches a biscuit for the boy, but he has already slipped down the hall and out of sight.

She can hear Jack rousing on him in the front room. 'What did I say about keeping out of everyone's hair?' and 'You're not to go in there without me, you understand?'

So he's the stepson, then.

Henrietta stands still, listening for a squeak of a floorboard or the click of a door latch. When she's certain no one is about to discover her, she slips the letter out of her pocket and holds it up once more against the light. She will read every word Andrew wrote to her from that horrible place. Again and again. Especially the words that have been blacked out.

JACK

The bats have begun their evening hunt. The sky is alive with them, flying—as if magnetised—towards the east. Sitting on my green box, looking out the window, I'm the only one who sees them.

The boy is here now, sitting on the edge of his bed and staring fiercely into the floorboards. I watch him closely, as if he might, at any second, sprout claws and wings and fly away.

'Any word from Mum?'

'No, kiddo.'

'Did you even go to the police?'

'No need for that.'

The boy misses his mother. He pretends not to need her, but the boy is like a sick animal, dragged away from water. I don't know what to do.

Out of the pub on the opposite corner, women stumble with their hair half undone and falling over their faces, and men stumble with their arms half lost in the women's blouses. They move in a slow dance, as if their bones have melted away, and I am melting into them, too. How is it possible to feel this seasick a mile away from sea?

The boy speaks.

'Crawford?'

'Yes, son?'

'Do you think, once I've saved some money and can buy us a house, Mum might come back?'

'Maybe.'

The boy is curled up on his side, his blanket folded over his hands under his chin. His eyes are bright—the light from the streetlamp outside has lit two fires in them. He is staring at me, as if every answer I give is something he can peg into the ground to keep himself from drifting away.

I sit in the crook the boy's body makes, and stroke the hair out of his eyes. He has his mother's wild hair, his mother's grey eyes, but some other man's jaw—a man who'd died years before and left the kid with nothing but a name and a jaw. How proudly the boy holds on to that name. It was the first word the boy learned how to spell, his mother said, and once he'd learned it he wrote it on every surface he could find to write on in the house. Everything was labelled Birkett. The underside of plates: Birkett. The address book: Birkett. The edge of the dishrags: Birkett. When I moved in, I was living a borrowed existence.

Daisy said the benefit to having her son grow up without a father was that all the boring, violent, less-than-perfect aspects of the man were not around. His empty name could be filled with the strongest, most honourable hero a boy could imagine. She never told him about the day his father moved to Newcastle so she couldn't nag him anymore, because she could see that there was something in the myth of the man that filled up the boy from within.

Sitting here, nursing another man's child to sleep, I can see how this boy might be my unravelling. This boy, who I have absolutely no claim to, who tries so hard to prove himself as a man that he lets his childhood slip through his fingers like sand.

The boy is asleep now, and I go back to my green box, watching the street below. Above the chimneys and spires of the city, the sky is a bruise, healing. Morning will come soon, but before it does my mind will wander in and out of sleep and memory, mistaking one for the other. Nothing will be left as it was found.

HENRIETTA

She is up to her elbows in blood and fat. She has so much to do today and there is Jack standing in the doorway, moaning, 'Are we having sausages for breakfast?' as if everything she does is for him. He is in the same rumpled suit he arrived in yesterday. He has not bathed, he has not changed; she wishes she had never let him into her house.

'No,' she says. 'These are for my son.'

'Where is he?'

'Where is your wife?'

A silence makes the morning light lemon-sharp in the eye and is not broken until her husband, sitting at the kitchen table, turns the page of his newspaper. His contribution, as it is most mornings, will be to read out the headlines from the paper, offering commentary when he deems it necessary.

'The Baltic Islands! Russians Hit Back!'

'Nothing to do with the war, please,' she asks.

'Grocer's Profits! Prices Raised Without Authority!—does that count, Hettie?'

'No—but so dull, Eduard.'

'Chatswood Mystery,' he reads next. 'Woman Not Yet Identified.'

'Alright, read that,' Henrietta says, because he will keep going on and on unless she lets him read something.

'The detectives engaged in clearing up the mystery surrounding the death of a woman . . .'

Jack drops his cup in the kitchen sink. 'Oh, Mother! Mother!' she thinks he says. Is he sobbing—or laughing?

'Jack, what is wrong with you?'

He is pale. 'I don't know,' he says, and shakes his head. 'I don't know.' But when he looks up to see the boy standing in the doorway he acts as if he does know and he takes the paper from her husband, the boy by the shoulder and says, 'Come and read for me in the room.'

JACK

The boy is sitting on the green box, glaring right at me.

'It's her, isn't it?' he says.

I look at the picture of the shoes in the paper. 'Now, calm down, we don't know . . .'

'What are you going to do?'

I say nothing.

'I suppose it doesn't help anyone,' he says.

'What doesn't?'

'Telling the cops that Mum's a slut and went off with another bloke—'

I take the boy's hand in my own. 'It's not your fault,' I say. He tries to pull away, but I'm holding on so tight my fingers have turned white. 'She left. That's all we know.'

But really, she hasn't left. I can see her in everything. She's right there in the boy's face.

HENRIETTA

Her husband is in the upstairs music room, galloping through the Paganini concerto he and his mother had played for the Russian tsar when he was only nine years old. He plays it when he wants to be back in old Europe, back at the beginning of his glittering future that never eventuated, and now the whole house is unsettled. Even the suds in the sink are collapsing with disappointment.

Henrietta looks up from her wrinkly hands to see Jack pass down the hall. Her husband's plaintive violin is drawing the bottle of Johnnie Walker that Jack clutches in his hand up the stairs.

The concerto lands on a low G and stops so suddenly Henrietta puts down her dishcloth and listens. She hears silence, footsteps, her husband's bold, generous laugh. The sounds of two lost men, finding something of themselves in each other.

An hour later the sound of the men has become raucous. They are probably halfway through that bottle of whisky, telling dirty jokes. The last thing she needs is for her loud husband to get on the bad side of the neighbours, or the boarders, or her own nerves, so she brews a pot of coffee and takes it upstairs.

'And so you see, the way we've been treated, I am starting to side with the German position in the war,' she can hear her husband saying as she makes her way upstairs. 'My family fled Germany over forty years ago for the exact same reason Britain is now at war with her, but here we are not allowed to own businesses. I have lost half my students. My wife's son—'

'Eduard!' she says so fiercely he puts the cap on the now half-empty scotch bottle and hands it to Jack without her needing to say another word.

She leaves the door open when she goes. *I am listening,* the open door says. *I am always listening for you to break your promises, Eduard.*

Descending the stairs, she hears the chink of spoons in coffee cups, the mutterings of goodnight, Jack's voice in the open doorway: 'Oh, and Edward—if two detectives come, remember: the boy and myself, we are not here.'

JACK

From my position on the green box I can see a figure walking down the footpath on the opposite side of the road. I can't quite make it out. I'm sure I can see a police helmet, but the figure crosses the road and the helmet becomes a mass of woman's hair, piled up on her head.

It is safer to sit here and watch than to try to sleep.

HENRIETTA

Returning home one afternoon, she can hear the sound of an axe splitting wood. Her paranoid heart speeds up, convinced that an intruder is at that moment smashing his way through her back door. She turns the key quietly and creeps into the house. She will not let that intruder get his hands on her husband's violin. He will have to cut her to pieces first.

In the back courtyard, Jack is hunched over the smashed remains of a green wooden box. Bits of lace and shreds of linen are strewn around his feet, making him look like a werewolf just turned back into a man. She sees him raise the axe over his head again—his shoulders broadening—and throw it down, scattering splintered wood across the yard. She's horrified—such good boxes, all broken up! They could be sold. And Jack, he owes her money. He has been paying her in lace and pretty pieces of wearing apparel that will never fit her even if she starves herself for a year.

'Jack!' she says, stepping out to take her husband's axe from his hands. 'Your wife will come back to you.'

He lets her take the axe and slumps, as if the feel of the axe in his hands was the only thing giving him strength.

A low animal moan comes from him then. It has its own heartbeat. It is almost a song. 'Oh no, no, no, I want her no more, no more, no more, she is no good, no good, no good, drinking too much.'

She puts a hand on his back—it is more bone than muscle when his arms have nothing to wield—and walks him into the kitchen to make him coffee.

She puts the kettle on the hob and feels safer, moving through the ritual she knows so well. She feels so safe she dares say, 'That is a funny thing that she leaves you without anything. Surely you had a row or something with her—she would not run away for nothing.'

'Yes,' Jack says, 'I had a jolly good row with her and I gave her a jolly good crack to go on with.'

Henrietta does not believe that this man, on the verge of tears, could be the sort of overbearing husband one reads about in the penny press. He is surely only violent the way a toddler gets violent, confused over how to hug a playmate without asphyxiating him to death.

'You should not hit a woman so hard,' she says with a pat on his hand. 'It is not nice.'

Jack puts his head in his hands, as if he is sorry.

JACK

Breaking up the box hasn't helped. Lying awake I can hear a noise coming from the corridor—a scratching made by flimsy nails. Closing my eyes only makes the noise louder, as if it's coming from the gas pipe, the window, the ceiling and the corridor at once.

I check the sleeping boy. He's out cold. Good. Sleep, boy, sleep sound enough for the two of us.

The hallway is so dark it's dimensionless. I have to pull back to stop myself from falling. After my eyes have adjusted, I run a hand down the hallway wall towards the sound. The sound is coming from behind a door. I open the door and in the middle of a small room I can just make out the metal horn of a gramophone. In the dark it looks like the bell of a giant, carnivorous lily growing out of the dust on the floor.

The gramophone is spinning a record. Its needle slips, comes back, slips, comes back to the last second of the record.

Beside the gramophone is a candle and a box of matches. I light the candle, and see that the room I'm in is bare, except for the gramophone. The room is too small to be a bedroom, too big to be a cupboard. It has no windows, no shelves. I move the needle back to the beginning of the record, and hear what sounds like my own voice. The record is playing at a very slow speed. I turn the handle of the gramophone, and a woman's voice comes to life.

'Take off your shirt,' she says.

'No,' my voice says.

'How is it we've been married for this long, and we've never slept flesh to flesh?'

'We aren't that sort of people.'

'And why not? Take off your shirt.'

'No. What's wrong with you? It's the middle of the day.'

'Are you worried I'll laugh at your breasts?' she says.

The record slows; the voices through the trumpet become deeper, until they are the voices of two men at the bottom of the sea. I look to see that I have spilled candle wax onto the spinning record. It has spread along the grooves and congealed around the needle.

A gust blows the door of the room shut behind me. I turn, and there I am, reflected in a mirror on the back of the door.

The shadows under my eyes look like dark pools of water corroding the soft rock of my face. How could she have loved this face? How could anyone have loved this face, steadily weathering into powdered bone?

The figure in the mirror moves his mouth.

'Jack,' the figure says.

'Nina,' I reply.

'What's troubling you?'

'I'm not sure. I can't seem to remember.'

'Surely you can, if you can only be still for long enough.'

Shutting my eyes, I can see a woman with her mouth frozen open. A girl in a too-small nightshirt standing in the cool light of the kitchen late at night. Cold bodies hanging from hooks. Me, or someone like me, waltzing with them. A giant fish with a hundred broken jaws suffocating in the open air. A boy growing, bursting out of his shoes. The boy has a woman's face. Her eyes are spinning like planets, her hair is as wild as weeds in a summer field.

I open my eyes.

'It's the boy,' I say. 'Sometimes I see him out the corner of my eye, and it's her.'

When she arrives at Central Police Station, the officer at the front desk does not get out of his seat.

'Sheep Lick,' he says, as he says every Wednesday just before lunch. Her presence is a punctuation mark in the digestive calendar of his week, nothing more.

'Yes, Henrietta Schieblich,' she says in reply.

There is a woman officer there too, who looks up at Henrietta with a fleeting smile. She's often at the front desk, helping the secretary with the typing. But once Henrietta saw her walk a fortune-teller through the station in handcuffs, and sometimes she overhears the policewoman giving a strumpety-looking girl a talking-to about how to turn her life around.

Henrietta walks past the policewoman, the bored officer, into the back room.

'Can you smell cabbage, Sergeant? I can smell cabbage!' the officer there says to his colleague, the same as he does every week. 'Been building any trenches down Cathedral Street, Sheep Lick? Manufacturing any mustard gas in your lavatory?'

She lets him have his fun. It does not bother her. Her mind evacuates the room to monitor the weather, to think about the mending or what she will buy for dinner that can stretch to feed six. But when the officer says, 'Sign here, Sheep Lick. And here,' as he inevitably does, her mind is brought back into the room.

This week, however, the officer has something to add.

'Going to be sending you over to the barracks, Frau.'

'To the camp?' she asks. She is terrified of the camp, but also drawn to it, obsessed by it. She could be with her son again. She could trade one set of anxieties for another; one set of comforts for others greatly missed. (Her son's face, when he tells her a joke; the way it lights up.)

'No. Listen. To the barracks. On Oxford Street. The army are handling you lot now. Krauts are apparently too dangerous for us.' The police officer looks disappointed and Henrietta smiles. The police station is a lion's den of men trying to climb on each other's backs. And his back—hunched over in the tiny office he had been allocated—supports much bigger backs than his.

When she returns home she forgets to tell her husband about the barracks, because there he is, meeting her at the door, pulling her in close, walking her up to the music room. He has not been this forthright with his affections since the Toowoomba Eisteddfod in 1908, when they first met: the miracle meeting in a Queensland backwater of two Germans who loved Schubert.

But this afternoon her husband is not about to kiss her behind the music stands. He shuts the door.

'There was a fire,' he says.

'What? Where?' She sniffs the air, looks around the room. Before the war the two of them were laughed out of Queensland after trying to claim insurance for their incinerated home. Now, especially now, they would never have their claims met.

'Under the boiler,' he says. 'It had been lit. And it was still burning with papers and lace. And there was a pair of scissors there, too, when I came home.'

He fetches the scissors from where they hold a Haydn concerto down on his desk. The scissors are black with soot.

*

A storm lands over the city like a blanket thrown over a birdcage. The darkness is suffocating, and Jack is in the kitchen, pacing back and forth. He is like an ant, unsettled by the promise of rain, desperate to scurry. She can see he needs to get something off his chest to someone—anyone—but tonight she would rather hear her knife slice potatoes than listen to him complain.

'I can't stand it anymore,' he says, without any prompt from her. 'The bloody bastard's no good, no good.'

'There is nothing wrong with the boy; the boy is real good,' she says, decimating a potato with five whacks of the knife.

'I must get rid of him,' he says. 'I must take him to his aunty up the line.'

'Tell me the address,' she says. She is getting sucked in. 'I can take him in the morning.'

But he will not tell her. He sits at the table wringing his hands like a hammed-up Lady Macbeth. Maybe he is a genuine lunatic. But what can she do? Get the doctor? Fetch the police? Not in this weather, and never to this house.

'Leave the boy here, and you can go elsewhere,' she suggests. 'Find a job somewhere. I'll look after the boy for a while.'

But this suggestion makes Jack worse. He stands up, sits down and stands up again, like a cuckoo clock out of touch with time, and when the boy comes in, already changed into comfortable clothes after his first day at a new job in the city, Jack shoos him out. 'Hurry up and dress yourself, and I'll take you to your aunty.'

The boy whines.

'Now!' Jack roars.

She doesn't understand why the boy doesn't stand up to Jack. He is taller than Jack. Stronger, too, probably. And yet he always skulks around like a reprimanded puppy. Jumping when Jack says jump. Going out whenever Jack says. But never smiling. Not once.

The two leave the kitchen and she hopes that's an end to the drama for the night. Jack will calm down. He will take pity on the boy, and calm down. But a quarter of an hour later they are back again. The storm is worse. Jack is worse. He is out in the hall, raging in a raincoat, but the boy, he is only in a thin summer coat. It's outrageous to take the boy out on a night like this. Why can't he take the boy tomorrow?

'Yeah?' the boy says. 'Why can't I go tomorrow?'

'Ah, get out,' Jack says, and pushes the boy out the front door.

The wind throws the door open, and the rain comes into the hall in horizontal streaks.

'Wait a minute, Harry,' Jack calls to the boy, and she thinks: yes, good man for changing your mind. Good man for taking pity on the boy. She is about to say as much but he goes into their room to fetch a brand-new shovel and is on his way again.

'What on earth are you going to do with that?!' she calls out to him.

'I'm going to kill the bloody bastard!' he screams. The door slams, and she almost collapses on the floor.

JACK

Out in the rain, things I was sure of now seem hazy. The boy's being good, the boy's doing what he's told. The boy's still asking questions, but they're thinning out now he knows I won't reply.

There are only a few people on the William Street tram. Young men going to the Cross—loud and calling to each other across the tram aisle; couples on their way home from the theatre. One woman, drunk, is abusing her husband for ogling one of the girls at the Tivoli.

The rain is streaking down the windows of the tram in floods. Two horses at the intersection wobble with rain. One shivers, melts, comes back together again.

We get out at Edgecliff and walk past trees backlit by lightning. The boy is silent. He's shaking, too; the clatter of his teeth sounds like distant hooves.

No one will find us on a night like this, and our footsteps will wash away. But despite the sticky blackness, the houses on Ocean Street are bright. They're fitted out with electric lights and it seems like every one is trained, like a searchlight, on me and the boy, throwing hundreds of our shadows down at our feet.

We come to a flight of stone steps and go up. On the left-hand side there's a thick scrub. I enter, and the boy follows. He always walks behind; he's somehow afraid to walk near me.

When we come to a space amongst the bushes, I begin to dig a hole some three or four feet wide and longer, and three or four feet deep. The rain helps. The earth is soft and turning into mud.

I stop digging a couple of times to drink spirits from a bottle, and after I have the hole about four feet deep I say to the boy, 'Now you get down and have a go.'

The boy digs the hole a foot or so deeper, but he's started asking questions again. He asks what I want the hole for. I won't answer. He keeps an eye on me all the time until he gets tired and drops the shovel in the bottom of the hole. He climbs out, so I jump down and have another go at it, but it's no good, the earth's too rocky, so I climb out and search for sandier ground. I walk in and out of the bushes, branches flinging back into my face, my arms and hands are scratched but it feels good, it feels right. The boy is behind me, though. Watching, always watching.

After a while, the rain still streaming, I find a good spot and dig again. I dig about the same in width and length, but not nearly as deep as the first place, and ask the boy to help. He digs for a while but doesn't do much because by then he's soaking wet and shivering violently. All I can hear is his skeleton rattling in his skin so I give in.

'That's enough,' I say, and take the shovel from the shaking boy.

HENRIETTA

The rain blends the hours together. People are passing through the rain outside and as they pass their shadows stretch across the wall. The shadows' umbrellas dig and dig at the sky, and once they have dug all the rain out, she sees a shape that makes her sit up. Perhaps it is a police helmet? The helmet crosses the road towards her house, and once it has reached her front step it turns into a shovel resting on the shoulder of Jack. Beside him, the boy, looking half drowned, is covered all over in sand.

When Jack comes in he says, 'Oh, Harry's a coward. He started crying and wouldn't go to his aunty.'

The boy is silent.

JACK

The memory of her will not be buried, and the boy has gone to Italian people up the road. On my first night alone I am kept awake by an image of my wife unbuttoning her blouse—perhaps reluctantly, but at least she's finally doing it.

HENRIETTA

Jack makes a point of standing before her while she's doing the mending to declare in her boarders' presence that everything is fine. The boy's mother has written, she is working in a hotel over in North Sydney. She needs time apart to get her head straight and try to get off the drink, that's all.

As he speaks, he seems to be waiting for Henrietta to breathe out, or nod, or give some other sign of approval. But she doesn't. She's sick of coming home to find perfectly good things smashed to smithereens, or burned, or drenched. The man is disruptive on a biblical scale. She doesn't need his money so badly that she has to put up with Jack and his ghosts chasing each other through her house. She simply says, 'Oh,' and prays that peace will soon be restored.

But peace is not soon restored. Her trips to the barracks are unsettling her nerves. The soldiers all look the same. They could have been put together in a factory, those lizard-green killing machines. She can't stop thinking about what they are doing to her son right now at the camp. And then there's her husband, spending his nights drinking with Jack. And the price of butter. And the ghosts stalking her mad tenant through the house, shuddering up the pipes when she sleeps. She can hear Jack muttering to them in his room, sometimes so loudly she wakes up.

On one occasion she runs into Jack in the hall as he flees from his room. He is quivering with terror, his hair tousled, his eyes red.

'Madam, madam, I think the room is haunted. I am haunted,' he says.

A part of her wants to calm him down. Another part of her— the weary, sleep-deprived part—has become as ruthless as those lizard-soldiers up in Paddington. *This is your chance*, that side of her thinks, *to exorcise your house.*

She looks him in the eye. 'I think your wife is haunting you,' she says. 'I think you killed her.'

JACK

At my new job, bodies swing off hooks, smooth and almost elegant. They have no heads.

The floor is littered with cigarette butts, swelling with blood like gorged leeches. Smoking helps mask the smell. But after the second or third day, the smell of blood and fat becomes sweet and almost metallic. A smell I could get used to.

The carcasses come out of the cool room on hooks. Headless, armless, they are the colour of candlewax, mostly, and glow a bluish pink.

It's late November, and even the high ceilings of the meatworks don't release the heat. Flies stick to our mouths. We shake our heads, but the flies turn a few circles in the air and come back.

The hooks hold the carcasses by the ankle joint, between the two long bones of the leg. Sometimes a hook gets caught up in tendon or membrane. The hook doesn't pierce all the way through, and the membrane stretches over the rusty metal. When that happens, I shove the heel of my hand against the joint, so the membrane splits. It's a satisfying feeling.

We hug every third or fourth carcass. Our ears press against the pig's thighs, our arms wrap around the haunch, the nook between our necks and shoulders lock against the meat. Braced like this, we walk the carcasses out of the cool room, and into the butchery.

The first time I walk in the procession of carcasses, I have the feeling I've been here before. It's the coldness of the skin. The touch of a woman who doesn't know how to love.

HENRIETTA

After being woken up again by Jack's mutterings, she stares steadily at the ceiling and tells her husband she can't stand it anymore.

Her husband rolls to face her. 'The detectives,' he whispers.

'What? Did they come?'

'They could have. Looking for him.'

'Ah!' She kisses her husband on the forehead, the cheek, both curls of his moustache. 'You are a genius, Herr Schieblich. This is why I married you.'

JACK

She is everywhere. She is sitting three rows ahead of me on the ferry. She is buying a pound of sugar at the grocer's in a suburb I never thought she'd visit. Wisps of women's hair fly up under the brims of their hats, the way hers used to. I see the flash of a green coat tailored sharply into a waist as small as hers. These things make me realise how often I think of her.

I see her standing outside Mark Foys with the boy. I walk towards her with my hat in my hands. She's standing in front of a window display of new dining room furniture, arranged around a fibreglass roast. A mannequin mother stands in the corner of the window display, watching me with a jug in hand, threatening to hurl boiling gravy in my face if I get too close.

Daisy sees me and grips the boy's arm. The boy's bigger than me now. Amazing how fast they grow.

'Hello,' she says. Her mouth has new lines around it; her neck is as shiny as plastic, as red as scalded skin.

HENRIETTA

Telling Jack about the detectives is easier than she thought. All she has to do is pull the same straight face she pulled for the insurance men when they came to inspect the ashes of their house in Toowoomba.

She waits until after Jack has paid his week's rent, then knocks on his door.

'Jack,' she whispers through the door.

'Mmm?' he says. He sounds drunk.

'The men you said about—the broad-shouldered men. They came looking for you.'

'Yeah?' he says; then, snapping out of it, 'Which men?'

'The detectives. They came just this morning, asking about a man who had come to stay with his stepson.'

Jack opens the door. Now she has to lie while looking him directly in the eye. The calm this gives her—a thrilling calm, the way one feels after climbing to the peak of a mountain—is surprising to her. She will soon be free. He is not her problem. When he slams the door in her face, and begins to rip the linen off the bed and hurl his belongings into boxes, his distress is nothing for her to worry about. And when, the next day, her other boarders begin to pack, when they nervously make apologies on their way out her front door, she is still calm, although colder now, and a little confused. They must have been told something, and the only clue is what Miss Johnson says, as she hastily pins her hat into place at the front door: 'I know you are different to the rest of them. I'm sorry.'

When two detectives eventually come to 103 Cathedral Street, asking if the collaborationist Herr Schieblich is in the house, she steps back and lets them take him. She has not been sleeping. She has been walking through the days as if she is asleep. She has been having visions, premonitions, strange fancies. They seep into her consciousness, are whispered through the creaks and groans of the house. She does not ask who reported her husband; she already knows. She does not protest—as she would have only a few months before—that he only said the things he said to feel alive and dangerous, the way his music used to make him feel. She steps back and watches them take him. Hadn't she invented these men herself? Hadn't she almost wanted them to come?

JACK

I leave the German woman's house for a small cottage in North Sydney. Here, I have Daisy all to myself. I run circles around her. Get up before her. Get the breakfast things out before the sun comes in through the window. And when I come home, I bring offcuts from the meatworks and cook her chops in extra fat. I don't want her to lift a finger, so she doesn't. She stops going to work. She sleeps in. She is tired all the time.

When I come home from work my hair is hard with blood and my cheeks are sticky with fat. She won't kiss me like that. We go through five boxes of soap that summer, and I have to spend at least an hour after work each day soaking in water so hot it turns my skin red.

The first night Daisy lets me touch her again she says she'll have to be drunk. I take two tin mugs down from their hooks and fill them up to the brim with straight whisky. We sit on the edge of the bed in silence, sipping and wincing at the sharpness of the booze. When she's sipped her way through a quarter of the mug, I put my hand on her knee. She flinches slightly, but leaves it there. I pull the mug away from her mouth, and hold her hands in my own. She's forgotten the feeling of my hands touching hers. The gentle electricity of it.

I stand up to turn out the light.

'No, leave it on,' she says.

I pull her by the ankles so that she falls flat on her back in the bed, her whisky spilling, filling the room with the smell of smoke. We are heady with it.

I draw patterns up and down her inner thigh, coil her pubic hair around my little finger, bring the juices of her cunt up to my nose. God, I've missed this. Her hips carve figure-eights in the mattress as I trace smaller ones with my tongue between her legs. She begins to shudder. I pull my head out from under her skirts. She's unbuttoning her blouse, unhooking her corset. Then—

I stop moving. There, in the centre of her chest, is a pit. I'd never noticed this when we made love before. I touch it. It's cold, and feels as if the walls of the cavity were made of bone. At the bottom of the cavity the skin is blue. The colour moves like a gas flame. I look up at her face. She smiles. Toothless. The way her tongue moves between the ridges of her gums looks like the head of a snake, blindly testing the air for warmth.

'Yeth, thomeome burmp my hearp oup. Burmp i' righ' oup of my chesp.'

She throws her head back and laughs.

Afterwards, I watch her sleep. It's the only time I can look at her without making her flinch. Through the water and the curve of the glass jar beside the bed, her teeth look huge, but also kind of crooked. Each tooth is traced with a fine black line. Her gums are turning black, too. All that sugar and brandy she hides in her tea is rotting her from within.

Even in her sleep she's gripping her jaw, and the skin around her eyes is tight. The scar on her temple is purple, like a mark on a rind of pork, and rises up off her face.

I can keep her with me, run circles around her, but I can never make her love me. When she speaks to me, if she's ever up before I leave for work, she sounds distant, as if her spirit wants to be somewhere she can only ever visit in her sleep.

I've killed her. I really have. I've killed what it was in her that loved me in the first place.

WOMAN NOT YET IDENTIFIED

LANE COVE RIVER, OCTOBER 1917

SYDNEY

Spring in Sydney is a confusion of winter and summer days jarring against each other. It is the beginning of the southerly buster season, with its window-shuddering winds and sudden thunderstorms. The air is hot with pollen from the London plane trees, reddening our eyes and throats; and on the streets horses are more irritable, their drivers quicker to take risks or tell those in motorcars to go to hell.

During the spring of 1917 we were still fuelling the Great War of the northern hemisphere with a steady supply of men, munitions and hand-knitted socks. Meanwhile, another war raged right under our noses. A new American-style card system designed to monitor labour efficiency was introduced by the Department of Tramways and Railways, and the workers at the Eveleigh train yards responded by walking off the job. Over six long weeks, union leaders lost their voices preaching like religious zealots in the Domain on Sundays—'Work slow, show the masters it is we who control them. They will all burn in the end.' The strike spread to the coalfields and the waterfront, until eventually every industry was affected, even those whose workers did not strike. Crates of rubber resin piled up on wharves. No one dared ferry them to Perdriau's upriver in Drummoyne, and the workers there were laid off one by one. 'I'm sorry, lads,' the foreman said. 'There's nothing for you to do.' A man named Harry Crawford returned home to his wife, hat in hand, hoping she'd understand. 'Well,' she might have said, 'that's it. We won't survive like this.'

Only a year before, twelve leaders from an anti-war socialist group, the Industrial Workers of the World, were arrested for treason and two were hanged for 'imagining the death of the King'. In spring 1917, some members were still interred in enemy alien camps without ever having seen a warrant for their arrest.

These were strange times. Strange measures had to be invoked. It was hard to know who was with us or against us, or who 'we' even were in the first place. If we were Irish Catholics, should we have been fighting on the side of an Empire that killed our cousins in Dublin the previous year? If we were workers, should we have been fighting a capitalists war? If we were Australian, should we have been fighting a European diplomats war over Belgium, a country half the size of Tasmania, whose citizens we doubted would ever return the favour? Those of us with sons, fathers and brothers brave enough to risk their lives for the Empire found it hard not to be personally insulted by those speaking out against the men who had signed up. Even if, deep down, we were not absolutely sure why we were fighting, too many people had died for us not to believe in the war.

By the Eight-Hour Day weekend of 1917, everyone knew someone who had been killed in a place few knew how to pronounce, but we were alright really, all things considered. Bodies were being found in our dreams, on the banks of rivers, but we were still attending the picture houses, the rowing regattas, the football. Strange men walked amongst us, but we were still milling on street corners on a Friday night to drink and gossip. Nothing was stopping us from betting a week's wages away at the Spring Derby, or from taking our beloveds out for a picnic, though we might have been quicker to snap if we were ever double-crossed.

EMILY HEWITT

MONDAY, 1 OCTOBER 1917

'Looks like you might never have to go back to work again, Em.'

Emily's mother raised her glass in the direction of the paper mills, where a twist of smoke was winding its way towards the sky.

Emily, her mother and the new girl from the mills were sitting on Emily's verandah enjoying a glass of holiday ale. Emily sat up straight and squinted at the smoke. It was definitely coming from a spot very near the paper mills. She hiccupped and held her fingers to her lips. If the mills really had caught alight, they wouldn't stay mills any longer than you could point and shout, *Look!* The storage sheds were crammed with stacks of odd papers and boxes gone wrong. The vats of woodchips were lined up ready to burn one by one. She thought of the gum trees rubbing themselves against the mills' roof like friendly, combustible cows, then sat back in her chair and poured her guests another round of ale.

As the women watched the smoke their thoughts dawdled towards help. What, should they notify the police? Take wet blankets and buckets full of water over there themselves? If Emily had a telephone, then maybe—but who would they call? Their husbands were lost to the chaos of the Eight-Hour Day parade, no one would be in the mills' office, or at the cornflour mills upriver, and the police were probably at the pub. On public holidays misfortune had to be taken with a shrug of the shoulders, and dealt with when those who could help were getting paid enough to care.

The three women continued to sit, mesmerised by the lilting dance of the smoke rising and falling and kicking out to rise again from a new, surprising angle. It was too late to do anything about it. An enthusiastic picnicker had over-kindled his bonfire, that was all. The women leaned back in their chairs and watched the waterbirds rise from the river, turn black against the sinking sun, and dissolve in a lick of smoke.

'To the Eight-Hour Day!' Emily said, and lifted her glass to a vision she fleetingly had in which she had set fire to the mills herself.

TUESDAY, 2 OCTOBER 1917

When Ernest signed up as apprentice at the Cumberland Paper Board Mills he did not think he'd be spending most of his days running messages between the manager and his wife. But he liked the walk to the manager's house. Crossing the canal, you could get a good look at the cranes moving like slow steel giraffes reaching for their greens, and up alongside the river, if you were lucky, you might get a look at that mad woman who'd been hanging around the place for the last week or so, chasing invisible monsters through the scrub.

But the walk was never as exciting as it was on Tuesday, October the second, when—about four hundred yards from the mill—Ernest saw traces of a fire. From the track, he could hear what sounded like ten thousand frenzied flies; he could see that the whole side of a gum tree was blackened with soot, its leaves shrivelled up or burned right off. He let the scene draw him closer until he found himself standing inside a circle of charred earth.

Once inside the circle, Ernest stopped short. There, at the centre, lay a woman. She was cooked, contorted. She was lying on her back, with her legs slightly drawn up. Her arms were above the chest, as if protecting her heart, and her hands were tightly clenched. Ernest saw that her left hand was nearly broken off at the wrist, it was that severely burned. Her clothes were completely burned off her body, with the exception of the shoes and the bottom of her stockings. He could see her whole body, or what was left of it. He could see where her vagina would have been, and her breasts. Something white was moving in her mouth and between her legs. Maggots. Hundreds of them.

He ran all the way back to the mills. He was flushed in the face, excited. He ran straight to the telephone in the office and when Emily the office girl asked him what was the matter, he laughed. Afterwards, he would be ashamed for laughing—*they'll believe I did it*, he'd think, *and maybe, if enough of them believe it, maybe it means that I did*—but at the time all he could do was laugh as if he had just been kissed.

THE POLICE

WEDNESDAY, 3 OCTOBER 1917

At first the police thought it was accidental. That she had accidentally set herself on fire. Standing on the perimeter of the black circle surrounding the burned body—between a large rock and a fallen tree—all they could see were objects and strange details glinting through the charred remains.

First, they made note of details they could be relatively certain about. They determined the direction of north and estimated that the rock was nine feet high. They paced the distance from the body to the paper mills and wrote in a notepad that the body was found forty yards from the mills.

The closer they looked, the more they could attribute causes to the damaged details that jumped out from the scene. For instance, there was a tall tree. The police could see that the fire had leaped right up to the top branch of that tree, where a single white cockatoo now sat. The fire had reached the rock, but on the right side of the body, the fire only extended six inches. Piecing these details together, they conjectured that the wind would have been coming, say, from the south, following the rise of the land.

Next, they turned their attention to the stiffened female found in the charred circle. Staring at the body, everything they didn't know swam out of the darkness into the foreground, but they stayed calm, professional, and pushed these unknowns back, remembering to pay attention only to what they could see.

The female lay on her back, facing the east. Her charred hands were fixed in the position they'd held at the moment of her death: grasping at the chest. Her right leg was slightly drawn up. All that remained on the body was a pair of stockings and a pair of shoes. Her head was in something resembling a peaceful position, although the forward part of the head—the forehead and the face—were burned beyond recognition.

They found things—incidental details, useless in themselves—and tried to divine a story from them, but couldn't. They found a piece of gabardine under the body. They found a full set of upper teeth, and some loose teeth representing the lower plate. They found a broken quart flagon with the name *Robert* blown into the glass. They found a glass, and an enamel mug. They found the locks and corner-pieces of what appeared to be a carry-all, or small suitcase. They could see where the corners had fallen as it had burned. There was no steel frame, which they thought odd at first, but then they remembered that some of those Japanese cases had cane frames, and there were others with a sort of fibre, with no frame at all. They found locks and a knife. A hat pin. Some hat wires, or remains of a medium-sized hat. They found a kidney-shaped greenstone that appeared to have been a trinket.

But they could not find any trace of kerosene or blood, or any signs of struggle.

The site was ripe for burning. Eleven years later, the mills themselves would burn down, and four years after that the building's remains would be laced with nitrate film, doused with petrol and re-ignited for a major motion picture directed by Frank Hurley. But at the time, if the police were honest with themselves, they really had no idea at all about the fire, let alone whose body was burned in it. That was the trouble. They could not get a start and they could not find out who it was.

THE MASQUERADER

SYDNEY, SUMMER 1917

LYDIA PARNELL

Couples were everywhere at the shops, walking arm in arm, padlocked to each other's elbows. Lydia preferred to shop alone. Too many times had she taken her husband to the shops only to watch him spiral into a pit of despair at the sight of how expensive butter had become or snap at a shopkeeper for asking how he was. 'DO YOU ACTUALLY CARE, OR ARE YOU TRYING TO SELL ME SOMETHING?' he would shout in their blank, professional faces. After a trip to the shops, he would go for long walks and come back wild in the eye, as if he had stalked up to the mountains, killed a shopkeeper with his teeth, and returned when the animal in him had been satiated. Yes, it was better for everyone if she shopped outside Drummoyne, and alone.

Lydia knew that when people were at the shops, they were simply playing the role of people at the shops. They held themselves upright and said, 'Hello, how are you?' or, 'Very well, thank you,' when what they really meant to say was, 'Give me your money,' or, 'Get away from me.' When they reached into their bags and fetched their wallets it was as if they were reaching into their soft bellies to pull out secret body organs they were ashamed of. Lydia preferred what people became at night in her backyard, after a few drinks. Then their raw, bared hearts insulated her against the cold and she became a kind of woman priest, listening to people's moral conundrums.

But when Lydia went to the shops in Rozelle for a change, and saw Harry Crawford in the butcher's laughing with her friend Emma Belbin, without a single wrinkle on his usually worried brow, her world flipped in on itself, like a sock getting turned out of its pair. This man had spent many late nights and early-morning breakfasts pouring the tale of his unloving wife into Lydia's spongy heart. There was a plumber she had gone off with. He had wept. He kept coming back to Drummoyne, to see if she had returned. Lydia had been humbled by the sincerity of his feeling. But seeing Crawford with Emma, content and about to buy chops, Lydia was hit in the chest with the realisation that perhaps the loose ease people arrived at after a few beers was a whole other world invented by, and for, drunks—a realm that felt more authentic when you were sobbing at its depths, but when remembered the next day was as ridiculous and invented as a description of hell.

For Emma Belbin, the summer of 1917 was a summer of beer parties, learning the foxtrot, and momentarily forgetting how bored she was at home. It was a summer that raced forward, but not from underneath her as other summers had—it carried her along, so that she was fully alive and inside every second as it heeled-and-toed into the next. It was the summer she became close with Lydia Parnell's friend Harry Crawford and—energised by loud, loose songs sung around strangers' pianos—managed to charm him out of the funk his wife had left him in.

Harry Crawford had left the area very suddenly that spring, after his wife had left him for a plumber, but he was always over at Lydia's house for breakfast or beers or to see if his wife had shown her face around Drummoyne since their house had been broken up. Emma had got poor old Harry Crawford drunk on more than one occasion (only sometimes by filling his glass when he wasn't looking), and they had often found themselves sitting in the corner of a stranger's kitchen in the early hours of the morning, plumbing their souls for sad stories worth sharing.

Sometimes Emma's husband came to these beer parties, and sometimes he didn't. Emma preferred it when he didn't. He would only stand awkwardly in the corner, holding his beer glass too high up against his chest, looking as if his trousers were constricting his testicles. He would watch her as she talked to Crawford, and worry about how the two of them came across. Then she would have to spend the whole walk home explaining that they were only close friends, that Mr Crawford was still very much in love with his wife, that she, Emma, was nothing more than a shoulder to cry on.

When her husband wasn't there, Emma let her shoulder be a little more available for tears. And when Harry Crawford told her he could not take his wife back, even if she begged him, Emma did notice something flutter up inside her, like a racing pigeon released from its box. But she quickly trapped and smothered it, in case its feathers should fall from her eyes and he should see. No, theirs was not a friendship like that. And besides, there was another woman, a neighbour she shared a wall with in fact, that he mentioned once or twice—only a good friend, he assured her—and Emma tried her best to be happy for him.

They sat in the corner, knees facing in towards each other, a bowl of peanuts balancing between. They nibbled and talked and reached for the nuts without even looking; they were so absorbed by the picture show of each other's lives. They had arrived at a kind of deep, sedimentary truth together, accessible only by the brutally honest conversation of best friends.

She told him how, after six months of marriage, when Mr Belbin was grunting away on top of her, she realised with a shock that the oceans of his eyes were mere puddles, and the caves of his soul that she had thought so mysterious were no deeper than potholes in a poorly maintained road. They were not filled with mystery, but with images of her husband: sitting in an armchair, reading the results of the boxing in the paper, smoking a pipe. *Is this it?* she had thought. *Is this the rest of my life?*

She could say these things to Crawford. She could be crass and horrible and he would understand. His eyes as they listened changed their colour—from hazel, to blue, to grey—as if they were windows into an underwater cave lined with shells.

When she finished speaking, he would tell her about his wife, how much she drank, how he was never good enough for her.

Emma was always slightly disappointed he never went into the same level of detail as she did for him, but she had to remember he was a man. It was a wonder he was talking about his feelings at all.

After their deepest conversations, Emma would need the walk home, to turn over the secret feelings that had been dug out of her guts and decide which she would ignore, and which she would return to later in her daydreams. She would arrive home to find her neighbour watching her through her lace curtains, and her husband asleep in his favourite armchair. She would fold up his newspaper, pick up his dropped pipe from the floor, and try not to catch herself thinking: *What if he fell asleep when his pipe was still lit? Perhaps he would burn to death.*

LYDIA PARNELL

He had seen her, he said when he was barely inside Lydia's front gate. He had seen her. Flush-faced—maybe even a little drunk—outside the Palais de Danse on George Street. She'd had her arm around the shoulders of another man, but when she saw him, she quickly took her arm away, adjusted her hair and walked towards him, swinging her strumpety hips. From five yards away he could smell the gin on her breath. And—as if the sight of her wasn't enough of a shock—she had the hide to ask him for money. Clearly things had not worked out in North Sydney with that plumber of hers and now she was reduced to this: earning her living doing the lame duck or the turkey trot to some honky-tonk band, charming pennies out of men with every flick of the head.

He told her he did not want any conversation with her and she asked him for money and he said he had not any to give her and he jumped on a tram and left her standing there. Of course, the sight of her shrinking into the distance had pained him, especially after the two worried months he'd spent imagining all the things that might have happened to her. But it was not as bad as it could have been, didn't she think?

'Yes,' Lydia said. She supposed so. Though she found it hard to imagine Mrs Crawford doing the lame duck. She found it hard to imagine that gangly woman dancing at all.

Lydia and Crawford stood on the front path, blinking at each other. Now that the mystery of his missing wife was so easily resolved, there was nothing much else to say. Everything seemed less urgent, less real.

Work had been good.

George was good.

Lydia coughed.

He didn't have time to stay long, he said, but he'd just wanted to tell her how overjoyed he was.

Well, overjoyed was the wrong word. How relieved he was.

He laughed like a man at the end of a film. The dark made a circle around his face, and closed in.

LILY NUGENT

Lily had been meaning to contact her nephew for three years, but things had got in the way, and now it was somehow 1920 and he was here of his own volition: a grown man sitting on the edge of her day couch, making it look too small.

Harry held his teacup as if it might crumble to dust at any moment, and spoke softly, careful not to blow it away with his breath. Since 1917, his mother had vanished without a trace; his stepfather had tried to push him off a cliff and bury him alive.

Lily looked at her limp hands resting in her lap. Why had these hands not sought her nephew's address? Written him a letter? Seeing him now—sitting in the seat his mother had once sat in, drinking from a cup she had drunk from—Lily flushed with shame. She had been angry at her sister, not this boy. It was her sister who had always been so impressionable; it was her sister who had stayed with that monster.

'If you will not shake Crawford off, goodbye and good luck,' was what Lily said to her the last time she had visited, in 1917.

Now, three years later, her nephew's face had Annie's refined angles. The poor thing must have been reminded of his mother every time he looked in the mirror. How could it possibly have taken him three years to start searching for her? Never mind, he was here now, and that was what mattered. They must put guilt and blame aside, roll up their sleeves, and take a practical approach.

First, she had to see if he knew about his mother. About the way she was.

'Harry, there's something you need to know,' she said, putting her hands to use by straightening out the kinks in her skirt. 'Something about your mother.'

Harry looked up from his cup.

'Some time in 1917, your mother wrote me a letter saying she had something to tell me. About your stepfather, how he was not . . .'

Oddly enough, the boy nodded. Perhaps he had been in on it after all.

'Do you know?'

'Yep.' He spoke out the side of his mouth the way Crawford had done. The boy had been shaped into a man by that freak of nature. The scenario did her head in. 'That's why I'm here, Aunt Lily. You always knew what to do.'

HARRY BIRKETT

They'd been saying the rains were about to come for days now, but tonight, by the look of the bruised, swollen thunderclouds rolling in from the west, Harry would believe it. He had been standing by the lamppost for an hour now. It had taken him three years to find out where Crawford worked, and even after his flatmate Frank had seen him at Richardson's Hotel it took him a week to pay a visit. Now it was taking him an hour just to cross the street.

Yes, the rains were definitely on their way, but Harry stayed where he was, looked at the sky, looked in the window of the warm pub over the road, and talked himself into moving.

Soon, he told himself. Soon.

The horses trotting down George Street were tetchy in the premature dark. Drivers were cracking their whips more than usual. Or maybe it was Harry who was on edge. Either way, he couldn't stand out here on the street forever. He would wait for that tram to pass. And the next. And then he would cross.

Two trams passed. Then a third. A drop of rain hit the middle of the road and Harry crossed.

The roar inside the pub and the boozy sweat coming off what had to be at least fifty men made Harry calmer.

'Yeah?' one of the bar staff said to Harry.

Harry blinked. 'Sorry?'

Four of them, the bar staff, were staring at him like gargoyles. 'Get you something or what?'

'Johnnie Walker,' Harry said. 'Two.' He didn't really drink the stuff, but tonight would be different.

Over in the corner of the room was a table, recently vacated, and leaning over it a man—short, wiry, forty-five maybe, and still in his jacket despite the humidity. He was collecting glasses, stacking them into a tower nestled into the crook of his elbow. The glasses wavered above his head, first to the right, then to the left, and Harry rushed towards them, but they did not fall.

'Crawford,' Harry said, gripping the glass at the top of the stack. Harry was a lot taller, or Crawford had shrunk. Crawford looked bad, anyway. Like the air had been let out of him.

'You look good, mate,' Harry said. 'You been well?'

Crawford laughed, thank God, and Harry laughed too. He was tall now. He was a man. But he felt as if he was still playing at being a man; as if his bones were two sizes bigger than he was used to.

He lifted the scotches. 'Johnnie Walker. Got one for you, too.'

Crawford eyed the drinks. 'Well, I'm working, so I can't, but thank you.'

'It's alright,' Harry said, placing a hand on the man's shoulder. 'See if you can get a ciggie break? Meet you out the front?'

'Sure,' Crawford said. He laughed again, and shook his head. 'Jesus Christ, Harry, it's been such a long time.'

Outside, the rain was feathering down onto the street. Taking its time, like it had a long time to take.

Crawford lit Harry a cigarette. Lit one for himself, too, and sucked the end of his fag as if it was filling him with life. Glinting on the ring finger of his smoking hand—four-fingered now—was a gold wedding band.

'You got a new missus, Crawford?' Harry asked as casually as he could.

Crawford pulled the hand away, covered the ring up with his thumb, but he was smiling. 'Lizzie,' he said. 'My Lizzie. She's a good egg.'

They both smoked and stared into the rain and were glad their cigarettes gave them something to do with their hands. Harry could see where he had been standing just a few minutes before, on the other side of the street. Now he was standing right inside the moment he had been both yearning for and dreading for three years.

'Hey, Crawford,' Harry said. 'I was wondering if you'd heard anything more about Mum?'

Crawford took a drag of his cigarette, and shut his eyes, as if he was trying his hardest to hold something inside him down.

'I'm sorry for asking,' Harry said. 'I know you took it pretty hard when she left.'

'Nah, it's fine.' Crawford said. But it wasn't. Crawford still had his eyes shut, and he was breathing slow. Even and slow.

Harry didn't ask anything more; he simply stood and smoked, and when Crawford opened his eyes, Harry saw that his face was wet—with rain or tears, he couldn't be sure.

'Why don't you come back tomorrow, Harry, when it isn't so busy? I'd like to talk. I'd like that very much.'

But when Harry came back the next day, Crawford had already quit.

LIZZIE CRAWFORD

For weeks, water poured out of the sky. A bridge near Newcastle had broken under the pressure. Farms out west were sliding clean off the sides of hills, taking roads and train tracks with them. In country towns, umbrellas could not stay up for longer than a minute, and men were left to wade across the wide streets with their coats up over their heads, looking like nervous, waterlogged geese. Although the weather had been bleak in Sydney, it had not been quite so destructive as it was out in the sticks. Here, the rain simply made the trams late, their brakes squeak, and was used as an excuse—by those who sought one—to stay in bed.

On the morning of Monday the fifth of July, however, the deluge above the little house at 47 Durham Street, Stanmore, paused, and a chink of blue was visible through the Crawfords' lace curtains. The sun tugged at Mrs Lizzie Crawford—*Go outdoors! Go outdoors!*—and she felt buoyant, full of life in a way she never had in all her fifty years of living.

Her husband was asleep. The parrots outside the bedroom window were tipsy and shrill with sun, and he slept through their shrieks so peacefully she could not bring herself to do anything other than sit on the bed and watch the miracle of his nose, his mouth, his rising chest breathe.

He was curled on his side, his right, four-fingered hand under his left cheek. They'd been married for eight months now, and Lizzie was still stunned by him and his unearthly effect on her. He'd been a prickly little man when they'd first met at the Coogee Bay Hotel—wounded by a cold-hearted woman who'd left him, a woman she'd never dared ask about. But, like an artichoke, underneath his prickles hid a tender heart and she believed she was the only woman who knew how to find it.

And find it she did. Eight months into her marriage, there it was: a decent, caring, tender heart that flourished in the light of their radiant love.

At her request, he stopped drinking. And when he made love to her, he focused his attentions not on his own pleasure, but on the magical conversion of her body into many unpredictable things. Sometimes it was the city at night seen from above—some streets flickering out, some surging with white light. Sometimes it was as if all her pores were wincing at the taste of sherbet. Sometimes she felt nothing but a spark on the roof of her mouth. Sometimes she wanted to swear loudly and kick, as if she were possessed. But she never told him any of this, because he was so painfully modest. Lovemaking was an otherworldly experience to be had in the dark, under the covers, and never spoken of in the light of day.

Because of this crippling shyness, Lizzie was not sure how to tell her husband that their love had sparked new life in her old but not-yet-withered womb. As she watched him wake, she wondered if she should tell him at all.

She held on to her news as she made him breakfast, as she ironed his shirt. She let the news tickle her on the lips until she leaned in to kiss him goodbye at their front gate and she couldn't hold it back any longer.

'We're having a baby, love. Isn't that wonderful? Did you ever think we would?'

He did not throw his arms around her neck as she hoped he would. Instead, he stiffened. Lizzie stepped back, held his face in her hands so that she might read it. He had a confused look, as if he did not understand how it worked—people growing inside of other people, coming out of them somehow.

'Are you alright?' she asked.

'Yes,' he said, pecking her on the cheek. 'Just late for work.'

He adjusted his hat, then turned and walked to work for the last time in their short married life.

JOSEPHINE DEANGELIS

If there was one thing Josephine DeAngelis knew, it was how to catch a sailor. She didn't know how to hold on to one, but she absolutely knew how to catch one, and that was the first step.

The Returned Sailors and Soldiers Imperial League's events at the Palais de Danse on George Street were always the best bet for catching sailors. But in terms of holding on to them, the problem was either you didn't sleep with them and they lost interest, or you did and then they wouldn't foot the bill when it came time to get rid of what they'd left up inside you.

As she grew older, Josephine became a better judge of who might stay catched once he was caught. She just had to avoid freefalling into a man's eyes within the first five seconds of meeting him. That was always the worst, when you fell in love too hard and too fast. Then there was no getting up off your back until they left.

She'd thought things would be different with Arthur Whitby because he was The One. Josephine could tell. The sound of her name and his together sounded so nice, repeated over and over in her head (Jo-*se-phine* Whit-*by*, Jo-*se-phine* Whit-*by*, Jo-*se-phine* Whit-*by*), and had spiralled her across the floor of the Palais de Danse with the help of a positively electrified band. Those horns. Just, wow. They'd turned her blood into gold glitter the minute their notes hit her ears.

After only a few weeks he moved into the boarding house she was staying in, but now he was prone to going out and staying out all night. She wasn't about to sit around worrying about his hand cupping some other girl's breasts. No, she was going to go out and get her own kicks. So here she was, back at the Palais de Danse, and a man with four stripes on his lapels was asking her to dance. Arthur was only a seaman, just a boy it seemed to her now that a real captain was slipping his arm around her waist.

She hadn't even needed a pick-me-up before hitting the floor. He was a captain in the Royal Australian Navy, that was pick-me-up enough. After three songs Josephine and the captain spun to the side of the hall, panting. He was a little soft around the middle. About twenty years older than Arthur, too. Probably more experienced, though, when it came time for the uptown shopping of a kiss to lead to the downtown business of fingers in the knickers.

'Do you know my father?' she shouted to him over the drum solo. 'What?' he shouted back, cupping his ear so he could hear her. 'He's a famous sea captain,' she said, 'Captain Martello.' The captain threw back a drink. 'No, I don't know the tarantella, sorry, love,' he said, and spun her back out onto the floor again, with Josephine thinking, *Love, love, oh my God, he called me love.*

Josephine's steps became longer and looser as the night spiralled on, but if she ever lost the rhythm of the band, she simply closed her eyes and let the music play her from the inside, as if her skeleton and all her internal organs were an instrument only the horn section knew how to play. And Arthur, of course. He knew how to play her exceptionally well, but then perhaps that was the problem, perhaps she had become boring and predictable and far too easy for his lithe hands.

The captain led and she followed without one misstep, and it felt as if the whole world was watching, as if all the women in the room were whispering jealously behind their hands, because she had undoubtedly done it. She had nabbed the most important-looking navy man in the place, and he was going to take her out for ice-cream afterwards.

But once the dancing had finished it was too cold for ice-cream. It was bitter, in fact, and George Street had turned into a river of mud, so Josephine thought, *Why not, just this once* (though it had happened before with other, less important men) *let him escort me home in a cab, and walk me up to my front door?* Arthur would probably still be out anyway, and even if he wasn't, maybe it would do him some good to see how fired up Josephine could make another, more important man than him. So, with a wave of her hand, Josephine hailed a hansom cab for the two of them.

By the time they'd reached her door his kisses had proved more delicious than she'd first thought. His hands inside the placket of her skirt gave her the feeling of stepping into a hot bath after a long day at the factory and every part of her let go, saying, *Yes, more of that, oh please more of that.*

She tried to be quiet with the front door of the boarding house, but it was hard getting the key in the lock when all the cells of her body were still doing the foxtrot, and the captain was kissing her right up the back of her neck.

'Josephine!' rasped a woman on the other side of the door, when she had finally thumped it open. It was the landlady, her hair in a mussed-up plait for sleeping. Josephine kicked the captain backwards out of the door and straightened up, but the woman did not give two hoots about the drunk old man who was feeling up her tenant. There were more pressing issues at hand.

'A detective was here again, Josephine. He wants to talk to you about your mother. Urgently.'

Josephine's blood lost all traces of glitter and booze. She ripped the captain's hand off the back of her skirt. 'I'm sorry, darling, but I need you to help me.' She could see in his eyes the flash of fear she'd so often seen in Arthur's when she asked him for a favour. This time, though, she was asking a captain, a man used to responsibility, so she did not feel so terrible asking him for it.

'I need you to help me move,' she said. 'Tonight.'

Standing to attention in front of the camp hospital in dungarees that have never been washed, with no undergarments on, and a rash on his left testicle he desperately wants to scratch, Herr Schieblich is about to burst. He can sleep on a mattress thrown over some rough-hewn logs he had to fell himself; he can sleep in a room with fifty other snoring Germans, Austrians, and Australians of socialist persuasion; he is prepared to share one lantern between ten men, and defecate in a group latrine with no partitions separating him from a man with diarrhoea. He has already planned to forget how Otto, whom he first met on the ship to Australia, died within his first twenty-four hours in Liverpool Internment Camp after being shot in the knee by one of the guards for no apparent reason. But the Great War is over. The Great War has been over for almost two years now and he is still locked up in Liverpool. He cannot stand not knowing when he can return to his wife. He cannot even write her a candid letter. He is only allowed to send two letters a week—each no longer than one hundred and fifty words in length—which will be opened, read and guffawed at by the guards. He is only allowed to see his wife in person once every two weeks between the hours of two and four on Sunday, and even then the guard present steers the conversation away from his concerns like a cautious cab driver steering a horse around a turd. And how Henrietta must miss the strength of his opinion! He saw how timid she could be as she stepped out into the streets of Woolloomooloo to take the boarders' whites to the laundry. Each day she stood in the doorway, looked up the street and back, and sometimes would not step out onto the footpath for three whole minutes. She moved so slowly through their house, it was as if they lived six leagues under the sea—but instead of water, the sea was made out of all the possible decisions Henrietta could make, floating around her, tangling in her hair and making the cotton of her skirts cling to her legs. At the end of the day, Herr Schieblich would sit next to her in front of the fuel stove as her slow hand passed a needle and thread through their residents' frayed clothes. Frau Schieblich would sew, look up, think, and sew, while Herr Schieblich read between the lines of a collection of papers, tied the loose ends of his deduced facts together and wove them into a flawless verisimilitude of the current state of the world. Or he would practise his violin, stop, turn to her and share his latest theory, before digging the bow back into a stormy Beethoven sonata. He kept talking, even when he knew that the connections he made between the ideas he shared were tenuously held together. But what Henrietta didn't know was that his assurance in his knowledge of the world was a perform-ance he put on to give her strength. He should have known that it was not wise to act too certain about sensitive political topics when their boarding house was full of spies. He should never have got drunk with Jack that night, especially not to the point where he felt loose enough to say Germany was in every respect at least equal, if not superior to, England. Or that in spite of the German strength and power, we bowed our head for twenty-five years before England, and kept quiet when Russia and England divided up Persia and the whole north coast of Africa. Or that Egypt and Morocco had been divided up between England and France, with a little strip for Italy, while all we got, as compensation, was a slight enlargement of Cameroon. And he most definitely should not have said, after the sixth or seventh scotch, that a second war would follow because if anything could breed revenge, it was this.

Now the phrase haunts him.

When the guard takes and drinks the pint of black-market Kölsch beer that Henrietta had brought to the camp from Woolloomooloo, when Henrietta turns away at the sight of the guard drinking what cost her a week's worth of groceries, as if blaming herself for making the wrong set of decisions that day, Herr Schieblich thinks: if anything could breed revenge, it is this.

But now the guard is busy skolling the beer, and his wife is whispering to him—'Eduard, Jack Crawford has been arrested, and I have been asked to appear in court.'

Herr Schieblich sighs. Perhaps that is revenge enough, for now.

JANE WIGG

Mrs Wigg of 7 The Avenue, Drummoyne, opened the door to the crown of a rakishly angled fedora and a slate-blue, broad-shouldered suit, and thought, *Oh, hello! Won't this make an interesting story for the Eisteddfod committee meeting this evening?* The hat tilted back to reveal the serious face of a man who required serious information—this was no ordinary door-to-door salesman.

'Good afternoon,' the man said, taking off his hat. 'My name is Detective Watkins. Might you be a Mrs Jane Wigg?'

A chill crept over her skin then, from the base of her neck—a chill born of genuine concern. What on earth did one offer a detective for afternoon tea? Poundcake? Honey jumbles?

'I'm sorry,' Detective Watkins said, squatting slightly to lift up her troubled gaze with his own. 'I haven't caught you at a bad time, have I?'

'Oh no!' She stepped backwards into the house. 'Please! Come in.' At the moment of retreat it came to her: a selection of fish-paste sandwiches, teacake and arrowroot biscuits would be the wisest selection for a detective—not too showy, nutritionally comprehensive.

'Please make yourself comfortable in our parlour,' she announced, indicating the kitchen.

After placing the afternoon tea in front of the detective, she turned the plate around as brazenly as one might spin a roulette wheel, so that the teacake (her signature cake) was facing him. Mrs Wigg perched on the edge of her chair, with her knees twisted away from the detective as she had been taught, and asked delicately, 'Detective, how may I help you?' (*Ten points!* cheered the Eisteddfod committee. *What a talented hostess!*)

The detective pulled up his trousers at the knees, leaned forward, and selected a fish-paste sandwich. He chewed quickly at first, then paused as if his tongue had discovered something illegal hidden between the slices of bread. A tooth? Or a limb? He swallowed hard.

'Is it stale, Detective?'

'No! Fish paste!' He coughed, and tried to smile. 'I thought it was chocolate butter, silly me.'

Mrs Wigg was horrified. Fish paste! What was she thinking! 'I'm sorry, Detective, it must have been quite the shock.' At that moment she felt for him the way she had felt backstage after last year's Eisteddfod, seeing the minstrel performers wipe the

PIP SMITH

black off their skin—how inferior their talent for singing suddenly seemed.

Detective Watkins placed the rest of the sandwich on the coffee table for them both to keep an eye on in case it leaped off its plate and swam around the room.

'Mrs Wigg, I am here to talk to you about the man-woman.'

Mrs Wigg laughed. 'Pardon, the what?'

'The man-woman. Have you not heard of her? She is in all the papers.'

'Oh,' she said. So he *was* a salesman. What a foolish woman she had been, to endow his slate-blue suit with such inflated import-ance. 'You are a gentleman from the circus, aren't you, come to sell me a ticket?'

'No, Mrs Wigg, I promise you I am a detective of the police.'

Mrs Wigg did not want to hear it. She had already been shamed by her husband after purchasing radium pills and blood tonic from a man who looked the spitting image of a doctor. Her work on the Eisteddfod committee was making her believe in first impressions, talent, magic tricks. It was exciting to believe in these things. To live a cynical life was to live like Mr Wigg, always grumbling sensible facts at a newspaper effervescent with sensation. But she was not going to be played for a fool so easily by this charlatan detective. The detective was reaching into his pocket, no doubt taking out a ticket book for a quack travelling freak show of trickery and fat women with beards. She stood up, ready to send him on his way, when he pulled from his pocket not a ticket book, but a police badge. It was police-grey—the colour of gaol terms and bullets. Too dull to be a prop, too ordinary. Mrs Wigg sat back down.

'Do you remember Mr Crawford, your neighbour at number five?' the Detective asked her.

'Yes, of course.'

'And did you notice anything odd about him, Mrs Wigg?'

Mrs Wigg wanted to answer yes, so that she would not seem unobservant. 'Yes, I suppose so.'

'What did you notice?'

'Well,' she said slowly, 'his wife seemed tall, so I suppose that would mean he was short.'

'Right,' Detective Watkins said, shaking the cuff of his sleeve back from his wrist in preparation to write. 'What else?'

'Ah . . .'

'Did you overhear anything at all?'

'Overhear anything?'

'Yes—any rows, or anything like that?'

'I heard a few groans coming from the house in the night.'

'Yes?'

'And once I heard a little scream, and then a door slam.'

'But did you notice anything in particular about Mr Crawford?'

'About his . . . ?' She leaned forward, hoping he would finish her question so that she might better know how to answer it, but the detective was not playing. He sat back in his chair.

'This is not a school exam, Mrs Wigg. It's alright to admit you noticed nothing at all.' He spoke in the same weary tone of her high school maths teacher when he insisted that a hypotenuse was not, as Jane then believed, an African animal that lived in a swamp.

Yes, now that she put her mind to it, she could remember the rumours that circulated in 1917, about Mrs Crawford going about with other men. About her penchant for plumbers. She remembered the last time she saw Mrs Crawford, too. She was carrying nothing but a small suitcase, and walking arm in arm with Mr Crawford in the direction of the tram. Funny behaviour for a woman planning to run away with a tradesman, now that she thought about it.

'Can you describe the suitcase for me, Mrs Wigg?'

'Well, it was a small square case.'

'Did it look oriental at all?'

'No.'

'No?'

'Perhaps a little.'

'Almost Japanese?'

'Yes, perhaps it was a little bit Japanese.'

'Thank you, Mrs Wigg.' And the detective wrote down some more notes.

As the detective walked towards the door, she felt relaxed enough to ask him, 'Detective, what does this have to do with the man-woman?'

'You do know that Mr Crawford is not Mr Crawford at all, don't you, Mrs Wigg?' the detective asked.

'Oh?'

'Mr Crawford is an Italian woman called Eugenia Falleni.'

'What?'

'Are you seriously telling me you never suspected?'

'My Lord,' Mrs Wigg said, and leaned very quickly against the wall. For a full nine months she had lived next door to a pair of sapphists and hadn't even known. Mrs Wigg remembered the groaning house, and the little scream, and flushed. Now that she thought about it, Mr Crawford never wore a five o'clock shadow at five o'clock, nor any other time either. And he walked as if he had something to prove. And he had a funny swing to his arm, like he was a child playing the role of a sailor in a play. *My God*, she thought, *am I so easily fooled?*

Yes, my girl. Yes, you are.

NINA, THE WRONG DAUGHTER

SYDNEY, 1898–1917

GRANNY DEANGELIS

It was late in the night when the girl came to Granny's door. It was a cold night—there was a wind whipping right off the bay. She was standing on the front steps in a big coat, and her belly was out here like *this*, like she had swallowed the moon. The girl was pregnant and the baby had hands and hair and fingernails already. She had been pregnant for seven months and Granny thought to herself: *No, this is not the daughter I was promised.*

Granny knew the girl's mother back in Wellington. Isola had sent the girl here because the Lord did not give Granny any children. He gave Isola so many, but he did not give Granny even one. The girl, Nina, she was five daughters for the price of one. She was too much daughter for Isola and so she sent her to Sydney to help out in the DeAngelis's laundry.

Granny foolishly thought, *How kind of Isola, giving away her oldest girl like this.* But when Nina turned up, pregnant and with short hair, short as a boy's, she saw that she was not her girl either. She would never be anyone's girl.

'Mrs DeAngelis?' she said. 'Is that you?'

'Yes, dear,' Granny said, but Nina did not come inside, she only stood there and burst into tears. She had saved up every tear from her life for this night, it seemed like to Granny, and now they were fighting each other, trying to come out first.

'I have to get rid of the baby,' Nina said through her tears. 'I cannot look after a baby.'

Granny folded the girl up into a blanket and when she did she could feel the baby move. *This is the daughter God promised me*, Granny thought. *She is still growing hair and eyelashes and toenails. She is the girl inside the girl.*

Sitting by the stove, sipping coffee, Nina did not say anything for some time. She only sat on the stool, with the blanket wrapped around her, and stared at the glass of the window. Her eyes did not look out the window; it was like they were two birds thumping against the glass.

'Who is the father?' Granny asked. 'Maybe he can help pay?'

The girl sipped the coffee and looked at Granny, but did not say anything. Granny thought: *She must be heartbroken, with him so far away.*

PIP SMITH

When the coffee was all gone and the stove was out, Granny took the girl to her bed. She told Mr DeAngelis, 'Get up, you're sleeping on the floor,' and he said, 'What? Sleep on the what? In my own house?' And Granny said, 'You have not paid a penny for any of this, it is my house and if I say the girl is sleeping in the bed she is sleeping in the bed.' So Mr DeAngelis went and slept on the floor like a dog.

Nina barely even touched the bed before she fell asleep; she must have walked such a long way to bring Granny her new daughter.

When the girl and the baby were all tucked in, Granny took her coat and clothes to the laundry and looked in the pockets for the money Isola had promised her, but there was nothing there.

Even though Granny gave Nina her own bed, Nina was up every night having hot baths and doing handstands against the wall, and one night Granny found her vomiting into the chamber pot after drinking half a bottle of whisky, but she put up with it because she knew her daughter was coming in the end. She had held fast for so long, there was nothing Nina could do to shake her out now.

Another night Granny found her with her head bent down between her legs. She had a knitting needle bent into a hook, and she was using it to poke up inside herself.

'Stop!' Granny shouted at her. 'Do not hurt my baby!'

Granny took the knitting needle away from her. There was no blood, but even so she crossed herself, crossed the baby in Nina's stomach, and left Nina for Our Lady to judge.

'Just send me to the home!' Nina said. 'I can't keep the child and neither can you!'

Mr DeAngelis stood behind Granny in the hall and shouted along with the girl, 'I don't want another mouth to feed!'

'What are you talking about?' Granny said to him. 'It's my laundry, I run the business—what do you do but scratch your scrotum and spit into the cabbages?'

'I don't want another man's baby here!' he said. 'Send the girl to St Margaret's!' But Granny did no such thing. She knew what would happen. Those frigid women, they'd take the baby and sell her to make money.

When the baby was born it was a beautiful night. The full moon popped out from behind a cloud just as the baby came screaming out of the girl. There was no wind. The whole night was holding its breath at the sight of the most beautiful of babies being born.

'A girl!' Granny said to the midwife. 'She will be called Maria, after Our Lady.'

'No,' Nina said. 'She needs an Australian name.'

'Maria can be an Australian name.'

'No,' Nina said. 'Call her Josephine.'

She was red in the face and tired, so Granny let her name the baby. She gave her that.

When the midwife handed over the baby, Nina turned her head and looked away. She was crying and didn't want the baby to see. Her breasts were weeping, too. They were weeping milk at the sound of the baby's voice. Nina pressed them down with her hands to make them stop, but they would not.

'You have to feed her,' Granny said. 'She will not stop crying until she is fed.'

Nina took the baby to her chest, and the baby was so thirsty, she drank her dry. Nina's breasts were not weeping anymore, but she was still crying, because there, in her arms, was her baby, and she couldn't do anything about it now.

All the next day Nina lay in bed, as grey as the sheets. She said she wanted to die, but Granny did not let her die, because she needed to feed the baby milk until Granny could feed the baby porridge herself.

The baby cried every time the girl did not touch it, which was all the time, so the baby was crying all the time. It sent Mr DeAngelis crazy.

'I have to sleep on the floor of my own house and listen to another man's baby cry?' he said. 'Get rid of the baby or I will leave you and go back to Italy!'

Granny looked at his fat belly, his lazy hands too stiff to work, his penis which could not make babies. She looked at his forehead, all wrinkles from frowning at the things he did not understand, and she looked at the baby: small and pink as a piglet, wailing so loud it was almost an aria, and she said, 'Certamente, Mr DeAngelis, see you in Italy,' knowing she would not.

Mr DeAngelis looked at her like a fish that had been hooked through the throat; he did not believe that his threat would work, and then it had.

Even with him banished from the bedroom, the baby kept crying through the night, and kept crying when the dogs started howling and the roosters started crowing and lights came on in neighbours' houses. During the day, the whole of Pelham Street walked about as if they were asleep, and at night, they would stay up and fight.

One night, the baby stopped crying very suddenly. Granny could see that Nina was not in her bed. She thought: *Ah, maybe now she has finally gone to her baby.* Granny saw Nina leaning over the crib. *Maybe she is about to pick the baby up,* Granny thought. But no, she was not moving. Her arms were strong, her elbows locked. She was holding a pillow down on the child.

'What are you doing?' Granny beat the girl's arms but she did not stop. Granny pinched her, pushed her. Nina was strong, but she stopped when Granny yanked back her hair. Nina stepped back and shook her head at herself. She was crying again, but the baby was crying louder than she ever had before. Granny picked the baby up and sang along with the dogs and the roosters and the screaming neighbours until the sun came up.

When Granny woke, she was sitting on the stool next to the stove with the blanket wrapped around her. The baby was in her arms and Nina was gone. She had taken everything she'd brought into the house. Everything, except Eenie.

JOSEPHINE DEANGELIS

Helping Granny in the laundry was as exciting (and ultimately disappointing) as a smoke and mirrors show at a carnival. Ghosts flickered in the shadows the steam cast against the walls, and sometimes those ghosts would become the spectacular figure of a man standing between fluttering sheets and drums of boiling chemicals—one of his hands resting on the handle of a sheathed sword, the brass buttons on his captain's jacket glinting as danger-ously as stolen doubloons.

Every time the man appeared, Eenie was sure it was her sea-captain father come to take her with him on his next voyage across the Pacific.

'Come on, Eenie,' the man would say. 'Come and help me deliver the laundry for Granny.'

Eenie would stare at the figure, wishing from the bottom of her toes that it was him this time, that they were going to deliver laundry to an exotic island in the middle of the sea, but when she stepped towards him he would turn into Nina, in trousers again, his hand on his sheathed sword nothing more than Nina's hand holding the end of a wooden pole used to poke boiling rags.

Even though the laundry cart was not a barque and Nina was not a famous sea captain, Eenie helped her mother deliver crisp piles of sheets and shirts to the houses all around Double Bay. If they rode through Queen's Cross, Nina would ignore the hoots and hollers of sailors unused to cart-driving, trouser-wearing women, and Eenie would eye each one of them, wondering if that man was a captain, or that man, or that. She would tug on Nina's sleeve and ask, 'Is that him?' And Nina would act as if she was only capable of fixing her eyes on the road ahead.

As suddenly as Nina could appear before Eenie's eyes, Nina could vanish, too, and be gone for months. Then Eenie would sit in the laundry shop window and watch the rabbit-oh skin his rabbits in the street, and the bloody rabbits twitch even in death. She watched for Nina, who came back sometimes to fight with Granny and try to take her away. She watched for the fruit-and-vegetable man, played by one of four different Chinamen whose name was always John. But she watched, mainly, for her father, who never came.

*

When Josephine turned twelve she left school to work in Granny's laundry full time. A gloominess seeped into the space her father should have filled. It seeped stealthily, under the cracks of doors at midnight. It pooled in the hollows under Josephine's eyes and weighed them down; it stuck to her thoughts and made them drag. Josephine thought the darkness might not stick if she kept moving, and so she spent her nights walking through the streets of Double Bay towards the Cross. She walked dangerously close to gaudy, feathered girls and men in high-heeled boots, but they let her pass silently. She wanted to be frightened so that she could leap out of her skin and feel lighter for a moment, but no one mugged her. No one even snarled.

She tried the walk on other nights, wearing Granny's lipstick, Granny's rouge. She piled her hair up on top of her head and practised sauntering. She burned messages into the hearts of the men she passed with her eyes. *Look at me*, her messages said. *I exist. I exist.*

After a few years of practice, Josephine's message finally landed in the heart of a waiter at Woodward's Oyster Saloon on King Street. Her message released itself as stealthily as a gas, so that all he could pay attention to was the miracle of Josephine's existence fogging up his field of vision.

She sat on a stool at the oyster bar, swivelling from left to right, left to right, holding his gaze fixed. He was tall, dark and handsome, just like the men she read about in books. Except he was very dark. Italian maybe. He would whisk her off to Livorno in an old fishing boat he made himself. He would place fresh mullets at her feet as an offering to her beauty. But before all this, he slipped her a glass of lemonade with complimentary bubbles.

'Can't let a beautiful girl like you go thirsty,' he said with a wink.

Like fleas, the bubbles leaped from her drink and into her skin and tickled the roots of her hair.

She covered her mouth and giggled to mask a little burp. 'No,' she said, and swivelled to face him front on. 'No, you shouldn't. The only problem is, I'm thirsty for something stiffer.'

Driving straight into the full-bodied attention of an unknown man without the brakes on gave her a thrill she did not think she'd be able to live without now she'd had a taste.

'How old are you?' he asked.

'Twenty-one,' she said, and outlined her lips with her straw in case he'd missed how full they were. What did it matter if she was seven years shy of twenty-one? She felt twenty-one. And so many twenty-one-year-old girls sat at home doing needlework, wasting the freedoms their age gave them. He looked as if he didn't care to know her real age anyway, in case it stood in the way.

'You got a feller?' he asked.

'Only you,' she said, and he clutched his heart and dropped his head as if he had been shot straight through.

'Coroneo!' his manager called to him from the back of the room. 'Are them tables going to clear themselves, you slack Greek, or what?'

So he was a Greek. That was very almost Italian. Josephine imagined the white house they would have on a hill rising out of a turquoise sea writhing with octopuses. He would come home in a toga, tasting of salt. She would turn olives into oil with her own hands. The ways of their ancestors would come back.

'I knock off at ten,' he said. 'Meet me out the back. I'll take you somewhere real nice.'

By eleven o'clock she was two drinks in and as syrupy as toffee on the hob. Jack Coroneo could have poured her into any shape he liked and she would have stayed and let him lick her all over, starting at the toes. He took her by the waist after the third drink and walked her through the streets, stopping to kiss at every intersection.

After they had walked for what felt like hours he smuggled her up the back steps of his parents' house, so that his mother would not wake. 'Shhh,' he said. 'We'll have to be quiet.'

It hurt, what he did to her down there under the sheets, but in a way that reminded her she was alive. All the same, she had heard stories of girls having to go away to the country after they'd let men keep their penises inside them for too long. She didn't ever want to go to the country, it sounded like the most boring place in the world.

'You can't stay in there,' she whispered, trying not to sound too frigid.

'It'll hurt me,' he said, not letting her pull away. 'If you make me this excited and don't let me get off it'll turn my balls purple and then they'll fall off.'

He was so frightened of losing his balls, he was beginning to shake. She did not want to make his balls turn purple because then he might not like her and above everything else that was the most important thing—that he should like her, that he should think she was maybe even worth loving. She moved a little, so that she could look him in the eye.

'Oh! Oh, Josephine!' he said, shaking more violently. The way he said her name, she didn't care anymore about his seed or going to the country. The way he said her name he may as well have said, *Let's go to the country together, you and me.*

The jolting of his body subsided until he was so still she thought for a moment she had killed him.

'Jack! Jack!' She shook him by the shoulders. 'Jack, I'm sorry! You don't have to come to the country!'

'What? Who's going to the country?'

'Oh, nothing. I thought you—nothing.'

He sat up and she leaned in for a kiss but he was reaching for an old singlet to wipe her blood off his penis. 'Can you be careful not to let the screen door bang when you leave?'

He pulled her hat from under his back where it had been crushed by the weight of them and threw it to her.

'Yes,' she said, still hopeful, always hopeful, and stinging a little between the legs.

The next time they met out the back of the oyster saloon. He loved her quickly, bent over the staff dunny. This time, he did not ask her to leave. After they dressed he placed his hand on the small of her back. Her nerves burned there, in the shape of his hand.

What followed was a week of saying, 'Alright, why not?' Not *yes*—a word of conviction—but *alright*, a gusty word that lifted her off her feet and carried her to places she had no real intention of visiting. The middle of Rushcutters Bay Park in the rain on Wednesday evening, for instance, or standing naked in the wash-room of his friend's boarding house on Friday, watching him wash his penis in the low sink, saying, 'It's probably too soon for this.'

When Josephine saw Granny's grey face, it seemed to her that the week had run out ahead like a wave and was now drawing itself up to crash over her head from above.

'Where have you been going at night?' Granny said in a frail voice. 'You are too much. You are just like your mother.' Granny coughed. Granny rubbed her swollen knees and groaned. She looked at Josephine as a stranger might.

I'm still here, Josephine wanted to say, *I'm still Eenie,* but it was too late to undo what she had done, and the shame of it only kept her out longer—made her drink four drinks, instead of three.

No one came to the house when Granny died, not even Jack Coroneo. There had been no notice in the paper, so no one had known to come. Customers rapped on the door, frustrated their laundry had not been delivered, but when they saw Josephine pregnant, in mourning, and wearing far too much make-up for a girl her age, they pressed their hands into their chests, muttered condolences, and quietly took their business elsewhere.

Josephine hung on. This was her house now, her cave. She was a mama bear going into hibernation, and if anyone tried to take her away, she would be fierce, too, just like a mama bear. She collected pretty things from the pockets of coats that had never been picked up from the laundry, and made a nest out of them. A silk scarf, a bright brooch made out of real diamonds, a playbill from a show. She was sick some mornings, but she hoped that meant she'd be thinner once the baby was out. They could live like this, together. She and the baby protected from the rest of the world.

And maybe a man would see her from across the street. Maybe he would be touched by her fierce instincts. Maybe he would save them from the withering gaze of neighbours. The daydream was a light, flickering at the mouth of her cave. It threw its shadows large against the shutters at night until it was hard to tell the difference between what could only be a dream, and what could ever possibly be real.

The first thing Nina asked Marcelina was could she write a letter.

It was 1910 maybe, and it was rare to meet new Italians in those days, seeing as the country wasn't letting any more in. They had been coming for years to the goldfields, and then suddenly: no. You have too many babies, you use too much garlic in your cooking—but that is another story, not for here.

Marcelina met Nina at the Italian laundry in Double Bay. Nina would come and go from that place: come to take her daughter away from the woman who brought her up, and when the woman chased Nina out the door with an open bottle of bleach she would go—no one knew where, but she would put on a man's clothes and go away for months. It was strange the way Nina went about in trousers, but she could do a man's work and got paid more for it, too, so what did it matter if she was a woman underneath her clothes? Marcelina couldn't think of any good reason.

Marcelina did write a letter for Nina, and after that Nina was a frequent visitor to her house. The two women would talk in Italian well into the night. Marcelina talked of the country and the family she left behind. They would re-create Italy right there on Cathedral Street, and it got so they could almost smell the place. Even though Nina had left Livorno when she was two, after Marcelina started on about the holiday villas studded into the mountainside, and the wine merchants brawling in the streets, and the fishermen always coming back with more fish than they could sell, Nina would get wet in the eyes. She remembered the place well, even if it was only Marcelina's memory dropped into her head.

Nina spoke of Wellington. Her Nonno and his horses, her Nonna always telling stories, pretty Ida, Emily and Rosie always wanting to be saints, and little spoiled William. They'd had their fights as all families did, but the life she was living here could not last. She had to run from job to job in case anyone caught her out for the man's pay she was getting. She was sick of looking over her shoulder every second. She was worn out. Maybe her family were right, Nina said, maybe she should have married a rich man when she had the chance, and put on a smile to show everyone she could take it. Her mother had sent her here to help Mrs DeAngelis, but now that Mrs DeAngelis had stolen her daughter she wanted to go back and start again.

'Will you write another letter for me?' she would say when she got like that, and Marcelina would smile and hope another memory would carry them away, but then Nina would say *'Per favore?'* and Marcelina would have no choice.

She began to dread writing Nina's letters, because they were always the same. *I want to come home*, her letters would say. *Per favore fatemi tornare a casa.* They had tried writing this to her sisters, her brothers, her Mamma, her Papà, her Nonna and Nonno Buti, and none of them ever wrote back. Anyone would have thought New Zealand had drowned itself under the ocean.

Nina must have started feeling as though Marcelina's house was a deep, dark well with no echo. You could shout all sorts of things into it, and no one would shout back.

Late one night, after they had talked their way to the bottom of a bottle of wine, Marcelina could see that Nina was on the verge of asking her to write another letter. 'You know what I think?' Marcelina said, before Nina could say another word. 'I think you need to take a lover.'

Soon after Granny's death, Josephine was shaken awake by a man she did not at first recognise. He smelled familiar—of salt, horses and sweat. It was dark, but she could just make out a blue work shirt with the sleeves rolled up and the cabbage-tree hat of a bum. He was opening and closing her drawers, throwing her clothes into a bag.

'Who are you supposed to be now?' Josephine asked.

'Your father,' Nina replied.

'What's become of Nina?'

'She's dead. Consumption.'

'Alright. So where are we going?'

'Balmain,' she said. 'A lolly shop in Balmain.'

'What, *now*? Can't we go in the morning?'

'No.' Nina pointed at her belly. 'Who did that to you?'

'No one,' Josephine said.

'Alright, Virgin Mary, who's going to pay for it?'

Josephine said nothing. And then, to make sure Nina said nothing else: 'I'm going to keep it.'

They rode in silence, through streets piled high on either side with boxes and bits of wood nailed together in a semblance of houses. They passed a pregnant cat lying on its back in the gutter, panting.

'So who is she?' Josephine asked Nina.

She was silent for a moment. She whipped the horse. 'A Mrs Birkett. She has a bit of money.'

'And does she know?'

'No.'

Josephine rolled her eyes. 'You know she'll find you out one of these days.'

'Oh, I'll watch it. I'd rather do away with myself than let the police find out anything about me.'

After midnight they arrived on a doorstep somewhere. A crisp voice called through the door, 'Who on earth is *that*?'

Josephine was looked up and down by a woman, pinched in the face and alarmed, like a crow that had just found a vulture in its nest. The woman lingered over the bulge beneath Josephine's dress.

'This is my daughter,' Nina said. The woman could not take her eyes away from the bulge. 'Can you let us in now, Daisy? We've been driving for almost an hour.'

Daisy smiled, though only her mouth moved. Her eyes were lead doors, sealed shut.

'Excuse us, dear,' Daisy said to Josephine, 'while I have a word with your father.' Daisy folded Nina into the house by the shoulders, careful not to open the door too wide in case Josephine made a dash inside and gave birth in the middle of the floor. The door closed in Josephine's face with a thud and she was left to lean against the nearest streetlamp and listen to Nina get torn into strips.

'Why didn't you tell me she'd been knocked up?' the woman was saying. 'Why didn't you *tell* me? I can't understand it.' As the woman got louder, her pitch rose. A glass canister smashed to the floor.

'Calm down,' she heard Nina say.

'Send her to St Margaret's!'

'I can't do that, Daisy—have you ever seen that place?'

And so the argument went on. Josephine listened, shifting her weight from foot to foot to give her back a break. It was surely one o'clock by now, or maybe two. She turned her attention to the street and the wind whipping the dust up into miniature tornados. An old woman passed, clutching a wicker suitcase. Even in the dim streetlight, Josephine could see that the woman's once-yellow skirt and blouse were filthy. She had a grand kind of hat on, though, with a big feather struck through the band. It flopped up and down as she lugged her suitcase up the hill, muffling and releasing the sounds of her mutters as it rose and fell. The woman was in her own world, but even so she saw Josephine's belly and gave Josephine a look of pity. How pathetic, to be pitied by a lunatic. Josephine turned her head away. *Come on*, she willed Nina. *Come on, let me in.*

The door opened a crack and Nina squeezed out. She had a gentle spattering of sweat across the brow. It had been a long and arduous fight.

'You can stay tonight,' she said, 'but we have to get you gone before she wakes up.'

Josephine pushed herself away from the streetlamp. 'Great, thanks.' Some man Nina was, she couldn't even keep that scrawny bitch in line.

'What can you expect, being up the duff?'

How quickly you have forgotten, Josephine thought, but she was too tired to fight. Nina picked up her bag and helped her up the steps into the shop.

Traces of the fight were scattered across the floor. Shards of boiled lollies and glass snatched at what moonlight made it through the windows. Josephine resolved to wake up and be dressed with all her things packed before that horrible witch cracked opened the slits of her eyes. Anywhere would be better than here. Even St Margaret's.

*

Josephine woke to the sight of two white shirts drifting from the sky towards the street. Upstairs, the banshee was holding Nina's things to ransom.

'Who *are* you?' she shrieked. 'Tell me!'

A pair of trousers drifted past the window. 'And who is that little madam's mother?'

Silence.

'Tell me!'

There was the sound of Nina's feet descending the stairs three at a time. She rushed outside to catch the rest of her clothes before they fell into the horseshit in the street.

'Well, good morning,' Josephine whispered to the bump under her dress. It fidgeted and rolled, and Josephine rolled too, onto her back. She was lying on a blanket on the floor of the shop under shelves of boiled lollies lined up in gradations of colour. The early sun shone through the jars, casting a timid rainbow across the room. At its end stood the stockinged feet of the woman, Daisy.

'I trust you slept alright,' the woman said. Her gaze could not quite hold on to Josephine's. Their eyes were two wrong ends of magnets forced to meet.

'Fine,' Josephine said. 'Except for the shard of glass that was jutting into my back.'

The woman let her smile drop. 'Perhaps the sleeping arrangements at St Margaret's will meet your standards,' she said. Her look added, *Though I doubt it.*

At St Margaret's there were the things you were not allowed to do, and then there were the things you did. These were often the same things. They were the things that happened at night, when Mrs Abbott was not stalking the hallways and the girls stretched their claws, ready for the hunt. Then Josephine snuck out the window and crab-walked across the roof to steal port wine and cigarettes from drunks asleep on the church steps, or stood watch in the hallway while boys were snuck into the bedrooms of other girls, and wondered when they would get to do the same for her.

Josephine thought about Jack Coroneo as she cleaned the nice toilets used by the pregnant women with proper husbands in the hospital next door. She thought of him as she hung washed sanitary napkins up on strings threaded through the laundry rooms, scraped charred fat out of the ovens in the kitchen, and watched unmarried girls go suddenly into labour, slumped in a puddle on a half-mopped floor.

On Saturday afternoons, Josephine sat in the garden out the back and stared deep into the earth, right down to where the skeletons of babies had been buried. They were supposed to have sprouted shoots and leaves and bloomed into less burdensome organisms, but instead they occasionally surfaced and were found scattered across the dirt after the dogs had got in through the hole in the fence.

Nina visited once a week, though Josephine had no idea why. They would sit on the furthest ends of the settee in the foyer. Nina would ask her how she was, and she would say, 'How do you think?' then pretend to read a pamphlet taken from a box on the wall. Something about St Margaret's protecting the country from white race suicide. There was nowhere else to look, there was nowhere else to sit. If Nina tried to bring up the subject of adoption, Josephine would say: 'I told you: I'm keeping it,' and Nina would shake her head and leave.

'I know it's hard for you to imagine!' she'd shout out after her. 'Wanting to keep a child!'

Josephine did not waste time being sorry, because she knew Nina would be back again the following week to take her daughter's moods like a cat-o'-nine-tails thwacked across her back. Nina was far more Catholic than she ever dared admit.

Jack Coroneo had no idea where Josephine was—she knew this—but still she hoped—assumed, even—that he would find out anyway, and walk in just as the crown of their baby's head was beginning to show between her legs. He would take up her hand in his own, kiss it, and only then would their baby slip out as easily as a word. He would say it: *Sorry*. And she would forgive him.

She had rehearsed the scene so many times it had the detailed clarity of a premonition, and so she was surprised when—as she breathed in for a final push—Nina walked through the door with her hat in her hands.

'Where's Jack?' Josephine panted. 'What have you done with him?'

'Now, now,' the nurse said. 'It's not your father's fault you got into this mess.'

'Yes it is!' Josephine screamed. '*Yes it is!*'

'I put an ad in the police gazette for the bloke that did that to you,' Nina said, nervous, 'but nothing came of it.'

'I don't believe you!'

Josephine grunted. She moaned. Nina looked fraught and slipped out into the corridor where she'd only be met with more wails and forty eyes from twenty bassinets staring up at her.

Josephine did not get to see her baby after it was born. It—or she, Josephine would later find out—was taken, big-eyed and squirming, to an empty bassinet in the corridor. 'It will be easier,' the nurse said. 'This way you won't form a bond.'

But what about the blood that flowed through both of them? The placenta she had made that it had been feeding off for the past nine months? 'I'm keeping it,' Josephine said, staring down the nurse. She wanted to call her a bitch, a fucking bitch, but she knew it wouldn't help.

'No, Josephine, the papers have been signed.' The nurse was turning back Josephine's sheets, tucking them in, strapping her arms down.

'I never signed anything.'

'Your father did, and with your best interests in mind. Now calm down.'

Her best interests? The hospital would probably sell her baby—for 'a donation'—to a barren, uptight family and she would not see a penny of it. The injustice made Josephine dumb. Couldn't they see how unfair this was? To have the most important decision of your life made by an ex-nun and a distant—possibly lunatic—parent who never wanted you in the first place? She kicked the sheets off her bed and crept out into the corridor to steal her baby back.

She was the only girl in the place on the darker end of European, and she realised that for the first time this could work in her favour. She would know which baby was hers by its dark lashes, black hair, melted chocolate eyes.

Josephine waited until the night-duty nurses were nodding off in their seats and snuck down the hallway, testing the handles on doors. At the end of the hall she opened a door onto a room full of pink-and-white babies in eggshell bassinets. The babies were bald, or with tufts of gold, blond or pale brown hair. Some were sleeping, some were wailing; their sausage fingers wriggled at the end of fat, edible hands. None of the babies were hers but they wailed anyway, because the cold air was nothing like the red warmth of a womb, and the scent of milk leaking from Josephine's breasts was driving them wild.

The night nurse came rushing after the wails and found her. Josephine's cheeks felt old and heavy. She could not turn and run. 'Where's my baby?' she whispered. 'None of these are mine.'

The nurse took her by the hand. 'I'm sorry, Josie,' she said.

'Why?'

'She is no longer with us.'

'She's still in the hospital though, yes? She's just in a different ward?'

'No, dear. I'm sorry.'

When the nurse pressed her gently in the small of her back, Josephine did not fight. She shuffled back to her bed, curled up to face the window and watched the bats fly home from their evening hunt.

Childless, with aching breasts, Josephine growled and sulked. Daisy let her stay in the flat above the shop with the rest of them, but her moods were not tolerated for long. 'You can live here,' thin-lipped Daisy had said, 'but you have to do a few chores until you feel well enough to go out and get a job.'

Ah, so she would be a slave here, too.

The shop was failing—anyone could see that. Josephine could have told Daisy she'd have to be a few degrees warmer than an ice chest if she wanted any child other than her dopey son to dare to set foot in the place, but Josephine did not care to give her insights as well as her labour away for free. And so she watched Daisy's shop fail from on her knees, where she scrubbed the hardwood floor, and smiled into the suds.

There is only so much scrubbing and genuflecting a charismatic girl of sixteen can handle before her claws flick out of their own volition and start scratching the plaster off the walls. To spare the walls and lives of others, Josephine dressed up like a movie star and caught the tram to the Cross, where boys flashed through the streets like flocks of gaudy parrots. She would buy a pie, sit on a bench, and try to catch the eyes of the dark-haired ones as they passed.

The navy men were her favourite. They were steeped in delicious man-smells, and were as bold and loud as trumpets. They strode across the road as if no one would ever dare run them down. They were lovely, and even lovelier when they were drunk. Then they would tell her how beautiful she was and, when she blushed, tell her again with one arm around her waist. They would ask to buy her drinks. They would breathe their whisky breaths into her neck and she would feel alive again, even something close to loved.

The next day, stories would have to be concocted, apologies dished out for stumbling up the stairs too loudly at three in the morning. By the incredulous look on her stepmother's face, she could have sworn Daisy had never had a womb at all—it was like trying to explain the cancan to a cornhusk.

When the shop finally failed, it was everybody's fault but Daisy's. They would fight about it in bed at night. 'It's because your daughter comes home too late at night,' Daisy said to Nina. 'Don't you worry for her? Anything could happen.'

Josephine called through the bedroom door: 'Ah, you frigid old bitch. Anything already *has*!'

It wasn't until they moved to Drummoyne that Josephine wondered if Daisy was not quite so frigid as she appeared. Returning home from work one afternoon, wondering where to go that night, she realised she might not have to go anywhere at all, for there, waving around in the air, were the firm buttocks of a young plumber. His arms and trunk were stuck halfway under the kitchen sink.

Josephine took off her hat. 'Hello,' she said, shaking out her hair.

The plumber did not look impressed. He was now all the way out from under the sink, and rubbing his hands down his grease-streaked trousers. He was handsome, but uninterested. This was not how it usually went.

'Thought you was Annie,' the plumber said.

He wasn't smiling. He seemed immune to her eyelashes, immune to the molten brown of her eyes.

At that moment, Daisy came in through the back door, hugging a basket of sun-warmed washing against her hip. The redness was gone from her cheeks—was she wearing powder? And her hair was done up—not in the harried way it usually was, but in a neat bun with a well-selected curl spiralling down from her temple. Now the man smiled, and Daisy did too. Their smiles were connected—it seemed for a moment—by a fine gold thread. The man looked away, looked at Josephine, rubbed his hands down his pants again, and started talking.

'Mrs Crawford, it appears I might need to come back tomorrow, to fix the, ah, balancing valve.'

'Yes, of course,' Daisy said. The saucy hypocrite.

'I suppose I should let Dad know,' Josephine said, her voice as strong as a wrench. 'So he knows how much money to leave?'

Daisy's smile hardened. 'Yes, I suppose so.'

So then, Josephine would have to go out to get her kicks after all.

*

She didn't come home until the weekend had worn down to dust, her clothes reeked of cigarettes, and the smell of semen wafted up from her underpants. The light in the kitchen was watery—it must have been four or five in the morning—but there, sitting in a meek shaft of moonlight, was Nina, head bowed down to a bottle of beer.

'More rows over you,' she said. 'I can't get any sleep at night.'

Josephine fetched a glass and sat opposite her. 'Should have finished me off all those years ago, like you wanted.'

Nina's head lifted, could not hold itself up. 'What a lovely daughter I've got.'

'What can you expect?' Josephine took the beer, poured herself a glass. 'A lovely mother I've got.' She leaned over the bottle and whispered: 'She had a plumber over. And I don't think it was the kitchen pipes he was fixing.'

She should not have said that. Nina sat up straight in her chair, every part of her paying attention.

'From Balmain? What was his name?'

'I don't know. It was probably nothing,' Josephine said, although she knew it wasn't nothing anymore.

Josephine thought it might be wisest to stay home in the evenings, only for a week or two, to make sure she hadn't lit any fires that couldn't be easily put out. But then actually standing in the middle of the room while her so-called parents glared at each other was another thing entirely. And actually staying put in Drummoyne was about as dull as living could get. The neighbours lapped up any sensational detail glimpsed in the lives of others. *Did you hear that Crawford lost his job at Perdriau's? Yes! As a result of that nasty strike! Lord, I thought it would never end!*

Eventually, one brazen neighbour found herself on the Crawfords' doorstep holding out a plate of homemade ginger snap biscuits.

'Hello, dear,' the woman said, looking over Josephine's shoulder. 'Is your father home?'

'No,' Josephine said, trying to close the door.

The woman pushed it back with her plate. 'Well, I made these for you, too.'

Now, after all this time, a neighbour was prepared to acknowledge—to her face—Josephine's existence. She opened the door wide and let the woman in.

The woman sat at the kitchen table and waffled on about the repercussions of the strike, and the horrible ways she'd heard Germans treated their pets, and the price of butter, and the unpredictable spring weather, and only after she had exhausted every mundane topic did she ask the question the whole street wanted to know the answer to: 'Dear,' she asked, 'where is your mother? Why aren't you living with her?'

The woman's eyes were bright with hunger for the attention she'd receive once she'd grown full and interesting with this particular piece of news. Josephine was sick of it. Why should her family live caged in by the opinions of bored women too frightened to be interesting themselves?

Nina was walking up the front path with her usual quick, overreaching strides. Her head was down; she was clutching a bottle in a brown paper bag.

'There is my mother over there,' Josephine said, 'dressed up as a man.'

The neighbour laughed but Josephine did not join in. The neighbour glanced over at Nina, who was standing in the kitchen now, quiet and alert. One look at Nina's cadaver-pale face had the woman stop laughing at once—'The potatoes,' the neighbour said, 'I have left the potatoes'—and she was careful to give Nina a wide berth as she made her way out into the street.

Nina did not rage or shout. She breathed in, and slowly sat in a chair at the kitchen table as if her joints were made of paper and easily crushed.

'I'm sorry,' Josephine said.

Nina said nothing.

'I should leave,' Josephine said.

Perhaps her mother would protest? Ask her to stay? There was a small part of Josephine that was afraid to live alone. She did not know how she would orientate herself without someone to live against.

'Maybe a place close to your work would be good,' Nina said.

'Yes.' Her lip began to tremble. *No*, she thought, *don't cry, not now, she will think it is a trick.*

But it wasn't a trick. A dam wall had ruptured and violent, ugly sobs were forcing their way out.

Hold me, she wanted to say, but she couldn't speak, she couldn't even breathe.

MARCELINA BOMBELLI

One night Nina brought a sneezing, shivering boy to her place. They had been staying at a German woman's house up the road, and the over-boiled cabbage had him wasting away. The boy's father was dead and his mother was sick in hospital with consumption,

Nina thought—could Marcelina take him in? 'Alright, if you pay me,' Marcelina had said, and sometimes, when Nina had money, she paid.

It is hard to explain the joy that is felt when you meet someone who speaks the same as the family you have left behind on the other side of the world. This person, when you meet her, becomes a substitute for the family you have lost. There might be other things this person brings. A hand gesture, a certain way of frowning—and maybe it was a combination of these things that meant Marcelina did not ask too many questions, and did exactly what Nina said.

'The boy calls me Crawford,' Nina said. 'It'd be better for everyone if you could too.'

So Marcelina did.

She knew it was her son Frank she had to watch. Little ones born in a new country, they feel an allegiance to the new place and the people in it, so that when you say, 'Now listen, Frank,' as Marcelina said to her son the day he left for Sans Souci with the boy Harry Birkett, she knew he would not listen.

Frank was a real good boy, but the two women could not trust what he might say when he'd thrown back a beer or two. Nina would stare at him long and hard and that would shut Frank up. He would look away; he never could stand her stares for long.

The boy Harry thought Frank was the best thing who ever stood on two legs. Frank was a motor mechanic then, and had a healthy appetite, and the hair on his arms and chest was good and strong and dark. After the boy moved in, he hardly noticed Nina when she came around to talk with Marcelina. He was too busy following Frank around like a baby bird, squawking: could Frank show him this, could Frank show him that, could Frank teach him a thing or two about girls? 'What, like how to tell them apart from a bloke?' Frank would say, and Nina would stare until Frank changed the subject.

Frank enjoyed having the boy Harry follow him around, and the two became as thick as motor grease, always tinkering with rusted engines or brewing beer in the bathtub, until eventually they moved to Sans Souci.

'Why must you go?' Marcelina said. 'My house is so much closer to your work.'

'I can't stand having Nina breathe down my neck,' Frank said.

God knows what he told the boy down by the beach. Whatever it was, it was not good.

'Where is the boy?' Marcelina asked, when she went to give Frank's place a clean.

'In town with the detectives,' Frank said. 'Learning how to tell the difference.'

JOSEPHINE DEANGELIS

After dancing for two hours straight at the Palaise de Danse, Josephine went outside to breathe. Arthur had become a little too friendly with a woman who lived on her street, and nothing could take her mind off it. Not the music or the booze, and the cocaine only made the cool air feel like shards of glass in the nose. And was that a man staring at her from the other side of the street? She blinked. A gentle rain took the edge off the electric dance hall sign, and—yes—a man was there, watching her. She leaned her head against the wall in a way that made her hair cascade over her shoulder.

Now the man was stepping forward. Perhaps he would offer her some snow? She waited until he was at smelling distance before she turned to look him in the face.

He smelled like Nina. Josephine turned and, yes, there was Nina: damp and on edge. Josephine would have slapped her across the face if so many people hadn't been nearby to see.

'Where have you been?' Josephine asked. She had not realised how angry she was until she opened her mouth and the words splintered out. She was speaking quickly, more quickly than she thought it possible to speak. 'I went back to The Avenue, and you weren't there, and Mrs Bone had no idea where you had gone. Do you know what that's like, to come looking for your mother and to be met by the dark rooms of an empty house and no note and no message, no nothing?'

Nina looked horrible. Her cheeks dragged down, her mouth was a limp line drooping towards the dirt of the street. 'Everything's unsettled and upside down,' she said. 'Daisy has found out I'm a woman. I'm going my way and Daisy's going her way, and if you ever go near her again, she'll go for you.'

Josephine thought of the costume brooch she had turned over to Daisy in lieu of board, the necklace that was hers that she had seen Daisy wearing about the house. 'Who has the jewellery?' she asked.

'Oh, she's got all that.'

That bitch had milked them of their precious things, then took it all and ran.

The rain was picking up, but Nina made no move to leave or step under the awning. She was standing in the mud, lingering in the rain. Why? Did she have nowhere else to go? Josephine remembered what Nina had once said to her, about doing away with herself before the police found anything out.

'Come and stay with me and Arthur in Darlington,' Josephine said. 'We're having a party tomorrow night. Will you come?' Nina thought for a moment, before drifting back out into the street.

Daisy had killed herself. That's what Josephine thought when she saw the picture of her shoes in the paper. She had doused herself in kerosene and thrown herself into a fire. It was a brazen way to go. Romantic, even. And Josephine thought: *Perhaps we were not so different after all. Both of us wanted to burn the place down.*

GENE, THE FATHER-IN-LAW

DARLINGTON, NOVEMBER 1917

GENE

What's that Arthur Whitby you think you can make me small
by looking at me like that   sitting me in the shadows of your
rank beer party so no one will see me   I know what you get
up to with that woman over there   that slut from down the
street   don't think I don't know   even her little girl   she
can't be more than four   she's in on it too right in front of my
daughter   I'll kill you if you hurt her you low down bugger
don't think I haven't done worse

Don't think I never shoved a crowbar right where it hurts you
    sailors swanning around in your white uniforms like baby
    lambs   like you wouldn't take what you could get away with
    if you knew you'd never get arrested

And if any of you come for me again I'll lock myself up in the
    toilet and I'll hold my back against the door and you can cut
    your way to what you want through my kidneys—go on try it
    I bet you can't—I bet you scream at all the blood like a pack
    of pansies   I'm no lay down and take it type of animal—

But it isn't my snatch you want is it   you'd probably think it was
    all shrivelled up and foul like an oyster in the sun   ha

No   you want to feel like you've swallowed something alive you
    want to feel that alive thing kicking and fighting for its life
    you want it to fill you up on the inside and make you more
    powerful than a god and you want me to shake like a leaf and
    beg you to stop please stop

You cunts wearing your gonads on the outside like you think
    they won't get hurt   I'll twist them off with a wrench   I'll
    tie them off with a belt until they turn black and drop off like
    the rotten fruit they are

Yes I will have another scotch—you call that a scotch?—that's it
    fill it up   of course I can take it Josie you think I'm weak—

Whitby I will drink you under the table and then we'll see who's
    the bigger man when I've cut you down the arm—

        yes it's a knife you dumb fucker—

Ha   what   you can't take a joke? Every man carries a knife

No Josie I won't calm down and don't you whisper anything into
that slimy cunt's ears like I'm the embarrassment   he's made
of the same rotten stuff you sprang from   course you'd end
up with something as low down as Arthur bloody Whitby—

Yes I had a day off the sauce yesterday   don't you patronise me
girl I am your father

What's that Whitby   what is it you want me to say? Yes I am her
father yes that's right and you know it—look at her she looks
just like me

What have you told him Josephine   what lies have you been filling
his hollow head with now?

Ah girl I'm sorry   thank you for putting me up love I know I am
a good for nothing—come here please sit with me it's cold over
here in the corner and everyone at this party is looking at me
like I'm a funnel web spider and I've been so lonely since that
trouble with Daisy and I just can't keep it together—

I'm sorry   it's just   can't you see the way he is looking at that
woman   who is she   it's your neighbour right? and her little
girl   look Eenie look   that girl is looking at your feller like she
is real familiar with him   like he is over at their place every
second night   like he is her *dad*

This is all happening under your nose girl you're being walked
all over—don't let them take your shoulders-back-tits-out way
of being in the world Josie don't just lay down and think of
England it's a horrible place it always rains

No I am NOT seeing things   look at him reaching over and
brushing beer off that slut's top lip   oh ha ha yes did he just
say the moustache Gene could never grow? Very funny Whitby
tell that bitch to get her own feller   I will go him I'll bloody
go him and smash his smirking smug face   I will pound him
in the head until his brains dribble out his cauliflower ears
that thick fucking cunt

What's that Whitby yes I'm talking about you

No I won't calm down

       No I WON'T   I have a RIGHT I know my—

       SMACK you in the BLOODY *HEAD*

Ha! Not scared are you?

   Here we go! Here we bloody GO—

THE MAN-WOMAN

SYDNEY, WINTER 1920

DETECTIVE SERGEANT STEWART ROBSON

Robson always thought Central Police Station looked as if it had been dropped from a great height onto the wrong street. It was a grand colonial building, but it'd been built on a laneway down the rough end of town, crammed between the boiler rooms of two buildings that fronted onto wider, more respectable streets.

When he'd first walked through the carriage entryway of the station as a young cop, he'd soon realised the place had been built around a lot of hot air—literally, a bare stone courtyard. The building itself was only a few yards deep. The plaster was cracking—you could see the brick underneath—but a few chips in the paint only made the place look tough. *You should see the other bloke*, the building seemed to say. And the thing was, you *could* see the other bloke. More often than not, he was locked in a cell underground, bruised and licking his wounds.

By the winter of 1920, Robson felt as battle-scarred as the building crumbling around him. For weeks the press had been drumming up an impending state inquiry into a few slip-ups he'd made four years prior, and now people were talking about it at his kids' footy games, the pub, the dogs, the place where his wife got her hair done. Now she was asking questions, too, and staring at him over her porridge spoon each morning as if she couldn't quite size him up. Look, he wanted to say, we might have set a warehouse on fire and planted some fire dope in a socialist's wastepaper basket, but the Superintendent had the Commissioner breathing down his neck, and the Commissioner had the Premier, and the Premier had the Prime Minister throwing tantrums over his failed conscription referendums, and the Wobblies were asking for it, waving pamphlets around in the Domain with *SABOTAGE* written in block letters across the front. He wanted to admit these things straight to his wife's hard, honest face, but he knew he couldn't. He would prefer to be a murderer of socialists than worse. A ball-less whinger. A snivelling excuse-maker. Mindless fingers at the command of a head office that now had a serious case of dementia. So when a young man and his uncle and aunt walked into the station that winter, mumbling something about a murder, Robson relaxed. Here, finally, was a chance to prove he could think for himself.

He was at the front desk trying to get Miss Armfield to make him a cup of tea when they swung back the door—the woman in her best pink dress, gripping her husband's elbow as if he might lose his way; the young man doing his best impression of a coat-hanger, awkwardly filling out a stiff, cheap suit.

Robson steered them away from the bright eyes of ambitious juniors and into his office, and before they had even perched their backsides on the edge of their chairs, the woman started whimpering that her sister had gone missing three years ago, around the time a burned woman was found on the banks of the Lane Cove River.

'Three years?' he said. '*Three years?*' He shook his head. There'd be little surviving evidence of any use. His fresh ambition was wilting faster than a cock in a rent girl who was drifting off to sleep. He was about to send the nervous woman and her family home with condolences, but then she lowered her voice and told him the reason they'd taken so long to come.

'The thing is, Detective,' she said, 'my sister's husband was not a man.'

Robson looked at her husband to see if they were having him on, but the man swallowed hard and looked up, as if he were afraid his wife might get struck down for sharing such a shameful thing.

'He was a woman, Detective. A woman in disguise as a man.'

Robson imagined the headlines. His photograph in the paper. *Happy birthday you old bastard,* God whispered in his ear. *Here's that case you have been waiting for your whole life, Stewart—now don't fuck it up.*

Then it came to him. Perhaps it would be best for her sister's reputation if the woman kept the bit about her brother-in-law being a woman under wraps, so to speak.

'Let us make that discovery,' he said. 'Allow yourselves—and your sister—the innocence of never having known.'

STEWART ROBSON.

About 11.30 a.m. on the 5th July
I went in company with D tective Watkins
to the Empire Hotel at the corner of Parramatta Road and Johnston Street Annandale,
- that is this year - and I
there saw the accused
in the office of the Licensees of that hotel
and said "What is your name".

The accused replied "Harry Crawford".

I said "How long have you been working here".
The accused replied "A few weeks".
I said " What nationality are you".
The accused said
"What do you want to know that for".

I said "I believe you are an Italian".
The accused re lied". No, I am
a Scotchman and was born in Edinborough."

I said "I have my doubts
about you and I am going to take you
to the Central Court or the
Detective Office to make further investigations."

SERGEANT LILLIAN ARMFIELD

The morning Robson went out to find the wife-killer Crawford, Lillian was rubbing cream into her hands under the front desk. Five years earlier she'd been one of the first two women police officers in the Commonwealth and still no one knew what to do with her. Get the boys a cup of tea, they'd say. Type out our reports. Dog a white slaver. Go undercover at a fortune-teller's. Stay out of the way until a case comes along with a woman in it, then sit in the interview room with your mouth shut to make sure no one puts their hands anywhere they shouldn't. The only thing she was certain of was that she wasn't there to replace the boys, she was there to complement them. If she wanted to keep her job, it was important to maintain some feminine habits. Hence the cream.

Detective Sergeant Robson had been flexing his muscles over this Crawford character for weeks now. All Lillian knew were the details of the ghastly remains of his wife. Lillian had seen the broken pieces of the dead woman's dentures, had held the woman's greenstone pendant in her own hands, had touched the square of fabric that remained of the woman's incinerated skirt. There was something about touching these objects that transported her three years back, to the moment the woman screamed and dropped to the ground.

When Robson and Watkins dragged Crawford in by each scrawny arm, she was disappointed. He was not the thug she'd been expecting—he was small for a start, even smaller than her. He was itching himself with his cuffs the way a mangy dog squirms inside his collar, and asked Robson, 'Are you going to lock me up?' When Robson said, 'We certainly are,' Crawford whimpered, 'What will happen to me when I'm put in jail?'

'Usually they bathe you and put you in clean clothes, and then in a cell,' Robson said.

'I want to be put into the woman's section,' Crawford said, and Lillian laughed because she thought it was an impudent joke.

'Don't we all, mate!' Truskett said, and they laughed harder then, everyone but Robson. He smiled and surveyed the room like a captain at footy training.

She liked Robson. He hadn't quite got the hang of the fact that she was an officer of the police and not a tea lady, but there was an earnestness to his virility that comforted her, the way her family's snarling dog had done.

An hour later she was called in to witness Crawford's examination by the Government Medical Officer.

'Strip,' the GMO said. 'We don't have all day.'

Crawford's hands were shaking as he reached for the buttons on his shirt.

'Hurry up,' the GMO said, giving Lillian a look of impatience, as if it was her fault Crawford was so useless.

'Here,' Lillian said. 'Let me help you.'

She watched her hands as they pulled Crawford's buttons from their holes. *Don't look at the wife-killer's eyes*, she told herself. *Or his—*

Breasts? Were they breasts? Why had Robson said nothing about *breasts?*

Crawford did not move.

'Well, Miss Armfield,' the GMO said, 'you don't need a medical degree to know what those are, do you?'

She laughed, nervous.

'Trousers,' he said.

'What?'

'Would you please remove the man-woman's trousers.'

She accidentally looked at the wife-killer's face then—why? to seek permission?—and as she reached for Crawford's belt she couldn't shake the thought: *Is this how your wife undressed you when you got ready for bed?* She'd undressed all kinds of crazed, violent women when she worked over at Gladesville Hospital, but she'd never undressed one who had reached so far out of her sex that she had fallen from its clutches entirely.

She undid the belt in three deft moves—you learn to be swift, strapping women into straitjackets.

'No need to take them all the way off,' the GMO said. 'Just around the ankles is fine.'

Lillian let the pants drop, hooked her thumbs around the elastic of Crawford's long johns and pulled down.

There was no doubt about it: Harry Crawford was more woman than man. The GMO stuck his hand down amongst the hair to check that nothing had been tucked back between the thighs, but it came back empty.

Stripped naked in the room like that, the man-woman was grief-stricken, her wolf eyes shot red. 'This is a terrible thing for me,' she said softly, 'and the worry of my life.'

Lillian knew she wasn't talking about the murder. She wasn't feeling bad for anyone other than herself.

STEWART ROBSON.

I went in withDetective
Truskett to a residence inStanmore
- 47 Durham Street Stanmore - and in the room there
occupied by the accused and the wife then
-the last wife that would be -
Imade a search.

A woman was there
who was supposed to be the accused's wife,
and the accused said to me
"Don't let her see anything."
The wife was there crying.

I openeda portmanteau
and in it I found a fully loaded revolver
and also an exhibit.

By "Exhibit" I mean an article.

No, first she said
"Let me open the bag and I will give you some-
thing that is init".
I said "No, I could not do that".
She said "Well, don't let the wife see it. "
I said "What is in the bag".
She said "You will find it,
something there that I have been using".
I said "What is it, something artificial"
and the accused said "Yes, don't let her see it."
I said "Do you mean to say that she doesnot
know anything about this".
She said "No, and I do not want you to
let her know."

I opened the bag.
I got the article from it and asked the accused
"Is this what you referred to
as having used on your wife."

And the accused said "Yes."

No. I said "Did your first wife know that you were using anything like this".

The accused said "No, not till about the latter part of our marriage, not till about the latter stages of our married life.X

I think somebody had been talking."

Many years later, Lillian would tell her biographer what she thought of the lesbian cult. How it was a problem the authorities had to face, even though it was difficult. It required the cooperation of the wisest and best medical specialists, police, clergy and welfare workers, because it was on the increase. Those who practised it were furtive and subtle, and the leaders in the cult shrewd and persistent in their eagerness to corrupt others. Sooner or later, and the sooner the better, this menace would have to be faced head-on. It was a menace too serious to be ignored just because it was such an ugly and unpleasant issue to drag out into the open. This was why it was important she tell her biographer about the woman who pushed through the front doors of the station at six in the evening on 5 July 1920.

Lillian had no doubt at all who she was. At the sight of her, and the thought of what she would soon find out, Lillian wished she was still strapping mad women into straitjackets over in Gladesville. Or that she was anywhere, really, other than there.

'Mrs Crawford, I'm afraid you are in for a terrible shock,' she said. She tried to coax the woman into one of the interview rooms before saying any more, but when she took her by the elbow the woman snatched her arm away. She seemed to want to stay standing there, in the middle of the foyer, for everyone to see.

Lillian had no choice but to come right out and say what needed to be said.

'The person you married can't be your husband.'

The poor woman looked lost. 'You mean he's a bigamist?'

'No,' Lillian said. 'The person we've locked up under the name of Harry Crawford is a woman.'

Mrs Crawford laughed. 'That's ridiculous.' And Lillian laughed too. It was a release of nerves more than anything, but she had to agree, the whole scenario seemed like it had been stolen from a terrible play, something with cloaks and cardboard swords. After a moment the woman appeared deep in thought—perhaps piecing together memories of lights turned out, sheets pulled up to the chin, and she now seemed genuinely stunned.

'The Government Medical Officer has checked,' Lillian said, 'and I'm afraid it's true, Mrs Crawford.'

The woman shook her head. 'Let me see him, please. Let me talk to him. I can't believe what you're saying.'

Lillian ordered one of the boys to get a glass of water for the woman and, without asking Robson or any of the others, went down to the cells to confront the man-woman herself.

Lillian found her curled up on the bunk in her cell.

'Your wife's here,' Lillian said. 'She wants to see you.'

The man-woman groaned and rolled over to face the wall.

'You owe her an explanation, don't you think?'

The man-woman was listening. Lillian could tell because her head was ever so slightly raised off the bunk, but when a howl came from her wife upstairs the man-woman played dead. Just as Lillian suspected, she was a coward through and through.

When she returned upstairs, she found Robson with the suitcase open in the middle of the foyer.

'And see this?' he was saying. 'This is what she's been using. So you see now, Mrs Crawford? You see what we've been trying to say?'

A STARTLING STORY.

IN MALE ATTIRE.

WOMAN CHARGED WITH MURDER.

Eugene Falleni and Her "Wives".

WHAT THE POLICE HAVE LEARNED.

SYDNEY

On trains and ferries and trams, in kitchens over wheat bran or marmalade on toast, we opened our newspapers expecting to read about the inquiry into the police.

When we opened the paper, there was that crooked detective. But he was not standing in the dock—he was standing tall and proud with his chest out, walking a wiry little man towards the police court.

The headline read: IN MALE ATTIRE. WOMAN CHARGED WITH MURDER.

We blinked. We looked at the picture again. *What? That is a woman? In male attire?* We read on.

She was an Italian. Of course she was. She had married a man named Martello in her native country, and had a daughter with him. She sailed with him to New Zealand, where they lived for a few years, and then she came to Sydney with the daughter. Here, amongst us, she lived as a man, she did a man's work. She met and married a widow named Annie Birkett who never knew she was a woman and four years later the widow was dead, burned alive on the banks of the Lane Cove River.

We looked up at our husbands. We looked up at our wives. 'But how could she not . . . ?' we asked. 'Didn't they ever . . . ?' we asked.

Apparently, no one knew.

DETECTIVE BILL WATKINS

He was on the train, Watkins was, a long way out of Sydney, and he was glad for it. With his thug boss Robson getting paranoid that Watkins was out to steal his job, and all the sideways talk around the Wobblies, and the station telephone ringing itself berserk with news from people desperate to be a witness on the man-woman case, it was impossible to get any perspective.

Nearly all the callers were women. Nearly all of them believed what they were saying, too, though not half of them were telling the truth. Or maybe they were all telling the truth—he'd heard that people actually bled from the hands in the parts of the world that believed in stigmata. It didn't take him long in the job to work out that 'the truth' was a room with the blinds down and the lights out. You could only see it if you pulled the blinds up to let in a little light, but then it wouldn't be a room with the blinds down and the lights out anymore, would it? It would become something else entirely.

In any event, the man-woman case file was littered with notes from mysterious female callers. After Walsh up at North Sydney had found the body (and no incriminating evidence), he'd received a telephone call from a woman who said if he looked again he might find a bottle of kerosene at the site and promptly hung up without giving her name. Another woman called Central Investigation Bureau to tell them a black girl had gone missing from a laundry in Double Bay around the time the man-woman had worked there. And a third woman called to say that both she and her neighbour had been screwing Harry Crawford while their husbands were out, until jealousy had her bore a hole in their shared wall to spy on the lovers in the act. She fainted when Watkins showed her the 'device', which had—presumably—been up her own snatch, and made them promise she would not be subpoenaed as a witness. *Why call, then?* Watkins wondered. *Just for the thrill of being involved?*

Wheatfields smeared across the train window. Watkins was on his way to Hay in search of the dead woman's dentist. How any dentist could recognise a singed and melted upper plate he'd made ten years ago beat Watkins, but then the dentist would see very different things in those dentures depending on what questions he was asked—Robson had at least taught him that.

Yes, the dentist would be easy to sort out, but what about the man-woman's daughter? They still couldn't find her, and Watkins wondered what she looked like. Going off her friends who'd been calling the station with gossip, he didn't figure her being as butch as her mother. He imagined her giggling about her eccentric mother's antics while she and her friends shelled peas into their aprons on their front steps. It was common knowledge—these girls had said down the telephone—that Josephine's mother got about in trousers, that Josephine and her mother had worked together at the Riverstone Meatworks, and that when her mother got her finger caught in one of the machines, she'd bandaged the stub of her amputated finger herself. Watkins could never imagine his wife being as tough as that.

To pass time on the train, Watkins played a game with himself. One by one, he imagined all the women he knew, in trousers. He started with Miss Armfield—she was a plain-looking woman anyway, and if it weren't for her hatred of sex perverts he could imagine her becoming something of a man-woman herself. He imagined his mother in plumber's overalls. Now that was a terrifying thought—his mother, with her fist up someone's pipe. He imagined his sisters dressed as butchers. He looked around at the women in his carriage and imagined them in police boots, carrying pistols, swinging batons above their heads, and began to feel afraid—not of being hurt, but of ever so gradually becoming obsolete.

In waiting rooms and parlours, in pubs and tea houses and milk bars, the story was changing. Every day we had to wind the pictures back in our minds and start again. She did not grow up in Italy, she went to New Zealand as a child, and it was there that she met Martello, the captain of an Italian ship. She became so attached to him, she left her parents to become his wife. They sailed in a vessel with their only child, Josephine, and eventually the mother and daughter were landed in Newcastle.

But what of the burned woman found in the bush? How did we know she was the man-woman's wife?

CONSTABLE WALSH

Constable Walsh was the first officer to see the burned woman in the scrub by the mills back in 1917. He could still remember how the red of her heart and lungs could be seen through the crumbled charcoal of her ribs. And her hands: he would never forget those two stiff talons clutching at that roasted heart. It had moved him then, almost to tears. At the Coroner's Court they'd said she'd probably been a mad woman escaped from Gladesville Hospital that the manager from the Chicago Mills had seen loitering about the place. Walsh had been told not to worry any more about it. But when, three years later, he found out the size of the lie this woman had been told, and the type of monster that told it, it fired him up so that he couldn't sleep at night. The picture of the man-woman he had seen in the *Sun* was seared into the back of his eyelids, he had stared at it that many times.

The case had been passed up the ladder to the boys in the city, and yet after weeks they still had nothing to prove the burned woman was this monster's wife, beyond the coincidence that one woman had vanished when the other had appeared. Surely someone at the mills had seen the picture, too; surely they'd remembered seeing him—her—stalking through the scrub, wringing her hands.

He decided to go to the paper mills again. He'd been a number of times, standing in the shadows of the city detectives, but they never let him speak. All they wanted to do was walk through the patch of scrub where the body had been found and look around. Parts of the gum that had been singed were still black, but new branches had begun to grow out of proportion to the rest of the tree, so that it looked like a tyrannosaurus rex—strong and ancient, with feeble child arms. *Let's go to the mill,* he'd wanted to say. *Let's talk to them, one by one.* But he never did say anything. He stood behind them, and nodded, and did what he was told.

'Not to be a cunt,' Detective Sergeant Robson would say, 'but do you think you could stand a bit further away?'

He started to become a little looser with the regulations. Or, another way of looking at it: he started to take initiative. He took a copy of the *Sun*, with the picture facing out, and went to the mills alone.

He spoke to the office girl, Emily Hewitt, about the fire she had seen. He spoke to the watchman on duty over that October long weekend, and another man, Hicks, who had seen a strange man look up towards the incinerators at the crack of dawn. He was amazed by what people would tell you, if you ever dared to ask.

When he got wind of a woman who had been telling everyone in the area she'd been stalked through the scrub around the mills by a suicidal-looking man that very weekend, he hightailed it over to her house.

Mrs Carroll's place was a newish bungalow, built of brick the colour of oily liver. She seemed to know that Walsh was coming, and seemed pleased about it, too, in a macabre sort of way. She was sitting by the only window that let in any light, and had herself turned at such an angle that her cheekbones glowed skeleton-white out of the shadows of the room.

Walsh lowered himself into a velvet club armchair and was nearly swallowed by it, so that his knees were like the knees of a huntsman: two sharp angles reaching up.

'Mrs Carroll,' he said, adjusting himself in the chair, 'I hear you've remembered seeing a man about the vicinity of the Cumberland Paper Mills in 1917?'

'Oh yes,' she said. 'A very strange man.'

He pointed at the paper. 'Is this the man you saw?'

'Yes, yes, that's him.'

'And when did you see him?'

'Good Friday.'

'What? In April?'

'Yes, the twenty-eighth of September.'

'So not in April?'

'Yes.'

From where he sat he practically had to throw the *Sun*, picture out, onto the table in front of her. 'Can you remember the colour of this man's eyes?'

'He had eyes of a grey hazel colour.'

'I'm sorry?'

'That is, they were neither brown nor grey.'

He tried not to look disappointed.

'They were a peculiar colour, Constable.'

'It appears so.'

He thought for a moment. Perhaps he was complicating things. Perhaps he should just let the woman talk.

'Mrs Carroll, would you mind simply telling me the story of when you saw the man, and I'll try and write it all down as quickly as I can?'

'Yes, certainly,' she said. She cleared her throat and, as she did, a breeze thrust a shrub up against the windowpane. The light that filtered through the leaves was a sickly green, and made the hollows of the woman's cheeks almost look burned out. She was thrilled, he could tell, by the thought that the burned woman could have been her.

ELIEL IRENE CARROLL:

On the Friday before '-Hour Day of 1917
I saw somebody who attracted my attention.

I was going to the Cumberland Paper mill
from my home in Tambourine Bay.
There is a canal leading up in front
of the paper mill and a moat on top.

When I got near the paper mill I saw a man
sitting out on a rock on a point
with his head buried in his hands.

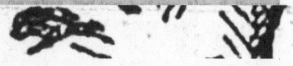

I know that district near the paper mills prett
well. I have been there since I was a child.
It is very dense.
There are very few habitations round.
It is very dense - thick scrub.

I passed within a few feet of this man.
When I passed within a few feet I startled him.
He dropped his hands from his face
and he startled and look up up.
I just looked him straight in the face,
but I got a good look at him for about
2 or 3 minutes side on before he saw me.

After seeing him there I went to the paper mill.

I passed on and went down to the office

I should say it was about three o'clock.

After I had done my business there

I returned half an hour after.

I saw that man again within about 20 yards

of where he was sitting first.

I missed him from the rock as I was coming back

and I looked towards the moat.

I thought perhaps he had gone down

to drown himself,

as I thought he was going to commit suicide.

He appeared to me at the time

He appeared excited

I looked for him on the rock and I missed him.

I next saw him  about 20 yards further round.

I heard a rustling in the rocks like

some one leaving behind the rocks,

and he jumped behind and he jumped over the rock.

He walked behind me for about 6 minutes.

I ju glanced round and looked back again.

I did not look back again the second time —

not till after he passed me.

I stood after he passed down the track

leading across the moat. I stood and
watched him cross on to the other side.

I told my mother when I got home that night.
I told two different people in the district
that afternoon before I got home
and several people after.

I said he had eyes of grey hazel colour;
that is, neither brown nor grey;
they were a peculiar colour.
I could not tell exactly what color they are
from here, but they struck me at the time
as being either grey or brown.
I cannot say that they are blue from here.
I would have to be very close.

I should say they are grey.
I would not call them blue. I also said that the man
I saw had a prominent chin and a straight droopy mouth.

I do call that a prominent chin.

I afterwards this year attended somewhere
for the purpose of identifying somebody.

About 20 men were lined up.

I was asked then to pick out the man that
I saw sitting on the rocks
to see if I could see him sitting   amongst the 20.

I saw him before I got to the gates. before I
got into the dock yard at all.

I can see him now.

THE ACCUSED

SYDNEY, AUGUST–OCTOBER 1920

THE PROFESSIONAL MEN

When dawn seeped meekly over the Tasman's edge on Monday, 16 August, the weather was cloudy and unsettled, as if all our evaporated sweat from the weekend's effort had curdled what should have been a crisp blue winter sky. On Saturday, the Roman Catholics of the city—some sixteen thousand—had filled the Domain to protest the British government's poor treatment of Archbishop Mannix of Melbourne, while His Royal Highness the

Prince of Wales had walked the golf links at Rose Bay and Louisa Lawson, mother of the New South Wales suffrage movement (and drunkard poet Henry), was laid to rest in the next best thing to a pauper's grave at Rookwood. Sunday saw solicitor Rod Kidston of the Crown Prosecutor's Office skip church to run through the proceedings of Monday's hotly anticipated man-woman case, while Maddocks Cohen, solicitor for the defence, aired his navy blue suit, knowing that by then the most he could do for his haggard client was look his dapper best.

And so, on Sunday night, the two solicitors put their nerves to bed, and woke on Monday energised, as if they had spent the night in an electrical substation and come out with surplus free electrons. They felt the way young directors do before the dress run of a play, for after over a month of remands they were finally about to attend the first morning of the man-woman's committal hearing.

The hearing afforded both men the opportunity to run their witnesses through the emotions they had set down for them, to see if that speech needed shortening, or that veil needed lifting and at what time, without the accused's life being wholly in the balance. Could the Crown prove that the burned-to-a-crisp five-foot-seven-inch body found by the Lane Cove River was tall Annie Birkett? Would Lily Nugent admit her sister had a weakness for drink? Would the accused's 'wife' be in attendance, and show support for her distressed spouse? These were elements neither lawyer could now control.

As both men shaved in the mirror before breakfast, their minds were as clear and indestructible as bulletproof glass. When they arrived at their respective offices, they greeted their secretaries with the same charismatic smiles they would soon try on the magistrate, Mr Gale. They lived for these Monday morning committal hearings, when the week ahead glimmered with the possibility of their success. Of course, both men could not succeed, and Maddocks Cohen, though calm, confident and dashing as always in his navy blue suit, suspected the forty subpoenaed witnesses were stacked ominously against him. So many infringements had been made by the prosecution—with the police parading the accused through the local court seeking remand after remand, sometimes without even telling him, her advocate, that she would be making an appearance. To make matters worse, they walked her from the cells to the court via the courtyard, instead of through the private indoor passageway as was convention. He could only presume they were trying to give the press ample photo opportunities, but he could not dwell on these details, or else he would likely lose his cool.

It was hard to imagine the ground where the police court stood as ever having sustained trees or grass or snakes burrowing under rocks. The imposing stone building rose from the earth like an uninhabitable slab of granite. But if the courthouse on Liverpool Street was imposing on the outside, its insides revealed that this impression of natural grandeur was exactly that—an impression— and one invented by lofty English imaginations before being built by calloused Irish hands. The furnishings were the colour of English parlours: maroons and dark, deciduous greens. The patterns on the carpet did not quite line up with the patterns the moving sunlight made as it shone past the beams in the ceiling and the joins in the skylights and refracted off the right-angles of the doorframes, so that it seemed to be a courthouse made from turning pieces always trying to connect, but never quite managing it.

Kidston did not notice these irregularities. When he bowed upon entering the court, he was bowing to the solid profession he had given his life to; a profession that had been worthy of his uncle's passions and mental energies and had done well for him, affording him a house in Mosman and two holidays a year. But Cohen—a former bankrupt who had stood on both sides of the dock's wooden barricade—knew that the law was not a divine decree received, Moses-style, from the clouds, but a tangled thing of sticky tape and string that had survived years of add-ons and subtractions and the twisting of language to the point at which it almost—but never quite—breaks.

At various positions along the front row of the gallery, journalists filled notebooks with furious scratching. They occasionally looked up, cocked their heads this way and that, and then scratched on, their hawkish eyes seeing more quickly, and in more detail, than those of the regular human onlooker.

They saw when, just after ten o'clock, Falleni, in man's attire, was ushered into the dock. She wore a grey suit, a blue tie, white collar, black boots, and her hair was plastered down in the ordinary masculine fashion. To their eyes, her face was pale and rather haggard, and while the charge was being read over to her her hands picked nervously at the dock rail. In answering she said 'Not guilty' in a low voice, and then sat down on the dock bench.[1]

---

1   *Evening News*, Monday, 16 August 1920.

Falleni, looking more effeminate than on any previous occasion, sat with legs crossed . . . and listened with drawn countenance and steady attention to the story told against her. Each time her advocate, Mr Maddocks Cohen, walked across to the railings of the dock to consult her those in the front positions of the galleries almost fell into the court itself in their endeavours to catch a glimpse of the man-woman.[2]

Constable Walsh was called to tell of how he found the remains of a body near the Cumberland Paper Mills at Lane Cove. He told the court that a mills worker named Hicks had identified Falleni as having loitered near the murder site around the time the body was found, and Mr Cohen did not waste the opportunity to point out that Hicks only identified Falleni after her picture had appeared in the paper and 'the whole world knew about the man-woman!'[3]

Dentists—with the help of ledgers—remembered making the very teeth that were found by the dead woman's body for a Mrs Birkett almost ten years prior. And Mrs Lily Nugent would recognise the dead woman's pendant and chain as having belonged to her sister, the very same Mrs Birkett for whom the teeth had been made.

Mr Cohen began his cross-examination with questions about Mrs Nugent's sister's drinking. If the burned woman was indeed Annie Birkett, mightn't she have been drinking metho by herself on the banks of the river, and mightn't she have spilled some on herself, and mightn't she accidentally have caught on fire?

---

2   *Daily Telegraph*, Tuesday, 17 August 1920.

3   *Evening News*, Monday, 16 August 1920.

Mr Cohen: Was she not under the influence of drink at the wedding ceremony?

Mrs Nugent: No.

Mr Cohen: Are you not aware that on the night of the marriage she had to be put to bed by a woman?[4]

The newspaper men, though impartial, could not resist a snigger. Of course Mrs Birkett had been put to bed by a woman. Hadn't she married one? Didn't she get naked and rub up against one in the marriage chamber?

Mr Kidston: Did ever the question of Crawford's sex come up?

Mrs Nugent: No.

Mr Cohen: He was always a nice man?

Witness made no reply.[5]

HARRY BELL BIRKETT, the deceased woman's son, was the next witness.[6]

Mr Kidston: What fluids did your mother drink?

Mr Birkett: She was a great tea drinker.

Mr Kidston: Did she drink ale?

Mr Birkett: She might have drunk ale at Drummoyne brought in by accused.

Mr Kidston: Did she drink spirits?

Mr Birkett: Not to my knowledge.

---

4   Ibid.
5   Ibid.
6   *Truth*, Sunday, 22 August 1920.

Mr Kidston: Did you ever see her under the influence of liquor?

Mr Birkett: No.[7]

[...]

Leaving Balmain, Birkett went on, he went with his mother to his aunt's place at Kogarah. They were there about 18 months, and Crawford, though his mother did not wish it, often went there. Then they went to Austral-street, Kogarah, and the accused lived with them there, but there were always the same rows. There was one big row.

Mr Kidston: What was that?

Mr Birkett: I don't know what it arose out of, but Crawford was wild, and smashed many a thing up.[8]

Cross-examined by Cohen, Birkett had to turn his head at a sharper angle to meet the lawyer's gaze, so that the late morning light fell harshly across his face, making his nose appear sharper, his eyebrows set at a more resentful arch.

Mr Birkett: I have heard my mother say that Falleni pestered her so much that she was practically forced to marry him. They did not live happily for long after the marriage. It was a matter of weeks. They would quarrel no matter who was there. They would row in the shop.

[...]

Mr Cohen: Has the accused been cruel to you, or chastised you?

---

7   *Evening News*, Monday, 16 August 1920.
8   *Truth*, Sunday, 22 August 1920.

Mr Birkett: He never had much to do with me, and he treated me with contempt. He has never been cruel to me.[9]

The light moved across the room, pulling Birkett from the stand, setting Mrs Bone, a grocer from Drummoyne, in his place.

Mr Cohen: Have you seen Falleni and Mrs Birkett out together?
Mrs Bone: Yes, I have seen them out on Sunday nights.
Mr Cohen: Walking arm-in-arm and going to church?
Mrs Bone: Yes, arm-in-arm, but I do not know where they were going.[10]

Mrs JANE WIGG, who lived at Drummoyne in 1917, deposed to seeing accused and his wife leave their residence together one morning late in September or early in October, 1917, and that she never saw Mrs Birkett alive again.[11]

After further corroborative evidence, and as the day's proceedings were nearing an end a young married woman entered the box. The lights had not been turned on. She told her story, which contained some startling evidence, in a dramatic tone. The court became hushed. Falleni shifted nervously in her seat. The witness was shaken by attacks of shivering.

This witness was Mrs Eliel Irene Carroll, living at Longueville, and she said that on the Friday preceding Eight-Hour Day, 1917, about 3 o'clock in the afternoon, she saw a man sitting on a

---

9   *Daily Telegraph*, Tuesday, 17 August 1920.
10 *Evening News*, Monday, 16 August 1920.
11 *Sydney Morning Herald*, Tuesday, 17 August 1920.

rock with his head buried in his hands looking across the moat near the paper mills.

[. . .]

To Mr Kidston: I did not speak to the police after the body was found because it was the body of a woman. Had it been that of a man I would have spoken up.[12]

Falleni was told to stand up, and Mrs Carroll said she was the 'man'.[13]

The further hearing was adjourned until Wednesday morning[14] and Maddocks Cohen came up for air. He buttoned his jacket, smoothed down his moustache and packed his briefcase as was his ritual at the end of a day in court. Although he moved with deft ease, he felt queasy, as if he had spent the day spinning in circles with his eyes shut, and not coolly cross-examining the Crown's witnesses in court.

If his client had gone into the police court a nervous wreck, now she was almost catatonic with worry. As she rose from her seat, she left the colour from her cheeks behind. Cohen had hoped word would reach his client's wife that the hearing was finally on (how could she miss it, when it was shouted by every newsboy at every tram stop in the city?), but she had not shown, and Cohen suspected the worst. Even the daughter—who had known his client's secret from the beginning—had not made any effort to support her mother. He—a lawyer—was the closest thing to a friend she had.

---

12 *Daily Telegraph*, Tuesday, 17 August 1920.

13 *Truth*, Sunday, 22 August 1920.

14 *Sydney Morning Herald*, Tuesday, 17 August 1920.

On Wednesday morning, the case was called on in No. 3 Court. There was not a dock there, and in order that she should not be exposed to uncomfortable scrutiny a green folding screen was provided by the police authorities. This was placed round a chair just behind the solicitors' table, so that the accused woman could be seen only by the magistrate, the witnesses, the members of the legal profession, and the court officials. Dressed in man's clothes, as before, Falleni was brought into court before the public was admitted.[15]

DR ARTHUR AUBREY PALMER, Government Medical Officer, said that he held a post-mortem examination upon a charred body on October 3, 1917. The upper portion was badly burnt, and the junction between the charred portions and the other was red and blistered.

Dr Palmer: This led me to believe that the burning took place before death.[16]

Mr Kidston: Can you say whether she was conscious or unconscious?

Dr Palmer: No.

The doctor then described his second examination at the Morgue, on July 22, after the body had been exhumed.[17] Several X-ray photographs were taken. These were produced.[18]

---

15 *Evening News*, Wednesday, 18 August 1920.
16 *Daily Telegraph*, Thursday, 19 August 1920.
17 *Truth*, Sunday, 22 August 1920.
18 *Sun*, Wednesday, 18 August 1920.

Dr Palmer: We found in the skull a number of fissures extending for the most part through the whole thickness of the bone. With one possible exception, these were all due to the influence of severe heat and the subsequent dissolving of the charred tissue.[19] That possible exception was a crack in the right side at the back of the head, which measured on the outer surface between two and three inches. This was in a situation, and had an appearance, which might have been caused by violence, such as a fall or a blow.

Mr Kidston: During life?

Dr Palmer: There was nothing to show if it was caused during life or death. It could have been caused during life.

[. . .]

Mr Kidston: Supposing the woman was injured, reduced to unconsciousness, and then burnt, would that be a possible theory of what happened?

Mr Cohen: I object to that.

Mr Kidston: I am only asking his opinion.

Dr Palmer: Presuming it was due to violence she would probably have been unconscious at the time. An injury which would produce that fissure would, in many cases, produce unconsciousness.[20]

Mr Cohen: Did you see any trace of bullet wounds?

Dr Palmer: No.

Mr Cohen: There were no marks of violence?

Dr Palmer: Only with one possible exception.

---

19 *Daily Telegraph*, Thursday, 19 August 1920.
20 *Evening News*, Wednesday, 18 August 1920.

Mr Cohen: How long were you at the locality on October 2?

Dr Palmer: About a quarter of an hour. Superintendent Tait was there with four or five other police.

Mr Cohen: Were the police searching the locality?

Dr Palmer: I think they were.

Mr Cohen: Did you see a whisky bottle?

Dr Palmer: Yes. It had a faint smell of spirits of some kind—probably kerosene or methylated spirits; but I would not be sure of that.

Mr Cohen: Would it have been possible for the woman to have fallen asleep and caught fire?

Dr Palmer: I think it would have been.

Mr Cohen: Did you notice any signs of a struggle?

Dr Palmer: I was not so much interested in that aspect.

Mr Cohen: Is it a fact women burn more quickly than men?

Dr Palmer: Yes; but that is on account of the nature of their clothing.

Mr Cohen: Would you say it would not be possible for the crack on the right side of the head to be caused by heat?

Dr Palmer: I would not say that.[21] Before I had studied the particular crack, I would have said it was caused by violence, but now I am not sure, it might be either.[22]

DR STRATFORD SHELDON corroborated Dr Palmer's evidence, but he still had the impression that the crack on the right side of the head was due to violence, but whether ante or post mortem he could not say.[23]

---

21 *Sun*, Wednesday, 18 August 1920.
22 *Daily Telegraph*, Thursday, 19 August 1920.
23 *Sydney Morning Herald*, Thursday, 19 August 1920.

The doctors were retired, and Kidston turned to see the gallery—his dress rehearsal jury—nod to each other, impressed by the gravitas of the doctors. Then, HARRY BIRKETT, the son of the dead woman, was recalled, and produced a copy of the 'Evening News' of October 16, 1917, containing a reproduction of a photograph of his mother's boots. The accused, he said, got him to read a copy of the 'Evening News' in which was a photograph of the shoes, but he could not remember the date. The photograph was similar.

Mr Kidston (reading from the paper): It was on page three of the issue of—

Mr Cohen (shouting): I object!

He snatched the paper from Mr Kidston's hand.

Mr Cohen: He was going to read the date out. I have strong reasons for objecting to it.

Mr Kidston: You've got strong hands. I don't know what your reasons are, but there's no reason to resort to violence.

Mr Gale admitted the newspaper.[24]

HENRIETTA SCHIEBLICH was the next witness, for whom an interpreter in German was sworn. The witness was ill, and after being sworn, sat beside the witness-box, with a lady friend who held smelling-salts. She gave her evidence mainly in broken English, but at times, when she could not express herself clearly, the services of the interpreter were necessary.[25] She said that

---

24 *Evening News*, Wednesday, 18 August 1920.n
25 *Truth*, Sunday, 22 August 1920.

accused came with his step-son to her place in Cathedral Street.[26] He took a room, and told her he had sold his own furniture the previous day.[27]

Mrs Schieblich: Accused's behaviour was as if he had been extremely excited or half-mad. He told me that if two big fellows, looking like policemen, came there and asked if he lived there, we must say he did not.

[. . .]

Mrs Schieblich continued her story in broken English, dispensing with the interpreter.[28]

Mr Kidston: How did Crawford speak to the boy?

Mrs Schieblich: He always spoke very sharply to him. Not cruelly; he spoke the same way to us all.[29]

Mr Cohen: This man became so confidential with you that he told you that he gave his wife a crack on the head?

Mrs Schieblich: Yes.

Mr Cohen: What did you say? Did you not say, 'Oh, you bad man'?

Mrs Schieblich: No, I said, 'You should not have hit her so hard.'

[. . .]

Mr Cohen: Is it not an invention on your part about Falleni saying he was haunted?

Mrs Schieblich: No, it is not.[30]

26 *Daily Telegraph*, Thursday, 19 August 1920.
27 *Truth*, Sunday, 22 August 1920.
28 *Evening News*, Wednesday, 18 August 1920.
29 *Truth*, Sunday, 22 August 1920.
30 *Daily Telegraph*, Thursday, 19 August 1920.

Accused left, but came back later, and said that he had been living with his wife at North Shore, but they had had another terrible row and parted again. Witness said, 'Bring her to me, and I'll bring you together again.'[31]

LYDIA PARNELL . . . was greatly agitated, and her body shook with sobs as she entered the witness box. She was sworn and was then given a chair on the floor of the Court. She took frequent drinks from a glass of water while giving evidence.

[. . .]

Mr Kidston: You know this person as Crawford; is that the person present in the Court?

The witness looked towards Falleni, and almost inaudibly murmured, 'Yes.' She broke down again, and had another glass of water and removed her hat.

Regaining her composure, Mrs Parnell said she asked the boy if he knew where his mother was, and he said he did not. About an hour later Crawford told her he had sold all the furniture. The next morning, Crawford told her that the boy was comfortable with some relatives.[32]

Mrs Parnell: In December of 1917 he told me that he had met his wife in George Street, and that she had asked him for money. He said that he told her he had none, and jumped on a tram-car. (To Mr Cohen): Falleni was always a very welcome

31 *Evening News*, Wednesday, 18 August 1920.
32 *Truth*, Sunday, 22 August 1920.

friend at our house. I only saw him under the influence of liquor twice. That was at parties. He was practically one of our own.[33]

GEORGE WILLIAM PARNELL, son of the last witness, said on one occasion Falleni asked him to read the paper, and see if anyone had been found dead or murdered. He read an account of a body being found in the bush at Chatswood, and Falleni exclaimed, 'That's the —! That's her!' For about a week witness was requested by accused to read the paper, and 'see if there was any more bodies found'.[34]

The hearing was adjourned until the following morning.[35]

From an early hour **on the Thursday** a crowd waited to gain admittance to the court, and about 10 minutes after the doors opened the public enclosure and the precincts of the court were crammed.

[. . .]

ERNEST BONE, husband of a previous witness, said he was in business at Drummoyne. The accused left The Avenue, Drummoyne, on the Wednesday after September 29, 1917.

[. . .]

Mr Kidston: Did you come into touch with the deceased?

Mr Bone: Yes. She was a very nice woman.

[. . .]

Mr Kidston: Did you ever hear the accused use an offensive name about his wife?

---

33 *Daily Telegraph*, Thursday, 19 August 1920.

34 *Evening News*, Wednesday, 18 August 1920.

35 *Truth*, Sunday, 22 August 1920.

Mr Kidston: Did you ever hear the accused use an offensive name about his wife?

Mr Bone: Oh, yes. One day when we were all down at the beach at Five Dock, prawning, I heard him say, 'Come here, you long, skinny—'[36]

FALLENI'S DAUGHTER . . . was dressed in neat navy serge costume, blue silk stockings, and black shoes. Her blue hat was trimmed with imitation fruits, and she wore[37] a grey motor veil. This she carefully kept down over her face all the time, so that not a glimpse of her features could be obtained.[38] She wept bitterly as she was escorted to a seat near the witness-box by a friend, and continued weeping while giving her evidence.[39] She became quieter for a time, but when asked if she was the daughter of the accused, she burst into tears again, crying loudly.[40] She sobbed all the time she was giving her answers, and her replies were difficult to understand.[41]

Falleni eyed the girl very closely. She kept tapping her left foot continually on the floor.[42]

She gave her name as JOSEPHINE CRAWFORD FALLENI and said she lived in Harris Street, Pyrmont. The first she

---

36 *Sun*, Thursday, 19 August 1920.

37 *Truth*, Sunday, 22 August 1920.

38 *Evening News*, Thursday, 19 August 1920.

39 *Truth*, Sunday, 22 August 1920.

40 *Daily Telegraph*, Friday, 20 August 1920.

41 *Evening News*, Thursday, 19 August 1920.

42 *Daily Telegraph*, Friday, 20 August 1920.

remembered was that her mother used to visit the house where she was brought up.[43]

Mr Kidston: Where did you first come into contact with Mrs Birkett, afterwards known to you as Mrs Crawford?

Miss Falleni: I can't remember the year.

Mr Kidston: Do you remember how many years it was before 1917?

Miss Falleni: I can't remember at all.

Mr Kidston: How old was Harry Birkett when you first knew him?

Miss Falleni: I don't know. I had very little to do with Harry.[44]

Mr Kidston: You always knew your mother was a woman?

Miss Falleni: Yes.

Mr Kidston: She went about in man's clothes?

Miss Falleni: Yes.

Mr Kidston: When did Mrs Birkett find the accused was a woman?

Miss Falleni: I don't know. She never told me anything about her business.

Mr Kidston: Did your mother ever say anything about the police?

Miss Falleni: No.[45]

Mr Kidston: Did she tell you whether Mrs Birkett knew she was a woman?

43 *Evening News*, Thursday, 19 August 1920.
44 *Truth*, Sunday, 22 August 1920.
45 *Evening News*, Thursday, 19 August 1920.

Miss Falleni: No. She told me nothing at all.

Mr Kidston: Do you remember when it was that Mrs Birkett came to live with your mother as her wife?

Miss Falleni: She was in the shop at Balmain.

Mr Kidston: Were you at the marriage?

Miss Falleni: No.[46]

Mr Kidston: What did you call your mother?

Miss Falleni: I never used to call her anything at all.

Mr Kidston: Did she tell you what to call her in Mrs Birkett's presence?

Miss Falleni: No.

Mr Kidston: Did you see if they occupied the same bedroom?

Miss Falleni: Yes. The same room and the same bed.

Mr Kidston: What terms were they on? Did they have rows?

Miss Falleni: They used to have rows over me.

Mr Kidston: What terms were you on with your mother?

Miss Falleni: Not very good terms.

Mr Kidston: Did you go to your mother's place at Drummoyne?

Miss Falleni: Yes, Mrs Crawford was there.

Mr Kidston: Did your mother ever tell you about Mrs Crawford finding out she was a woman?

Miss Falleni: She never told me.

Mr Kidston: Did you ever tell anybody in your mother's presence, at a table, that your mother was a woman, or that Mrs Crawford would find it out?

Mr Gale: Her mother would naturally be a woman.

---

46 *Truth*, Sunday, 22 August 1920.

Mr Kidston: But dressed in men's clothes. (To witness): Did you ever tell anybody in your mother's presence that your mother was a woman, dressed in men's clothes?

Miss Falleni: I don't remember.

Mr Kidston: Did you ever ask your mother about Mrs Crawford's jewellery?

Miss Falleni: No.

Mr Kidston: Do you remember the last time you saw Mrs Crawford?

Miss Falleni: No, I don't remember.

Mr Kidston: Did your mother ever tell you Mrs Crawford had disappeared?

Miss Falleni: No.

Mr Kidston: Do you remember reading in the paper about a body being found in the bush at Chatswood?

Miss Falleni: Yes.

Mr Kidston: Do you remember your mother telling you anything about it?

Miss Falleni: I forget now.

Mr Kidston: Did you ever remember?

Miss Falleni: I don't remember at all.

Mr Kidston: Did you ever remember?

Miss Falleni: No, I did not.

Mr Kidston: Do you think you will ever remember?—

Mr Cohen: I object.

Mr Gale: We can't have that, Mr Kidston.

[. . .]

Mr Kidston: Did your mother ever drink?

Miss Falleni: Not in my company. I never saw her under the influence of drink.

Mr Kidston: Did you ever make a statement to the police?

Miss Falleni: Yes.

Mr Cohen: I object.

Mr Gale (to Mr Kidston): You can only have that fact.

Mr Kidston (showing witness a document): Will you look at that signature? Is that yours?

Miss Falleni: Yes; I did sign that.

Mr Kidston: That is your signature to the statement you made to the police?

Miss Falleni: Yes.

Mr Kidston: Before you signed it, it was read over to you?

Miss Falleni: Yes, by Detective Robson.

Mr Kidston: Were you satisfied it was correct?

Mr Cohen: I object.

The objection was upheld.

Mr Cohen: In what condition of mind were you when you signed that statement?

Miss Falleni: I was too upset.

Mr Cohen: Did you understand what Detective Robson was reading at the time?

Miss Falleni: I was too upset and sick of it all.[47]

Mr Cohen: Some time ago you received a letter from me, asking you to call at my office?

Miss Falleni: Yes.

Mr Cohen: And I believe you took it to the Police Department, and they advised you?

Miss Falleni: Not to go to your office.

---

47 *Evening News*, Thursday, 19 August 1920.

Mr Cohen: What were the rows about between the accused and Mrs Crawford?

Miss Falleni: Mrs Crawford said she didn't get enough board money out of me.

Mr Cohen: Did you ever see Mrs Crawford drink?

Miss Falleni: Yes, beer.

Mr Cohen: Did she take whisky?

Miss Falleni: I never saw her take it, but she smelt of it.[48] She used to smash up things when she was like that.

Mr Cohen: You remember on one occasion—

Mr Kidston objected to Mr Cohen breaking new ground in his cross-examination.

Mr Gale: It is quite evident that she is giving evidence willingly now where she was unwilling before, but the poor girl is in a trying position, and I'm sorry for her.

[. . .]

Mr Kidston: Your mother has been dressed as a man ever since you can remember?

Miss Falleni: Yes.

Mr Gale: I think we will adjourn for lunch now, and that will give the witness a chance to pull herself together.

Mr Kidston: She's been crying for three days, and I don't think it will be any better.

After the adjournment, Miss Falleni was asked further questions. She was still sobbing.

---

48 *Truth*, Sunday, 22 August 1920.

Mr Kidston: In view of the attitude taken by the present witness towards Mr Cohen and the answers she gave to him, I ask permission to treat the witness as a hostile witness.

Mr Cohen: I object for this reason: The unfortunate girl is very upset, and she has answered Mr Kidston to the best of her ability.

[...]

Mr Gale (to the witness): I'm very sorry for the position in which you are placed, but in fairness to your unfortunate mother and everybody else we want the whole truth, you understand, and any information you can give. We want to know all about it.

Mr Cohen: She's perfectly justified in saying she cannot remember if she can't.

Mr Gale: No, but if she can she must tell us.[49]

Mr Kidston: You said that your mother never drank in your company.

Miss Falleni: Yes, it is right.

Mr Kidston: You remember making a statement to the police?

Miss Falleni: Yes.

A statement was shown to the witness, but she said she did not want to read it. [...] Mr Kidston then read the statement, as follows:

Mr Kidston: 'My mother often used to smoke a lot, and drink a lot of whisky, and she smelt of whisky a lot ...'

Mr Kidston then asked that the young woman be treated as a hostile witness.

---

49 *Evening News*, Thursday, 19 August 1920.

Mr Gale: I allow it.

Mr Cohen: I formally object to your ruling.

Mr Kidston: Did Detective Robson, in the taking of this statement, treat you with harshness or kindness?

Miss Falleni: With kindness.[50]

Mr Kidston then asked the witness a few more questions, and tendered the statement made by her to detective Robson.[51]

Mr Gale pronounced that the accused would stand trial at the Central Criminal Court, and bail would be refused.

Leaving court, the young Kidston smiled at Cohen. *Nice try*, the smile said, *but we got around your tricks in the end.*

Winter mutated into spring. Sunlight pushed against the borders of day and night and Cohen found it harder to sleep. A trial meant life-and-death stakes, a bigger courtroom, a jury of twelve men whose prejudices and opinions actually mattered. A trial meant a barrister would do all the talking and word on Phillip Street was that William Coyle, KC—also known as 'The Bulldog'—was booked to represent the Crown. How on earth could Sydney's best barrister be matched? What Cohen needed was a maverick, or some upstart graduate full of bravado and bite, immediately ready to take on the most difficult case of his career. But Cohen would not be the man to decide who should represent his client at trial. No, such decisions were to be made by the Crown, and the Crown chose Archibald McDonell.

---

50 *Daily Telegraph*, Friday, 20 August 1920.
51 *Truth*, Sunday, 22 August 1920.

Archie McDonell was a man of soft edges. He was not plump, but his gentle eyes, generous moustache and heaviness of step gave the impression he was an eater. Far from the bright-eyed pup Cohen had hoped for, McDonell was an old man, but without the experience or wisdom that was, sometimes, the saving grace of old men. He was new to the legal profession and painfully reclusive. Rumour had it he would rather spend an evening in his bedroom at his brother's house (he did not even own his own house) reading through his collection of books on sexual perversion than share a scotch with a colleague at a Phillip Street bar. Anyone would have thought that he—a bachelor at fifty-two—was a sexual pervert himself, but being too shy to meet his kind in the Hyde Park toilets, had to resort to his library for like-minded company. Perhaps he would bring a certain specialised knowledge to the case, Cohen hoped, because by then he could hope for little else.

THE MIDDLE-CLASS WOMEN

We rose early, when the light filtering through the London plane trees was a pale yellow and green. We took the tram into town, or our husbands drove us in on their way to work, or we travelled into town on the train. It was a novelty, seeing the men on their way to work, bleary-eyed in their overcoats and hats. Some of them read the paper. Some of them read cloth-bound books. Some looked out the windows and flicked their eyes past telegraph poles and the red-tiled roofs of houses. How we would have liked to know what they were thinking. Did some of them have mistresses? Secret harems they visited in the privacy of their imaginations? We wondered if they knew we were there, watching.

We arrived at the court when the air was still fresh and the sandstone steps had not yet been warmed by the sun. We caught sheepish glances from each other. Some of us had never been to a murder trial before, and felt guilty for taking such an interest. Our husbands thought we were morbid—they could not understand it—but we weren't the only ones there. Young men gathered outside the court, too, with bloodlust in their eyes. We all had our own reasons for attending the trial, and few of them were known to us. For some, the man-woman was a thing of wonder. We could not imagine running away to sea, we could not imagine passing as a man through the streets of Sydney or learning what it was men talked about when we were not around. She had done all these things, and more. Some resented her. We might have wanted to be sailors, too, but were not precocious enough to entertain the fantasy. And what of the daughter? The dead wife? The man-woman's freedom came at great cost to other people. Let that be a lesson.

The lawyers snuck up on us like a stealthy circus in the night. They wore anaemic clown wigs and slapstick gowns that smacked their ankles and rose up in gusts of wind as they ascended the court steps. When the large metal doors were pushed open, we made our way into the gallery, making new friends as we did. And where did you travel from today? Ashfield. Oh, do you know Mrs So-and-so? Yes, she is on the school committee. Et cetera. If there was a lull in conversation, we marvelled at the building, at the grandness of it. We watched the dock for signs of a small man in a suit, but he never turned up. Instead, at ten o'clock, a woman. She was frail, in black buttoned boots with brown cloth tops, a white linen dress and a black woollen coat. Her shaking hand was hiding under the lapel of her dress like a mouse under a leaf. She glanced at our faces, as if they were the faces of cats, with needles for teeth and sharp, extracted claws.

The barrister for the Crown—the man they called The Bulldog—stood and told us in a loud clear voice that he found it hard to refrain from referring to the accused as a 'he', but when he did we were to understand he meant the accused, who posed as a man, and definitely stated that she was a man, and married two different women as a man. So many lies were told, he said. He told the jury they must closely examine all her statements and ask the reason for them. They must ask themselves: why all these lies and subterfuges? But they must not convict on them. He may as well have told them not to think of a white elephant. Don't, he might have said. No elephants. *Tusk-tusk*.

The Bulldog paused. He looked at us. Was he turning red? He looked like a schoolboy who had seen a woman in a bathing suit for the first time in his life. 'There is another matter,' he half whispered to the judge, 'although it is an unpleasant subject to speak of in the presence of women.'

'We must not hesitate for one moment on account of the women,' the judge said. He was wearing a red gown and a white wig. He looked like Father Christmas but less likely to fly through the clouds on a sleigh. 'If women choose to come to a criminal court,' he said, 'they cannot be considered.'

We looked at each other and raised our brows. It is funny what men think we shouldn't know.

The Bulldog changed his voice so that it was as cool and loud and strong as a mountain stream. 'The accused has been through the form of marriage with two women,' he said, 'and later I will suggest something like a motive for getting rid of Mrs Birkett. The accused was so practised in deceit as to deceive these two women into the belief that she was a man. It was only in the end, when that deceit was discovered, and there were quarrels, that this person sought an opportunity to get rid of the person who would possibly broadcast her deceit.'

We listened to witnesses say what we had already read in the paper. Our eyes wandered. We scrutinised the man-woman's face to see if she looked guilty, but she only looked calm. *How about now?* we thought, looking quickly to try to catch her out. *Or now?* No, she had turned her face into an iron wall, she was not going to give any more of herself away.

We tried to piece the facts together. Over the 1917 Eight-Hour Day weekend, Harry Crawford had been darting about like a skittish fish. The Bulldog was suggesting Crawford went to the riverbank three times: to kill his wife on the Friday, to clean away the traces he left behind on the Sunday, and to dispose of the body on the Monday. Or maybe the accused had stayed by the body from Saturday night through to Monday afternoon, was that what he was saying?

When the court adjourned for lunch we cleared the matter up over sandwiches and tea. The gun, we said. Remember, they found a gun in her portmanteau. Alright, so the man-woman shot her 'wife' twice through the heart, and burned her chest, and shoved her fist into the blistering wound to pull out the bullets. We shrieked in delight. Oh, how gruesome! One of us choked on a crust and had to be thumped on the back. No, we said, she made the wife drunk with whisky, or perhaps she poisoned the whisky and then shot her through the heart, and when she fell she hit her head on a rock, and then the man-woman doused her in kerosene and burned her. But there is no evidence of bullets, we said (our tea had gone cold, we pushed it aside), there is no evidence of poison, no evidence of violence. So? Are the only events that happen the events that leave a trace?

After lunch we saw a skull. The real skull of the burned woman. A doctor pulled it out of a box as if he were in *Hamlet* and this was his only scene. We looked to see if the man-woman flinched or winced or blinked out of rhythm. She didn't. This was probably because she had seen it before. It had a large crack up the back. *So there*, The Bulldog seemed to be saying. *There is your evidence of violence.*

The man-woman's barrister, the one who looked more like a walrus than a bulldog, started asking the doctor about men and women, about how some men were more like women, and some women were more like men. *Sex inverts* they called them. He asked the doctor about sexual inversion, and the doctor said yes, a lot of literature had come up, but the red judge didn't know what they were talking about. 'Are you setting up insanity or not?' he said to The Walrus. 'Oh, certainly not,' The Walrus said. Then he carried on his conversation with the doctor, asking if it was not a fact that when the hands were extended normally in front of the body, palms upwards, the elbows of a woman were closer together than those of a man. 'That might have some bearing on the case if you were setting up insanity, but as you say you are not, I cannot see what it is leading to,' the red judge said.

'I want to show,' said The Walrus, 'that the accused had the masculine angle of the arms.'

We looked at our elbows, to see what shapes they made.

As our lunches digested, the afternoon dragged. One of the jurymen yawned. A willie wagtail rested on the windowsill and sang. When a large female witness was asked if she knew the accused, she looked the man-woman straight in the eye and said, 'I know the accused and she knows me.' How many women did this man-woman know, we wondered, and not just know, but *know*? Had we missed out? Was she somehow more potent than the average man?

On the trains and trams that took us home to our husbands we talked. What happened to the girl? we asked. The daughter? She had been a hostile witness at the hearing, there was no way they would bring her back. But some of us missed her. She was beautiful and fierce and fragile. One of us said she had a cousin who had a friend who lived in Darlington, where the daughter lived with Arthur, her husband. Husband? Yes. And guess when they got married? When? The day before she gave evidence at the police court. No! Yes. And she gave evidence as Josephine Falleni, not Whitby, which would have been her proper name. Well. Maybe she thought she could lie under oath if she gave a different name. Poor girl. And my cousin's friend, she says that the man-woman worked her passage from New Zealand on a steamer. She had to sleep with a lead pipe under her pillow, and one day she was in the ship's bathroom when a sailor bashed down the door and had his way with her. So the girl is the product of a rape, then? And do you know something else? The man-woman once stabbed her daughter's beau Arthur with a knife during a fight. No! Yes, possibly because he got the girl into trouble. Or perhaps the man-woman was jealous she didn't have the girl to herself anymore. Or perhaps she did not want the same thing to happen to her daughter that had happened to her in the ship bathroom, who can say?

Once our travelling companions alighted, we had a few moments to ourselves. We had been swept away by the thrill of getting to the bottom of things, but at the bottom of things was a woman who was fierce and fragile and beautiful in her own way, too. We wondered what she was doing. Was she sitting in her cell, rocking back and forth, going over and over the Eight-Hour Day until she had completely forgotten where, or who, she was?

The next morning we heard the policeman, the main policeman. He was big, with a muscly neck and an excellent memory. He could remember when he and Watkins arrested the man-woman and brought her into the station to give a voluntary statement.

He remembered when she volunteered to take off her clothes for the Government Medical Officer and then said, 'This is a terrible thing for me and the worry of my life.' He said they went to the man-woman's house and the wife was there crying, and then they found, in a locked portmanteau, they found—

The Bulldog held a prosthetic phallus by a thin leather strap. He held it out from himself, with his face slightly turned, as if it was a rotting rodent he'd pulled from a drain. He walked towards the jury, to make sure they had seen it. They reeled back, ever so slightly. He turned to face us, and we craned our necks so that we could see past the fascinators and hats. It was large, but not too large. More intriguingly, it was soiled. It was made of rags and capped with rubber. We imagined that it smelled, but of course, from where we were sitting, we couldn't smell a thing. We looked at the man-woman. *Now? Will she cry now?* She looked pale, perhaps. Drained of life, that's all. Now The Bulldog was showing us a gun, but all we could see was that other thing, the 'article'. It was like a gun, in a way. Hard and black and dangerous. We felt a tingle between the legs.

The Walrus stood. He said the accused was in a very nervous state, and would make a statement from the dock. *What*, we thought, *after her phallus has been shown to all and sundry?*

We watched her grip the railing hard. She was speaking, apparently, but no one could hear what she said. 'Speak up,' the red judge said. 'Your Honour and gentlemen of the jury,' she repeated. Her voice was thin, about to break. 'I have been three months in Long Bay Gaol and am near a nervous breakdown. I would like to make a statement, but my constitution will not allow me. I do not know anything at all about this charge. I am perfectly innocent, and I do not know what the woman done. We never had any serious rows; only just a few words, but nothing to speak of. Therefore, I am absolutely innocent of this charge against me.'

She trailed off and there was a silence. We looked to The Walrus. *Will he ask her any questions? Will he remind her of her lines?* He looked as if he were drowning and praying for a wave to end it quick.

The Walrus called a manufacturer, a Mr David Horace Love. In 1917 he had managed the cornflour mills up the river from where the body was found. He had seen a madwoman about the area, whose appearance matched the description of the burned woman. *What?* we thought. *Is he trying to say the burned woman was not Annie Birkett at all?* Next it was The Bulldog's turn to ask questions. No, Mr Love said, he could not swear to the woman again. Yes, Mr Love said, he knew that the madwoman had been located.

That was the case for the defence. The Bulldog had called twenty-seven witnesses. The Walrus had called one.

He will fix things, we thought. When he sums up, The Walrus will say it was an accident, that they had gone to the bush to make amends, drank more than they had intended and had a fight. She tried to leave, and he grabbed her by the wrist, and then she fell. She fell and hit her head on a rock, that's what the defence will say. We were on the man-woman's side now, because she was near a nervous breakdown and we felt guilty, just a little, for having wanted her to cry.

The Walrus stood. He cleared his throat. He said it was not only possible but probable that Mrs Birkett was still living and hiding her identity at the present time. His client was in no way at fault. We should look at the matter from this point of view: if a man commits a murder, he can live again, and in time become respectable; but if he commits a sexual crime, can he lift his head and ever assume respectability? And if a man would be so ostracised, what would happen to a woman when her mistake became public? He asked us these questions, and we weren't sure if he was talking about the man-woman or the wife or who. Then he sat down.

The judge spoke for half an hour and sent the jury on their way. They were young men, and seemed pleased they had been given such an important job. Even the man who had yawned seemed more sprightly now that he was given a task.

The doors of the court were opened and we weren't sure what to do with ourselves. *We have sat here for this long,* some of us thought, *it would be a shame to miss the verdict now.* Yes, but was she guilty of murder beyond reasonable doubt? That would surely take years to determine.

Some of us left. *It will be in the paper in the morning,* those that left thought. *There is no chance we will miss what happened.* And yet some of us felt more useful if we stayed, as if our presence might make a difference somehow, and so those of us with companions ate light meals in cafeterias on Oxford Street and imagined we were the jury, deliberating over the man-woman's guilt.

After our meals, we returned to the waiting room, knitting, reading, watching the doors of the court. When they opened, we took our seats in the gallery, a little ashamed at being the last women there. We watched a juryman hand a slip of paper to a court official, who handed it to the red judge. As he read, he did not give any emotion away. Two young men pulled the black curtains off the wall behind the judge and held them up on either side of his face. From the gallery, he looked like a black, mythical bird, lifting into the clouds.

Then he said it: she was guilty, and would hang from the neck.

The man-woman somehow managed to speak. 'I am not guilty, Your Honour. I know nothing whatsoever of this charge. It is only through false evidence that I have been convicted.'

Some of us were glad she had got what she deserved.

Some of us were sick to our stomachs.

We could feel the skin beneath our collars. How tender it was, how soft. For a second, we thought we could feel the scratch of a rope being slipped around our necks.

PORTRAIT OF AN INVERT

Being the Recollections and Digressions
of an Australian Surgeon

By

HERBERT M. MORAN

It was acting from an impulse provoked in me by my old friend W. T. Coyle, once Crown Prosecutor at Sydney, now a Criminal Court judge, that I first went to see her. He knew that I possessed some Italian, and thought that it might bring her a crumb of comfort to have a visit from someone who could understand her in her own Tuscan language (for she had the Tuscan tongue, if not the Roman mouth of the proverb). It was his Irish way, you know, first to prosecute the poor creature successfully—was there ever a greater prosecutor in Sydney?—and then to send his kindly wife and some of his friends to ease for her the pain of imprisonment.

The Long Bay penitentiary stands like a fortress on the coast a few miles south of Sydney. The Pacific Ocean is at its back-door as if to provide a contrast of turbulence unharnessed. The day W. J. McKell, M.L.A., gave me a pass to enter it, all was bright and cheerful until the key grated and the iron gates swung back. Then a wind—a cheerless wind blew upon us. The dejection of the prisoners, their hang-dog looks, their earthy complexions in spite of the exposure to sunlight, the dull eyes of those who were obviously practising the solitary vice, the slow footsteps which had lost all alertness—all these things appalled me. Merriment seemed gone for ever from their lives. In its place was a sort of brooding hopelessness. The horizon of these men was a wall ! and yet there was an ocean outside and beyond. The turnkeys all seemed to have hard iron eyes. Their faces bore the mark of alcoholic bouts. Were they seeking thus to exorcise the phantoms which pursued them? They must surely have always around them the spectre of these murdered lives. What a place to live in! Existence itself had a growth of green mould upon it.

A benevolent matron and I awaited Eugenia Falleni in the reception-room. The stiff uncomfortable chairs symbolised the attitude towards life within the prison. She came in shyly and suspiciously, a woman of fifty-four years. The stature was short and the gait slouching. She still seemed to be deliberately exaggerating the stride of a man. The grey eyes were restless and afraid; the face olive-tinted, lined, hairless. Such a head would easily pass for a man's. Her hair

indeed was still short. It was brushed straight back and there were patches of grey. The nose was thick and undistinguished. She was flat in the bust. The voice was low-pitched and raucous, the manner subservient but distrustful. Obviously her intellect was fixed permanently in low gear. The hands were large and spade-like, suggesting those of a manual labourer.

I told her my mission was to help her in any way I could (at that time I had foolish ideas of getting her returned to her native country). She replied cautiously complaining chiefly of the monotony. She said she was there "only on suspicion" (which was not true and which no intelligent person would have affirmed). She was always deceiving herself as to reality. But all the time she remained on guard, watching me narrowly. At no time then or later did she try to dramatise herself.

Obviously this was a woman with the mental capacity of some lower animal. She had none of the brilliant attainments of so many perverts. Nor was she aggressively masculine. There was nothing of the bearded woman about her. She had no religious sentiments of any kind, and not the slightest evidence of any spirituality. She was just a half-wild creature who felt herself apart and different, who had grown cunning and furtive, hiding her secret and satisfying her needs. She must have long since learned how the common people hated the habit she practised. She must have gone always harassed with fear. It is only by the light of that ever-present fear we can hope to

understand her problem and her crime.

I am not competent in the modern researches which have made so great a contribution to our knowledge of psychical phenomena, but even now we know so little of the subconscious. It appears at times like an unlighted dungeon from which come scurrying forth the famished rodents of our senses. I cannot say then if Falleni's perversion was or was not a perturbation of the Œdipus Complex. I do not know if in hiding herself from the realities of her environment she was seeking refuge under the maternal skirts and near a mother's breast. This, at least, seems clear. Falleni was not of that group which seeks fresh novelties of sensation in the lucky dips of a sexual bazaar. Hers was not a jaded palate asking for violent stimulation. Nor was she of that over-sophisticated class of artists

and literateurs who are bewildered by beauty or crazed by a longing to create something new. Still less had she kinship with those whose dammed-up normal desires seek new vents and hollow out new channels. She was condemned even from her birth and her abnormality derived from the very nature of her being. The temperamental outbursts, the vulgar debauches, the filthy speech, were but minor manifestations of her interior disorder.

SOME LOWER ANIMAL

ANIMAL

SYDNEY HOSPITAL, 9 JUNE 1938

Bugger the morphine, I'm clinging now: onto the hollow coughs resounding in the bedpans, the groans of the crook woman next to me, the rattle of a metal bed wheeled down the hall. I've been in a hospital before, long ago now, but it's all coming back—

Riding the tram to gaol the pain I felt was too big for moans. With Lizzie gone, and my daughter given up on me, I'd no one to live for—but I didn't want to die at the hands of old men in white wigs, and what were they hiding under there anyway? If I was going to go, it'd be by my own hand, thanks all the same.

The concrete floors, the single-file lines, the mosquitos that rose in clouds from the drains—to execute a person at Long Bay Gaol is worse than killing your wife in a drunken rage at a picnic and is much worse than not killing your wife and getting told by all of Sydney that you did.

I hope you never believed those stories about your grandma, Rita; it's important to me that you don't. I almost began to believe them myself when Sydney's million eyes twinkled in the electric courtroom light. Thinking of those eyes now, it's hard not to imagine them attached to butchers' aprons and bloodied arms clutching spears and stun guns. I was supposed to make a statement from the dock, but standing there in my meat and bones, all

I could see were the jurymen's smug faces grimacing at the sight of my member dangled before them—a poor cousin to what they had between their legs—and my mouth could not make a sound. Every word was suddenly right and wrong depending on how it came out, and I was stuck and drowning in the lost eyes of my barrister.

My gun and thing they found in the box made the jury sure I killed her. By the looks on their faces, you would have thought my member fired bullets out of its rubber shaft. Obsessed with secrets, people are. If I was a woman in man's clothes, there must have been other bad things I was hiding, too; things I'd want to kill to protect. They didn't think that my woman's skin was hiding another true thing that the man's clothes were bringing out. *Did you want to be a man, then?* the cops asked, confused, and what to say? *Yes? No? I don't know?*

All I knew was I wasn't good at being the way a woman was supposed to be, so I tried the only other option and it was better, for a time.

All I know is, if Harry Crawford had been on trial, the best they could have pinned on him was manslaughter; they'd never have sent him to hang.

That barrister they gave me was not so easily put off. He was waiting for me in the prison interview room the morning after I arrived.

Fight them, he said. *I know you want to give up, but we have to fight them, not just for you, but for inverts everywhere.*

So I was an invert now? He seemed so sure of the word, like it suddenly made sense of who I was. And others, too, apparently. We were part of a secret society of inverts who were *everywhere*, walking around with our penises sucked up inside ourselves, our breasts punched into our chests, our skins flipped around, so that the muscles and veins were flailing around in the wind.

Poor old Archie McDonell could smell my resistance. He couldn't stop mopping his brow and dropped my case file on the floor so that the pages lost their order. His cheeks burned red, and he apologised to his shoes because he couldn't look me in the face after we had lost.

We had lost. He didn't want to feel he'd failed alone.

You were convicted on circumstantial evidence. Circumstantial evidence!

His eyes were wet, and I wondered if he was about to cry.

I took his hand—something we weren't supposed to do, in case forbidden things passed from palm to palm.

It's alright, Mr McDonell, I said. *You did everything you could.* Which wasn't saying very much at all.

He appealed—or *we* appealed—and lost.

One month later, in a snap cabinet meeting, the Premier and his men overruled the decision anyway. In a matter of hours, my death was turned back into life. All of Archie's fretting and sweating, the months of being walked to and from the court in front of the flashing bulbs of photographers, the whole trial was suddenly revealed to be little more than a drawn-out freak show, an excuse to put journalists to work, a quick dose for readers addicted to their own outrage, so they could sit at their kitchen tables and point and comment and feel like they'd contributed to the running of things.

*

I spent the first few months of my new life sentence swallowing snail pellets in the prison fernery or sneaking sips of detergent in the kitchen. The old bod got the hint and ran with it. I was wheeled into the hospital wing. My insides were being scoured out, that's how it felt, and the doctors thought they'd help the process along by forcing vials of bitter medicine down my throat. Soon only my skin would remain: a costume to wear on New Years Eve. *Look, it's the man-woman!* a giddy kid might shout, but no one would believe him. By then my skin would be that of a shrivelled-up old lady—a spinster aunt or a librarian or a nun—as interesting as dregs of tepid tea left in the bottom of cups. Not a man, never a murderer, nothing as exciting as that.

A nurse pressed her fingers into my stomach to watch me wince, then whispered, *Cancer.*

A terminal illness. What a relief!

Turned out cancer was an alien creature, living off my stomach acid, knocking me out for days at a time. And as the weeks dragged on, I wished it could've been a bit more clear on when it was planning to terminate.

When I came to, I watched the walls move under their bugs. What never moved were two rows of steel cot beds, their starched sheets tucked stiffly in. Down my end was a curtained-off corner, the curtains embroidered with cross-stitched religious scenes. I saw Jesus wash Mary Magdalene's feet before a gust blew the curtains back, revealing the drawn face of a woman sitting on the bed beside me. I wondered if she was an angel. Her face was long and thin, her nose beak-like; the curtains moved like wings. She sat, staring at the medicine cabinet on the far wall.

Mary, I said.

She didn't flinch.

Mary, I said again.

I felt a rush of love for her, possibly because I'd rolled off my morphine drip, but at the time, with the light shifting from white to yellow in her wings, I thought this woman could save me. She rose and walked towards the locked cabinet on the far side of the room. Was she walking? She seemed to float. She scanned the room slowly, coolly, then picked the lock with a bobby pin drawn from her mass of dark, wavy hair. She took a vial from the cabinet, drank it, replaced it with something hidden in her blouse, locked the cabinet and floated back.

What did you put in there? I thought, or maybe asked.

Don't worry, she said, *only something I found in the cleaning cupboard. Nothing you people could distinguish from the filth you drink at the pub.*

When I next opened my eyes, she was unconscious. Her nose was an arrow aimed straight at God.

Later, I woke to hear the woman sobbing, to see the bones of her spine nudging up against the silk of her petticoat—silk, not the rough cotton of our nightshirts. The sharp blades of her shoulders rose and fell, almost cutting the silk from underneath. She was sitting on the edge of her bed, hooked over, facing the wall. She had a cathedral dome for a sinus, her sobs lifted towards the roof like miserable angels of their own.

Are you alright? I asked.

She couldn't hear me.

Mrs, what's your name?

She stopped sobbing for a moment. *Di,* she said. *Lady Diana Reay.*

And what's the matter, Lady Reay?

They hate me, she said.

Who hates you?

All of them. They snigger behind their hands when they come to the library.

I'd heard of Lady Reay. She was an aspiring film actress from Sydney's North Shore. She didn't have to sew buttonholes on pillowcases or clean out the loos. When she was well, she got to be prison librarian. And she slept in the hospital wing whether she was ill or not, never in the cold stone cells below.

I guess you're a novelty, I said. *A lady from the north side of the harbour.*

Yes, in this place I'm even more of a novelty than the wife-killing man-woman.

My cancer throbbed, releasing a wave of nausea as it did. Lady Reay turned, saw my pale face, and lifted her hand to her mouth.

Oh, she said. *That's you? But you're just an old woman, you look nothing like a man.*

Thank you, I said. I supposed she'd meant it as a compliment. *You can call me Jean.*

She turned her back on me again, hung her head low. *I'm terrible at this.*

What, talking to people?

Yes, she said. *I suppose they are people.*

The light behind her dimmed then flared. Her wings quavered. She lifted her head to the pale green light coming in from the high window.

Finally, a storm, she said. *These are the wildest moments of my life, now.*

The first drop hit the roof, dragging others down with it. They rattled in the gutters like pebbles thrown from the clammy fists of little boys. The sound filled the ward, and it was the closest thing to silence you could hope for in a place like that.

Thank you, she said over the roar. *This has been a comfort to me, Jean. This little chat.*

When I was well enough I was allowed to meet Lady Reay in the library between two and four, before I was locked up with my conscience and supper for the night. Yes, Rita, we had a library and even a fernery, but it was hardly a holiday camp.

The library was where the prison's dust gathered to mate— under dustjackets, between pages—and if you opened a book it escaped into the air only to hang, unsure of where to go next. Lady Reay ordered me to sit at a table piled high with newspapers. On top: a photograph. Two men, one short and tense, one bulky as a rugby thug. I knew the angle of the small man's cocked fedora, remembered the feel of that sweaty hatband against my forehead. It was a picture of Harry Crawford leaving court with Detective Robson. The picture was only months old, but the small man in it was so different to the woman looking at it now, in her grey cotton dress, with grey hair long enough to curl behind the ear.

The next paper also boasted Harry Crawford's face. There were hundreds of newspapers open at pictures of Harry Crawford, and too many Crawfords, all of them slightly obscured. As Lady Reay proudly pointed out, some were from as far afield as Western Australia.

I closed my eyes to shut them out and felt Lady Reay watching for signs I might break down. Perhaps she was as mad as her lawyers had made out.

I think it's time you took charge of all this, don't you? she said.

I thought there was nothing more they could do to me now, but there was. They could take what life I'd lived and cut it to bits, then twist each bit into a sinister, mangled mess. These Crawfords lived their own lives, separate from mine. I looked at them from high up, outside of time and my own skin. I read syllable by syllable, each detail stretched out, stammered through, wrangled by the tongue. Lady Reay sat patiently by, her long breasts resting on the table, her neck craning over the paper in front of us.

The tree . . . al . . .

Trial, said Reay.

Trial off . . .

Of, said Reay.

The trial of Eugene Falleni, the . . .

Man-woman.

Man-woman . . . on . . . the k-ha . . . k-har . . .

Charge. C-h is ch.

Charge off . . .

Of—

It was exhausting, but I wanted to know what happened next. Would your mother testify against her own trouser-wearing mother? What would Lydia say, who had been Crawford's closest friend? There was a chance they'd say something different in the world of paper and ink.

Two weeks of reading lessons was all it took for the cancer to return. The pain was easy to ignore while scrubbing pans in the kitchen, but in the library Harry Crawford twisted the wedding band around his finger as he waited for his hearing to start, and I was standing in the dock again, searching for Lizzie's plump cheeks, her earnest Scottish brow, her gloved hands clutching the handle of her handbag propped on her lap as if it was holding her together. I never did see her for the parade of former friends taking it in turns to stand in my line of sight and speak as if Harry Crawford never minded their kids or shared a scotch; as if they'd never heard of loyalty. How eager they all were to be part of the show.

Soon I was down one end of the hospital wing again. The doctor was playing the role of a man at peace with the company of prisoners, but behind his composed face he was mentally checking that his wallet was safely out of reach of the grasping, grubby fingers of convict women.

Mrs . . . ? he checked his clipboard. *Falleni?*

Yes?

You will have to stop imbibing cleaning products if you want your condition to improve.

Doctor?

We've run tests, he said. *I've no idea how you've managed to smuggle mouthfuls of the stuff, considering we've a warder watching you twenty-four hours a day.*

A warder was, in fact, sitting in a hard-backed wooden chair where Reay's bed had been.

I panicked. Please, no. Reay can't be dead, too.

Where's Lady Reay?

Who? the warder asked. *No ladies here, love.*

Lady Diana Reay. Where is she?

Oh, her. The warder laughed and nodded at the neatly made bed under the window behind me. I could have sworn the room had flipped. *You mean Mrs Dorothy Mort? She's at the Coast Hospital seeing the head-shrinkers. Don't worry, she'll be back soon enough.*

The warder said Mrs Mort's expensive lawyers got her off a murder charge by claiming she was mad. The warder said she called herself Lady Reay and shot her doctor lover in the parlour of her Lindfield home. The warder said she spent Sundays reading poetry in bed because she didn't like the way the prison chaplain pronounced his vowels. The warder said she was highly educated. *And look where it got her.*

She said this as if I hadn't heard it all before.

I wondered if, when a woman with a nose like Reay's looked up, even just to make out the pattern of a stain on the ceiling, it'd be hard not to think she was giving herself airs. But was she giving them to herself, or did these airs swarm around her? She'd had advantages I'd never had. They said she was insane to excuse her for behaving like a member of the criminal class, but she was no more insane than me. If we were weighed in the justice scales, they'd be down on my side. I knew this, but right then I decided: me and Reay would be friends. There's something about a proud woman that gets me on my knees. I want to build pedestals for them, so they never have to see how grotty the world really is.

That night I dreamed of Daisy, for the first time since she left.

That house of ours was a cold dark place full of cheap furniture, but the way Daisy cleaned, it always looked brand new. My face looked back at me from every polished surface and I felt as if I couldn't sit down anywhere, or play music on the wireless in case it made the curtains flutter out of their folds. After a few drinks, she'd loosen up, and maybe sit on my lap on the front porch for the whole street to see. But something died in her after I lost my job; it didn't matter how many glasses of ale I poured, she sat stiff and cold as a frozen pig on the hook.

Hooked on songs my next wife was. After Daisy's icy silence, Lizzie was my barrel organ wife. She hummed tunes under her breath and our curtains always danced.

After Lizzie disappeared, I decided to build a wall inside myself, with music on one side, where it could play without me having to hear it.

But then sometimes it would come at me from the outside.

My wall was still hardening when the gangster Pretty Tilly organised the first concert for us. She treated her Long Bay stints like well-deserved R&R and this time she was going to have the best singers you'd ever pay two pounds to see in the posh theatres of Sydney.

Are ya coming to the concert? was all she asked anyone. *Are ya coming? Are ya coming? I got youse the next best thing to Dame Nellie, you'd be a fucken deadshit if ya didn't go.*

I shook my head. Too old for concerts.

Don't give me that shit, Jeanie.

I smiled, or the muscles tightened on my face—I couldn't tell the difference anymore.

Everyone had to go to the concert, even Lady Reay. If you didn't go, Pretty Tilly would take it personal. There'd be a mix-up in the kitchen: concrete dust in the hominy, gravy in your underwear.

I pulled a lot of strings to get these girls to come out here and sing to you, so you—

She coughed up a fruity one. At twenty-five, her voice was already curdled with phlegm.

Alright, I said. *What's the worst that could happen?*

Exactly.

She cocked her head, sweet as a puppy that just shat on the floor.

*

We sat on wooden benches straight as church pews and even the warders seemed uneasy. The skills of the theatre usherette were not part of their job descriptions.

Sit down and shut up, and if ya even think of heckling there'll be no more concerts, you got it?

That was Mavis, number-one warder. She seemed nervous that we might start enjoying ourselves—or, worse, that she might crack a smile, and the smile would lead to God knows what carefree emotions cartwheeling up to her tear ducts. What if she cried in front of us? Her eyes moved from face to face, looking for a whisper to catch.

Pretty Tilly had it worked so we got the most handsome couple currently treading the Tivoli boards. No nightclub tarts for us. They were decked out in diamonds and furs and really gave the first-timers something to daydream about. *You could dress like this too if you worked for me*, those furs said.

The man at the piano began with such gusto that the warder who played hymns winced with every clang, but the young girls up the front jiggled their shoulders in time to the sounds and looked at each other and clapped their hands.

Oh, this one! I love this one!

The look on Pretty Tilly's face was that of a shark who'd just cruised past a school of bream.

The singer's first notes quivered over our heads like bubbles frightened of popping and I was taken off to the Coogee Palace Aquarium with Lizzie, my hands small on her generous arse. She showed me how to dance and laughed at the stiffness of my shuffle across the floor. She'd wanted to be out amongst young things jostling across the dance floor, each woman the star of her own penny romance, and so Lizzie moved me through clusters of sideways glances, her own eyes stubbornly looking straight into mine. What could she see there? Only what she needed, because she smiled, her teeth all angles, her cheeks as round as puddings, in love with her Harry.

Her Harry. No one else's, not even mine.

Around us drifted schools of tropical fish dozing in water murky with their own shit. There must have been a thousand bright humans in that aquarium-walled room, the notes of the band floating up, up, up.

> *By the sea, by the sea, by the beautiful sea,*
> *You and me, you and me, oh how happy we'll be!*
> *When each wave comes a-rolling in,*
> *We will duck or swim,*
> *And we'll float and fool around the water.*
> *Over and under, and then up for air,*
> *Pa is rich, Ma is rich, so now what do we care?*
> *I love to be beside your side, beside the sea,*
> *Beside the seaside, by the beautiful sea.*

And afterwards, outside, eating ices with our toes in the sand, she said, *I'll look after you like a wife, but if they ever find you out I'll say I never knew.*

I should've told her that she was not the first, that Daisy had tried and not lasted the distance, but I only said, *Of course.*

A wave licked the sand along the shoreline and I thought of her toes, how they'd taste. My skin tingled like algae lighting up at night. *It will be different this time*, I told myself, because by then it was impossible to tell myself anything else.

That conversation eventually weathered away and it got to a point where I—then Harry—couldn't be sure it had happened.

I played to our story. Took care to strap on my member with the door locked, in case she stumbled in to see how alien the thing was that gave her pleasure. But she knew. Of course she knew. How could she not have known? She must have unlearned the knowledge, so she didn't have to feel so strange.

One year was all it took for her dream husband to turn real.

I'm pregnant! she said one morning, her teeth in an akimbo grin.

She went red because pregnant made her think of what we'd done in bed for her to end up that way.

She was almost telling the truth. We had both given each other a feeling as new and fragile as an egg. We spoke to each other tenderly, in case it should break.

Where was Lizzie now? I imagined her walking to the edge of that rickety pier at Coogee, the pylons collapsing under the heaviness left in her when they took me away.

I heard her howling in the foyer of the CIB from my corner of the overnight cell, two storeys below sea level.

Christ, an old drunk said. *Sounds like a whale giving birth up there.*

A girl pissing in the corner laughed.

I could've smacked their criminal heads together, but I was heavy myself and could not move.

Like Daisy before her, Lizzie was older than me. She knew more than me, but she didn't know how to swim. Maybe drowning for her would be like dancing for me: spinning delirious past the blank stares of fish.

*

By the sea, by the sea, by the beautiful sea / You and me, you and me, oh! How happy we'll be, the couple sang last. The skin beneath my eyes began to twitch. A warder was watching. Don't cry. Don't cry now.

Talentless tarts, Lady Reay said on our way out of the hall. All the same it took me two days to recover. Sentimental songs are unnatural spells. They make your blood flow backwards, your memories start speaking in tongues. I was not strong enough for Pretty Tilly's concerts.

What's the worst that could happen? I'd asked.

Two wives dead, over and over. That's all.

When I next made it to the library, Reay pulled me behind the library shelves to say she had news. They wanted to take a piece of her brain away, she said.

You're not going to let them, are you? I was worried by the look of wonderment on her face.

Of course I am, she said, *if it means they'll let me out.*

But will it turn you into a vegetable?

Perhaps, she said, *but I don't have much to lose anymore.*

They discussed Reay's operation in the press, and a woman recently released thought she'd contribute by gabbing about Mrs Mort's special treatment in gaol. After that they were even more eager for bits of her brain, but not so keen on the idea of letting her loose. When they told her she wouldn't be released—not even to gain strength before her operation or to recover afterwards—she flat out refused to let them take any of her brain, not a single grey worm of it.

She found me tugging at weeds in the fernery and shouted at me as I did, but the fierceness of her conviction was too strong for her delicate frame and she looked about to break.

They shan't do it. What's the benefit to me? she said. *That I might not become so drearily bored staring at the walls of the prison hospital, day in day out? I would rather be an hysteric in this place; at least it gives me plenty to think about.*

I sprayed a fern with pesticide, and Reay enjoyed the nervous release of a sneeze.

Lovely, she said, suddenly calm. *Thank you, Jean, I needed that.*

A psychiatrist came, and Mr Mort, her husband, and an old family doctor who had stitched up the heads of her brother and mother after her father had attacked them with the blunt end of an axe. She decided to have a cold when they came to talk her into the operation. She wanted them to find her in bed, because it gave her an opportunity to wear her navy kimono with the pink irises. The men fluffed her pillow and asked the warders how she was. After they left she was right as rain, not a sniffle in sight.

You see, there is a taint, Reay whispered to me in the exercise yard.

We were doing our stretches. All of us in grey cotton, Reay in silk. Occasionally she joined in.

I never was mad until my father woke up that night, and hacked into Mother's head with the axe, she said, arms up straight as a pole. *It was the fear of madness that finally pushed me over the edge. When you stare straight into the eyes of whatever it is you are most afraid of becoming, you start emulating it, despite yourself.* The warder leading us through our routine had one leg forward. She lunged and we did too, as far as our stiff hips let us go. *They always said I had my father's eyebrows,* Reay said. *That's all I could think of when they told me what he'd done. I should have been grieving, or crying, but I was thinking of his eyebrows.*

Above us, the blue sky stretched up into forever. From where we lunged in the exercise yard, it looked like that was all there was beyond the prison walls. I wondered if her father thought he was doing his family a favour, slicing off the tops of their heads so they could find release.

But then, in the library, she told me she'd changed her mind again. She'd been reading plays, she said, and had an epiphany. *It was all an act*, she said. *My fainting at my trial, my muttering about world trips and babies. And yet the strangest thing began to happen. I couldn't tell the difference anymore between acting and its opposite. Or, rather, I realised I didn't know what its opposite was. Truly, the only time one is not acting is when one is out cold, and that is only because one has no memory of it. Even whilst lightly sleeping one plays picture shows behind the eyelids.* She took me by the hands. *Jean, don't you see? If everything is acting, then nothing is genuine. Or, rather, everything acted is all that is genuine. So perhaps I am as mad as I have affected to be. And by that logic, yes, they should take a piece of my brain.*

They eventually did operate on Reay. They came at night and took her to the Coast Hospital in a slick black motorcar. She was gone for two weeks, and when she came back she did nothing but sleep for months. I missed her ibis-beak nose, her pendulum breasts, her knees like the knees on a giraffe. I missed her coolly watching on as I worked like every other prisoner in the place, but I had my own ghosts to worry about. No one was allowed to distract her, the library was closed, and even the other prisoners stopped slagging her off behind her back. Most of us resented the special attention she received, that was true, but the special attention of psychiatrists was something no one envied.

In the fernery, I squashed the bright green caterpillars between finger and thumb, and let the slaters roam free. To be brown or grey, I thought, is not such a terrible fate.

Ever since the concert I hadn't been sleeping right. And the problem with not sleeping right in a place where every day is the same is that days take on the feel of dreams, and dreams become as dull as days. One moment no longer leads to another; it threads back into itself, from the future into the past, like the backstitch on Lady Reay's curtains.

I was in the prison fernery, with a frond curled around my finger. A currawong descended from the sky. He'd found something in the tree fern—a matted feathery thing. Walking closer, I could see that it was the nest of a small bird; walking closer still, I could see how the feathers came to a smooth red point, as if they'd been dipped in blood. The currawong cocked his head, and I knew what he was about to do before he did it. He took the nest in his beak and tore at it. He shook the pieces away, gripped the nest and, eyeing me, tore at it again. I couldn't see any reason for the bird to do this. Unless, of course, it had been his own nest.

To start again, Rita, I'll start with you.

I'd known you were about to be born because your mother wrote, asking if I was on a prison pension and if so could I help her out the way a mother should when her daughter's up the duff. Well I wasn't, and I couldn't, but I would've liked to see her nonetheless.

I planted a sapling in the fernery the day you were born and spoiled the fragile thing nearly to death with all the chicken shit it could absorb into the threads of its roots.

If it sprouted a new leaf, I imagined you had likewise grown a tooth.

You wouldn't be that little now.

By now you can probably walk and talk, can probably read and write. My God, I've never stopped to think, but you'd be, what, fifteen? Sixteen? Maybe you are married! Don't get married, Rita. You'll only end up having visions of your spouse lying dead in every room of the house. I tried to say as much to your mother, but she never did listen.

Josephine, my changeable daughter. I can't shake the sweet smell of pigs' innards from the memory of her. She looked like a page two girl from the magazines, even in a blood-smeared apron with her hair shoved up under a net. There was a rage in her that crackled under the skin, like a wireless being tuned. She hadn't found a frequency that made her sing, but the crackle kept her sharp for men and girlfriends eager to have adventures they could blame on a bad influence. One week she'd be living in Marrickville, another in Pyrmont, another in Darlington, always chasing that pig Arthur. He was a gunner in the navy, she said. He got his charm from the same sea she thought her father vanished into—it was too late to tell her anything different.

Who was my dad? she asked when she was little. We delivered laundry to the houses around Double Bay and the driving was long, the questions inevitable.

I told her about the steamer that went the wrong way to Sydney—from Wellington via London. I told her I saw the Queen at her silver jubilee, and that she looked like an old toad dressed up in lace and a hoop skirt big enough to hide a family of twelve.

Tell me who he was, she said, and I said I thought England would've been everything New Zealand only dreamed it could be, because anyone who was from there looked at you all smug if you said you were from anywhere else. They shared a secret, those people, a special mark in their blood. But when I got there it turned out to be a vague, grey country where the rain didn't fall so much as hover above the ground. Children worked in factories and everyone got by on bread and dripping if anything at all, unless you were the Queen. In that case, you got by on children basted in bacon fat. It was no wonder half of England came to live on the far side of the world, where the sky was big and bold and there was space enough to be whoever you damn well wanted to be.

That's not true, she said. *You never visited the Queen.*

You bet I did, I said.

She sulked, so I told her about the island traders I met in the Pacific on the way back; I told her about how they dived for pearls when pearls were still plentiful and offered themselves up in clams the size of dinner plates.

Just tell me his name, then, she said, exhausted, because by then we had arrived at a house and she knew I'd use the unloading of sheets as an excuse to change the subject.

Martello, I said. *Captain Martello.* It was a grand-sounding name, just like she would've wanted.

A name was never enough.

Even after she fell in love with Arthur, the idea of him at least, she had to know the sight of her could wind every man in the street. If not, something needed fixing. Her hem was too low. Her feet too flat. The sheen of her eyes too dull.

Nina, she announced when we worked side by side in the meat-works, *I'm gonna take up a typing career.*

Yeah? I said. Her hands were gloved in pig grease. I couldn't imagine them any other way.

Yes, she said, throwing a scrap of skin on the floor. *Why don't you ever believe me?*

There was no use responding. I wanted to believe her, which was almost as good, but it was never good enough.

Those were our closest years. She couldn't leave in a huff; we could only look at the frozen meat as we passed it under the saw.

She never did come to visit me in gaol. Our love, if you could call it that, was a mess of finger-pointing, fierce loyalty and silence.

I wished we could start again.

The beginning is a hard place to start. And now my toes are freezing and, try as I might, I can't warm them, can't even wiggle them. I can feel the cold skin of them, but can't see it, can't shift it. My toes must have turned blue by now, they must be smoking like dry ice. You'd think a nurse would notice the smoke, notice the serious reduction in temperature my toes have caused in the ward. I can feel all this, but I can't move a muscle.

A muscle. A twitch of that tiny blue muscle under her flat foot. She hadn't been able to move then, either, I was holding the pillow down that hard, but then that twitch of her muscle. It was so particular. She wasn't a baby anymore, she was a person, my daughter—a very particular person—and when I let the pillow go, her chest flooded with life.

Now it aches, my chest. There is phlegm building up behind my sternum, but I can't cough, can't shift it. I'm drowning in battlefield mud. *Suck it out of me*, I want to say, but I can't, and even if I could they wouldn't listen.

Listen, I'd say to her now, instead of holding the pillow down. *Listen, we can work it out together. I can be the father you always wanted. Listen, stop crying, let me paint him for you:*

He'll be a strong man. He'll be small, sure, but let's call him lithe. He'll have delicate features—let's call them boyish. He won't be able to read a word, but you can be in charge whenever there's some reading to be done.

In return, he'll show you how to fend for yourself in a world that wants you to cower.

I remember the day I found out your mother had died. It was hot at Long Bay, and for all her airs and graces, Lady Reay smelled ripe. In the library, the newspapers crackled to the touch. It was too hot to talk, so I didn't think much of Reay's silence when she set down a newspaper open at the obituaries. A strange choice for a reading lesson I thought, until I saw her name:

Whitby, Josephine Rita.
Beloved wife of Arthur. 26.

Tuberculosis, they said. She suffocated to death.

In the fernery, your leaves curled up, clutching at nothing but air.

*

Over the months that followed, I found it was best to stay out of the way of other people, in case they reminded me of someone or something or stirred the silt that had gathered at the pit of my stomach. Journalists asked after me at the front desk and the warders met their questions with blank stares the way I'd suggested. *Scare the vultures off with silence*, I'd said. *I don't know what to tell them, and they'll only write the story the way they want anyway.*

Lady Reay played a very different game. She had her friends write to the papers and anyone else important enough to be effective. They gave details—of her illness, prison life, how she was struggling—and gradually the accumulation of words turned like a flock of gulls on the wind. She was no longer a middle-class murderess, she was a fragile woman wrongly incarcerated, and lo and behold she was released.

I began to wet myself. Little drops that only came out when I coughed, but I was coughing a great deal at the time.

Poor dear, the warders said as I bundled up my damp bedding in the morning, *she's lost another queer chook and now she's falling apart.*

They gave me Reay's library job to cheer me up. What they didn't know is I wasn't pining for Reay. I was furious. She'd killed her lover just as I'd supposedly done. The difference was, there was no doubt at all she had done it. The pieces of her story lined up, there were no jarring contradictions. She was a spoiled brat who couldn't have the man she wanted, and so she shot him twice in the brain and through the heart as well. Nine years later she was released. *Prison is a great leveller*, the warders used to say, marvelling at my friendship with Reay. At first I believed them, but after seeing how easily she was released, I wasn't so sure.

A safety net followed her wherever she went. She could mess up, even murder a man, and she'd still wind up relaxing in her Mosman garden afterwards, surrounded by lavender and bees.

Perhaps it's time to tell them how it happened, Mavis said.

And how was that?

You know, she said. *Whatever it needs to have been to get you out before you die.*

I shrugged.

Think of your granddaughter, she said. *Wouldn't you like to see her?*

Right then. What it needs to have been.

When the police showed me where the burned woman was found, I was supposed to remember the long walk through the scrub. Why this spot for the picnic? Had I convinced myself the smell wouldn't be streaming from the chimneys of the cornflour mills upriver because it was a long weekend? Did I choose that spot because I thought I could lift her into one of the furnaces at the paper mills nearby?

Who planned it all: the picnic, the fire, the direction of the wind?

Wouldn't I like to know.

Wouldn't they just kill to know.

I told the warders: Alright, I'll try to talk. For Rita, you understand.

The first man who came was a doctor I'd never met before. He sat awkwardly in the reception room, beside a warder who was trying not to smile at his awkwardness.

I told him the parts of my story I could remember—mainly things I'd read about in the papers. I assumed they were the things people wanted to hear, but he seemed unimpressed, like he'd heard it all before.

Why are you here, then? I might have asked him.

He blundered through some sentences. Something about sending me back home.

And where is that?

He spoke slowly, in a clipped Italian learned from books. *Italia, avrei pensato . . . ?*

My Italian is very rusty, I said. *Seeing as I left the place when I was two.*

He lowered his notebook. *Mr Coyle arranged the visit,* he said.

I said nothing.

You know, the prosecuting lawyer in your trial?

How could I forget.

I hope that hasn't put you off speaking to me?

My cell's stone walls were warmer company.

Coyle meant for no harm to come to you, he said. *He feels sorry. He was only doing his job.*

Oh really? What a relief.

Hours later, the doctor returned in my sleep.

Would your faces like the chance to be killed? he asked.

The offer seemed sensible enough.

We're all going to die sooner or later. Probably when we least expect it. Would they prefer to control the timing of their deaths? To take the element of uncertainty away from the fear of their inevitable end?

To my surprise, all my faces said yes. I sensed relief in their voices, maybe guilt for letting the care between us lapse. I felt responsible then, for the nature of their deaths, and suddenly anxious that I had not quizzed the doctor enough. How would our lives end? Would we be in pain?

When the doctor proposed the plan to me—the anatomy department was struggling to get its hands on bodies these days—it seemed like a brave experiment. I didn't understand the practical reality until I saw Tally Ho, Crawford, Jack, Gene, Nina, all behind soundproofed glass, having our heads spliced open and the skin stripped from our scalps and necks while we were still alive. Their skin was elastic, unreal, it stretched for ages before it finally snapped. What was real was the horror in our faces.

In the morning, all I could see were bodies twisting in the fern fronds, vertebrae in the yellowed books stacked on the library shelves.

Try again, Mavis said.

The next man's card read: *Harry Cox, Journalist.* What a name. Like Harry Crawford but with multiple cocks. I imagined them squirming in his pants like Medusa's head as he sat opposite, holding his smile just out of reach.

It was a charming smile, full of teeth that were brighter than teeth, the way fishing lures are brighter than fish.

Why did you do it? he asked.

I had no choice.

He couldn't scribble in his notebook fast enough.

Wait a tick, I said. *Why did I do what? Dress as a man?*

Hmm? he said, half listening, still writing. *So, you came to Australia on a Norwegian barque . . .*

Did I? This was news to me.

Tell me a little about your time at sea . . .

My time at sea? I tried a smile. *Haven't I lived most of my life at sea?*

In his notebook he wrote: *At sea—six years.*

What I'd wanted to tell Harry Cox and his multiple cocks is this:

I was once a partner in a laundry business with a woman my family knew. Mrs D'Angelis ran the shop while I carted starched linen around Double Bay with my daughter by my side. Because we worked separately, the old woman didn't see how I slogged. She thought she was a tortoise, carrying the weight of the business on her back. Her limbs swelled in the steam until they looked like loose-skinned sausages that jiggled when she walked. This was evidence, she moaned, that she was doing all the work. She didn't count the work of the black girls from Parramatta. She only noticed them when something went missing, or when they themselves disappeared.

Everything was in her name: the house, the laundry, my daughter's future. *Sit down and write a will*, I urged her, and she did, but the old hag never signed it. When she eventually kicked the bucket, she did so instantly, pulling a string of starched sheets down as she went. They sat around her, as stiff as sugared egg whites, and sweated in the heat.

As a mother with no husband, no work and nothing to any of my names, what else could I do but try on the suits her dead husband left in their wardrobe? They were moth-nibbled and old, but they fit like skin. Wouldn't you have done that, Rita? If I'd stayed a woman I'd have earned half the wages of a man. I had two mouths to feed. It was simple maths.

But Mr Cox didn't ask the right questions, so he never heard any of that.

The next journalist met me in a room empty of furniture or decoration, save for a big table, two chairs, and a long form against the wall. I entered the room and waited for instruction. Asked by a distant warder's voice to take a chair, I chose the form. I wanted to lean against the wall, did not want my back exposed to the unpredictable hands of others.

The journalist noted my choice, and when I pulled a pink handkerchief from my pocket, it was not wasted on him.

J.D. Corbett was clean-shaven, his cheeks and chin still red from the razor. He smelled of soap and his eyes were a soft gravy brown—a comfortable brown, though he couldn't have been more uncomfortable in his scratchy suit. I wondered for a moment if he'd rather be wearing a dress.

What do you miss most? he asked. *George Street? The shops? The lights scrawling across the harbour?*

He asked me these questions and I forgot who was supposed to be wringing whose heart.

Please help me, I said. *I have no friends, no money, no influence.*

He was trying to believe me. He nodded a concerned nod.

I was convicted on circumstantial evidence, I said. *I was what other people made me.*

But sitting on either side of that large table we were making each other up as we danced around what we thought the other wanted us to say.

I told J.D. Corbett that soon after I lost my job, I found Daisy drinking at home. Maybe she hadn't drunk as much as I thought, but I knew we wouldn't make rent and she was at the table with her feet up, swishing a nip of gin as if she were the landed gentry. I didn't hold back and said she should go off with that plumber I heard she was so keen on if she was going to drink like that and I tried to remember the rest of our conversation but my memory wouldn't give it over. I know I went for a walk to Five Dock Bay and watched the prawns get frisky in the moonlight and when I came back half her clothes and she herself were gone.

After three days of waiting, I sold up the furniture and took her boy and together we went to lodgings. I know I should have gone to the police, but I hoped she'd come back after that plumber had had it up to here with her drinking too. Also, I worried (and I was right) that if the police got one whiff of the breasts under my suit they'd make up hidden murderous agendas to go with them.

It was hard living with her boy because he looked so much like her, and asked questions about her, none of which I could answer. He began to be like a flea, biting at the one sore over and over, so we went our separate ways after a time.

Have you noticed that when you assume people think you are guilty, you answer their questions in the manner of someone who is guilty? When I was a kid someone stole the scissors from Sister Katherine's desk, and even though I didn't steal them I thought, *They will think I did*, so I said in a loud voice, *I WONDER WHO DID THAT? GOSH I'M GLAD IT WASN'T ME*, after which everyone, of course, decided it was.

This is what it was like after Daisy went away. Neighbours asked after her, so did old friends. I could see that if I said, *I don't know where she is*, they'd think I was lying, so I tried to sound as though I knew where she went. To one woman I mentioned she'd gone to North Sydney, to another I said she'd left with the plumber from Balmain. I couldn't admit I knew nothing about my wife—where she'd want to go, and who with.

Three years later the police dragged me out of the cellar at the Empire Hotel to tell me I had murdered her, then locked me up and asked again and again: *What happened?* When I didn't say anything, they worked out a past for me, and my God it was convincing. I began to wonder if it was more convincing than the truth.

They took me to a hallway in a building without signs and held me against the closed door of a room. I could hear hammering and sawing inside. Eventually they opened the door and lead me to a long box on a high table. The air was thick with dust and the dank smell of underground animals. Inside the box I caught glimpses of bone through traces of dirt and I was surprised by the whiteness of her skeleton despite the worms and clumps of clay and smell of rot. It was as white as the coats of the doctors who leaned with metal instruments clanking at the end of their hands.

The detectives held my face up to the hollow eye sockets and toothless grin of a skull. *This is the woman you murdered*, they said. They had me by the neck so I couldn't look away. I closed my eyes but that grin burned red through my eyelids. Its toothless bone mouth was open wide in an expression of delirious joy. *I've got you now!* it seemed to say. *They'll never let a freak like you off the hook!*

The story made *Smith's Weekly*, page one. Mavis brought it to the library and in her best out-loud voice she read: *To-day Eugene Fallini, pink handkerchief in her gnarled hand, makes a humble, feminine gesture of entreaty. She beseeches her freedom. She does not want to die in gaol . . .*

I had them read me the article again and again. I committed the words to memory. All week I fluttered the handkerchief for show, using it to wipe the corners of my mouth to great imaginary applause, but one week revealed that the article had a very different effect to the one I'd hoped for.

Young Birkett and the detectives had spent the past ten years sitting in a circle, stewing on their rage, until I emerged between their blazing lines of sight, more animal than a salivating werewolf of the steppes. *Eugene Falleni, that murderous human monster* . . . the *Truth* wrote on their behalf. *This harsh-voiced, obscene-tongued, evil-featured person* . . . they went on to say, before declaring that it was in the interests of justice that I have no right whatever to be allowed loose amongst society again.

As I read, I felt something harden behind my sternum. Like a tree, I was growing a layer of brittle wood around my green core. I coughed up whatever was left. It came out thick and yellow, and eventually I could no longer walk.

When the air was drier they wheeled me out into the fernery. Sitting beneath the tree fern was a short, stocky man with a landslide chin and thick glasses. He was Italian, and you could see that, like me, he was haunted by some aspect of himself he wanted to cut out and burn. He asked me questions I would've answered, but the coughing had changed my voice into the echo of a voice, heard at the end of a drain.

One week later, Joe Lamaro, son of Italian fruit vendors and Attorney-General, took pity and announced my release.

I should have been overjoyed, but I couldn't eat my hominy the morning of my release.

Don't be nervous, Jean, Mavis said, watching me move my spoon through the glop. *What's the worst that could happen?*

Outside the prison gates, the journalists who followed me from court would be crouching behind their flashbulbs. Their beards long, their hair grey, they'd be waiting to solve the riddles in the story of their careers, drafted ten years back and set aside until this very moment. *Why did you kill her? Who is your daughter's father? Were you raped, is that why you are the way you are?* The worst that could happen was that they'd begin to swarm, reaching for bits they could keep in formaldehyde. A tooth, an eyeball. *Is the iris grey or hazel?* They'd ask their colleagues. Some would say hazel and some would say grey. An argument would ensue. The story of the eyeball's host would be told—*She was a man and a woman at the same time!*—until news would be received of a man, this time, in a dress. They'd rush to find him, leaving the rest of me to feed the currawongs and feral cats. That was the worst that could happen.

But when I walked through the prison gates it was already dark. I passed an old, veiled woman. Her hands gripped a plate of homemade biscuits. I smiled as she passed, but she didn't notice. I checked my hand—I was not invisible—and looked up to see my face reflected in the window of a brand-new automobile parked half up on the kerb. I'd seen my face in the prison mirror and hadn't paid much attention. But here, in the stark electric street-light, I looked like a woman I did not recognise.

From the forehead down my reflected face peeled away, revealing the face of another woman behind the glass. It was the woman they called the Silver Lining, rolling down her window. A nervous smile flashed across her face.

Hello, Jean, said another woman, leaning across from the front seat. As she waved, her white-gloved fingers looked like tentacles feeling around for a meal. It was Lady Reay, gloved and hatted and ready to collect me for 'rehabilitation' at her friend the Silver Lining's house. *I would have hosted you myself,* Reay said, *but Mr Mort tries to ensure we lead an unexciting life.*

They gave me the front passenger seat so I could sit next to Reay—or Dorri, as her friends called her. I hadn't seen her in over a year, but she was not making eye contact with me. I wanted to touch her hand resting on the gearstick, but she tugged it and the clutch rasped as if gasping for breath. It was a miracle anyone let her drive, considering what they'd done to her. But she was still Reay, just better-dressed and duller in the eyes.

She instructed us to stay quiet and slump down in the seats to be out of view of the prying eyes of journalists. *The plan is,* Reay said, pulling off the kerb, *to throw them off our scent.* She was convinced the road was lined with journalists hiding in the shadows behind trees. She assured us it was best to drive along the road closest to the sea, where the fierce onshore wind meant no trees could ever grow, and thus no journalists could hide behind the trunks of said trees in order to take down the coordinates of her car at every turn.

Are you sure you've driven one of these before? the Silver Lining asked, gripping her seat with two hands.

Reay's headlights set the pupils of a possum alight and for a moment we glimpsed the hell that burned inside the furry shell of its body.

Thump.

The Silver Lining screamed. *Oh, Dorri, was that a cat?*

No dear, just a possum.

Oh.

We were all rattled after that, and when white light could be seen, an anaemic dawn rising above the curve of the road, Reay switched off the headlights and turned into the nearest laneway too sharply. She mounted the kerb and winded a postbox. Headlights swung past, and I could feel the Silver Lining analysing the moving angles of my profile as they did. I tensed my jaw to give it a more masculine edge and made that sound men make when they clear their throats to help her see how I could have been the man-woman after all, and she had not been jilted.

Yes, Reay said, starting up the motorcar again, *hard to imagine how anyone ever took her for a man, isn't it?*

The Silver Lining quickly turned to look at the lights out of the window.

The lights. My God, the lights. Since I'd been inside Long Bay the city had been electrified. The whole place was trying to dazzle us. What was it trying to hide?

The curtains in the Silver Lining's house were embroidered with flowers of a dangerous size—the kind you might find in a rainforest, baring teeth. The fabric of the curtains was so heavy that even if you'd been standing in the room in the middle of the day, you'd never have known. At night, the electric lamps were left on and the hours hummed along in a dim haze. In that house, time evaporated into the high ceilings. The carpet looked as if it had never been stepped on, the lounge never sat on, and the moment a person moved, a half-caste girl materialised from the shadows to erase any trace of the movement.

The madness of the rich was more sinister and ordinary than I'd first suspected. When I saw that my shoelace was undone, the Silver Lining nudged the girl until she said, *Here, Mrs Ford, let me do that.*

It's fine, I said. *I can tie my own shoelaces.* And with that the girl melted back into the shadows.

There were black girls at Long Bay—more than I'd ever met in the outside world. Most of them had been locked up for no reason at all. The Silver Lining collected them when they were released, though they often vanished in the night, never to return, not even for their pay. *It's a common problem*, she said. *Those girls are like cats; you can make up a warm bed for them, but they are determined to wander off wailing in the night to sleep wherever they want.*

I lay awake that night thinking of all the half-caste girls in the wealthy houses across Sydney, rising from their beds and vanishing the way the black girl had done at the laundry in Double Bay. Where did she end up? The police couldn't find her, but they never looked that hard. Years later they became convinced she'd been my first victim; that I'd boiled her in the laundry tubs and turned her into glue.

How do the wandering girls know where to go? It bothers people that there is no fixed place. When dawn broke, I thought I saw a girl close the door behind her, and turned to see that my clothes had been replaced with a dress—somewhere between blue and green—and a possum-skin stole. I wanted to ask the girl if she knew a black girl who'd worked in a laundry in Double Bay, but I could hear the girl pad down the hall and I thought how stupid of me, to think they all know each other.

I wondered what was worse—to be invisible, or to become the kind of thick-skinned person who could ignore what they didn't want to see. Both were reason enough to leave, and I packed the following day.

Don't be a fool, the Silver Lining said over her boiled egg. *You've a house over your head, free meals, women who care for you. Where on earth will you go?*

No fixed address, I said.

She eyed me from across the table with a pitying look. I was too old and stubborn to change the way she'd hoped.

Rita, did you ever see an old woman watch you from the street? I was on my way to collect you when I left the Silver Lining's place, only once I was outside the convent gate I couldn't move. You were in the yard—there was no doubt it was you. Your dark curls were springing in all directions as you leaped over a statue of Our Lady without running up to it first. I thought to myself: *You're no granny for her, Jean Ford. She is at the beginning, she could go anywhere from here, and better ways than you ever did.* How would I begin to explain where I'd been? I could blame Arthur for leaving you with the nuns, but I'd have to say something for myself, too, and I couldn't say anything good. Once you'd run inside, I turned and walked back to the railway station. *I should make something of myself first,* I thought. *I should be the sort of granny a girl wouldn't be ashamed to climb all over.*

It's now many years later, but I am something. I was a boarder at first. Then I cleaned the boarding house instead of paying rent. And then I cleaned for pay, and cooked too, and fixed the pipes when they were leaking. I scrimped and saved until I could afford to take up the lease on my own. I spruced it up, and offered clean, no-fuss housing at affordable rates. I kept myself to myself and my tenants kept to their rooms.

Luckily no one at my boarding house ever looked at the legs of the kitchen table. If they did, they might've noticed how one leg resembled the leg of my first wife. It tapped its toes occasionally, demanding to be noticed, until I kicked it in the shin. There was quite a collection of bruises up that leg, all at different stages of the healing process. Some were blue, some were plum purple, some were yellow. Some were the colour of the sky before a storm. My guests never noticed the table leg, but they noticed the sound of my shoe thumping bone. I knew what they thought. I'd seen their eyes slide from side to side in their heads, looking at me then looking at each other. It got so I was always standing in front of the table, trying to shield the leg from view. *I can't go on like this*, I thought, and I sold the business with the intention of moving us to a place where table legs look like table legs, and grandmothers can live with granddaughters without any questions asked.

One hundred pounds seemed to be enough for a new life. I had it in my purse today—was it today?—leaving the bank, crossing Oxford Street, thinking: *How will I find her?* Then two shrieks in quick succession. A cockatoo above. I looked, remembering another I had seen. An automobile braked. The face of the driver rushed at me from a past no longer mine. I wondered if it was him as the car hit my hip and I flew back, carried by a tidal wave to smack my head against the—what was it?—against the side rail of the ship, and there's Horse tickling me, although it isn't a game anymore, is it?

Your grandfather's face. Dates. Names are slipping.

Drunk. At sea. Only paying attention to our bodies and the urges that made them paw flesh, we came to life in the places the other had touched. I pinned him down. He tried to roll me over, but he was drunker, or I was stronger—not in terms of muscle, in terms of fight. I had his hips gripped between my knees, his penis in my palm. *This is why I love you*, he mumbled. *You take matters into your own hands.* It looked like a large purple mushroom, alien to us both. It grew out of black hair that could have been mine or could have been his, and when I touched it I felt the nerves spark up its length, as if they had been mine.

—Detective Sergeant Watkins of the Central Police. This is the woman?

—Yes, Detective, but I'm afraid—

—A finger missing on her left hand. How old did you say she was?

—It's hard to say. She had one hundred pounds on her. No identification.

—Thank you, Sister. We'll handle the body from here.

AUTHOR'S NOTE

In 2005, Sydney's Justice & Police Museum hosted *City of Shadows*, an exhibition of early twentieth-century police photographs recovered from a flooded warehouse. Many of the accompanying files that would have given the photographs context had been lost, so they were mostly selected for their provocative compositions, the half-stories they told and the eerie, alter-Sydney they invoked.

Visiting the exhibition was like witnessing a séance. From the walls of the museum, forgotten ghosts of the city gazed through us. For many of the photographs' subjects, this would have been the only time in their lives they'd been photographed, and so— despite the trauma of their recent arrest—they'd made the most of it, dressing in their best clothes, possibly performing their role as criminal for a camera associated with the burgeoning popular art form of the movies. Even in the mugshots we did not see the deadpan expressions we have come to expect; instead we saw emotion—either performed, or caught when the subject was off guard.

I left the exhibition with the accompanying book, and later poured over the photographs for traces of suburbs I thought I knew. One picture in particular captured my attention: a mugshot of a man in a cheap suit and tie, his short hair combed into a sideways part. What struck me most was the melancholy that haunted the man's eyes. He seemed to be performing his normalcy, not his criminality, and only just managing to hold himself together.

I flipped to the back of the book to read a brief footnote:

Eugenie Falleni, 1920, Central cells. When hotel cleaner 'Harry Leon Crawford' was arrested and charged with the murder of his wife three years earlier, he was revealed to be in fact Eugenie Falleni—a woman and mother who had been passing as a male since 1899 . . .

Turning back to the portrait of the sad man, his face—or my perception of his face—morphed into that of a woman's. But in the moment that he, the sad man, morphed into she, the 'cross-dressing murderer', I have to admit that the thrill I felt was associated with my own jolt in perception, like the moment Escher's black birds turn into white birds, flying in the opposite direction. The portrait was of an indeterminate person: an unstable man and a reluctant woman at the same time. One look at Falleni's harrowed expression, however, and the thrill quickly turned into a chill. What would it have been like, to cause these jolts in perception? What would it be like to live your life oscillating between the different roles others expected to see?

Half Wild is a work of fiction written through and around historical sources related to the various lives of Eugenia Falleni (1875–1938). Throughout my research, I have tried to get the facts of Falleni's story as straight as I can. For me, it's been important to remember how my city *actually* behaved in the presence of someone who called our assumptions into question. The problem is, genuine facts have been hard to come by, and in their place I have often found elusive, shape-shifting, fact-seeming fabrications. But these fabrications have proven just as revealing about our past: they show us what we, as readers and writers, have *wished* to believe is true about the people we struggle to understand.

When so much of Falleni's story is uncertain, a range of narrative scenarios opens up. Many of these imagined scenarios have already been recorded as 'fact' by eager journalists of the 1920s, and continue to be referenced as credible to this day. I have chosen a slightly different tack. My challenge has been to turn these occasionally contradictory scenarios into a narrative, without collapsing them down into yet another singular, factually problematic, account of 'what happened' to Falleni.

I do not claim to speak on behalf of Falleni with any authority, and although I have, at times, written from Falleni's various points of view, these voices are imaginings, performances, and attempts at creating an empathetic bridge between then and now, archives and feeling, Falleni and us.

In order to accommodate contradictory possibilities, I have refracted Falleni's story by dividing the novel into four parts. Each part is informed by a selection of sources, although the sources that inform different parts might contradict each other. 'Who She'd Like To Be' is based on Suzanne Falkiner's interviews with Falleni's New Zealander friends and family, as well as newspaper articles that appeared in the New Zealand papers of the late nineteenth century. 'As Far As He Can Remember' is based on Harry Crawford's initial statement to police. 'To All Outside Appearances, At Least' relies primarily on the transcript of Falleni's trial for its foundation, while 'Some Lower Animal' uses Falleni's *Smith's Weekly* interview as its foundation. In it 'Eugene Fallini' [sic] protested her innocence, and provided her own version of what took place over the long weekend of October 1917. No one part is intended to be presented as 'more accurate' or even 'more probable' than the others, only more appropriate to the perspectives from which they're told.

While I have laid out all the facts as far as I could determine them, I have also borrowed from sources that themselves were partially invented, and have invented my own newspaper article (guess which one!) and framed it as a source. I don't do this to trick you, but to niggle at the borders of truth and narrative flourish in fiction that presents itself as fact. Also, to keep you asking questions.

Amelia Grey is an invention of mine, although according to New Zealand newspapers, a friend did report Falleni to the Salvation Army after seeing her outside the Wellington Opera House 'in male attire'. Harry Crawford, the stevedore and butcher boy in New Zealand, is also an invention, although it is true that a stevedore called Harry Crawford was murdered by a man named Raines in a drunken brawl shortly before Falleni left for Australia. Another Harry Crawford, 'Ethiopian song and dance artist and legmania champion of the world', toured New Zealand in the late nineteenth century. Fuckit and Buckit are inventions, although school records and histories indicate that the girls were notoriously 'more crude' than the boys at Newtown Public School in the late nineteenth century. Horse is also an invention, although a Horatio de Courcey Martelli (sometimes misprinted Martello in newspapers of the time) was born in Timaru, New Zealand, in 1876, and worked on sailing ships between New Zealand and London before becoming the third mate for the Eastern and Australian Steamship Company in 1897, around the same time that Falleni left New Zealand. His sister's name was Rita (Josephine's middle name, and her daughter's name), and he later became a captain and harbourmaster in Hobart. Beyond these coincidences, there is no evidence to suggest that he is Josephine's father, let alone that he committed rape. I doubt his sister's name would have been carried over to his daughter and granddaughter if that had been the case, but it is possible.

Almost all other character names (including Captain Gunion) have been drawn from sources, and while I have often taken dialogue and small biographical details verbatim from these sources, this is where the likeness between my representations and their warm-blooded referents ends; I cannot vouch for having accurately captured what they thought and felt. If I have caused any offence to living members of their families, I sincerely apologise.

In the interests of keeping the novel relatively succinct, I have left out Falleni's appearance at the Masterton court for vagrancy (read: trying to obtain work as a man) before Falleni left New Zealand. Another small distortion I will come clean about: Baby William was born to the Fallenis much later, although a son, Giuseppe, was born when Falleni was eleven. If you are interested in Falleni's life, and would like to read a biography sensitive to the mysteries and uncertainties of Falleni's story, I recommend Suzanne Falkiner's *Eugenia: A Man,* in particular the 2014 edition. For a thorough analysis of her trial, I recommend Mark Tedeschi's *Eugenia.*

In this novel I have attempted to oscillate between various versions of Falleni's story in order to capture the feeling of motion sickness that might rumble at the core of an indeterminate life. For me, the contradictions, mysteries and factual aberrations that colour the various 'true' accounts of Falleni's story are intrinsic to how Falleni lived their lives, and how those lives have been played out in the media since the late nineteenth century. To resolve them would be to ignore what is most provocative and alluring about Falleni's story: how it resonates with the common experience of being multiple, mutable and socially determined, and how difficult it can be to reconcile our many selves.

ACKNOWLEDGEMENTS

This novel began its life as *Portrait of an Invert*, a work of devised theatre that never found an audience. Thanks are due to Lexi Freiman, Anna Houston and Rochelle Whyte for indulging my mad ideas and meeting them with their own, as well as the University of Sydney's Theatre and Performance Studies department for giving us a room and time to play. The project then turned into a creative thesis, written within the supportive environment of the Writing and Society Research Centre at Western Sydney University. I would never have survived the five-year slog without the support of an Australian Postgraduate Award—may our governments continue to appreciate and fund deep and ongoing research forever more. Sincere thanks are due to my supervisors Ivor Indyk, Chris Andrews and Sara Knox for their guidance, and knowing when to curtail my exploration of infinite possibilities, as well as Matt McGuire for tactful advice on how to be less pretentious, and Melinda Jewell and Suzanne Gapps for humouring my requests for tall-ship insurance.

I salute the under-acknowledged staff of trove.com.au, the National Library of Australia, the Mitchell Library, the National Library of New Zealand, Wellington Library and Archives and State Records NSW—what a treasure chest you are all sitting on!

The novel's final part was written at the Faber Academy, under the guidance of Kathryn Heyman. I was especially lucky to study amongst a cohort of particularly generous readers and writers. Without attending the Faber Academy I would never have met Grace Heifetz, my energising Australian agent; Catherine Drayton, my discerning US agent; and Jane Palfreyman, my lioness of a publisher.

I'd like to thank Ali Lavau for her sharp eye and sensitive edit, Sarah Baker for her patience with my complicated layout requests, and everyone else who is responsible for Allen & Unwin's stellar reputation.

Thank you to Tom Cho and Kaya Wilson for sharing their views on trans identities, who should write them, and how they should be written about. Thanks to Dean Robinson for helping me understand the legal process; Jan Dickinson and Clea Mhilli for their assistance with the Italian; everyone on board the STS *Lord Nelson* and STS *Tenacious* for help with sailing terminology (and keeping me alive while traversing the Tasman); David Finnigan and René Christen for tolerating and even encouraging my obsession; and especially my parents, Ross and Sally Smith, for their patience and support.

Thanks are also due to Chad Parkhill for his knowledge of whiskey (or should that be whisky?) and dedication to the hunt for anachronisms; to David McLaughlin for taking on the oddest acting job of his career, and performing Harry Crawford in my flat; to my early readers Tom Hogan, Lucy Parakhina, Lauren Crew, Cameron Foster and Paul Jones for their feedback; to writing friends Rebecca Giggs and Fiona Wright for their moral support and time for wine; to Peter Doyle, Nerida Campbell and all at the Justice & Police Museum for the fresh insights on Sydney's history that were brought to light in the *City of Shadows* exhibition, which provoked my initial interest in Falleni's story in 2008; and to Suzanne Falkiner, Ruth Ford, Mark Tedeschi and Lachlan Philpott for their fresh perspectives and rigorous contributions to research on Falleni's lives.

And lastly and most importantly, to Eugenia Falleni, Annie Crawford and all who have suffered trying to live and love in ways that don't fit. My hope is that our cultures will evolve to accommodate more possible ways of being, and being in love.

ILLUSTRATIONS AND INSERTS

To give a sense of how it feels to open an archival box and piece together the first draft of Falleni's story, the illustrations and inserts included in 'To All Outside Appearances, At Least' (page 129) are facsimiles of original sources. Clippings from the original transcript of Falleni's trial—complete with its wonky typing, corrections and erasures—have been included on pages 134, 276–7, 281–3 and 294–9, though I have sometimes rearranged the words to create a ransom note from the past, to the present, and back again.

The newspaper headlines on page 286 are from the following newspapers:

'A Startling Story': *Truth*, Sunday, 11 July 1920
'In Male Attire': *Daily Telegraph*, Wednesday, 7 July 1920
'Woman Charged With Murder': *Daily Telegraph*, Wednesday, 7 July 1920

'Eugene Falleni and Her "Wives"': *Truth*, Sunday, 11 July 1920

'What the Police Have Learned': *Daily Telegraph*, Wednesday,
7 July 1920

Here are the references for each sketch:

Page 135: Harry Birkett, *Truth*, Sunday, 22 August 1920

Page 177: Henrietta Schieblich, *Truth*, Sunday, 10 October 1920

Page 205: Annie Birkett, *Truth*, Sunday, 22 August 1920

Page 213: Lydia Parnell, *Truth*, Sunday, 22 August 1920

Page 237: Josephine Falleni, *Truth*, Sunday, 22 August 1920

Page 268: Eugenia Falleni, *Truth*, Sunday, 22 August 1920

Page 272: Eugenia Falleni and Detective Sergeant Stewart Robson,
The Daily Telegraph, Wednesday, 7 July 1920

Page 300: Maddocks Cohen, *Truth*, Sunday, 24 September 1922

The collage on pages 335–7 is taken from Herbert M. Moran's
*Viewless Winds: Being the recollections and digressions of an
Australian Surgeon*, Peter Davies, London, 1939, pages i, 230,
233, 234 and 235.

The sketch of Eugenia Falleni used on pages 6, 10, 128 and 338
is from *The Sunday Mirror*, Sunday, 10 September 1967.